In the COMPANY of SECRETS

Books by Judith Miller

FROM BETHANY HOUSE PUBLISHERS

BELLS OF LOWELL*

Daughter of the Loom

A Fragile Design

These Tangled Threads

LIGHTS OF LOWELL*

A Tapestry of Hope

A Love Woven True

The Pattern of Her Heart

FREEDOM'S PATH

First Dawn

Morning Sky

Daylight Comes

POSTCARDS FROM PULLMAN

In the Company of Secrets

*with Tracie Peterson

07A

POSTCARDS *from* PULLMAN • 1

In the COMPANY *of* SECRETS

JUDITH MILLER

In the Company of Secrets
Copyright © 2007
Judith Miller

Cover design by Koechel Peterson & Associates

Unless otherwise identified, Scripture quotations are from the King James Version of the Bible.

Published by Bethany House Publishers
11400 Hampshire Avenue South
Bloomington, Minnesota 55438

Bethany House Publishers is a division of
Baker Publishing Group, Grand Rapids, Michigan.

Printed in the United States of America

Paperback:	ISBN-13:	978-0-7642-0276-6	ISBN-10:	0-7642-0276-6
Hardcover:	ISBN-13:	978-0-7642-0352-7	ISBN-10:	0-7642-0352-5
Large Print:	ISBN-13:	978-0-7642-0353-4	ISBN-10:	0-7642-0353-3

Library of Congress Cataloging-in-Publication Data

McCoy-Miller, Judith.
In the company of secrets / Judith Miller.
p. cm. — (Postcards from Pullman)
ISBN 978-0-7642-0352-7 (alk. paper) — ISBN 978-0-7642-0276-6 (pbk.) — ISBN 978-0-7642-0353-4 (lg. print : pbk.)
1. Cooks—Fiction. 2. British—United States—Fiction. 3. Illinois—Fiction. I. Title.
PS3613.C3858I5 2007
813'.54—dc22 2006038412

To

Roberta Stuke

With a thankful heart for your friendship!

JUDITH MILLER is an award-winning author whose avid research and love for history are reflected in her novels, many of which have appeared on the CBA bestseller lists. Judy and her husband make their home in Topeka, Kansas.

Visit Judy's Web site at: *www.judithmccoymiller.com.*

Wherefore putting away lying, speak every man truth with his neighbour: for we are members one of another.

—Ephesians 4:25

Chapter One

London, England
April 1892

Run! Faster! Hurry! The warnings tolled in Olivia's mind like a death knell. She raced toward the kitchen door, the rear stairway now in sight. Approaching the final obstacle, she rounded the kitchen worktable at breakneck speed. Her momentum abruptly slowed as the pocket of her starched white apron caught on the table's corner. The rasping tear of the cotton cloth echoed in her ears, and she quickly cast a downward glance at the frayed pocket. Still hoping for time enough to flee, she urgently yanked at the apron. She'd not been fast enough.

Chef Mallard's long fingers surrounded her forearm in an iron grip. She winced as he tightened his hold, certain she'd be bruised by the morrow. Shoving her against the table, he eased his grip only slightly and leaned his full weight against her. The edge of the heavy worktable cut into the small of her back, and she groaned.

A look of triumph shone in his small dark eyes. "Do not toy

with me, Miss Mott. I know you desire my affections."

"*Desire?* You disgust me! Turn me loose or I shall report you to the countess."

Her angry rebuff served only to incense him further. Instead of releasing her, he pinched her chin between his thumb and index finger and pressed his thin, hard lips against her mouth in a bruising kiss. The legs of the massive worktable scraped across the stone floor as she struggled backward, trying to gain her freedom. He captured her waist with his arm and pulled her into a fearsome embrace. A lustful gleam lurked in his watery eyes and penetrated her very soul. He traced his tongue across the vindictive smile curving his lips. She shuddered.

Beneath the collar of the chef's white tunic, his Adam's apple bobbed uncontrollably. "Quit fighting me!"

"Never! I'll not yield to you." She spat the words into his face.

With a wicked laugh, he grabbed at the hem of her skirt. *How dare he!* Without hesitation, Olivia stomped the heel of her shoe atop his foot. The despicable chef yelped and his grip loosened. Wresting free of him, she hastened to the opposite side of the table while straining to remain calm. Across the expanse of the wooden table, she stared at him. The man was a lecherous fiend.

He bent forward and rested his palms against the table. "You'll find speaking to the countess will do you no good." He wagged his index finger at her. "The Countess of Lanshire needs an excellent chef on her staff. Scullery maids can be found on any street corner. Be advised that others have tried that tack and none have succeeded." His stale breath wafted across the table and assaulted her. "You will permit me the pleasure of your body whenever I so desire, or you will find yourself among the unemployed, *Miss Mott*. You have but two days to give me your decision."

Outwitted! Olivia should have known the calculating chef would have a trump card at the ready, and that he would use it whenever and wherever he saw fit. Each of his words hit like a blow to the midsection. Swallowing hard, Olivia forced down the lump in her throat. If she disgorged herself of the morning meal, the chef would offer yet another serving of his brutal humiliation.

He moved away from the table and gestured toward the stairway. "I'll not detain you further. Consider your options carefully, Miss Mott. Either you'll be my mistress or you'll be unemployed."

Careful to maintain her distance, Olivia sidestepped toward the stairs on wobbly legs. She hoped to maintain some sense of decorum until she finally escaped the kitchen. He was watching her every move. Only when she reached the stairs did she turn her back toward him and race up the flight as though the devil himself were on her heels. She didn't stop running until she reached the third floor.

Leaning against the far wall, she gasped for air, her chest heaving. As her breathing slowed, she realized those few minutes in the kitchen had changed the course of her life. She'd seen her dream evaporate as quickly as ice melting on a summer day.

When she'd arrived at Lanshire Hall fourteen months ago, she had hoped Chef Mallard would lead her on the path to a successful career. Like everyone else who had eaten his expertly prepared delicacies, Olivia had been in awe of his culinary abilities. Until today the desire to become a renowned chef had outweighed all other dreams. Unfortunately, the Mallard, as she privately referred to him, had drawn a line in the sand—a line she would never cross, no matter how deep the desire to achieve her goal. Today he had proved himself to be the odious man about whom she had been forewarned.

With a quick swipe she brushed away the tears that stained her cheeks and dejectedly walked to the end of the hall. She sniffed loudly and pushed open the door to the room she shared with Ludenia, Lady Charlotte Spencer's personal maid.

At the sound of the latch, Ludie glanced up from her stitching. Her eyes opened wide, and she dropped the embroidery on the side table as she rushed forward to enfold Olivia in a gentle embrace. "Now what's this all about, dearie? Tell Ludie what's troubling you."

Olivia fell into the warmth of the woman's fleshy arms and wept, her body heaving up and down with each giant sob. When her wrenching wails subsided, Ludie loosened her hold and handed Olivia her handkerchief. The woman's eyes shone with sympathy as she lovingly patted her shoulder.

"Now, then, sit down and tell me what has happened."

They settled themselves on the only two chairs in the small room. In between hiccoughs and sniffles, Olivia explained Chef Mallard's sordid ultimatum.

"If I don't give in to him, he says he'll make certain I never work in another reputable kitchen in England." She wiped her tears on the linen hankie. "Oh, Ludie, what am I going to do?"

"Oh, my dear! Surely there's an answer. We merely must find it." She jiggled her knee up and down, a sure sign she was deep in thought.

Olivia remained silent, waiting for words of wisdom to pour from the older woman's lips.

"What about your aunt Eleanor Mott? Could you go and stay with her? You'd be safe from Chef Mallard."

Olivia slumped in her chair. She didn't want to go live with Cousin Albert's mother. She'd be required to work in one of the local shops or, worse yet, take a dreary job in a factory to support herself. Not that she didn't love Aunt Eleanor, but Olivia had expected a more resourceful solution from Ludie. Though Olivia's dream seemed outlandish to most, Ludie had encouraged her to pursue training as a chef from the first day she'd arrived at Lanshire Hall.

Suddenly Ludie's shoulders squared. "Didn't your cousin Albert move to America? Perhaps you could follow him there. Chef Mallard's malevolent threats to ruin your future can't follow you all the way to another country." She beamed at Olivia. "What do you think, luv?"

Olivia's heart pounded with a mixture of fear and excitement. Could she possibly do such a thing? She'd never even seen all of her native England, or even London for that matter. How could she consider such a journey on her own? Her heartbeat slowed as she remembered how many months Albert had saved for his voyage to America. Even if she could garner the courage, she didn't have money to purchase her passage.

Ludie jumped up and adjusted her bodice. "I'm late. If I don't hurry, I'll be the object of Lady Charlotte's wrath. I know her sharp tongue all too well." She stopped when she reached the door. "We'll keep thinking. There is a solution; we've just got to find it." After one final embrace and a warning to remain upstairs, where she would be safe from Chef Mallard, Ludie disappeared down the hallway.

Olivia slouched in her chair, settling her gaze on the scuffed toes of her black work shoes. One thing was certain: she would be a resident of Lanshire Hall for only two more days. Instead of staring at her shoes, she must pack her belongings. With a sigh, she pushed herself up from the chair and pulled open the wardrobe. She would be greatly relieved to never again see Chef Mallard, but she would surely miss living and working at Lanshire Hall. Even more, she would miss the woman whom she'd grown to love like the mother she'd never known. Tears threatened at the thought of leaving Ludie. Saying good-bye would be difficult.

Olivia's starched white cap wobbled precariously above her left eyebrow. She gaped at the formidable Lady Charlotte Spencer. Perhaps Olivia wasn't quite awake yet and hadn't heard correctly. "You want me to *what*?" Olivia blurted the words without so much as adding a polite "your ladyship" to the question.

The only daughter of the Earl and Countess of Lanshire Hall, Lady Charlotte was twenty-three, older than Olivia by two years. More often than not, however, she acted like a spoiled ten-year-old. Shoving her hat back toward the center of her head, Olivia prayed she'd misunderstood the young mistress.

With a hefty yank, Lady Charlotte pulled Olivia into the darkness of the linen closet and bid her remain quiet. She squeezed Olivia's arm in a viselike grip while she whispered a detailed and upsetting plan. When she'd hissed the final words, Lady Charlotte nudged Olivia toward the door and back into the hallway. Trembling, Olivia hurried off to the kitchen. She pinched herself as she descended the steps. Perhaps this was merely a dream. Unfortunately, the painful pinch revealed she was wide-awake.

She should never have confided in Ludie! The older woman meant well, but she chattered constantly. Even now, Olivia could picture the scene: Ludie serenely brushing Lady Charlotte's hair in long flowing strokes while regaling her ladyship with the daily gossip that circulated throughout Lanshire Hall. Unfortunately, this day's tittle-tattle had included the possibility of Olivia sailing for America once she accumulated funds enough to pay her passage.

Instead of dealing with Chef Mallard, she must now submit to Lady Charlotte's threats and demands. And this time, she couldn't ask for Ludie's help.

Chapter Two

From the time she was a little girl, Olivia had hearkened to her aunt Eleanor's admonitions against lying. Now she found herself trapped in the mire she'd been warned against during those formative years. Thus far, her journey with Lady Charlotte had been filled with deceit and a host of lies. So many that she remained uncertain whether she could remember all of them. What had her aunt called lies? The scourge of mankind! Yes, that was it—a scourge that entangles man like a sticky spider's web.

"Tell one lie, and you'll need two or more to cover the last." She couldn't count the number of times Aunt Eleanor had repeated those words to Olivia and her cousin Albert. Olivia had never quite understood the saying. Until now. To this point, she'd followed along in her usual submissive manner, doing Lady Charlotte's bidding without question. However, once they reached Pullman, Illinois, Olivia intended to free herself from the clutches of the young mistress.

Not that Lady Charlotte technically remained her mistress any longer. Nevertheless, she did maintain a hold on Olivia. A very strong hold. After all, she had paid for her passage from London to New York and then to Chicago, and she had offered to force the Mallard to write a letter praising her abilities and culinary expertise. Knowing that such a letter would open doors for her, Olivia had accepted the offer, an act she took no pride in admitting. But she did intend to use the letter once they arrived in Pullman. If all went according to plan, Olivia's future would be secured in the celebrated community that George Pullman had built for his employees. And so far as she was concerned, she couldn't reach her destination quickly enough.

As with everything since their departure, all things would happen according to Lady Charlotte's schedule. They would spend one night at the Grand Pacific Hotel on LaSalle Street before departing the next morning. Olivia's attempts to hold sway over Lady Charlotte's decision to remain in Chicago overnight had, as with all of her other suggestions, gone unheeded. Lady Charlotte declared they must be refreshed and rested before their departure for Pullman.

Exiting the glass-domed carriage rotunda at the Van Buren Street Station, Olivia gasped at the surrounding sights and immediately gave thanks for the safety the carriage provided. Monstrous buildings towered heavenward as a mere sliver of sunlight fought its way through to the ground below. Inside the carriage, they were assaulted by the noise of pounding steam hammers, clanging gongs, and teams of screaming horses frightened by the cable cars that nosed through the streets at breakneck speed. A cacophony bombarded them on every side. Olivia had never been in such a place as this. And she wasn't at all sure she ever wished to return.

She sighed with relief when the coachman reined the horses to a stop in front of the hotel. A uniformed young man hastened to assist them inside, and soon they were escorted to rooms that rivaled the opulence of Lanshire Hall. Once settled amidst the elegance, Olivia quickly pushed aside all thoughts of the treacherous carriage ride. Before embarking on this journey, never before had she been privy to such luxury and elegance. For throughout their trip, she had traveled as Lady Charlotte's equal, enjoying the same privilege and luxury as that afforded her companion. But tomorrow all of that would change. And tomorrow she must remember all of the lies.

Though she would never broach the topic, Olivia secretly wondered what Lady Charlotte planned to do if Randolph Morgan refused to marry her. Would she return to Lanshire Hall in her condition? This had been yet another of Lady Charlotte's lies. She had never planned to visit for only a few weeks and then return to England. Once they were well at sea, the mistress had confided she was going to have a child—Randolph Morgan's child. The news had been unnerving. It still was. Lady Charlotte didn't even know the man's address, though searching for him in the town of Pullman shouldn't prove overly difficult. Mr. Morgan was, after all, one of Mr. Pullman's most valued employees, if she could believe what Lady Charlotte had told her during their voyage.

Olivia remembered Mr. Morgan well. He'd visited Lanshire Hall on several occasions during the past few years and had been instrumental in hiring many young men who had come to work in Pullman. Artisans who gilded the coaches with gold leaf or etched perfect designs into the mirrors and interior glasswork—her cousin Albert among them. What would the Earl of Lanshire think of Mr. Morgan once he realized *all* that had occurred on the man's visits to London? The entire matter caused Olivia's head to ache.

Looking down on the street below, Olivia considered what would happen to her should she be unable to locate a culinary position in Pullman. What if there was no need for additional kitchen staff at the hotel restaurant? She didn't want to work in one of the factories, nor did she want to accept a position in the frightening chaos of Chicago.

Lady Charlotte entered their opulent sitting room and waved two tickets in the air. "I secured passage on tomorrow's nine-o'clock train to Pullman. The hotel clerk was most helpful."

After tucking the tickets inside her reticule, she dropped it atop a decorative mahogany table and gracefully stepped across the room. Olivia wondered how much longer Lady Charlotte could hide the fact that she carried a child. Already she was required to wear a long cape when in public. Soon the mistress would develop the sway and posture of an expectant mother, and a cape would no longer hide her condition. Hopefully she would be Mrs. Randolph Morgan when that time arrived.

After removing her cape and dropping it onto one of the heavily padded brocade chairs, Charlotte sat and folded her hands in her lap. "I also elicited a great deal of information regarding the town. Would you like to hear?"

Suddenly Lady Charlotte was an authority on Pullman, Illinois. Olivia found the idea utterly annoying. Only a short time earlier, her ladyship had sniffed at the idea of making a home in the small town. She avowed Randolph would be easily convinced to live in London once their wedding plans had been arranged. Why, then, had she taken time to discover details about the town?

Olivia offered a tight smile. "I'd be delighted to hear whatever information you'd care to share with me."

Charlotte arched her perfectly shaped brows. "My, you seem rather stuffy and abrupt this evening. I thought you would be delighted to hear about the town. I even obtained information regarding the hotel where you hope to work." She assumed a quick pout before hastening to continue. "It's called the Hotel Florence, and the clerk tells me it was named after Mr. Pullman's eldest daughter. He says Mr. Pullman hosts huge parties for his business associates, and there's a full-time chef on staff. According to the clerk, he's French and highly acclaimed."

Olivia sighed. Most chefs were arrogant—especially the French. She wondered if he could rival the Mallard, or if she'd even have an opportunity to find out. She doubted he would consider hiring her to do anything more than scrub pots and pans. Once again, a mere scullery maid. Olivia shuddered at the thought. But perhaps her letter of recommendation from Chef Mallard would help her avoid such a fate.

"All this talk of the hotel reminds me that you've not yet furnished me with Chef Mallard's recommendation."

Charlotte nibbled her bottom lip and glanced toward the window.

When her ladyship failed to reply, Olivia's stomach muscles tightened. "Did he refuse you?"

Charlotte arched her back and assumed a regal pose. "He wouldn't *dare* refuse me. However, I was fearful he would consider my request peculiar and consult my parents." Her lips tightened. "I couldn't have him arouse suspicion. He could have ruined *my* plans."

Olivia immediately pictured herself scrubbing dirty pots or, worse yet, spending her days toiling in a dreary factory. Though she longed to voice her anger, she remained silent. She'd spent far too many years in servitude to actually say what she was thinking. Besides, she should have known better than to take Lady Charlotte at her word. Hadn't she spent a lifetime doing that very thing? Trusting in what other people said, believing they would tell the truth and honor their word. She'd been duped once again. Aunt Eleanor always referred to her as a trusting little soul. Cousin Albert considered her naïve.

"Without a letter of recommendation, I won't be considered for any position other than scullery maid or factory worker." Olivia's words were as frosty as a winter wind.

"Oh, I didn't forget my promise to you, Olivia." Charlotte hurried to one of her trunks, dug deep inside, and retrieved her stationery box. "Look here!" She waved a piece of paper overhead like a parade banner. "I managed to *appropriate* several pieces of the *official* Lanshire stationery." She winked and placed the sheet of paper in front of Olivia. "I'll pen your letter of recommendation and sign my mother's name, and no one will be the wiser. Besides, a letter from the Countess of Lanshire will carry *much* more influence than that of Chef Mallard." With a look of triumph, Charlotte sat down opposite Olivia.

A large red and gold *L* emblazoned the top of the page. Directly beneath, "Earl and Countess of Lanshire" had been printed in a delicate script. Olivia feasted her eyes upon the sight. What would Aunt Eleanor say? What would Cousin

Albert do? What would God think? She forced the nagging questions from her mind and traced her index finger across the raised lettering. With a degree of fear and trepidation, she pushed the sheet of paper toward Lady Charlotte. She needed the reference.

Lady Charlotte beamed. "I'll see to it before I retire for the night."

When Olivia arose the next morning, the letter was sealed in an envelope and propped against a vase of flowers. Forcing herself to ignore the impropriety, she carefully tucked the letter into her purse before departing their rooms. By now she was becoming quite practiced at overlooking prevarication. Perhaps she would finally outgrow the naïveté of which her cousin so frequently spoke.

The short journey to the Illinois Central Depot proved as harrowing as their carriage ride the previous day, though by now Olivia was somewhat prepared for the onslaught of noise and mayhem. Their trunks had already been delivered to the train station, thanks to the desk clerk Lady Charlotte had befriended the previous afternoon. Once the train departed the station, Olivia settled into her seat. She peered out the window, pleased to leave Chicago behind her. For the first few miles, the train skirted the shoreline, a magnificent park, and several rows of fashionable homes. Even Charlotte perked to attention at the sight of the opulent mansions.

Shortly thereafter, the railroad tracks turned away from the lake front and entered the open prairie. Lady Charlotte tapped Olivia on the arm. "I've decided it would be best if you referred to me as your *friend* Charlotte, from this point forward. Do not address me as 'your ladyship' or 'Lady Charlotte.' Do you understand?"

Olivia shook her head. "I couldn't possibly, your ladyship. I don't understand why you would ask me to do such a thing."

Lady Charlotte sighed. "Because I want to surprise Randolph. If others know that a member of the English nobility has arrived in Pullman, Randolph will hear and my surprise will be ruined." She pointed her gloved finger toward Olivia's purse. "In addition, I might be expected to answer questions about you and your cooking abilities, which would never do. Our stories would likely conflict, and then where would you be?"

Obviously Lady Charlotte didn't expect a response, for before Olivia could reply, she spouted off a list of additional directives that made Olivia's head swim. She wished she could write down at least a few of the details, but a glance out the train window revealed they had traversed the fourteen miles and were nearing Pullman. One matter was certain: Lady Charlotte had given a great deal of thought to her reunion with Randolph Morgan, as well as to any possible obstacles.

Well, if her ladyship wanted to surprise Mr. Morgan, so be it. Personally, Olivia thought the expected child would be surprise enough for the man. Nevertheless, Olivia did agree her future employment in the Pullman hotel could be jeopardized if Lady Charlotte was questioned regarding Olivia's suitability. After all, Lady Charlotte had barely spoken to Olivia prior to the formation of their alliance to leave England. Their stories would undoubtedly differ.

Hat pulled low on his forehead, the conductor navigated his way through their coach. "Next stop, Pullman!" His announcement was as crisp as his navy blue Pullman uniform.

Olivia immediately pressed her nose to the train window. A sparkling lake with an ornamental waterfall spread in front of the Pullman factories. Olivia motioned to the conductor.

He stepped to her side. "Ma'am?"

"What's the name of that lake, sir?"

He leaned down and peered through the window. "That's Lake Vista. Mr. Pullman had the land excavated to create a lake that would collect the condensation water from his Corliss engine." Olivia's eyes widened as the train slowly inched forward and the conductor pointed to the huge glass window. "That's the Corliss, sitting right out there in plain view for all to see. It powers all these factories and produces 350,000 gallons of condensation water a day. Sure does keep that lake full." He shook his head. "Hard to believe, but I reckon it's true, or Mr. Pullman would set the record straight."

Her cousin Albert had written Aunt Eleanor about the Corliss engine shortly after his arrival in Pullman. Now she, too, had the opportunity to see the magnificent machine. A huge water tower sat to the rear of the factory buildings, along with another attractive building. Rather than depressing, Olivia thought the acres of brick factories looked gracious and inviting.

As the train slowly rolled forward, she pulled away from the window and turned. "Look! I believe that must be the hotel."

Charlotte grasped her arm. "Do sit down, Olivia. We can see the town once we've made arrangements for our baggage. I'll inquire about securing the trunks here at the train station until we've made definite arrangements."

Olivia hadn't even considered their baggage. Of course, *her* belongings didn't require several trunks, a variety of Gladstone bags, and three or more leather valises. She could manage her own two valises, but she didn't argue. The moment the train jerked to a halt, Olivia jumped to her feet and hurried Charlotte off the train. Once inside the station, Charlotte again took command, and Olivia patiently waited while her mistress spoke to the stationmaster. The man quickly agreed to keep a vigilant watch over their belongings. Olivia wondered if he would have been so pleased to help had *she* been the one to request his assistance. While Lady Charlotte's appearance spoke of wealth and status, Olivia's plain taupe gown clearly proclaimed her to be a member of the working class.

The stationmaster raced ahead of them to open the door. With an air of authority, Lady Charlotte turned toward Olivia. "I believe we are now ready to depart."

The town was even more appealing than Cousin Albert had told them in his occasional letters. Of course, most men didn't concern themselves overly much with the beauty that surrounded them. It soon became evident, though, that Mr. Pullman had given a great deal of thought to the details of his town. The small square yards that fronted the brick houses were evenly shorn, and the shade trees that lined the wide macadam streets were pruned to perfection.

From the depot, Olivia could glimpse the grandeur of Hotel Florence. A landscaped park sat to the front of the redbrick-and-stone hotel, which had been designed in the popular Queen Anne style. The magnificent four-story structure spread across an acre of ground. Rows of elm trees lined the paved boulevard. Unlike the pandemonium of Chicago, Pullman evoked a quiet perfection that beckoned her forward.

Olivia directed her steps toward the hotel but was suddenly stopped short when Charlotte grasped her arm and pulled her to a halt. "I believe that building straight ahead is the Arcade. The clerk at the Grand Pacific Hotel stated it would be a perfect place to spend several hours shopping or enjoying a cup of tea. Once you've been accepted for your new position, you can come and join me there."

"But, Lady—"

"Do *not* refer to me as Lady Charlotte. Have you forgotten my instructions so quickly?"

"No, your ladyship—I mean . . . no, Charlotte." Olivia shook her head. "Please understand that it feels quite unnatural to address you in this informal manner." Olivia straightened her shoulders when she saw the beginnings of a pout on Lady Charlotte's lips. "But I shall do my very best."

"Excellent. And don't forget to inquire about Randolph—Mr. Morgan." Lady Charlotte raised her parasol, turned, and sashayed toward the Arcade as though she'd lived in the town for years. Olivia watched for several moments and then a sudden jab of panic attacked her. "Charlotte! Wait!"

The loud command brought her ladyship to an immediate halt, and Olivia slapped one hand to her mouth. What had she been thinking to screech out Lady Charlotte's name in such a manner? She stood motionless as her companion walked toward her.

"Olivia, I am pleased that you addressed me as Charlotte, but you must also remember that ladies do not shout in public. Now, what is it you wish to ask?"

A gust of wind whipped at her cloak and Olivia shivered. The weather seemed uncomfortably cool for late May. However, she had little idea of the weather patterns in the area. Perhaps the warmth of springtime didn't arrive until June in Illinois. "How am I to locate you inside that huge building? I could wander around forever without setting eyes upon you."

"Dear me, it isn't all *that* large. But I'll make an effort to remain on the first floor. However, if the shops are upstairs, you'll likely find me there." Lady Charlotte reached inside her reticule, pulled out an extra pair of gloves, and handed them to Olivia. "And do wear these for your interview. We don't want these Americans thinking we've lost our English civility."

"But the chef at the hotel is French, not American."

Lady Charlotte's eyebrows raised a notch, and Olivia obediently donned the gloves. Murmuring her thanks, she marched off toward the hotel. As she neared the picturesque building, her pace slowed considerably. Perhaps she should wait until she'd had an opportunity to seek her cousin's advice. What if there was a specific method or protocol one used when applying for a position? She didn't want to embarrass herself and possibly ruin her chances of employment. She had mentioned her concerns to Charlotte, and the mistress thought her worries ludicrous. But then, how could she trust Lady Charlotte's judgment? What did her ladyship know about securing employment?

Olivia's legs weakened as she halted in front of the hotel. She wanted to run, yet worried her knees would buckle if she tried. Instead, she lifted her trembling fingers and adjusted her hat, straightened Lady Charlotte's lace gloves, and climbed the three steps leading to the enormous wraparound porch. Olivia forced one foot ahead of the other until she reached the hotel's main entrance. She glanced over her shoulder, worried someone might approach and shoo her away from the premises before she could enter. That thought propelled her forward. Taking a deep breath, she twisted the fluted brass doorknob and stepped inside.

A tight-lipped graying man stood behind a highly polished front desk and peered across the wood expanse that divided them. Wire-rimmed spectacles balanced upon the tip of his thick nose, and an involuntary shiver coursed through Olivia when the man settled his austere stare upon her. He had obviously judged her as someone who didn't belong in these opulent surroundings. Though she attempted to bid him good morning, a warbling squeak was all that passed her lips.

The man scanned the registry book before he once again focused his attention upon Olivia. "May I be of some assistance, miss?"

She bobbed her head. "I've come to apply for a position in the hotel kitchen. As a chef's assistant." She bravely added the final words.

"I didn't realize either our chef or Mr. Howard had advertised such a position. I'm the hotel supervisor, and *I* know nothing of such a vacancy." Brows furrowed, he came from behind the counter. "You may wait here. I'll return shortly."

Though Olivia wanted to explain she hadn't arrived in answer to an advertisement, she remained silent. The man was much too forbidding. He'd likely throw her out on her ear if he knew she'd boldly entered the hotel without any knowledge of a possible opening. Once he talked to the chef, she suspected that's exactly what would happen.

Catching sight of her reflection in the huge gilded mirror that hung across the room, Olivia tucked a stray curl behind her ear. At the sound of approaching footsteps, she turned and straightened her shoulders. Walking alongside the hotel supervisor was a rotund man whose puffy jowls, sagging eyelids, and wrinkled forehead reminded her of a bulldog. She detected a slight smile as he neared.

He dipped his head ever so slightly. "Chef René."

Uncertain what was expected, Olivia gave a brief curtsy and then realized her behavior was likely inappropriate in this country. "Pleased to meet you. I am Olivia Mott of London, England."

His smile broadened and he winked. "I would not make that confession when applying for a cooking position, Miss Mott. We Frenchmen do not believe *any* Englishman can cook well enough to be considered a chef."

In spite of her fear, Olivia giggled in response. Chef Mallard would be appalled by such a remark.

The nameless hotel supervisor squared his shoulders. "Do you have a reference, Miss Mott?"

For a brief moment, Olivia considered telling the truth. However, if she divulged she carried no reference from her previous employment, she would be promptly escorted from the hotel. Opening her reticule, she extracted the letter and extended it toward the chef. Without a moment's hesitation, the hotel supervisor snapped the envelope from her hand, sliced it open, and unfolded the letter. His eyes moved back and forth in rapid fashion as he read the page. On several occasions, he lifted his gaze to peer at her before he completed his review of the missive. A low whistle escaped his lips as he handed the letter to Chef René.

"I must say I am impressed, Miss Mott. You are of tender

years to have held such a responsible position with the Earl and Countess of Lanshire." He turned to the chef. "No doubt you will want to speak further with Miss Mott?"

"But of course, Mr. Beelings." Chef René waved a puffy hand in the air. "Follow me."

Billings. So that was the hotel supervisor's name. Olivia enjoyed the sound of the chef's voice, though she wasn't certain what to think him. True, he had smiled and winked like an old friend, yet she'd heard the French could be difficult taskmasters. Surely he could be no worse than the Mallard. Bolstered by that thought, she followed along as they passed the hotel barbershop and turned down a long hallway. She could see the kitchen at the end of the passageway, but Chef René stopped and escorted her into a tiny office situated outside the entrance.

As he stepped around a small table, he dropped her reference letter atop a sheaf of papers piled on one corner. Olivia longed to know the contents of the letter. Lady Charlotte had obviously been quite complimentary. If she could answer the chef's questions to his satisfaction, perhaps she would secure a position.

Chef René gestured for Olivia to take a seat while he squeezed his rotund body into the chair opposite her. "Having this uncomfortable chair in my office keeps me at work in the kitchen." His jovial laugh filled the room and set Olivia at ease. "Tell me, Miss Mott, what brings a lady of your accomplishments to Pullman, Illinois?"

His dark brown eyes sparkled beneath his eyelids. Pleased by the ease of this question, she explained that her cousin Albert Mott was employed in Pullman and that his letters had expounded upon the advantages of the community and lured her to the town.

"It seems to me that a talented chef's assistant with your astounding qualities would have remained in England. With luck, you might have ascended to the position of chef to the Earl and Countess of Lanshire." Chef René rubbed his fleshy jowl. "When I review this letter, I am awed by all you have achieved. And at such a young age. Astounding!" The chef waved the piece of stationery in the air.

The engraved red and gold *L* winked at her as the letter fluttered back atop his desk. Olivia silently scolded herself. She should have insisted upon reading the contents before presenting the missive as a reference. *What* had Lady Charlotte written? She edged a bit closer, hoping for a glimpse, but her efforts proved fruitless.

"Well, you have arrived at the perfect time." The chef slapped his beefy hand on the table.

Startled, Olivia's purse dropped from her lap, and she jumped to retrieve it from the floor. Securing the handbag, she peeked across the desk as she returned to an upright position.

The chef was watching her every move and obviously awaiting her response. "I have? Arrived at the perfect time, I mean?"

"Indeed!" He rose from his chair. "Mr. Pullman is in his upstairs office. I will speak to him. You may wait here for my return."

The chef pried himself from his chair and edged his way through the small room, obviously not expecting a response. When he didn't pick up the letter, a silent sigh of relief escaped her lips. She waited only long enough to be certain he wouldn't immediately return before reaching across the table, retrieving the letter, and reviewing the contents. What had Lady Charlotte been thinking? Olivia marveled that Chef René hadn't laughed her out of his office. Why had he even condescended to speak to her? Surely he didn't believe she could perform the myriad duties detailed by the mistress of Lanshire Hall. Most any chef would have simply called her a fraud and pointed her to the door. Why hadn't he?

At the sound of footsteps in the outer hall, Olivia dropped the letter back in place. If she had an ounce of sense, she would run from the room while there was still time. What would she do if Chef René actually offered her employment?

Chapter Three

Chef René lumbered through the doorway. "You are hired, Miss Mott. Come with me."

She couldn't move. Her backside felt glued to the chair. If she didn't stand, he would think her a complete fool. Better now than when he discovered she couldn't perform the numerous duties outlined in that overblown letter of recommendation.

"No time to dally. We are to meet with Mr. Howard, the company's agent."

The chef grasped her by the elbow and propelled her out of the chair. Without so much as a word, she followed in his broad shadow. Once outside the hotel, he motioned her onward.

"May I inquire where we're going?"

He pointed a thick finger across the street toward the artificial lake and clock tower she'd viewed from the train. "To Mr. Howard's office in the Administration Building. He will assign your living quarters and arrange for payment of your wages. You will begin work in the morning."

Who would have thought a man of Chef René's girth could walk so rapidly? Didn't he realize she couldn't keep pace with his long stride? The chef continued across the wide boulevard, with Olivia following in his wake. When Chef René arrived at the Administration Building, he pulled open the heavy walnut and glass door and turned. Olivia sighed. Finally. Perhaps he would see her lagging and take pity! Instead of the contrite apology she'd expected, he waved her on like the exasperated bobby she'd seen directing traffic in Chicago.

The chef shook his head in disgust when she stopped long enough to readjust her straw hat that had slipped to one side.

"Why must we hurry so?" she asked.

"Mr. Howard will leave his office promptly at eleven thirty. He is unavailable for employee appointments after that time. Mr. Pullman instructed me to speak with Mr. Howard today. Consequently, we hurry." He pointed down the hall. "Follow me."

Did she have any other choice? At least the end of this race to meet Mr. Howard was in sight. Somewhere along this hallway she would enter an office and perhaps even be permitted to sit and rest for a moment. Unaware they had reached their final destination, Olivia bounced into René's broad backside as he came to an abrupt halt. She muttered an apology, but the chef seemed completely oblivious. After all, he had several layers of padding. She stifled a giggle. She *must* cease her desire to laugh when she found herself in these embarrassing circumstances.

Chef René knocked on the door and patiently waited.

"Come in! Come in!"

The deep voice emanating from the other side of the door sounded annoyed. Not a good sign . . . not a good sign at all. All thoughts of laughter immediately took flight. She followed the chef's gaze to a clock hanging at the end of the hall. Eleven twenty. Mr. Howard was likely anxious to be on his way home. In all probability, he had a wife who expected him home for the noonday meal. She could only hope his proclivity to remain on schedule would work in her favor and he wouldn't bombard her with a multitude of questions.

Before she could further weigh the possibilities, Chef René ushered her through the doorway and into the agent's office. She had anticipated a bald man with spectacles and a tight frown. To her astonishment, the man sitting across the desk was none of the things she'd expected. Perhaps this man was Mr. Howard's assistant.

He pushed aside a stack of papers and stood to shake hands with the chef. "How may I help you, Chef René?"

"May I introduce Miss Olivia Mott. She recently arrived from London with an incredibly fine recommendation from the Countess of Lanshire. Mr. Pullman instructed me to offer her a position as my assistant. She is to begin tomorrow morning."

Mr. Howard glanced in her direction before returning his attention to Chef René. "Any other instructions from Mr. Pullman?"

Olivia remained a silent observer while the two men discussed her future. From all appearances, nothing was expected of her. She stared at the ticking clock on Mr. Howard's desk. With its hand-painted violets and miniature roses, the china timepiece seemed strangely out of place on the massive unadorned desk.

The hands of the clock settled on twenty-five past the hour. If only she could reach across the desk and push the minute hand forward to eleven thirty, the agent would then surely shoo them from his office and hurry home to his wife. Her gaze remained fixed on the hands of the clock, which appeared to remain stuck at eleven twenty-five.

"Miss Mott? Miss Mott?"

Discomfited, Olivia met Mr. Howard's perplexed stare. He likely thought her a complete dolt. Even worse, he might believe her apathetic. "I'm terribly sorry. Instead of admiring your clock, I should have been listening to the conversation. Please forgive me."

She attempted one of the coy looks she'd seen Lady Charlotte assume in the past. But when Mr. Howard raised his eyebrows and peered at Chef René, she feared her endeavor had fallen short.

"I need to know if you are planning to arrange for living accommodations outside of Pullman or if you prefer to rent from the corporation." He poised his pen above a ledger. "I recommend the latter, don't you, Chef René?"

"*Oui*. You will find your life much simpler if you reside close to the hotel. You should not consider any other arrangement." He wagged his index finger back and forth.

With a bob of her head, Olivia agreed. "I prefer to rent from the corporation."

"Excellent." Mr. Howard made a check mark beside her name and closed the ledger. "Once you've completed your paper work, I will show you to your new living accommodations and explain a bit about life here in Pullman." He pulled a printed page from the desk drawer and slid it toward her. "*After* you have completed your application for employment."

Olivia swallowed hard. The first paragraph of the application was an oath avowing all information submitted by the applicant would be true and correct under penalty of discharge. Combined with the oath was an additional warning: *Under such circumstances, repayment of any wages paid would be required.* She didn't want to answer the numerous prying questions, and she certainly didn't want to sign her name to the oath.

"Is my letter of recommendation insufficient?" She did her best to offer him the lovely dimpled smile that seemed to render success for Lady Charlotte. However, her lips wouldn't cooperate. Best she couldn't see in a mirror, for she feared her attempt had more closely resembled a quivering snarl.

"All employees are required to complete and sign this paperwork. Even Chef René was required to fill out our application. Of course, we are always appreciative of recommendations such as the one you've supplied. Unfortunately, we've received an occasional letter of recommendation that couldn't be trusted."

If she questioned the matter further, Mr. Howard would surely become suspicious. *More lies.* And this time, her false statements would be in written form—and bear her signature, as well! After penning her answers, she crossed her first two fingers and signed the paper. She truly didn't want to continue with her lies, yet there appeared to be no alternative. She hoped God understood the meaning of crossed fingers. She slid the paper back toward Mr. Howard.

He scanned the responses before placing the form with her letter of recommendation. "Now then, let's go and see your new accommodations."

"Now?" Her voice warbled.

Mr. Howard pushed his chair away from the desk and stood. "Unless you have some other matter that requires your immediate attention."

The desk clock chimed a soft tune. Eleven thirty. Finally! Wasn't it time for Mr. Howard to depart for his noonday meal? Why didn't he ask her to come back tomorrow? "No, but I can return later if it would be more convenient. I don't want to interrupt your schedule."

"Now is fine, Miss Mott. I'm eager to hear more about you, and I know Chef René is anxious to get back to the hotel kitchen and oversee his staff."

Taking his cue, Chef René rose from his chair and started toward the door. Olivia wanted to run after him. Though she feared failure in his kitchen, she dreaded time alone with Mr. Howard more. He would surely subject her to a multitude of questions that she didn't want to answer. That fact aside, she didn't want to be the cause of his late arrival home. Years of servitude had taught her the foolishness of angering an employer's wife.

He escorted her out of his office at a leisure pace and walked at no more than a saunter as they retraced the path she'd taken with Chef René only a short time earlier. Apparently Mr. Howard had forgotten he was expected home for the noonday meal. Once across the boulevard, he turned to the left. The houses that lined this street proved to be substantially larger and more ornate than those Olivia had previously viewed. They were, she decided, most impressive.

Mr. Howard pointed to his right. "This is my home. As you can see, I'm situated close to my office."

He looked quite young when he smiled. "I'm sure your wife

appreciates that fact." His smile disappeared as quickly as it had arrived.

"My wife is dead, Miss Mott. She died nearly three years ago. Though this house is much too large for only one person, Mr. Pullman thought it best I remain in the housing assigned to the company agent."

"I'm sorry to hear of your loss, Mr. Howard. Please forgive me." Olivia stared at the scuffed toes of her shoes, afraid if she looked up she would detect a tear or two in his eyes. Why had she mentioned his wife? She needed to *think* before speaking. Perhaps she should change the subject. "I was wondering, Mr. Howard, do you perchance count a Mr. Randolph Morgan among your acquaintances?"

He stopped midstep and stared down the length of his six-foot frame. "I know *who* he is, but we are not personally acquainted. Mr. Morgan is an investor and stockholder who executes special tasks for the Pullman business interests from time to time—primarily in England and other countries. However, the Morgans and their young children visit Pullman on occasion. Like most of Mr. and Mrs. Pullman's acquaintances, they attend the summer games hosted in Pullman each summer."

He waited as though he expected some response. But Mr. Howard's revelation had rendered her speechless. She could barely believe her ears. Randolph Morgan was married and had children? How could that be? Worse yet, *she* must be the one to deliver this startling news to Lady Charlotte. Her ladyship certainly didn't expect to hear that the man she planned to wed was already married—and a father! There must be some explanation, but she could imagine none at the moment.

Once she'd gathered her wits, Olivia forced herself to speak. "Somehow, I believed Mr. Morgan was a resident of Pullman."

Mr. Howard remained close by her side while they continued to stroll down the shaded sidewalk. "No. Like Mr. Pullman, he lives in Chicago. So you're acquainted with Mr. Morgan?"

Olivia shook her head and clasped an open palm to her bodice. "Oh no. I've never personally met the gentleman." Careful to avoid any mention of Lady Charlotte, she explained that Mr. Morgan had interviewed and hired her dear cousin Albert Mott on one of his visits to England.

"So *that's* why you've chosen Pullman as your new home. I knew there must be a sound reason for you to forfeit your position at Lanshire Hall."

Olivia didn't bother to respond. What could she say that wouldn't compound the lies she'd already told? She focused her thoughts on Lady Charlotte and how she would react to the news. Where would Charlotte go and what would she do? Perhaps she could spend the night at the hotel and return to Chicago in the morning. And then what? Would her ladyship go home and tell her parents the truth? She doubted whether Lady Charlotte would consider that suggestion a realistic solution to her problem. Olivia was uncertain how long they'd been walking when Mr. Howard led her toward a set of wooden steps that fronted one of the brick row houses.

He pulled a key from his vest pocket. "I can offer you two choices for your housing arrangements. Since you'll be furnished many of your meals at the hotel, I thought you might want to room with another family. If not, you may rent one of the smaller row houses and take in a boarder or two if you wish. Otherwise, you'll find that alternative rather expensive." He turned the key in the lock. "Perhaps your cousin would like to rent one of the rooms."

Moving in with another family held little appeal, yet she must talk to Albert before agreeing to rent the house. "May I withhold my decision until I speak with my cousin? Perhaps I could take a room in the hotel for tonight." Surely Charlotte would pay for a hotel room for one night.

"I understand your dilemma, Miss Mott, but our hotel rooms are rather expensive." Mr. Howard tugged at his collar. "Most of our guests are wealthy businessmen. . . ."

Obviously her suggestion caused him discomfort. "I see. Then I wonder if you could offer some suggestion to aid me?"

He brightened at the request. "I shall be at home this evening. Once you've talked to your cousin, the two of you may come to my house and advise me of your decision. I'll make the necessary arrangements so that you can move into the lodgings of your choice tonight."

Well, she couldn't ask for any more than that! "I believe you've offered me a suitable solution to my problem. Thank you, Mr. Howard."

"My pleasure. Shall I accompany you on a tour of the Ar—" He stopped midsentence and stared toward the park.

Olivia followed his gaze. She couldn't believe her eyes. Charlotte was sitting on one of the park benches—*waving*. Whatever was she thinking!

Mr. Howard shaded his eyes and took a step forward, his eyebrows furrowed. "I don't believe I know that young lady."

Olivia clasped his arm. "She's signaling me. She's a friend who accompanied me from England." The words spilled out of her mouth before she could stop them.

"With you? Is she seeking employment?" The moment he'd asked the question, a gust of wind captured Charlotte's cloak and whisked it aside. Her bulging midsection protruded like a small watermelon. Mr. Howard arched his brows. "And does your friend have a husband, Miss Mott?"

"She's a widow. A dreadful accident."

The lies slipped over her tongue like butter. In her haste to prove the validity of her response, Olivia chattered on. Mr. Howard visibly paled as her words flowed with unbridled ease. When she eventually fell silent, he stared at her, mouth agape. She'd woven a masterful story that even the brothers Grimm would have applauded.

Mr. Howard shook his head while he commiserated over Charlotte's future.

Best to strike when opportunity availed itself, she decided. "Is there any rule that would prohibit her from residing with me should she so choose? With her small inheritance, she could pay enough that I could afford the house." She offered him a bright smile. "And my cousin wouldn't need to make any change in his current living arrangements."

"Highly unusual." He massaged his forehead. "Residents of Pullman are either employees or relatives. *Is* she related to you, Miss Mott?"

Did he want her to change her previous comment? Was he encouraging her to lie? She couldn't be certain.

"Might she be a distant cousin?"

Olivia bit her lower lip. "Perhaps." Her voice was no more than a whisper.

"Excellent! Then I see no problem. Why don't we go and tell your *distant cousin* the good news?" With a conspiratorial wink, he grasped her elbow and began to walk toward the park.

Olivia jerked to a halt. "No! We don't want to do that."

"We don't?" He appeared dismayed by her behavior.

She wagged her head back and forth. "No, we don't. Her loss is so recent that she becomes extremely emotional." Olivia dropped her voice a notch. "She's embarrassed by her outbursts—especially in public or with strangers."

The company agent's enthusiasm deflated as quickly as a punctured balloon. "Having experienced a similar plight, I thought I might be able to lend a word of comfort." He tipped his head to the side and frowned. "I'm somewhat surprised to see your friend has already given up her mourning attire."

Olivia silently chided herself. Why hadn't she thought of her ladyship's dress? Any respectable widow would be wearing a black mourning gown rather than a pink and white silk stripe.

Mr. Howard awaited her response.

"Questions! Charlotte detests having strangers interrogate her about her husband's death."

When he slowly nodded, Olivia continued. "Charlotte donned her normal daytime attire at my recommendation. She loathed the idea. However, she soon discovered my plan freed her from a plethora of prying questions."

Yet another lie! If she didn't soon record this entire tale, she'd surely forget one of the details. Worse yet, she must see to it that Lady Charlotte learned every minute facet of her story. Otherwise, they would most certainly be found out. "If you would permit me a moment alone with my friend, I'll advise her to wait for me while we tour the house."

Mr. Howard glanced in Lady Charlotte's direction. "You're quite sure she wouldn't like to join us? It might relieve some of her worries, even cheer her a bit to see the fine dwelling where she'll be living."

"No!"

Mr. Howard startled at her sharp response.

Olivia silently chastised herself for her careless behavior. After a gentle reminder of Charlotte's fragile emotional state, she said, "I truly believe it's best for us to go alone. I'll return straightaway."

Olivia hurried across the grassy expanse and wasted no time issuing her brief instructions to Lady Charlotte. "You *must* do as I've requested. I'll explain everything upon my return."

She hastened back to Mr. Howard's side. There was little doubt he'd been carefully watching the exchange, and Olivia forced herself to assume a nonchalant demeanor. "I was correct in my assumption. Charlotte much prefers to remain in the park and enjoy the fresh air."

During their walk and the subsequent tour of the house, Mr. Howard plied her with questions. In order to avoid telling any further lies, she responded with varying and sundry inquiries of her own. For the most part, she was successful. And when she could think of no further questions, she expounded upon the beauty of Pullman, a topic that Mr. Howard was more than willing to dwell upon.

Although Olivia had explained Charlotte's aversion to visiting with strangers during her time of grief, Mr. Howard remained close at hand as they started toward the park. She must find some way to escape him and speak privately with Charlotte. There was so much to tell her ladyship. "I would be grateful for assistance with the delivery of our baggage from the train depot to the house," Olivia said. "If you could direct me to someone who could help?"

"Please allow me. All of the horses, carriages, and wagons are maintained in the Pullman Stables." He nodded toward the clean and quiet streets. "Makes for a tidier community. I can stop and make the arrangements before returning to work."

"I do appreciate your kindness, especially when I've already taken far too much of your time."

"My pleasure. As I mentioned earlier, I'll be at home this evening if you need anything further." He tipped his hat. "I'm pleased that you've joined our community, Miss Mott."

Waiting only until he was out of sight, Olivia hiked her skirt and hurried off to meet with Lady Charlotte. Though glad to be free of Mr. Howard, she feared revealing the news of Mr. Morgan's marriage. What if Lady Charlotte caused a scene and drew unwanted attention? Olivia maintained a steady gaze on her former mistress, suddenly struck by the realization that Charlotte might not want to remain in Pullman any longer. If so, what would she tell Mr. Howard?

Don't borrow trouble. The words played over and over in her mind as she approached. Lady Charlotte stepped forward with an air of expectancy. "Well?"

Olivia forced a smile. "Chef René has hired me as his assistant. I begin tomorrow, though I fear I'll be an utter failure. Your letter was much too—"

"No." Charlotte shook her head and frowned. "I want to hear about Randolph. Did you secure his address?"

"Why don't we go over there?" Olivia didn't wait for Lady Charlotte to protest. Instead, she pointed toward a bench along the far side of the park and marched off. If her ladyship wanted to hear anything further, she'd be required to follow. At least the woman would be somewhat closer to the ground in the event she fainted. Callous thought, perhaps, but Olivia had heard many a story about her ladyship's petulant behavior. As Charlotte's lady-in-waiting, Ludie had always taken such conduct in stride, but Olivia wasn't accustomed to dealing with high-strung women who succumbed to fainting spells and tantrums. Ludie would know how to handle this situation, but Ludie wasn't in Pullman.

Charlotte panted for breath as she yanked on Olivia's hand and plopped down. "This bench will do! Now tell me about Randolph."

Olivia hesitated, searching for the proper words, but nothing came to mind.

"Well, come on, girl! Tell me what you've discovered!"

It might have been Lady Charlotte's angry tone, or the fact she'd called her *girl,* or perchance it was the final realization there would be no easy way to convey the information. For whatever reason and without further thought, Olivia blurted out the dreaded words. "He's married."

Olivia clenched her fists in expectation of a scream, a denial—some show of emotion. She waited. But only silence reigned. Lady Charlotte merely stared at her as though she hadn't spoken. Olivia forced her gaze away from the woman and looked down at her scuffed shoes. She should have polished them before going on the interview. But she shouldn't be thinking about her shoes at this moment.

Giving herself a silent rebuke for her callous behavior, Olivia stole a glance at her former mistress. "Did you hear me, Lady Charlotte? I said that Mr. Morgan is married—he has children. He and his family live in Chicago, not in Pullman."

This time Olivia *should* have clenched her fists. Lady Charlotte's tirade was like nothing she had ever witnessed. The woman appeared to experience a state of delayed hysteria as she shrieked, wailed, and accused Olivia of lying. But when the outburst finally concluded, no more than an occasional sob or hiccough escaped Lady Charlotte's lips. The emotional explosion had taken its toll. Bright red splotches mottled her ladyship's porcelain complexion, and pillowed half moons slowly formed beneath her azure eyes.

"Your information must be incorrect. Are you certain you asked about *Randolph* Morgan?" A loud hiccough followed the question.

Olivia gave an authoritative nod. They *both* knew the account was correct, the only difference being Lady Charlotte's reluctance to accept the truth. "I know you're unnerved by this dreadful news. However, you *must* make some immediate decisions."

After one glance at Lady Charlotte's quivering lower lip, Olivia revealed the housing arrangement she'd made with Mr. Howard. When she'd finished, Charlotte silently looked toward the horizon.

Not knowing what else she should do or say, Olivia added, "Please don't feel obliged to remain because of the living accommodations. I can ask my cousin to share the house with me."

The comment had the desired effect. Charlotte glanced at her protruding stomach. "Where else could I go? I certainly cannot go home in this condition. Neither my parents nor I could abide the gossip that would be whispered throughout

London. I'd ruin any possibility of a proper marriage." She rested one hand upon her stomach. "If only I'd taken care of matters earlier." She slumped back against the bench.

Olivia didn't know if Charlotte meant she should have contacted Mr. Morgan several months ago or she should have done harm to the child before arriving at this stage in her pregnancy. And Olivia truly didn't want to know. For if it was the latter, she would think far less highly of the woman.

"Why don't you sit here while I check to see that our luggage is on the way? Then I'll take you to see our new home." Charlotte didn't argue. She'd transformed into a docile and submissive companion. How had their roles so quickly changed?

Olivia wished she had given this matter more thought before offering Charlotte a home. But when? There had been no time for well-thought-out decisions. She'd been too busy improvising. Too busy *lying*. She must commit all she'd said to paper. Otherwise, she would surely forget and become ensnared in that tacky spider's web of which her aunt had warned.

Crossing the wide street to the stables, she attempted to remember everything she'd told Chef René and Mr. Howard and Mr. Billings. Had she spoken to anyone else? Suddenly she wondered if Charlotte had spoken to any strangers while she shopped in the Arcade. *First things first*, she warned herself. She had issues of greater concern. What if she couldn't perform her duties? What if Chef René declared her a fraud and banned her from his kitchen? By this time tomorrow, she and Lady Charlotte could both find themselves dispossessed in this foreign country.

CHAPTER FOUR

As he walked toward home, Samuel Howard briefly glanced over his shoulder at Olivia Mott. A pretty girl with dark brown eyes and curly hair the color of freshly brewed coffee—*and* exceptional references. He ran his hand along his jaw. Almost too exceptional. His years with Mr. Pullman had made him a fair judge of character, and something seemed amiss in this case. Had Mr. Pullman not sensed a problem?

Instead of passing by the hotel and going home for the noonday meal, he bounded up the steps. Offering Mr. Billings a hasty wave, he continued down the hallway to the kitchen. The hotel dining room had already filled with guests—likely not the best time to visit Chef René.

The rotund chef immersed a wire basket of asparagus spears into a large kettle of boiling water, looking up only long enough to acknowledge Samuel's presence. Undoubtedly, his primary concern was cooking the asparagus to perfection, not an unexpected interruption by the company agent. Samuel waited, extending the same courtesy he expected from others.

Moments later, the chef motioned an assistant forward. "You may arrange the plates while I speak to Mr. Howard. Make certain you do it properly, as I will be watching." The chef raised his eyebrows and rolled his eyes heavenward. "Good help is impossible to find, is it not? How may I be of assistance, Mr. Howard?"

Samuel motioned the chef out of the assistant's hearing. "About Miss Mott."

Before he could elaborate, Chef René slapped a hand to his forehead and shouted at the assistant. The asparagus hadn't been properly positioned atop the toast points. Samuel didn't understand why it should matter, but placing toast points beneath the asparagus seemed a matter of extreme import to the chef. He stomped across the room and, with a flair normally expected only in a theatrical presentation, rearranged the food.

Taking a step back, he studied the dinner plates. "Oui! You see how much better that is?" The thick ham steaks were centered on the plate. Asparagus spears, aligned on the toast points and topped with a creamy hollandaise sauce, were positioned down one side of the ham steak. Along the opposite side of the plate in a perfect semicircle was a serving of buttered potatoes sprinkled with parsley.

The quaking assistant bobbed her head, loaded the plates onto a serving tray, and beckoned for one of the servers while Chef René returned his attention to Samuel. "You were asking about Miss Mott?"

Samuel tilted his head a few inches closer. "Did you find her letter of recommendation somewhat astounding?"

The chef shrugged. "Who can say? Soon enough we shall

see if she possesses talent. Let us hope so. As you can see, I am surrounded by people who are better suited to raising asparagus than cooking or serving it." With a hearty laugh, he grasped Samuel's shoulder. "However, Mr. Pullman made the decision to hire her, so there is little responsibility on your part—or mine. If it pleases Mr. Pullman to have her work in his hotel kitchen, then it will please me. I would surmise he doesn't want to offend one of his investors. At least Miss Mott is a pleasant young woman, and she seems bright—unlike some of the others working in this kitchen." The chef winked. "Attractive also, don't you agree?"

A flush of heat rose from Samuel's tight collar to the top of his head. "Yes, she is attractive, but my concern is her suitability to work in your kitchen. I want you to inform me of any problems."

"If she is inept, it will be *my* problem. Until Mr. Pullman tells me she is to be dismissed, I will be forced to adjust. We can only hope her recommendation is well founded." He leaned a bit closer. "Of course, who can trust the judgment of the English? The country has produced few who should hold the title of chef."

Chef René waved at his assistant, who had piled another batch of asparagus in the wire basket. "If there's nothing further, I must see to my food preparation." Without waiting for a reply, René lunged at the wire basket and rescued the asparagus before it could be immersed in the kettle of boiling water.

Samuel didn't wait long enough to hear what was sure to be an upbraiding of the kitchen assistant. He wondered how young Miss Mott would withstand such a tongue-lashing. Then again, if she truly possessed all of the talents described in her letter of recommendation, there would be no need for such a remonstration.

Like Chef René, Samuel thought Miss Mott quite attractive. Yet there was something elusive about her behavior. In any event, he would make it a point to stop by this evening and see if she and the young widow were settling into their living quarters. It was the least he could do—a kind and welcoming gesture, he told himself.

Lady Charlotte stood in front of the brick row houses that lined Watt Avenue. Her lip curled as she peered up the front steps leading to number 341. "This is it?"

Olivia forced herself to remain civil. What did Charlotte expect? The woman had already seen a great deal of the town. She knew it consisted of similar brick dwellings, most of them sharing common walls and small front yards. Olivia thought the houses charming. Obviously Lady Charlotte found them objectionable. Had her ladyship expected a fine castle to suddenly appear in the midst of these row houses? Even if it had, such a fine home wouldn't be offered to the likes of Olivia.

With a true sense of satisfaction, she retrieved the key Mr. Howard had given her and proudly unlocked the front door. Never before had she lived in even a room she could call her own. Now she was the renter of her very own row house—almost. Of course, she couldn't afford the entire amount of the rent without assistance from Lady Charlotte. But still, the rental agreement bore *her* name.

"Where is the furniture? Are we to sit on the floor? I trust there are at least beds and linens."

The look of disdain was enough to erase Olivia's excitement. Why hadn't she considered the absence of furniture when Mr. Howard escorted her through the residence? "I was concerned only that there would be accommodations adequate for both of us, your ladyship. I didn't think to ask about furniture."

Regaining her air of authority, Lady Charlotte patted Olivia's shoulder. "It wasn't my intent to injure your feelings. This has been a trying day for both of us. Until we can furnish the house, I suggest we check into the hotel. We certainly can't sleep on the floor."

Though Olivia thought she could sleep on the floor without too much difficulty, she didn't argue the point. "Mr. Howard mentioned the hotel rooms are costly. I think he would find extravagant spending out of character for a chef's assistant and her widowed friend."

"Widow?"

"When your cape flew open and revealed your condition, I had to tell him something."

Lady Charlotte continued to glare at her as if a further explanation was expected.

"He asked if you were married." Olivia wanted to add that if Charlotte would have remained in the Arcade as they'd arranged, she wouldn't have been forced to provide Mr. Howard with a string of lies.

"Since Mr. Howard is so interested in my welfare, perhaps *he* can suggest where we might locate some furniture." Hands on her hips, Charlotte stared at her.

Did her ladyship truly think she should attempt to locate Mr. Howard? "My cousin Albert will be home from work before six o'clock. I obtained his address from Mr. Howard. I think he may be a better choice to help us with this dilemma."

"We cannot possibly wait until then. What if he can't help? Nightfall will be upon us, and if the hotel is full for the night, we'll be forced to remain in this uninhabitable dwelling." Contempt reverberated in Charlotte's words as clearly as a pealing bell. "Go and talk to that Mr. Howard again." She motioned toward the door.

Lady Charlotte's list of priorities differed from Olivia's in the extreme, with Olivia's two primary concerns consisting of committing their story to paper—she much preferred to think of their lies as a "story"—and reuniting with her cousin. She could ask Albert for assistance, a much more agreeable solution to their problem, to her way of thinking. And if her culinary abilities proved less than what Chef René expected—no doubt they would—the two of them might not be in Pullman long enough to need furniture. That thought was reason enough for her to reestablish control of their situation.

"No. We're going to wait here. Right now, I'm going to tell you all that we must remember. Once our trunks arrive, I'll commit our story to paper. While I'm at work tomorrow, you must memorize *all* of it."

Apparently her voice had commanded authority, for Charlotte sat down on one of the steps. Perching an elbow on one knee, she rested her chin in the palm of her hand. "Well, go ahead then. Set forth your list of lies."

Olivia flinched at the remark. Charlotte had worded her comment as easily as though airing an inventory of lies were a daily occurrence. And as if all of the lies belonged solely to her. When had Charlotte surrendered ownership of their deceit? Olivia forced away the thought. She was too deeply enmeshed in this tale to now act the innocent.

A short time later, the sound of an approaching wagon rumbled down the street, and soon a knock sounded at the door. Fortunately, she had told Charlotte most of the story. Olivia hoped she herself would remember everything when she finally had time to commit their lies to paper.

As Olivia rose from the stairway to answer the door, Charlotte tapped her hand. "Don't forget the forged letter of recommendation and the pieces of jewelry you stole from my mother. Be certain you put those on your list, too."

Olivia's heart thumped wildly. Each thought of the falsified document she had presented to Mr. Howard caused wild palpitations, but *stolen* jewelry? Why would Charlotte accuse her of theft? "You told me it was *your* jewelry!" She ignored the knocking at the front door. Her fear rose like a tidal wave as she waited for Charlotte to affirm the truth of her response.

Instead, Charlotte brushed past her and opened the door. "Do come in." When the men had deposited the first two trunks in the hallway and turned to retrieve the others, Charlotte blocked their exit and batted her lashes. "Would you strong men kindly consider carrying our trunks upstairs? As you can imagine, the two of us couldn't possibly manage such a burden."

Both men beamed at Charlotte and nearly knocked each other over in their attempt to do her bidding. Had Olivia not been so angry, she would have laughed at the spectacle. She waited only until the men had lumbered up the stairs before grabbing Charlotte by the hand. Olivia yanked her into the parlor. "Was the jewelry I sold yours or was it not?" She hissed the words like a snake preparing to strike its prey.

Twisting out of her grasp, Charlotte nodded toward the

stairs. "We don't want our conversation to be overheard. There will be more than ample time for discussion once we're alone." She smiled demurely as the men returned downstairs. "You certainly are strong."

Had she been a pigeon, Charlotte couldn't have cooed any better! Olivia merely shook her head in disgust and stepped into the parlor until the men had unloaded the final baggage. They adamantly refused Charlotte's attempt to pay for their assistance. "It has been our privilege to help you," they insisted. With a coquettish giggle, she escorted the men outside and waved as they drove off in the wagon.

Charlotte's flirtatious behavior was truly beyond the pale. Olivia could only hope that the men hadn't misconstrued the unseemly behavior. Normally, Charlotte's expectant condition would deter any interest or advances by men. However, in the short time it had taken the Pullman employees to unload their belongings, Charlotte had mentioned her widowhood several times. No doubt she would be offended if one of those men should attempt to come calling on her. Yet Olivia noted her ladyship didn't hesitate to use her womanly wiles for her own gain.

With a mixture of false bravado and anger, Olivia tapped the toe of her shoe on the hardwood floor. "Well?"

"I suppose the jewelry could have been considered jointly owned by me and my mother."

"*What?* But you—"

Charlotte waved her hand. "Let me finish. The jewelry has passed through our family from mother to daughter for generations. Since I am her only daughter, the jewels would pass to me at her death. It's a matter of interpretation and timing." She shrugged. "No doubt my mother considered the jewelry hers rather than mine."

Olivia clutched the newel-post for support. "And she has no doubt reported the items stolen?"

"I imagine Father would take care of that. Mother wouldn't—"

"Oh, forevermore, Charlotte! I don't care which one of them might have gone to the authorities. I'm concerned with the fact that they would believe the jewelry has been stolen."

Charlotte nonchalantly bobbed her head. "I would surmise they think of the missing jewelry as stolen rather than my claim to an early inheritance."

Olivia nibbled at her lower lip as she sought to unscramble the frightening news. "When you instructed me to go and sell the items, you specifically told me they belonged to you. If the authorities locate the shop where I sold the jewels, the owner is bound to give my description. I'll be considered a thief!"

"Do cease all this fretting. The authorities are not going to travel from London searching for you. Eventually Mother will give up on finding the items and will simply purchase new ones." A faraway look glistened in Charlotte's eyes. "I do wish I could be there to help her choose."

The remark was so totally ludicrous Olivia didn't know whether to laugh or cry. How could the woman even think such a ridiculous thought? "Forgive me if I don't lament with you, Lady Charlotte."

"No need to be derisive." Charlotte tilted her head and looked down her nose. "I thought we were getting on rather nicely, and I was beginning to consider you a confidante. In the future, I'll keep my thoughts to myself. Just remember—you need me."

Olivia clenched her hands together and forced a grim smile. "And I hope you will remember that you are in need of *my* assistance, your ladyship."

Charlotte's hand rested on her bulging midsection. "Well, then, we need each other, don't we?" Waving Olivia forward as though not a cross word had been exchanged, Charlotte headed up the stairs. "Come along. Let's begin memorizing that story of yours."

Olivia balanced the tablet of paper on her perched knees while she delineated the items that must be committed to memory. After completing the list, she tucked the pencil behind one ear. "I do wish I had told Mr. Howard I met you on the ship. Now he's going to expect me to know about your previous life, and so will everyone else we meet. And that means we'll have to memorize more lies." She sighed at the remembrance of Aunt Eleanor's admonition.

Seemingly undeterred, Charlotte pointed to Olivia's ear. "Please remove that pencil from behind your ear. It is most unladylike and, even more, unfashionable, I might add." She tapped the writing tablet. "If you're uneasy about anything, let's decide right now. You can annotate the story of my life on our list, and we'll memorize it along with everything else."

For the next half hour, they were storytellers. After one of them suggested an idea, the other would embellish or correct it until they were both satisfied and ready to begin the next thread. Each piece of Charlotte's recently created life history was added to the page when they were both in agreement.

Cupping her chin in her palm, Charlotte balanced her elbow on one knee. "Read it to me one last time so I'm sure to remember."

"You'll have all day tomorrow to memorize—" Startled by a loud knock at the door, Olivia mashed her lips together. Who could be calling on them? Not giving heed to the time, she jumped to her feet, filled with an expectant joy. "Perhaps it's Albert." Her eager smile disappeared when she rushed downstairs and yanked open the door.

The glint in Mr. Howard's eyes faded. "You were expecting someone else?"

Olivia couldn't tell if Mr. Howard was disillusioned, angry, or merely perplexed by her lack of enthusiasm at his arrival. "I thought perhaps it was my cousin."

"Why, how would he know you've even arrived in town?" Mr. Howard pulled his pocket watch from his waistcoat and then shook his head. "In addition, it's only two forty-five. I thought I mentioned Albert doesn't finish his workday until five-thirty." Without waiting for an introduction, he peered around Olivia. "I'm Samuel Howard, the company agent. And you must be Miss Mott's friend."

Olivia's throat constricted. Would Charlotte act like a grieving merchant's widow instead of the flirtatious daughter of English nobility? Olivia sent a prayer winging toward heaven but quickly recanted. Had she actually thought God wanted to help his children promote lies and deceit? She shuddered at her own irreverence and silently requested forgiveness.

[illegible] [illegible] [illegible] [illegible] [illegible] [illegible] [illegible] [illegible] [illegible] [illegible] [illegible] [illegible] [illegible] [illegible] [illegible] [illegible] [illegible]

[illegible] [illegible]

[illegible] forgiveness.

Chapter Five

Olivia wedged herself in the doorway and stared at Mr. Howard. Words failed her. She silently chastised herself. With all their scheming, how had they overlooked selecting a proper name for her ladyship? Mr. Howard raised his brows. "Yes, this is my friend." She hesitated. "La—Char—Mrs. Horn . . . Hornsby. My friend Mrs. Hornsby—*Widow* Hornsby." Olivia raised her voice by at least an octave and hoped Charlotte would heed her prompting.

When she continued to block the doorway, Mr. Howard stared at her as though she'd lost all sense of propriety. She had no choice but to step aside and permit him entry. The moment he crossed the threshold, Charlotte jumped to her feet. Olivia glared, but to no avail. The woman batted her lashes and coyly smiled at Mr. Howard while she explained their dire need of furniture and household goods.

Drastic measures would be needed to gain control of her ladyship's behavior. Olivia moved to Charlotte's side and covertly pinched her arm. When Charlotte squealed in pain, Olivia hastened to allay Mr. Howard's obvious concern. "She's fine—merely a stitch. From time to time Charlotte, Mrs. Hornsby, is overcome with an occasional pain that quickly subsides." Olivia directed a warning look at her ladyship. "The doctor in London remained uncertain if the bouts are caused by her present condition or her profound *grief*." She virtually hissed the final word.

Sympathy emanated from Mr. Howard's eyes as he pushed the wave of hair from his forehead. "You poor woman. So young to have suffered such tragedy. I do admire your bravery—setting sail and coming to a new country so soon after your loss." He briefly glanced at Charlotte's expanding waistline. "And in your present condition."

Olivia heaved a sigh of relief when she saw recognition spark in Charlotte's eyes and the smile fade from her lips. *Finally!*

"I attempt to do my best under the circumstances. Even Olivia can attest to the fact that I force myself to feign cheerfulness. In reality, my grief appears to make those around me uncomfortable. And far be it from me to cause others discomfort."

Olivia glanced heavenward at Charlotte's final remark. "Mrs. Hornsby finds questions about her husband's death most distressing."

Charlotte bobbed her head up and down. "Indeed. I find such inquiries intrusive and disquieting—*and* a breach of proper etiquette."

Clasping a hand to his chest, Mr. Howard offered a sympathetic nod. "I *do* understand. Perhaps Miss Mott mentioned that I lost my wife to a terrible bout of pneumonia?"

Olivia gulped. "No! I didn't share your personal information with Mrs. Hornsby." Apparently Mr. Howard was grieved by her oversight, for all evidence of his earlier smile vanished. Suddenly, Olivia felt required to absolve herself. "I try to avoid any talk of death with Mrs. Hornsby." She leaned a tad closer and lowered her voice. "Upsetting."

Her explanation seemed to appease him.

"Yes, of course." He glanced about the house. "Now, then, I must do something to aid you in locating furniture for this place. Without a proper bed to sleep in, I can't expect our new chef's assistant to arrive prepared for work in the morning, can I?"

Olivia didn't know if he expected an answer, but she needn't have worried. Charlotte immediately seized upon the moment and soon parlayed their situation into a promise of furniture before nightfall. Mr. Howard departed with a purposeful stride, clearly pleased he had come to the aid of two damsels in distress—as Charlotte fancifully described their situation.

Olivia had cringed at the woman's behavior. Charlotte had used every advantage in her portrayal of a grieving widow. Indeed, she'd taken the role to new heights. Olivia wondered if Charlotte possessed even a smidgen of decency. Was this considered normal conduct for members of the aristocracy or simply a reflection of her ladyship's ever-indulgent behavior? She wondered if Ludie was pleased to be free of her duties as Charlotte's lady-in-waiting. Had the maid been assigned a new position or instructed to simply await Charlotte's return? Olivia hoped it was the latter. After caring for Charlotte all these years, Ludie deserved a good long rest.

Olivia climbed the stairs, anxious to be alone for a few moments. Though her bedroom was the smaller of the two, a narrow bench seat had been fitted beneath the double windows, a feature that pleased her. The men had placed her baggage along the north wall, and she hefted the smaller valise onto the bench. Surprised by a sudden urge to connect with her sparse memories, Olivia unclasped the leather strap and dug inside the suitcase. A euphoric sigh escaped her lips when she touched the smooth wood of the rectangular box. Clutching the keepsake recipe box, she lifted it from the bag and pressed the cool wood to her cheek. A poor substitute for a mother's love, yet, along with her mother's Bible, the only reminders she had ever known.

Aunt Eleanor had always said she was much like her mother, but Olivia couldn't be certain. Her father had never confirmed such facts, but then she'd seen little of him. He'd taken to drinking after her mother died—at least that's what she'd been told. She'd been only two years old and had few memories of him, though he hadn't died until shortly before her fifteenth birthday.

Lifting the lid, she removed the recipe located at the front of the box. Sunday Scones. Aunt Eleanor said they had been her mother's favorite. Olivia traced her finger across the exacting script that listed each ingredient as well as the mixing and baking instructions. If only she could step into Aunt Eleanor's kitchen and mix a batch of the current-laden pastries right now. Instead, she'd been forced into this horrid predicament, wherein she must carefully weigh every word she spoke. Not only did she fear a slipup each time she spoke, she dreaded failure in her position at the hotel. More frightening, what if she should be accused of theft by her former employer? And, of course, the forged letter of recommendation could not be forgotten. Her future hung in a delicate balance. All because of Charlotte!

And what of you? Do you have no responsibility in this maze of deceit and lies? The quiet voice pricked her conscience. Hoping to silence the condemnation, she jumped to her feet. A walk to the Arcade might prove to be just what she needed. Once she began work in the morning, she'd have few opportunities to leisurely browse in the various shops. Retrieving her mother's recipe from the box, she tucked the paper into her pocket. Perhaps she would purchase the ingredients to bake scones.

She grabbed her cloak from the bench and watched as the writing tablet dropped to the floor with a thud. She couldn't leave the list in plain sight. There was no way of knowing who might pass through the house delivering furniture. She ripped the pages from the tablet and folded them into a neat rectangle. She stared out the window. Where could she hide them? Suddenly she knew exactly where the list would be safe. She picked up the wooden recipe box and shoved the list inside. With a quick snap, she closed the lid and headed toward the stairway.

Charlotte remained perched on the step where Olivia had left her only a short time earlier. Edging her way around Charlotte, Olivia offered a slight wave. "Since you've already seen the Arcade, I thought you could wait for Mr. Howard." Without an effort at decorum, Olivia plopped her hat atop her head and turned the doorknob. Once she reached the sidewalk, her escape from Charlotte would be assured, she thought, but then she heard Mr. Howard calling her name. She turned and spotted him. He was a block away, waving his hat back and forth to gain her attention. If only she hadn't heeded his call, she could have been well on her way to spending a bit of time at the emporium.

He hurried his pace, his long legs permitting a lengthy stride as he approached her. Panting, he held one hand to his chest. "It appears I'm not in the same physical condition as the men practicing to compete in the athletic games."

Olivia didn't know what Mr. Howard was referring to, but she wasn't interested at the moment. "I had planned to go and do a bit of shopping at the Arcade. Lady . . . Mrs. Hornsby is inside awaiting your return." Olivia silently chided herself for the near slipup with Charlotte's name. She must quit thinking of her as *Lady* Charlotte.

Mr. Howard moved to one side and blocked her escape. "I'd be most pleased to escort you. My earlier invitation to show you about the town remains open, and I do hope you'll accept."

How could she refuse? He was, after all, the company agent. "What about the household items?" She hoped she could still divert him.

He nodded. "Taken care of. They'll be delivered in short order. Mrs. Hornsby can take charge of directing the men. She shouldn't have any need for my assistance." He offered an apologetic shrug. "I can't guarantee it will be everything you need, but the two of you will have beds and linens, along with a divan and several chairs. Perhaps Mrs. Hornsby should plan to take her meals at the hotel until you've adequately supplied the kitchen."

Olivia nearly laughed aloud. If only he knew that cooking utensils were the least of Charlotte's concerns. She wouldn't care a whit if a carving knife or platter ever made its way into the kitchen, for her ladyship would never use them! "I'm certain she'll be delighted to partake of Chef René's fine cooking."

"And yours."

The note of pride in his voice was unsettling. *Wait until he discovers that my letter of recommendation consisted mostly of false praise.*

Olivia noted the throng of workers who filled the streets, and she searched their faces for her cousin's familiar blue eyes and broad smile. Mr. Howard removed his pocket watch and checked the time. "I believe your cousin should be arriving home about now. Why don't I escort you to his residence?"

With a bob of her head, Olivia accepted his offer. Mr. Howard explained that most of the men working the day shift worked from seven in the morning until five-thirty in the evening with a half hour lunch break. "There are a few employees who are required to work longer hours, but most work a ten-hour shift."

She wanted to hurry him along but continued at his snail's pace like a proper lady.

"Of course, your hours will be somewhat longer in order to accommodate the dining habits of our guests. However, Chef René will have the final say in that regard." They came to a stop in front of one of the redbrick tenements. "This is where your cousin resides. I'll bid you farewell. I'm certain you'll want time alone with your cousin after your separation."

She thanked him for his kindness and hurried up the front steps. She knocked and waited, her heart fluttering with excitement. The door opened and Olivia jerked back. Instantly she knew she'd made a mistake. In a slow motion ballet, her foot teetered to one side and slipped off the top step. The lurching movement sent her arms flailing about like propellers as she attempted to regain her balance. She stared into the questioning blue eyes of the man whose strong arms now encircled her.

"You're not Albert." She could feel the heat rise in her cheeks. What a foolish thing to say—of course he wasn't Albert.

He grinned and released his hold. "No. I'm Fred DeVault. Why is it Albert has all the luck? He already has Martha, and now another lovely young lady has entered his life."

By now her face had likely flushed bright red. "I'm Albert's cousin, Olivia Mott."

He brightened and waved her toward the door. "In that case, do come in. Albert should be home soon." He glanced down the street one final time before leading her inside. "If I didn't know better, I'd think Mr. Howard had escorted you to our front door."

"So he did. With a few simple instructions, I believe I could have found the place myself, but he has been ever so helpful. He's quite the gentleman."

"There are those who might argue that point," he muttered. "Come along and let me introduce you to my mother. She's the one who's in charge of keeping Albert and me on a straight and narrow path."

Olivia giggled as he led her down the hallway. "I didn't realize Albert had changed so much. His mother will be sad to hear such news."

The blue eyes of the short, stocky woman who was standing in the kitchen sparkled. "Don't you go believing Fred. *He's* the one who needs watching. Albert's a fine young man, ready to settle down with his Martha."

"So Albert *has* met someone special."

Fred leaned against the kitchen table. "You could say that. I'm thinking he and Martha Mosher will be married before the year ends if Albert has his way. Are you here for a visit or planning to make your home in Pullman, Miss Mott?"

"Where are your manners, Fred? Offer the lady a chair before you start with your questions."

Mrs. DeVault placed a cup of tea in front of Olivia and continued paring potatoes. Fred plopped down in the chair opposite her. "Now tell us about yourself, Miss Mott. With that accent, I take it you're from London, too?"

"Yes, I am. I worked in Lanshire Hall—in the kitchen." She must turn the conversation away from herself. "I've only seen a small portion of your town, but I must say that I am most impressed and pleased that I will be making my home here. Mr. Pullman must be a wonderful man."

Fred leaned across the table. "*Wonderful?* Let me tell you a little about the man who founded this town. Like most of the capitalists in Chicago, George Pullman came up from nothing. Unfortunately, once these men begin to make money, greed takes over and they want more and more—they're consumed with accumulating more wealth. Pullman started out in the house-moving business. When the Chicago city council declared the grade of the city had to be elevated for new sewers and streets, George Pullman arrived on the scene. He and his brother operated a business that elevated buildings like the Tremont Hotel."

Olivia gasped. "Truly? I can't imagine such a feat."

He nodded. "While twelve hundred men turned five thousand jackscrews to raise the building, business went on as usual inside the hotel. And not a pane of glass was broken in the process."

"Mr. Pullman must be quite the innovative man."

Fred hesitated. "I suppose I'd agree on that point. He went on to Colorado and had good luck in the gold fields. After that is when he expanded upon the idea of the sleeper train car. There are some who think the concept of the sleeper car was all his idea, but it wasn't. He improved upon the idea by developing better sleeper cars. Now he's created a monopoly by buying out his competitors."

Olivia didn't understand the rancor she detected in Fred's response. "You don't find his story inspiring? Look at the good he's done by building this town for his workers."

He shook his head and laughed. "This town wasn't constructed as a kindness, Miss Mott. It was erected for two purposes: to make money and to control the employees. Mr. Pullman expects a minimum six percent profit from this town, and he sets the rules for how we are to live. Those seeking work with the company agree to rent from him, because those who do not are laid off during lean times—or are not hired at all."

"Yet you must agree—" Olivia stopped midsentence when she spotted her cousin walking down the hallway. The wooden chair clattered to the floor as she jumped forward to greet him. "Albert!" He pulled her into a warm embrace. Their words soon tumbled over top of each other with questions and news from London.

Finally Albert grasped her hands in his. "Are you here for a visit, or do you plan to remain in America?"

They gathered in the kitchen while Albert inquired about the voyage and her brief visits in New York and Chicago as she journeyed to Pullman. Most importantly, he wanted to know how she'd been able to afford her fine travel arrangements—it had taken him over a year of meager living to save funds for his ticket in steerage. She didn't want to go into details regarding Charlotte on her first meeting with her cousin. In fact, she hadn't truly decided how much she wanted to reveal at all. But with two strangers in the room, she decided she had best adhere to the tale she'd given Mr. Howard. Relating only meager details might prevent any possible misstep in the tale and permit an early exit from the topic.

Several minutes later, with her explanation complete, Olivia pushed away from the table. "I was hired as an assistant chef at the hotel and will begin work tomorrow." She snugged her hat more firmly atop her brown curls.

Albert slapped his knee. "Then you'll be in good company. Martha works at the Hotel Florence—she supervises the maids." He grinned. "You'll like her. I know you will."

Olivia nodded. "I'm certain you're correct." She stole a look at the clock. Charlotte would be furious if she didn't soon return. Besides, she felt as though she might drown in the steady stream of questions. She needed to come up for air. "Charlotte will be wondering what's happened to me. Perhaps you could come over this evening for a visit?"

The question had been directed at Albert, but the three of them nodded in unison, and it was Mrs. DeVault who answered first. "We'd love to meet Mrs. Hornsby." She patted Albert's shoulder. "And you can bring Martha along and introduce her, too. Olivia will already have a friend at the hotel when she begins work in the morning." She seemed pleased with herself and beamed at Olivia. "Won't that be nice?"

What could she do but agree? Too late she thought of several responses that might have forestalled the arrival of the extra uninvited guests. She hurried toward home, anxious to add notations to her list of lies—necessary documentation of who had been told what. If she didn't keep everything straight, this house of cards she'd built would soon tumble around her.

As expected, Charlotte greeted her with an angry jibe, and although Olivia offered a flowery apology, Charlotte insisted upon detailing every tiny incident that had occurred during her absence. She trailed behind Olivia like a newborn pup fearful of losing its mother. How could she possibly concentrate on her notes while Charlotte continued her incessant jabbering?

She shook her pencil at Charlotte and furrowed her brows. "Please give me a few minutes of silence so I may think."

Charlotte dropped onto one of the chairs that had been delivered during Olivia's absence and assumed a childish sulk.

So be it. Olivia could deal with Charlotte's pouting so long as she remained silent.

When she finished writing, Olivia handed her notes to Charlotte. "The furniture looks very nice, and you've had it arranged in a lovely fashion." She tapped her finger to the paper. "You have little time to read and memorize what I've written. We're entertaining guests this evening."

Chapter Six

While Albert raced upstairs to wash and change clothes before supper, Fred remained settled at the table, watching his mother move about the kitchen. She was humming a soft tune as she worked.

Fred rested his chin in his hand and peered across the room. "What did you think of Albert's cousin?"

His mother offered a brief glance. "She's a beauty, no doubt about that, and she seems nice. The question is, what did *you* think about her?"

Fred laughed. "Much the same as you, although she seems a poor judge of character. And I thought her quite young to be hired as an assistant chef."

While his mother wanted nothing more than his marriage to a suitable young woman and grandchildren she could spoil, Fred thought ample time remained for such life-altering events. All the same, he considered Olivia an engaging girl with a charming smile. He'd be more than willing to show her about town—unless

Mr. Howard had already claimed that opportunity.

His mother shrugged. "Martha is near the same age, yet she holds a position of responsibility, even supervises maids older than herself." His mother bent down and peeked in the oven to check the dinner rolls. After opening the oven door, she shifted the tin baking pan and quickly stepped back, her cheeks rosy from the heat. "And what do you mean she's a poor judge of character? You've only just met Miss Mott."

"Appears as if she may be keeping company with Mr. Howard. At least he escorted her to our front door." Fred walked to the stove and helped himself to a cup of coffee. Wrapping his large hand around the cup, he ambled back to his chair and sat down. "If she plans to keep company with the likes of Mr. Howard, then she's not figured out how to separate the wheat from the chaff."

His mother flapped her hand. "She's only just arrived. It's too early for her to make a judgment on the man's character. And you'd best keep your voice down. The windows are open. No need giving the neighbors something to talk about."

Though she smiled with the admonition, Fred knew she feared his remarks would be overheard and eventually reach the ears of company officials, which was only one of his many complaints about living in Mr. Pullman's *perfect* town. Though no one would ever admit to such behavior, there was little doubt in Fred's mind that spies lived among them in the row houses—men and women willing to report on their neighbors for an extra favor or an added dollar or two in their pay. Fred found such actions appalling and had proposed moving to Roseland or Kensington on several occasions.

However, his mother feared moving from Pullman. Too many of her friends' husbands had been laid off once they moved outside the town. She worried the same would happen to Fred. And though he'd attempted to assure her there was little chance of layoffs in the foreseeable future, she'd been reduced to tears at the very thought of moving. He'd finally given up on the idea—at least for the time being.

Fred gulped a final swig of his coffee as Albert returned to the kitchen. "This certainly has been a surprising day! I never imagined I'd come home and be greeted by my cousin Olivia. Difficult to believe!" He smoothed his damp hair with the palm of his hand. "She *was* here, wasn't she?"

Mrs. DeVault chuckled. "Indeed she was. And she seemed a very nice young lady. It's fortunate that she's located a position so quickly, too. Some of the women in our sewing circle have had their names on the waiting list at the laundry for nearly three months now." Careful to use a folded towel to protect her hand, she pulled the baking tin from the oven and placed it on the wood worktable. "Of course, Olivia has lots more experience and training, what with her education and skills in cooking."

Fred watched his mother brush melted butter atop the perfectly rounded mounds. He was thankful they had enough income that she wasn't required to seek work in the huge laundry or sewing departments where some of the town's women labored. Intermittent income from her midwifery duties provided a bit of money for what she often referred to as her rainy-day fund.

He'd seen the arrival of carloads of soiled uniforms and linens that needed to be washed and then pressed on the huge mangles and shirt-pressing machines. Occasionally he'd visited Homer Lindsey on the second floor of the laundry, where fifteen hundred pounds of soap were made each day, then piped downstairs and delivered to the huge washers, where the dirty items were restored to snowy white perfection. Homer's wife worked as a seamstress in the linen department, and they hoped to save enough to buy a house of their own in Roseland one day. Fred doubted they'd ever reach the goal, given their wages, but he didn't voice his opinion to Homer.

"Martha mentioned one of the hotel maids has quit her position to take a job in the knitting mills next week." Albert appeared pleased he'd remembered to pass along the information. "You might tell some of the ladies they could apply at the hotel."

While most everything required for the building and repair of the Pullman railroad cars had purposefully been incorporated into the multiple buildings that formed the Pullman Car Works, the positions for men far outweighed those available for women. And it seemed Fred's mother was often searching out prospects for one lady friend or another.

"If George Pullman paid a decent wage, the women wouldn't be required to work in order to make ends meet."

Once again, his mother waved a warning. "Enough of such talk. Let's enjoy our supper. I'm anxious to go visit with Albert's cousin and meet Mrs. Hornsby."

Fred grinned at his mother. "You win, Mother. I promise I'll not say another word against Mr. Pullman or the town—at least until after supper."

Charlotte remained sound asleep while Olivia prepared to depart for work the next morning. She was grateful she wouldn't be forced to listen to her ladyship whine about their poor accommodations or her need for a maid to help fashion her hair. Upon seeing the sparse furnishings in the kitchen last evening, Mrs. DeVault had insisted Charlotte come and take her meals with her the next day.

After the guests had departed the night before, Olivia had once again shoved her notes at Charlotte. "Study these again before you go to sleep and before you depart for your visit with Mrs. DeVault."

Though Charlotte had immediately objected, she conceded defeat when Olivia mentioned several errors made during the evening. Had it not been for Olivia's quick recoveries, they would have been subjected to a genuine interrogation. Now she could only hope Charlotte would heed her advice.

Attempting to assure herself all would go well on her first day in the hotel kitchen, Olivia squared her shoulders as she entered the room.

Chef René was on duty, his gaze darting about the kitchen until it finally came to rest upon her. "So you have arrived." He grinned. "I wondered if you might flee during the night."

With a flourish, he pointed to her flower-adorned hat and sensible broadcloth cape. "Place your personal items in the outer hallway. Never bring them into the kitchen." Upon her return, the chef greeted her with a double-breasted white cotton jacket. He extended it toward her. "It will be too large, but it is all that is available at the moment. We can have one tailored for you." The words rolled off his tongue in his lilting French accent.

She shrugged into the oversized jacket and gingerly rolled up the sleeves that extended well beyond her fingertips. The two rows of buttons were at her sides rather than running down the front of the jacket, but she didn't complain. However, she took a backward step when the chef pointed to a tall white toque that resembled his own chef's hat.

"Put it on. All chefs in my kitchen must wear a jacket and hat—it sets them apart."

Olivia wasn't certain she wanted to be set apart, especially by the oversized jacket and huge white hat. Even with her hair pulled into a knot at the back of her head, the hat slipped down and balanced precariously over one eye.

When the remainder of the kitchen staff arrived, they surveyed her with what she could only guess was a mixture of curiosity and amusement. Perhaps she could borrow a needle and thread from Martha or one of the other women and tighten the band of her hat.

She was still engrossed in dealing with the problem toque when Chef René stepped to her side. "Would you like to prepare a cheese soufflé, or do you have a breakfast specialty with which you'd prefer to surprise me?"

Her stomach catapulted into a frenzy of unwelcome activity. She hadn't eaten before leaving home, yet she was forced to swallow down the lump in her throat. "I thought for my first day it would be helpful if I could watch and learn where you keep your utensils and what methods you prefer to use in your kitchen." Would he see through her reply?

A slow smile curved his lips. "You have a valid point, Miss Mott. For today, you may observe. Tomorrow you will cook."

She didn't fail to notice the frowns she received from the kitchen staff. While they scurried about in a frenzy of activity, she sat on a stool and watched, her hands primly folded in her lap. With each course, she studied the chef's movements, as though merely watching this man would cause her to immediately evolve into a chef. She'd been observing Chef Mallard for over a year and hadn't mastered *his* techniques. However, she used the time to advantage today.

There were, she discovered, differences in this kitchen. Each person knew exactly what was expected, and the staff moved to and fro like a well-oiled machine. The plates were removed from the warming oven at the precise moment the eggs Benedict were coddled to perfection. The hollandaise sauce peaked to a rich, creamy texture at the exact moment it was to be ladled over the eggs. The tall Negro servers appeared at the door of the carving room, where they retrieved the silver-domed plates from the hot closets and silently carried them to the awaiting hotel guests. Unlike the harried frenzy and crashing pots and pans in Chef Mallard's kitchen, a quiet accord of movement surrounded Chef René's staff as they accomplished their purposes.

Breakfast was served until nine o'clock each morning, at which time the doors to the dining rooms were closed, and the entire staff ceased their work promptly at ten o'clock. Some departed out the side door and gathered under one of the large maple trees that flanked one side of a budding flower garden; others hurried off in diverse directions. Chef René departed toward his office, and Olivia remained perched atop her stool.

"Olivia!" Martha Mosher stood outside the kitchen door and crooked her finger. She grinned as Olivia jumped down and the toque bobbed forward and once again sagged across her right eye. "Is all going well?"

Pushing the hat from her eyes, Olivia shrugged. "I'm merely observing today." She glanced toward the side door. "Some of the others have been casting angry looks in my direction."

"I don't doubt it. They're hard at work while you relax. Is

there any reason why you couldn't assist them washing the dishes once the meal has been served?"

Martha was correct, and Olivia decided she'd do just that after the noonday meal. When Chef René returned, she carefully watched his food preparations. Later, when the dishes began to accumulate, she slid from the stool and made her way to the sink.

However, Chef René called an abrupt halt to her activity. "Chefs cook. Dishwashers wash dishes. Waiters serve. Sit down and observe! I am going to prepare a dish that is enjoyed by our hotel guests: Aubergines Bohémienne. You will be expected to prepare this dish from time to time."

She didn't understand what the chef would be cooking, but Olivia compliantly returned to her stool and watched as he began to dice a large eggplant.

When the workday finally ended, Martha met her in the park across from the hotel and explained there were likely hard feelings because the chef was showing her preferential treatment. "It makes the others feel less important." Martha attempted to reassure Olivia before she headed off toward home. "Things will be better tomorrow. Once you actually begin working, their resentment will disappear." She pointed at Olivia's toque. "I hope you plan to put a tuck in that this evening."

Olivia laughed. "I think that will be my first order of business tonight." Although she could easily stitch the hat so that it would fit snugly, she knew her lack of culinary abilities could not be so easily remedied.

Chapter Seven

Olivia bent forward and rested her head atop her folded arms. How had she survived the past five days? Chef René had looked at her with disdain when she'd attempted to carve the mutton with an unsharpened knife; he'd scowled when she'd not whisked the eggs to perfection; he'd slapped his forehead in disgust when she'd ordered the potatoes cubed instead of sliced; and he'd abruptly exited the kitchen when she had prepared a lumpy lemon sauce. Through it all, the staff continued to hold her at bay with their frowns and silence. Instead of offering sympathetic words, they ignored her. She wanted to ask what she had done to cause their dislike but feared what they might say.

When she asked Martha that very question after work, her new friend gave her a sidelong glance. "Have you not noticed Chef René is forgiving when you make a mistake, yet with the other staff he is relentless?"

"He scowls or hurries from the room when I fail," Olivia defended.

"Perhaps, but he is much harsher with the others."

Olivia had been too concerned over her own failures to notice the chef's reaction to anyone else. In fact, she couldn't say with authority that she'd had time to observe anyone else make a mistake. She'd been too busy attempting to resolve her own messes. "I can't say that I've noticed."

Martha nodded. "He treats you differently, Olivia. They don't know why, nor do I. It makes them jealous, and you've become the object of their anger rather than Chef René."

Now what? She could hardly march into Chef René's office and ask him to yell at her. On top of thinking her an inept cook, he'd think her a blathering idiot. "What can I do?"

"I truly don't know. But for tonight, let's not worry over work. Mrs. DeVault invited us to supper. Fred and Albert are going to practice with the baseball team and want us to come and watch. We can cheer them on."

Martha's words had a rallying effect upon Charlotte, who had been lying on the divan ignoring them since they'd entered the house. "How can you even think of such a thing? I'm alone all day long, and now you're going to go off and enjoy yourself for the entire evening?" She formed a pout and folded her arms across her chest.

Waving a hand, Martha shook her head. "You can join us for supper, too. Mrs. DeVault said she'd walk you home afterward."

But Charlotte's displeasure didn't completely dissipate.

"Seven o'clock. Don't be late," Martha said on departing.

Although Mrs. Hornsby had made every attempt to force a change of plans, the men remained steadfast. They wanted Olivia and Martha to accompany them to their baseball practice. Though Fred sensed Olivia's hesitation, he hoped she wouldn't succumb to Mrs. Hornsby's wishes. The woman appeared to have a certain power over Olivia that he couldn't quite figure out. Then again, perhaps Olivia merely gave in due to her friend's recent loss. Still, he didn't think Mrs. Hornsby acted like a woman in mourning. She behaved more like a petulant child set upon having her way.

Fred found her conduct most annoying and wondered if his mother would tire of the woman's immature antics before the evening drew to an end. He felt a brief tinge of guilt as they departed and left his mother alone to entertain the sullen woman.

They automatically formed into couples, with Albert and Martha walking a few steps ahead of Fred and Olivia. Once they settled into a comfortable pace, Fred broke the silence. "How are you enjoying your work?"

"I can't say it's going very well," she said and told him of the myriad mistakes she'd made throughout the week.

Fred found her admissions puzzling. He couldn't imagine how she'd been hired for her position if she didn't possess the proper training and abilities. "When I secured my job," he told her, "I was required to sign a contract as well as submit recommendations. The Pullman representative who hired me even talked with my previous supervisor. Were you not required to do the same?"

She looked like a frightened animal hoping to find an escape, yet there was no reason his questions should make her fearful. He waited, anxious to hear her response. She stammered a reply that made little sense, but before he had time to ask for an interpretation, she changed the subject.

"I understand Mr. Pullman has a library located on the second floor of the Arcade for the town's residents." She chattered on for several minutes about the good-hearted gesture and Mr. Pullman's thoughtfulness in making such a fine donation to the city. "Do you frequent it often?"

"The library? No, and it's not free, you know. Residents must pay twenty-five cents a month in order to use Mr. Pullman's *gift*." He looked toward the second floor of the Arcade building. "I don't consider something a donation to the town if I must pay to use it."

"But still, I've been told there are thousands of books to choose from."

Obviously Mr. Howard had already indoctrinated her with the wonders of Mr. Pullman and all his good deeds. From all appearances, Miss Mott had taken his propaganda to heart. "As I told you on the day of your arrival, profit is crucial to Mr. Pullman and his shareholders. Whether machinery or people, Mr. Pullman believes control will increase profit. Consequently, he controls everything that happens in the town and factory."

She was silent for a moment, seeming to ponder his words. "But what of this athletic field we're going to? How does it bring profit to Mr. Pullman?"

"The athletic fields and playgrounds don't bring a direct profit, but they do result in public accolades for Mr. Pullman. And they indirectly produce revenue when the games are held. People throng to Pullman to participate in or watch the events." Fred grinned. "On the other hand, I'm certain the cost of the facilities far outweigh any plaudits Mr. Pullman receives. I do praise him for providing fine recreational opportunities for the town's residents."

"And there's the beautiful Greenstone Church. I made a special point to go and see it. You must admit a church isn't profitable for Mr. Pullman."

Fred laughed and pronounced her gullible. "That beautiful church remained unused for several years. The company required more rent than any small congregation could afford. Of course, Mr. Pullman thought one church was sufficient and everyone should worship together. That way, the excessive rate would appear tolerable. Unfortunately for him, folks didn't agree; they built churches outside of the city limits. And that, Miss Mott, is why Mr. Pullman finally gave in and lowered the rent."

"The church issue aside, don't you think it was wise to have the town well planned? It is a beautiful place, with all these redbrick buildings and wide streets."

There was little doubt Olivia was bedazzled. He wished Albert or Martha would join in and tell her a bit more, for they, too, knew the way of things in Pullman. But they were engaged in their own private conversation and had moved several paces ahead. Fred knew that he should refrain from further disparaging remarks and forced a smile in an attempt to lighten his mood.

Olivia took his cue and smiled. "I saw many buildings as we arrived on the train, though I've not had a closer view. It appears there are train tracks running in and out of some of them, as well as around the perimeter. I was surprised to see the tracks."

Apparently Mr. Howard hadn't yet versed her in the operations of the Pullman Car Works. "There are tracks so that the railcars being worked on can be moved from building to building and tracks to deliver lumber or supplies needed in the various shops." Although she appeared interested in hearing more, Fred decided he'd already said more than was needed for one evening. "That's enough talk of the town and the railcar works. I'm going to bore you to death."

Olivia shook her head. "Oh no, I'm truly interested. What's it like to work in the shops? Do you enjoy your work?"

He was surprised she wanted to hear about his dreary job. None of the other young ladies he'd courted had ever expressed an interest in his work. Her eyes sparkled with obvious interest. He longed to tell her he found fulfillment and challenge in his work, but such a declaration would be a falsehood.

"I'm afraid I can't say that I enjoy my work. You see, I thought I had been hired to design and etch the mirrors and decorative glass inside the cars. Instead, I was assigned to a position where I spend my days electroplating everything from screws and bolts to cuspidors to be used in the older cars as they are refurbished. The same is true with Albert. Pullman doesn't make use of your cousin's etching talents, either."

She removed her gloves and tucked them into her reticule. "Perhaps after you've proven yourself a while longer, you'll be moved into the department that interests you."

"Perhaps," he said, unconvinced.

The sparkle vanished from her eyes.

He bowed his head and picked at an imaginary speck on his shirtsleeve. "I'm sorry for my boorish behavior. If you truly want to hear about electroplating, I'll be happy to explain the process."

Olivia bobbed her head. She truly appeared interested as he explained how the articles to be refurbished were cleansed, suspended by copper hooks, and then plunged into a wooden tank lined with gutta-percha, and filled with a solution that included nitrate of silver and cyanide. Olivia appeared to remain interested, especially when he mentioned that the silver used in each of the bathing solutions was valued at nearly four thousand dollars.

She clutched her reticule to her chest. "Did you say four *thousand* dollars?"

"I did. No expense is too great for the railroad cars produced at the Pullman Car Works. It's with his employees that Mr. Pullman cuts his overhead." They continued on toward the athletic field.

"What happens after you dip the items into the silver?"

He gave her a sideways glance. She was obviously attempting to deflect him away from any further negative comments. "No more talk of my work or Pullman politics. If you want to know more about electroplating, I'll explain at another time."

Though she mildly protested, Fred insisted. He wanted to learn more about Olivia. She was a vivacious and engaging young woman, and he enjoyed her company. "Albert mentioned the girls in the kitchen have been giving you a time of it. Are things getting any better?"

Color heightened in her cheeks. Too late he realized he had embarrassed her. He wished he could withdraw his question.

She bowed her head. "I suppose Martha told him about my difficulties."

"I believe so, but we need not discuss them if it makes you uncomfortable. I had hoped for a good report."

"I suppose matters are somewhat better." They walked across a small bridge that led to an island. She studied the expansive area that stretched before them. "So this is the athletic island."

Fred nodded, pleased they'd arrived. He hoped that by the time their baseball practice ended, Olivia would forget her embarrassment. After escorting the two young women to the grandstands, he and Albert loped across the grass to join their teammates.

Olivia's responses to Fred had constituted additional falsehoods in the mounting inventory. Soon her notes would reach book-length proportions. Her stomach roiled. How much had Martha revealed to Albert and Fred? There was no way of knowing, but Olivia suspected Martha had heard plenty from the kitchen staff.

She attempted to concentrate on the baseball game. Martha claimed that both Fred and Albert were showing excellent progress with the game. Though Olivia knew nothing of baseball or its rules, she asked questions and cheered along with Martha. Anything to avoid talk of her past or her work in Chef René's kitchen.

She clapped loudly when Albert swung the bat and the ball flew far into the field. She inched a bit closer to Martha. "Albert loved to play cricket back in England."

"He told me." Martha's eyes were following Albert as he ran to second base and stopped, leaving one foot touching the bag, the other outstretched in preparation to race to third. She continued. "Both he and Fred play on the cricket team, and they're on the rowing team, too."

"They must be busy every evening."

"Not quite, but we'll be here a lot throughout the spring and summer. Especially while they're preparing for the athletic games. Mr. Pullman likes his employees to make a good showing at the competitions. Fred and Albert say it's an issue of pride for Mr. Pullman. He'd be embarrassed if one of his teams got routed."

These must be the games to which Mr. Howard had referred when she had first met him. She certainly hoped there weren't any competitions for the women. Trying to navigate in the hotel kitchen without a daily catastrophe was enough of a challenge for her!

While the members of the teams exchanged positions on the field, Martha scooted closer. "You're planning to attend church with us tomorrow, aren't you?"

Where had that question come from? One minute Martha was talking baseball; the next she was asking about church. Unprepared for the question, Olivia floundered for a response. "Us?"

"Yes." She motioned toward Fred and Albert. "Mrs. DeVault, too. And you can invite Charlotte. We don't want to leave her out, poor dear. I know the trauma of losing her husband and now having to adjust to a new home in a different country are most stressful. No doubt she's come to rely heavily upon God through all of this."

Martha eyed her with an expectancy that required a response. "Thank you for inviting us. I can't answer for Charlotte, but I'd be pleased to join you." She nibbled her lip—that wasn't exactly true. The thought of sitting in church and attempting to worship God while her life was a complete charade would be more than a little uncomfortable and likely abhorrent to God, also. But what could she do? A tiny inner voice reminded her that telling the truth would be a good starting point, but she squelched the thought and asked Martha where they would meet.

A number of young women soon joined them, and the remainder of their time together consisted of squeals and cheers each time one of the men came to bat. Olivia took careful note of the girls who worked at the hotel. Most ignored her, though she observed a critical look from one or two. The girls remained at Martha's left, distancing themselves from Olivia while visiting with Martha. She could feel their cold stares when Fred approached after the game and took her arm. The four of them headed off toward home, and Olivia resisted the urge to turn to see if they were still watching her.

Discomfort followed on her heels like a stray animal, but she forced herself to accept an invitation for a glass of lemonade at the Arcade. Once they were seated, the conversation centered around the missed home runs and improperly fielded balls—whatever those terms meant. Thankful nothing was required of her, Olivia silently kept pace with the men's animated discussion over the prospects of winning their game on Tuesday evening.

"You'll come and watch us play, won't you?"

Before she could respond, Martha interceded. "Of course she will. And she's agreed to come to church with us tomorrow, too."

Olivia's schedule was being planned without her input, but

she didn't object. Right now, she wasn't confident she'd still have a job next Tuesday. But as long as the conversation didn't require her to answer any questions about her cooking qualifications or Charlotte's past, she was pleased.

When the foursome finally returned to the DeVaults' residence, Mrs. DeVault and Charlotte were sitting side by side on the divan. The older woman was attempting to teach Charlotte how to knit. This was a feat for which Mrs. DeVault should receive a special award for patience. With each wrap of the yarn, Charlotte dropped or twisted a stitch and then whined in overt frustration. The minute she spotted Olivia, Charlotte dropped the needles and tightened her lips into her familiar pout.

"I thought you were going to be gone only an hour. It's nearly ten o'clock." She pushed herself up from the sofa. "I'm ready for bed."

Olivia sighed. She wondered if Charlotte had ever experienced genuine weariness. The woman hadn't performed a day of work in her life. How could she possibly be tired? But Olivia couldn't argue or make disparaging remarks in front of the others, for they'd think her callous and cruel. After all, what kind of person would treat an expectant widow in such a manner?

It took a good five minutes to convince Fred and Albert that she and Charlotte weren't in need of an escort for the walk home. They said their good-nights with a promise to meet the group at church on Sunday morning. Olivia hoped Charlotte hadn't slipped up during her conversation with Mrs. DeVault, and she wanted to ask what they had discussed. However, if their chat had gone amiss and Olivia found out now, she'd likely be unable to sleep a wink. Best to wait and inquire tomorrow.

Chapter Eight

The church service had been as uncomfortable as Olivia had expected. She was certain God had whispered into the ear of the preacher. Why else would he have chosen that particular Sunday to preach about lies and deceit? Frocked in his black suit with white collar and cuffs, the preacher had opened his Bible with a flourish and read Ephesians 4:25. He had stared directly into Olivia's eyes when he'd repeated the passage for the second time: *"Wherefore putting away lying, speak every man truth with his neighbour: for we are members one of another."* For the next thirty minutes, he had expounded upon the necessity of truthfulness, especially among those who considered themselves God's children. Then, as if to emblazon the words upon her heart, he had once again repeated the verse before leading the congregation in a final prayer. She had wanted to run out the door. And, as if she hadn't already felt guilt raining down on her, Charlotte had elbowed her in the ribs each time the preacher had mentioned liars.

Thoughts of the sermon came to mind as she donned her work dress on Monday morning. She slipped her arms into the white jacket and carried the toque in her hand, almost pleased to be returning to work. *Almost.* Sunday had been filled with church, dinner with the DeVaults, and an afternoon of fielding questions, all of which had left her exhausted and angry that she found herself in this position. She could only hope things would go smoothly today.

Chef René stood at the ready when she entered the kitchen and beckoned her to his office. Her stomach coiled into a knot. He pointed to a chair. She sat and then waited while he perused several notes on his desk before dropping his bulky body into the chair across from her. "We will be hosting a contingent of important guests tomorrow. Mr. Pullman is hosting a delegation of Chicago businessmen who will spend the day in our hotel. We will serve their noonday meal."

Olivia gulped. She hoped he wasn't going to ask her to plan the menu. "How may I be of assistance?"

He looked heavenward for a moment, and she wondered if he might be seeking divine inspiration. "I recall that your letter of recommendation stated you are well qualified to deck tables for dinner parties. Rather than helping in the kitchen, I believe I'll have you take charge of the tables. Arrange seating for fifty. The waiters will need two buffets for serving, and make certain there is adequate space for them to enter and exit the room."

Her heart pounded at a frenetic pace. For a moment, she thought it might leap from her chest. Had he actually asked her to deck the dining room tables? Mrs. Wright had always been in charge of such matters at Lanshire Hall. Olivia didn't have the first idea of how to decorate for a formal gathering. Mrs.

Wright had expertly created all types of arrangements for dinner parties hosted by the countess, and Chef Mallard often carved ice sculptures for the large events. But she'd never helped with such matters. A fleeting glance as she passed by a bedecked hall was the most experience she could bring to such an assignment. Why had Charlotte been compelled to go to such lengths in the spurious letter of recommendation?

"Miss Mott!"

Wide-eyed, Olivia started. "Yes?" She wondered how many times he had called her name.

"There is a closet off the main dining room where you'll find items that may be of use to you. Since this is merely a business meeting and no ladies will be present, please refrain from using a *theme* for the decorations." He curled his lip in distaste when he mentioned the possibility of a theme. "Of course, it goes without saying that you will want to impress Mr. Pullman and his guests."

She opened her mouth, but the words stuck deep in her throat, all wadded up and cottony. Unable to offer an objection, her body trembled at the thought of what lay ahead. Chef René waved her toward the closet with an admonition to return to the kitchen once she'd chosen the items she would need. Although today she could decide what would be needed, the room couldn't be decorated until morning because hotel guests would dine in the room this evening. Not that it truly mattered. Even if she'd been given an entire week, she couldn't accomplish the assigned task.

Her mind raced while she reviewed the contents of the musty closet. Vases and bowls of every size and shape, candelabra of crystal, silver, and gold, and crisp table coverings and napkins lined the shelves. She could stare at the items for the remainder of the day, but she'd still be unable to accomplish the task at hand.

While Olivia traced her fingers along one of the silver bowls, she had an idea. With her years of attending dinner parties and other social gatherings, surely Charlotte would be able to lend insight. Olivia leaned against the closet door. She longed to race back home and inquire, but her questions would have to wait until this evening.

"You are done so soon?"

She hadn't heard Chef René's approaching footsteps. "Yes. I discovered a lovely assortment of pieces."

"Then I shall expect something magnificent."

Olivia cringed. The chef could anticipate magnificence, but he would likely observe disaster.

The moment Chef René dismissed her for the evening, Olivia hurried home in not exactly a full-fledged run, but close. She didn't want to appear completely unladylike, but she'd moved quickly enough to remain breathless after she entered the house. "Charlotte!" The name came out as more of a gasp than anything else. She sucked in a breath of air and tried again.

She caught sight of a flagging handkerchief waving from the divan and entered the parlor. "Are you not feeling well?" Panic clung to her question.

"Just resting. I'm bored."

"Good. I've just the thing to resolve your boredom."

"What?" Charlotte remained in her supine position and eyed her suspiciously.

Undeterred, Olivia wiggled into a spot on the end of the divan and explained her plight. Charlotte's eyelids drooped to half-mast as she shifted positions. "And what do you expect from me?"

"Help! I need your help." She jumped up from the sofa. Panic clutched her in a viselike grip as she noted Charlotte's languid expression. "Get up!"

Charlotte sighed and slowly pushed herself into a sitting position. "I'm up, but I don't know what good that will do for you. I've never decked a room." She gave another flit of her lace handkerchief. "That was one of Mrs. Wright's duties."

"Yes, I understand you've never performed the actual work. But at least you know how the room should appear and how I might decorate the tables." Olivia clenched her teeth. "Besides, this is your fault. *You're* the one who wrote that ridiculous letter stating I was accomplished in every imaginable task."

"I wrote an eloquent recommendation, and this is the thanks I receive. You wouldn't have been hired had it not been for that letter."

With a forced effort, Olivia agreed with the woman and then requested her expert advice. The words of praise and flattery had the desired effect, along with a promise to bring home a plate of whatever Chef René prepared for the guests attending tomorrow's meal.

Charlotte paced back and forth and then stopped in front of the parlor window. She pointed toward the blooms that dotted the Pullman flower beds in a profusion of color. "You can use those. Along with some greenery and several candelabra on the sideboard, the flowers will be sufficient." She turned to Olivia and shrugged. "Simple enough."

Perhaps in *her* mind, but not in Olivia's. "Will you go to the hotel and help me choose the vases and candelabra later this evening?"

After Olivia offered to prepare a lemon dainty for dessert, Charlotte agreed. Since arriving in Pullman, Charlotte had given little thought to her meals, but she had developed a fancy for sweets that was insatiable. A good thing for Olivia, since baking was her one area of expertise, but not good for Charlotte, whose girth seemed to balloon with each passing day.

While Olivia dined on baked chicken and a generous helping of green beans, Charlotte devoured the lemon dainty. When she finally pushed away from the table, Charlotte had eaten the entire dish of pudding. Rejuvenated by the sugary treat, she willingly accompanied Olivia to the side door leading into the hotel kitchen. Olivia motioned her to wait while she checked on Chef René's whereabouts. She certainly didn't want to run headlong into the rotund chef. Fortunately, his office was unoccupied.

She waved her ladyship toward the decking closet. Their selections didn't take long, and Olivia deposited the items in the dining room. The hotel seemed eerily quiet. Except for the desk clerk who relieved Mr. Billings each evening, no one was about, and he appeared more interested in reading a book than seeking an explanation for their presence.

Behind the closed doors of the dining room, Charlotte assisted while Olivia covered the tables with crisp white cloths. With surprising deftness, Charlotte arranged a place setting, surrounded it with the proper glassware and silver, a napkin, a salt cellar, and the remaining necessities for a proper meal. When she'd finished it to her satisfaction, she instructed Olivia to arrange eight settings at each of the tables and place Mr. Pullman at the head table, along with the largest of the floral arrangements.

"Be careful to keep the floral arrangements low to the table. You don't want to block Mr. Pullman's view of his guests." She wagged a finger. "Tall, bushy arrangements will mark you as an amateur. Cut the flowers first thing in the morning and use fresh water in the vases. They will be perfect for the noonday meal."

On the way home, Olivia made a mental note of the instructions. She had no hope of arranging flowers with the expertise of Chef René, but with a plethora of showy flowers, she could arrange something that should prove at least acceptable. In a burst of desire to please, she decided she would rise early, complete her duties in the dining room, and then offer her services to Chef René in the kitchen. Yes, that should impress him and also reinforce her genuine desire to learn and succeed as a chef.

Later that night she fell asleep while mentally calculating exactly how many flowers she would need for each arrangement and how long it would take to cut and arrange them. Her dreams were filled with visions of flowers and candles.

Shears in hand, she departed the next morning before sunup. While most of the residents of Pullman slept, Olivia visited the public flower gardens, careful she didn't cut too many from any one area. Occasionally she located a few late blooms of one variety or the early blossoms and buds of yet another, pleased when each addition provided another delicate hint of color.

She arrived at the hotel with four overflowing baskets. Delighted with her find, she filled containers with water and carried the vases into the dining room. In the rosy hue of sunrise, Olivia arranged the plethora of flowers—mostly peonies, dotted with a few early daisies, mock orange, and wild sweet William—in the squat vases Charlotte had chosen. After circling the base of each container with sprigs of greenery and inserting tapers into the candelabra, she silently declared she'd done her best. If nothing else, the aroma should delight the visitors.

Donning her chef's attire, she entered the kitchen before breakfast preparations had been completed. Chef René scowled and pointed at the door. "The banquet room, Miss Mott."

A tinge of pride colored her words as she announced completion of the assigned project. "I began decking the dining room at sunup and have completed the task. I wanted to be free to assist you in the kitchen."

The chef's white hat ascended an inch as he raised his bushy eyebrows. "I'm impressed, Miss Mott. Perhaps you're going to work out after all."

Her spirit soared like a kite sailing on a stiff March breeze. Amazing what a few kind words could do for the soul. Chef René set her to work and offered encouragement as she buttered and seasoned croutons and prepared the ingredients for the potage of puréed peas that would be served with the delicate croutons. As she continued to work with confidence, he assigned her the preparation of the Allemande sauce that was to be served atop the fish course.

"You know, Miss Mott, it is said the British have but three sauces and three hundred sixty religions, whereas the French have three religions and three hundred sixty sauces. However, I agree with our famous French chef, Antonin Carême—all can be placed into four families. From those four, all others descend."

She truly wanted to know the four sauces, but at the moment she merely wanted to remember the recipe for Allemande sauce. She had watched Chef René prepare it only twice previously, and the man's recipes were locked away in his memory. She hoped she'd be able to recall the measurements and few ingredients. In any event, the sauce couldn't be prepared this early in the morning. She thanked him profusely for his show of confidence and hurried to retrieve another tray of croutons from the oven.

"We have a few moments before I must turn my attention to the leg of lamb. Take me to see what you've created for the tables." René wiped his wet hands on the towel tucked at his waist.

One of the pastry assistants and a dishwasher grinned as he made the request. Olivia remained convinced neither of the young women liked her. Most likely they were hoping he'd find her decorations unsuitable. She, however, remained confident. Certainly Charlotte knew more about entertaining than those women could ever imagine. Olivia pushed open the doors to the dining room and, with a flourish of her arm, bid Chef René enter.

His thick lips curved upward as he surveyed the tables from afar. But when he approached one of the tables for a closer review, his smile deteriorated into a harsh scowl. He turned and pointed at the tables, his eyes wide as they reflected either anger or horror—she couldn't determine which. "What were you thinking? Look at these tables!" His words echoed throughout the huge empty room like a clanging bell.

With the timidity of a small child, Olivia edged nearer and then gasped at the sight. Countless ants marched up and down the table in long formations that occasionally veered off to circle a bread plate or climb the stem of a water goblet before making a return descent to the starched white tablecloth. And not only on this table closest to her. She raced to each of the perfectly arranged tables and then skidded to a halt. At each one, she was greeted by the same sight—ants.

She checked the windows, but they remained tightly closed. How had this happened? "The tables were perfect when I came to the kitchen this morning." She pointed at the windows as if to affirm that she'd not been the one to permit the insects entry.

The chef marched about the room waving his arm at the offending insects. "We are on a time schedule, Miss Mott. I need everyone in the kitchen helping with meal preparations. Instead, my helpers will be required to spend their time washing dishes and glassware. All because I trusted you to deck the tables." He stopped pacing and massaged his forehead. "Why me? Why must I be plagued with employees who cannot perform the simplest of tasks without supervision?"

Olivia wasn't certain if he expected an answer, but when he once again began pacing the floor, she muttered, "The tables were quite beautiful only a short time ago. I truly don't know what happened."

He yanked the towel from his waist and waved it in the air like a banner. "The *flowers*, Miss Mott! You've placed *peonies* in the vases."

She watched in horror as he plucked flower after flower from her artfully designed arrangements until she could stand it no longer. She grappled for his arm. "Wait! You're ruining them!"

He shoved the handful of flowers beneath her nose. "Look at these. Do you not see the ants crawling on them?" Fire danced in his dark eyes.

She meekly nodded. "Yes, but the ants are everywhere—not just the flowers."

"Oui! But you carried the ants in here with the peonies. They love the sweet nectar of the budding flower." He shook his head in disgust. "You must get busy and remove and change the linens. The table settings must be replaced. You will be the one to tell the girls they must wash all of these place settings. They will likely be as unhappy as I."

Olivia listened to the remainder of Chef René's orders. She dreaded telling the dishwashers, but there was no choice. She'd doubled their work for the day and must now attempt to rearrange the flowers without the colorful peonies. Her thought outside the closet door yesterday morning had been prophetic: Chef René had indeed observed disaster rather than magnificence in the dining room.

Chapter Nine

Samuel Howard stared out his office window toward Hotel Florence and considered his emerging feelings for Olivia Mott. A burst of hot air drifted through the open window. He tugged at his shirt collar and longed to unfasten the top button, but Mr. Pullman would never approve of an open collar. The weather had been unseasonably warm this summer. And with more than a month remaining in the summer, there would likely be no reprieve from the heat.

Samuel had never been a man who dallied during working hours, yet he'd become decidedly less productive of late. Instead of poring over his daily ledgers and correspondence, his mind now wandered and filled with thoughts of the lovely young woman working in the hotel kitchen.

He had marked the third anniversary of his wife's death two weeks ago. Though he truly had believed he'd never find another woman who would compare with his Lydia, there was no denying the young English woman had captured his attention from the moment she first stepped into his office. He had waited to call on her, allowing her time to settle into her new position with the company and become accustomed to her new home. Undoubtedly, there had been much for her to learn, and he hadn't wanted to appear overly forward. But now he believed the proper amount of time had passed, and he could make his interest known.

He hoped he hadn't waited too long. On several occasions he'd noticed her in the company of Fred DeVault. At first he had shrugged off the notion that she might be interested in Fred. After all, they were practically thrown together, since her cousin lived with Fred and his mother. But he had observed the two of them alone on several occasions, and now he wasn't quite so certain there wasn't something more than friendship on Fred's mind. If Olivia proved to be the woman who could replace his Lydia, he'd fight for her.

He picked up the china clock and traced his finger over the hand-painted violets and miniature roses. The timepiece had been a gift to Lydia, purchased while traveling abroad on their honeymoon. She had fallen in love with the beauty of the delicately painted flowers and greenery. Though he'd known the clock was grossly overpriced, he'd secretly purchased it and then presented it to her when they returned to Pullman. If he closed his eyes, he could still imagine her touch as she'd embraced him and whispered her thanks for his thoughtfulness.

He shook his head, determined to move forward with his life. A year after Lydia's death, he'd given away her clothing and sent several items to her parents as remembrances. Although he doubted whether he could ever do the same with Lydia's precious timepiece, he knew the time had arrived to pack away this final reminder of the past.

At eleven thirty, Samuel carefully tucked the clock into the crook of his arm and returned home. He wrapped the clock in a soft cloth and laid it in the bottom of the chest of drawers, prepared to open a new chapter in his life. If he hurried, he would have sufficient time to walk to the Arcade and purchase tickets for the Saturday night band concert.

He hurried out of the house and down the sidewalk with a spring in his step. Suddenly life seemed much brighter. He was still a young man—perhaps not as young as Fred DeVault, but young enough that he wanted more out of life than working every day and coming home to an empty house each evening. He wanted to share his life with a wife and a child or two. Shaking his head, he stifled a laugh. He was getting a little ahead of himself. First he must ask Olivia to attend the concert—later he could think of marriage and children.

Olivia couldn't decide if she'd grown more fatigued with Charlotte's ongoing complaints of boredom and loneliness or with Chef René's expectations. Weary from yet another day of rushing about in the hot kitchen, Olivia picked up the next day's guest list and menu, as well as the two stacks of cards that needed to be handwritten before tomorrow's dinner party. She'd promised Chef René she would inscribe them this evening, and he had readily agreed the chore could be completed at home. Olivia was certain he would have assigned her the task anyway. But offering to perform the duty carried a distinct advantage—at least that's what she told herself. And she hoped it was another way to compensate for her previous mishaps.

Ever since the incident of the marching ants, as Chef René so aptly referred to it, she'd done everything in her power to regain the man's confidence. And he hadn't refused her offers to work extra hours while he relaxed or read his books, yet always maintaining a watchful eye on her progress. She soon discovered that he borrowed library books that detailed diverse cooking methods and recipes. Mostly he would sit in the kitchen, book in hand, and occasionally read a recipe aloud before scoffing at the directions or at ingredients—especially if authored by a British chef. Nothing delighted him more than a good argument with the pastry chef, who attempted to extol the merits of English cooking.

When the pastry chef had been assigned to cook on the Pullman dining cars last week, Chef René had attempted to spar with Olivia. However, she ignored his contentious remarks. She didn't care whether he found the English recipes unsavory or wondrous. She merely wanted to go home, soak her feet, write the menu and place cards, and retire for the night.

Fortunately, Chef René had offered her leftovers from this evening's banquet—his compensation for her willingness to prepare the menu and place cards, she'd decided. At least she wouldn't be required to cook Charlotte's supper. After retrieving a basket from the decking closet, Olivia packed two portions of salmon, a generous serving of both the potatoes and rice, and a jar of fish chowder. She placed the menu cards and place cards atop the basket while Chef René continued to read. He grunted his disapproval of some item in the book as she bid him good-night.

"Don't forget we must begin early in the morning, and don't forget to write out the menu and place cards this evening."

Olivia adjusted the basket on her arm and continued out the door. How could she forget? She would be up until at least eleven o'clock working on the cards unless she could convince Charlotte to help. Perhaps she'd hold the Salmon à la Rothschild hostage until Charlotte agreed to help. After all, the woman did little but mope about. Her appetite increased with each passing day, as did her weight. And though she complained about her escalating size, she continued to eat everything Olivia prepared or brought home from the hotel.

True to her nightly ritual, Charlotte was pacing in front of the parlor window when Olivia arrived. "You're late and I'm hungry." The scowl on Charlotte's face matched her angry words.

"Good evening to you, too." Olivia forced a smile as she brushed past Charlotte and headed for the kitchen. "I've brought home several delightful dishes." As expected, Charlotte followed on her heels. Olivia placed the basket atop the kitchen table but grasped Charlotte's wrist when she attempted to remove the enticing offerings. "Only if you help me write the menu cards for tomorrow's dinner at the hotel."

Charlotte stepped back and wrested her arm free. "You're bribing me? I pay most of the rent on this hideous dwelling, and yet you're going to force my help before you'll serve me supper?" Charlotte clutched her bodice as though she might faint from hunger.

Olivia nearly laughed aloud at her theatrics. "You truly should consider the stage, Charlotte." She removed the menu and place cards from the basket and pointed toward the hall. "Why don't you retrieve two pens and the ink, and we can begin."

"*Before* we eat? I truly can wait no longer, Olivia. I promise I'll help as soon as I've had my supper."

Though she questioned the wisdom of her decision, Olivia relented. Better to let Charlotte work on a full stomach. While Charlotte devoured the main course, Olivia explained they would likely be done in less than two hours if they both set their minds and hands to the task.

As she finished the final bite of her meal, Charlotte perused the items being offered at the next day's dinner, her attention settling upon the final entry on the list. "Oh! Chocolate meringues with whipped cream and chocolate shavings!" The words rolled off her tongue as though she could almost taste one of the delicacies. "I do wish Chef René had prepared meringues for dessert tonight." She peeked inside the basket, no doubt hoping one of the desserts might appear.

"There's nothing more to eat, Charlotte. Besides, we need to begin."

Charlotte reached for one of the place cards, and Olivia shook her head. "I'll do the place cards, and when I've finished, I'll help you complete the menu cards," she said, adding that Charlotte's delicate script was much finer than her own. But from Charlotte's pout, she knew that her compliment hadn't hit the mark.

Charlotte continued to pout as she took up her pen and perused the menu. "This is quite a feast. A special gathering, I take it?"

Olivia shrugged. "Business associates, investors, and foreign dignitaries, I'm told." Usually, she cared little about who would attend festivities at the hotel. However, a name at the top of the list she'd received from Mr. Pullman's secretary had immediately captured her attention: Randolph Morgan. After having inscribed his place card, she'd been certain to leave it at the hotel, and before departing work, she had dutifully drawn a line through his name on the list.

If only Mr. Pullman's secretary didn't insist upon the return of all grocery lists, menu items, and guest lists related to the events their employer hosted at the hotel, Olivia would have eradicated Mr. Morgan's name with a giant ink blot. Instead, she'd be forced to keep it out of Charlotte's sight. She didn't want to do anything that might reawaken Charlotte's thoughts of confronting Randolph Morgan. The two of them had struggled through enough arguments about Mr. Morgan after their arrival in Pullman. Olivia had finally convinced Charlotte that contacting him would be of little use, and she didn't want to revisit the matter. As far as Olivia knew, Randolph Morgan had no idea Charlotte was in Pullman. Olivia hoped it would remain that way.

The meal appeared to have sated Charlotte's hunger for the moment, and she penned the menus with only an occasional question or comment. They were making fine progress except for the need to share a single blotter. Each of them seemed to require it at precisely the same time. When Charlotte sighed for the third time, Olivia conceded. "I'll go and fetch the blotter from my room."

She was gone only a few moments, but fear struck her like a bolt of lightning when she returned to the room and saw Charlotte hastily pushing papers about the table. Olivia feared the woman had been reading the guest list during her absence, though she couldn't be certain. The list had indeed been moved, but so had the other papers.

[illegible]

[illegible]

[illegible]

[illegible]

Chapter Ten

Kitchen preparations had gone smoothly throughout the morning, but as the hour of the guests' arrival drew near, Chef René grew impatient. After sending one of the young dishwashers scurrying on an errand, he pointed to Olivia. "Make certain the menu and place cards are on the tables."

She wanted to object, for one of the kitchen boys could check on the cards while she continued stirring the hollandaise sauce. But her objection would only cause disruption in the kitchen, and that wasn't needed during the final moments of meal preparation. She marched down the hall, her shoes slapping heavily upon the tiles—in case Chef René hadn't noted her level of agitation.

As she rounded the corner, the sound of loud angry voices drifted in through the open windows along the veranda. A tall Negro waiter, his white jacket as stiff as the menu cards, stood sentry outside the dining room door. He moved aside as Olivia approached. If he heard the shouts outside the hotel, it wasn't reflected in his stoic expression. While she quickly surveyed the room, the heated argument escalated. She exited the dining room and stopped in her tracks, straining to listen. *Charlotte!*

She cast a look toward the front desk. Mr. Billings, who normally would have hastened to arrest any commotion, was away from his usual post. Fear gripped Olivia's heart as she raced to the front door. She weakened at the sight that greeted her. Stomach bulging, hair flying in total disarray, and blue eyes darkened with fury, Charlotte looked like a woman gone mad. She was clinging to Randolph Morgan's arm, obviously intent upon forcing him to listen to her. Olivia glanced at the clock. The other guests would soon be arriving.

Chef René would expect her hasty return to the kitchen, but she couldn't ignore the unfolding spectacle. Throwing caution to the wind, she hurried down the front steps of the hotel and looped arms with Charlotte. "Why don't we go home? I believe Mr. Morgan is expected inside."

Charlotte turned a wild-eyed stare at Olivia while still maintaining a fierce grip on Mr. Morgan's arm. "He's denying his own child, Olivia. What kind of man would do such a thing?"

Olivia leveled a steady bead on the man. "One who is both married and a coward, your ladyship. One who cares only about himself, I would assume."

"How can you possibly expect me to think this child you're carrying is mine, Charlotte?" He leaned a bit closer. "I'm certain you were as free with other men as you were with me."

Charlotte broke loose of Olivia's hold and swung her arm. A gust of air passed Olivia's face as Charlotte landed a perfectly aimed blow across Mr. Morgan's cheekbone. Shock registered in his eyes, and he slowly rubbed his face. When he lowered his hand moments later, red streaks emblazoned his cheek. Charlotte took another menacing step toward him. "How *dare* you speak such an outrageous lie! You know this is your child I'm carrying."

He shook his head and smirked. "I know nothing of the kind. And should anyone inquire, I would be forced to tell the truth: the only time I've been in your presence is while dining at the home of your parents in London."

Charlotte gasped and lunged at him while Olivia attempted to wedge herself in front of Mr. Morgan. "Please, Charlotte, don't!"

He tilted his head to one side. "You should listen to your maid, Lady Charlotte."

Olivia glared at him. Couldn't he see her uniform? She longed to tell him she wasn't Charlotte's maid and if he considered himself marginally intelligent, he would discontinue his argumentative remarks and go inside. However, she dared not say anything to a man of Mr. Morgan's stature. Olivia inwardly groaned when Charlotte's chin jutted forward.

"I do wonder what *Mrs.* Morgan would think about her husband's behavior—or Mr. Pullman." Charlotte tapped the toe of her shoe and pursed her lips. "Indeed, you might find yourself unemployed should the London shareholders begin withdrawing their investments with Mr. Pullman's company. You surely recall that my father carries a great deal of influence with the overseas investors, Mr. Morgan."

"You can't prove your allegations." He smirked and sidestepped her advance.

A gust of wind swept across the expanse, and Charlotte's unfettered curls spilled over her shoulders in wild abandon.

"Don't be so certain, Randolph. I have an item in my possession proving we were *much* more than acquaintances who met over supper in my parents' dining room."

His eyes narrowed and his lips tightened into an ominous line. "How *dare* you continue with these threats! You stay away from me and my family. And if you know what's good for you, you'll stay away from Mr. Pullman, too."

Obviously undeterred, Charlotte pressed on. "It sounds as though *you* are the one making threats. But you have no control over me, Randolph. If I decide to write a letter or two, you'll have no control over that, either."

He yanked Charlotte close, whispered into her ear, and then shoved her away. With anger still shining in his eyes, he turned toward Olivia. "I suggest you see that your mistress returns to wherever it is she lives." He stomped away without a backward glance.

Olivia grasped Charlotte's shoulders and looked into her eyes. "I *must* get back to the kitchen. Please promise me you'll go home."

Charlotte's lips trembled and her complexion paled several shades. "Randolph said he'd see me dead if I said anything further about the baby." Her eyes clouded. "I believe he meant it."

Olivia folded her into an embrace. "He's angry." She leaned back and forced a reassuring smile. "You caught him unaware and confronted him with unwanted information. Besides, you were making idle threats. There's no need to worry." She turned Charlotte toward home as though she were a small child and then raced to the kitchen. No doubt she was the one who needed to be frightened of retribution. Chef René would likely greet her waving a wooden spoon and venting his anger.

Fortunately for Olivia, Chef René had been too busy scolding the headwaiter, who hadn't made a timely appearance to confer over details of serving the meal. René didn't even notice when she entered and reestablished her position at the stove.

The remainder of the day passed in a flurry, and she had little time to dwell upon the earlier scene. It wasn't until she was packing one of the meringues into her basket that she recalled Charlotte's frightened words.

Lost in her own thoughts, Olivia picked up the basket and left the kitchen. If nothing else, the food should help calm Charlotte's mood.

She hadn't heard the sound of approaching footsteps and started when Mr. Howard approached.

"May I carry your basket for you, Miss Mott?"

"I can manage, thank you." Instinctively, she grasped the basket handle a bit tighter. Mr. Howard's unanticipated appearance was unsettling. It seemed as if he had a way of appearing when least expected. Had someone mentioned her involvement in the skirmish outside the hotel? Though she hoped the confrontation had gone undetected, she realized the three of them had been standing in full view of many of the hotel's windows—including those in Mr. Pullman's office. He could have observed the entire incident without difficulty.

She wondered if Mr. Morgan had already departed for Chicago. If not, perhaps he had sent Mr. Howard to elicit information. Or had Mr. Pullman sent him to inquire about the confrontation? She now wished she had checked the hotel registry to see if Mr. Morgan had registered as an overnight guest, though with Mr. Billings standing guard over the leather-bound tome, it would have proved awkward, if not impossible. The hotel manager guarded the book as though it held the world's greatest secrets.

"I wondered if you might enjoy a stroll through the Arcade or a visit to the library with me this evening," Mr. Howard said.

A stroll? Her feet ached, and he was inviting her to accompany him on a walk through the Arcade. Obviously he had little idea what her work entailed. "I'm rather weary this evening." She tapped a finger on the basket handle. "Charlotte and I haven't yet eaten our supper."

"How thoughtless of me. I wasn't thinking about the busy day you've had. What about tomorrow evening?"

Even his enthusiasm couldn't erase her memories of the wearisome day. Between Chef René's ongoing demands and the encounter with Charlotte and Mr. Morgan, Olivia was exhausted. She truly didn't want to think about tomorrow evening, but the question remained open between them.

"Tomorrow evening would suit," she finally said, "after seven o'clock."

He glanced at the basket swinging from her arm. "Right. You'll need time to have supper with Mrs. Hornsby."

"Who?" She quickly caught his look of surprise. "Oh yes. Charlotte. I seldom think of her as Mrs. Hornsby." Without missing a beat, she turned their conversation to the weather and the beautifully maintained flower gardens and lawns they passed by.

He glowed at her remarks, as though his personal touch had produced the blooms. "I've purchased tickets for the band performance on Saturday night in hopes you'll attend with me." He patted the breast pocket of his suit jacket and grinned. "I'm asking now so you won't make plans to go with someone else."

She'd heard Albert and Martha mention the band concert, but nothing more had been said. Likely both Albert and Fred would have cricket or baseball practice on Saturday evening. Unless there would be no practice due to the concert. The thoughts jumbled about in her mind while Mr. Howard continued to peer at her.

"May I look forward to enjoying your company at the concert?"

"Yes, I suppose that would be agreeable." She bid him goodnight, wondering why she felt obligated to accept his offers. He was a nice enough man, but it was Fred who had truly captured her interest. Fred, with his spirited laughter, could lift anyone's mood—especially hers—in the wink of an eye. Perhaps that was it. Mr. Howard was somber and serious, a more thoughtful man. Though he wasn't much older than Fred, he seemed more the fatherly type. However, she should at least get to know him a bit more before judging him as stodgy and boring.

"Finally! I thought you'd never get here. I'm starving." Before Olivia cleared the threshold, Charlotte's assault of words reached her.

No matter how much Olivia's feet ached, Charlotte's attitude was enough to make Olivia want to turn on her heel and run back to the hotel. She sailed past the door to the parlor and headed directly for the dining room. No need stopping to argue or defend herself. She'd tried that tack often enough, to no avail. She could only hope Charlotte's mood would improve once she set eyes upon the chocolate meringues.

Grasping her back with one hand as she lumbered into the dining room, Charlotte surveyed the table. Her eyes appeared to glaze at the sight. Food seemed to be her only pleasure in life. Olivia couldn't be certain, but she thought Charlotte had gained at least twenty pounds since their departure from England back in April.

"Mrs. DeVault came over this afternoon." Charlotte dipped her finger into the center of a meringue and licked the whipped cream.

Olivia shook her head and moved the dessert aside. "This is for after you eat your meal." With each passing day, Charlotte acted more like a two-year-old. "What has happened to your manners, your ladyship?" She hoped referring to Charlotte's position and title would give the young woman pause.

Charlotte shrugged. "No need for formalities in this place. I'm just another nobody living in a rented tenement. Randolph made my station in life abundantly clear this morning. Wouldn't you agree?" She jabbed her fork into a piece of the creamed quail with chestnuts.

Olivia helped herself to a serving of the grilled mushrooms and puréed potatoes while Charlotte stuffed a bite of quail into her mouth. "Well, don't you agree?"

Now her ladyship had taken to speaking with her mouth full! What next? Would she soon give up bathing? "Your station in life is whatever you choose to make of it, I suppose. You're not treated as anyone special in this country, but if you made it known that you are Lady Charlotte, daughter of the Earl and Countess of Lanshire, you would undoubtedly receive a great deal of attention."

Her cheeks now swollen with far too many grilled mushrooms, Charlotte bobbed her head. Her neck extended a few inches as she swallowed the mouthful. "Exactly my point." She aimed the tines of her fork in Olivia's direction. "We both know

I can't reveal who I am, yet I detest this boring existence."

With her swollen feet and aching shoulders, Olivia didn't want to hear Charlotte's complaints, so she attempted to change the subject. "You said Mrs. DeVault stopped by. Did you have a pleasant visit?"

Charlotte reached across the table and heaped the remaining potatoes onto her plate. "I accompanied her to the Arcade, thinking I would borrow a library book, but they said you hadn't paid the fee." Her lips formed a slight pout.

"You could have paid it, Charlotte. I don't have money for library fees, nor do I have time to read."

"I found the librarian rather rude. I chose to leave the book and walk out." She raised her nose into the air.

Olivia shrugged. There would be no making the woman happy this evening. While Charlotte finished the second meringue, Olivia cleared the dishes. Once she'd finished in the kitchen, she would retire for the night and leave Charlotte to complain to the walls.

"Oh yes. Mrs. DeVault said to tell you that Albert and Martha have tickets for the band concert on Saturday."

Olivia popped her head around the corner. "Is that all she said?"

"No. Fred purchased tickets, also. He's hoping you'll go with him." Charlotte licked her fingers. "I told her I was sure you'd be more than pleased to leave me alone for yet another night."

With a sigh, Olivia plunged her hands back in the soapy dishwater. Two escorts for the band concert. She hoped Mrs. DeVault wouldn't take Charlotte's word and relay an acceptance to Fred. What would she do with two gentlemen callers arriving at her front door on Saturday night?

[illegible]

Chapter Eleven

After brief consideration, Olivia decided against having Charlotte deliver a message to Mrs. DeVault. Charlotte had already determined Mr. Howard would be the preferable suitor for Olivia. And knowing Charlotte, she would intentionally forget to deliver the message, an embarrassment that would likely terminate any further pursuit by the younger man. Olivia remained uncertain how Charlotte could consider herself an accomplished judge of men. Hadn't she chosen a true scoundrel for herself? Olivia dared not mention that opinion for fear of igniting the woman's wrath or sending her into a crying spell that would go on for untold hours.

Instead, she'd send her message through Martha. Though the two women saw little of each other at work, Olivia would make a special effort to go to the upper levels of the hotel and locate her today. She'd explain what had occurred, and perhaps Martha could lend some advice on how to best handle Mr. Howard's advances in the future.

Although Olivia had little time to think about her conflicting escorts for the band concert, Chef René soon offered the perfect opportunity. Before placing a tray of croissants in the oven, he checked the temperature and beamed at the stove. *"Magnifique!"* He slid the baking sheet into the Goodwin gas range—the pride of *his* kitchen. "Georgie is missing, likely hiding out somewhere on the fourth floor. I need you to go and find him."

On any other day, his request would have annoyed her. Normally she preferred to be at Chef René's side, observing every move, hoping to gain his expertise. But today was different. Today she must make certain Fred knew exactly why she couldn't accompany him to the band concert. Taking the steps two at a time, she looked down the hallways before proceeding to the next floor. Not seeing Martha on the second or third level, she continued upward. She'd first locate Georgie, a task that should prove rather easy. The fourth floor was occupied by kitchen boys and the servants who accompanied some of the hotel guests, all of whom would be—or should be—out of their small stuffy quarters before dawn. She need not take precautions before flinging open the doors on this floor. The oddly shaped spaces had been wedged into the crannies surrounding the dormers or fitted to the varying slants of the roofline. Little care was given to their size or shape, for they'd not be used by anyone except the lower class.

Nearing the end of the hallway and still having no success, Olivia wondered if the young man had run off without telling anyone. She'd been told that from time to time one or two of the boys would jump a train passing through town. The boys all thought they'd find a pot of gold at the end of their ride on the steel rails. So far, three had returned. They'd found neither their pot of gold nor gainful employment. Chef René was forgiving, saying young men should explore their opportunities before settling on their life's work. She doubted whether he believed the same about women.

Pushing open the final door, Olivia heaved a sigh. Finally! There was Georgie. He appeared to be asleep. She clapped her hands together and called out his name.

The boy rolled over and groaned.

"Chef René wants you in the kitchen this moment. Are you ill?"

He held his stomach. "Yes." He jumped to his feet, waved her away, and then raced down the hall toward the bathroom. Two empty liquor bottles sat in the corner by his bed. Apparently Georgie had been celebrating throughout the night and was paying the consequences this morning. Chef René would not be pleased. Georgie was still holding an arm across his stomach as he staggered back to the room, obviously weakened by constant visits to the bathroom.

"Please don't tell," he said in a raspy voice and fell back onto the narrow cot. "I just received word my mum died last month. I didn't even know she was sick."

"Well, you'll not pay her tribute by falling into a drunken stupor every night. Will you promise this is the last of the drinking?"

He groaned an affirmative reply.

"I'll tell Chef René you've taken ill, but if he asks about alcohol, I'll be required to tell the truth. I'll not lie for you, Georgie."

He rolled back toward the wall. "Yes, ma'am. I won't ask you to go against your religious convictions."

His words burned through her conscience. Though she had lied to protect herself, she was quick to tell Georgie that truth must be spoken when it applied to him. *Self-righteous!* The words echoed in her mind as loudly as if someone had shouted them down the empty fourth-floor hallway. She ran to the staircase and started down, her shoes clattering on the bare oak steps, clinging to the railing for support. At the third-floor landing, she collided with Martha and jerked to a halt.

She clutched Martha's arm as she gasped for air. "I've been looking for you."

Martha's thin eyebrows lifted and formed two perfectly shaped arches. "On the fourth floor?"

"No. I went up there looking for Georgie—at Chef René's request." She tugged Martha's hand and pulled her to an alcove that overlooked the rear of the hotel. After explaining her predicament with Mr. Howard, she leaned against the windowsill and looked into Martha's hazel eyes. "What can I do?"

Martha lowered her voice as one of the maids walked down the hallway. "You must go to the concert with Mr. Howard. You've already accepted his invitation. It would be impolite to break the engagement in order to attend with Fred."

"But what do I say should he extend a future invitation? I'm to be with him both this evening and tomorrow evening, yet I'd rather be with Fred." Her cheeks flushed at the admission.

Martha giggled and looped arms with her. They walked toward the stairs. "Then tell him no thank you. It's as simple as that."

Olivia shook her head. "I worry my refusal could jeopardize my position at the hotel."

Martha stopped at the head of the stairs. "Why should it?"

Olivia couldn't respond. Outside of another lie, what could she say? *Because I was hired based upon a fraudulent letter of recommendation, and if I make an enemy of Mr. Howard, he may delve into my background*? Such a reply wouldn't endear her to Martha.

"You aren't still concerned about those ants marching all over the dining room, are you?" Martha stifled a giggle.

"No, but I've continued to have my share of mishaps in the kitchen, and I know I try Chef René's patience from time to time—even though it's not my intent." She glanced toward the stairs. "I had best get back to the kitchen, or he'll be sending someone to fetch me as well as Georgie. You will explain to Fred?"

Martha nodded. "I'll do my best, but he's bound to be disappointed."

Olivia didn't say so, but she truly hoped he would be. Leaving behind the pine woodwork of the second and third floors, she descended into the main lobby, where rich cherry woodwork and Minton tile gleamed to polished perfection. Mr. Billings stood behind the front desk, guarding the enunciator box, call button board, and registry like a mother hen protecting her chicks.

"Chef René has inquired concerning your whereabouts, Miss Mott." His lips remained in a tight line as he relayed the message.

"Thank you, Mr. Billings." The man's demeanor remained unchanged. Olivia was convinced he didn't like her. He'd never warmed to her. She could only assume that being hired without his stamp of approval resulted in the man's ongoing displeasure.

Of course there was no way of being certain. With the exception of Chef René, no one else had been hired to work in the hotel without Mr. Billings's endorsement—at least that's what Martha had told her.

"Oh, and Miss Mott . . ."

She turned and met his austere stare. "Yes?"

"I'm told that some liquor has been disappearing from the hotel bar. Two to three bottles a week." His eyes darkened. "I'm told these occurrences began at approximately the same time you came to—"

She stepped closer to the smooth marble-topped counter. "Are you accusing me of—"

Mr. Billings leaned forward and waved his index finger back and forth. "Do *not* interrupt me, Miss Mott." He stood back, grasped the hem of his vest, and tugged with such vigor that she thought it might soon reach his knees. "The only persons who have keys to that room are Chef René and me. Even the barkeep does not have a personal key, and the bottles are counted each evening before closing."

Olivia waited until she was sure he'd finished speaking. "And for that reason you feel you should accuse me of this despicable act?"

He cleared his throat and looked down his nose as though she were a fly that he was anxious to swat. "I believe I stated more than one reason, Miss Mott. The keys *and* the timing. In addition, I don't believe Chef René or Mr. Howard performed a proper check into your background or references."

Perspiration dampened her hands and beaded along her upper lip. She swallowed the lump that had begun to form in her throat. Should she mention that Eddie and Georgie had been hired two days after her own employment at the hotel or that Mr. Billings could find two empty bottles in their room at this very moment? Oh, how she wanted to shout that information across the desk and watch Mr. Billings's arrogant look evaporate. But what right did she have to accuse Georgie or Eddie? She had no proof the bottles had come from the hotel bar. Her accusations would be as tenuous as those of Mr. Billings.

Best to take the offensive. She squared her shoulders and jutted her chin, hoping her deportment somewhat resembled the demeanor she'd seen Charlotte assume from time to time. "I am *highly* offended." When he glowered, she remained steadfast. "I plan to report your false accusations to Chef René. He may proceed to investigate further, if he so desires. I believe the chef will confirm that I have never had access to his keys. And I do not imbibe alcoholic beverages." She turned on her heel and marched off, careful to keep her head high and her back as straight as a broomstick.

"I will talk to Chef René myself," Mr. Billings called after her.

Olivia pretended not to hear. She'd see Chef René long before Mr. Billings would. Indeed, the rotund chef now stood in the kitchen doorway with his beefy hands on his hips and a scowl on his face as she approached. Had she not known better, she'd think Mr. Billings had already alerted him.

"Where have you been, Miss Mott? I sent you to locate Georgie, and you finally come back after almost a half hour and"—he bent back and forth and pretended to look behind her—"I *still* don't have Georgie in my kitchen."

"My apologies, Chef René. Georgie is ill, and I remained

long enough to ensure he wasn't in need of immediate medical care. Then as I returned to the lobby, Mr. Billings detained me." She lowered her voice and leaned closer. "I must speak to you privately when you have a few moments."

All discussion of Georgie was forgotten. Chef René was much more interested in what Mr. Billings had to say. He crooked his finger for her to follow. "Out here where the staff will not hear." Marching to the side door, he led her outside to a grassy expanse well beyond the kitchen door. "Well? What did that pompous man say to you?"

Chef René folded his thick arms across his chest, and a haughty expression slowly took form as she explained Mr. Billings's accusations.

He raised a finger into the air. "Ha! Who does that man think he is to question my employees? We shall *see* about this! I will talk to Mr. Howard—to Mr. Pullman, if necessary! Mr. Beelings's accusations have been directed against Chef René as well as against you, Miss Mott." He shifted his head with a vigor that sent his white hat fluttering to the ground in a graceful landing.

She stooped down and retrieved his hat. "Mr. Billings said I shouldn't speak to you about this matter, but I pretended I didn't hear him."

The chef rubbed his sagging jowl. "*Did* he?" He winked and nodded. "Then I shall be well prepared when he approaches me. Thank you for bringing this matter to my attention, Miss Mott. I knew you were a young lady of integrity—someone I could trust."

His praise set her mind awhirl. If he knew the truth, he'd think her far from trustworthy. In fact, he'd likely discharge her that very moment. She dug the toe of her shoe into the grass, her face warm with embarrassment.

With his thickly padded thumb, Chef René lifted her chin until their eyes met in a somber gaze. "I know your letter wasn't genuine. Nevertheless, I still believe you are a young lady of integrity."

Hot tears began to pool in her eyes. "How did you know?"

He laughed. "I was certain before I hired you, Miss Mott, but it took only two minutes in my kitchen to confirm what I already believed." He shook his head. "You worked in a kitchen, but you held no position of responsibility. However, you are a good student—how you say? Inspired. Chef René will make you into a fine chef, a true protégée, so long as you stay committed to learning."

She enjoyed the way he referred to himself as though he were some distant third party. "I'm very committed and honored that you consider me talented enough to be your protégée." She gave him a shamefaced glance. "But why is it you never said anything about my lack of training?" The moment she'd spoken the words, she wondered if he had been setting a trap. Her heart pounded against her chest and her stomach roiled. She hoped she wouldn't faint.

His lips curved into a wide grin. "I did the very same thing when I was your age because I knew I was destined to become a great chef." He patted her shoulder. "We shall survive Mr. Beelings and his accusations. Mr. Howard and Mr. Pullman will prove to be strong allies."

She didn't want Mr. Howard to be her ally—or Mr. Pullman, either. She'd rather they stay out of the matter. Chef René might be willing to accept her forged credentials, but Mr.

Howard and Mr. Pullman would be another story altogether. Chef René appeared unconcerned as they walked side by side to the kitchen door, but her worries continued to mount. Now that she'd admitted to one of her lies, he could use it against her at any time. Thoughts of Chef Mallard's unwanted advances flitted through her mind. Would Chef René expect some favor in return for his silence? She could only hope he would prove trustworthy.

When she finally was dismissed from the kitchen to partake of her late midday meal, Olivia raced to the fourth floor. Gasping for air yet unwilling to waste a moment, she continued down the hallway and flung open the door to Georgie's room. He didn't appear to have moved since she'd last visited him. He turned his bleary eyes upon her.

"I don't have much time, so listen carefully. And you'd better tell me the truth, Georgie." She gave him a stern look.

Her legs continued to tremble, and she longed to sit down and rest a moment. The sparsely appointed room contained only two narrow cots, two suitcases, and a stack of boxes that served as a makeshift bureau for some of the kitchen boys' belongings. No chair in sight. And she would never consider sitting on the edge of a young man's bed. Leaning her weight against the wall, she hoped she would soon regain her strength.

Georgie rolled over and flipped his gangling legs over the side of the bed. His bare feet slapped against the wood floor. The room would seem a bit more homelike if Georgie would put a rug between the beds, but she didn't mention that. The empty bottles remained in the corner of the room. Olivia pointed at them.

"You stole those from the hotel bar, didn't you?" She narrowed her eyes. "And don't you lie to me."

"Maybe, maybe not."

There wasn't time for his nonsense! She leaned forward and pinched his ear. "Your thievery is going to get Chef René in trouble, and maybe me, too, so quit playing your silly games."

"Eddie stole it, but I drank most of it. Don't tell him I told you."

Eddie—the tall redheaded boy who was always winking at the young girls that passed by on their way to work at the laundry. "Is that Eddie's bed?" She tipped her head at the unoccupied cot.

"Yes, ma'am. He's down at work, ain't he?"

She nodded. "How'd he get Chef René's key to unlock the door to the bar?"

"He didn't need it. Eddie can pick a lock quicker than I can unlock it with a key."

The thought of the boy running about the hotel picking locks was more than a bit disconcerting. "*Any* lock?"

"Don't know about that, but he's done pretty good so far. Some nights he goes back to the kitchen and gets us extra food. Other nights, he wants a few drinks and goes to the bar. He's never had trouble with either of those doors."

"Mr. Billings has discovered the missing liquor. He's accusing Chef René of being careless with his keys. Either you or that hobbledehoy with whom you share this room need to tell the chef the truth."

A shock of greasy brown hair fell across one eye as he looked up at her. "Or?"

How she wished he hadn't called her bluff. Conflict wasn't her forte. But Georgie must understand this was serious. "If one of you doesn't tell him, then I will." She hoped her voice had been firm enough to convince him. A picture of Eddie picking the lock on her front door flashed through her mind. If he became angry over her interference, he might break in during the night and harm her. The mere thought caused her to shudder.

Georgie hunched forward and buried his pasty-complexioned face inside his cupped hands. "I'll tell Chef René. But not until I have a chance to talk to Eddie."

Olivia strained to hear the muffled response. "You must go to him before morning."

Georgie bobbed his head.

"Does that mean you will?" She needed to hear him give his word.

He lifted his face from his palms, his eyes bloodshot and watery. "Yes. I promise."

"I'm going to trust you'll do as you've promised." She left the room and closed the boy's door. Only time would tell if he would keep his word.

CHAPTER TWELVE

Mr. Howard arrived at precisely seven o'clock. The moment Olivia opened the front door, he handed her a small bouquet of daisies. She sneezed—three times—and wondered if her reaction to the flowers signaled an evening of disaster.

Feeling awkward and unsure of herself, she muttered a thank-you for the flowers and apologized for the sneezing episode. She hoped the brief expression of regret covered all of her social blunders thus far. Before descending the front steps, Mr. Howard offered his arm. When she pretended not to notice, he lightly grasped her hand and tucked it into the crook of his left arm. Apparently she'd made yet another faux pas.

Offering a reassuring smile, he patted her hand. The softness of his palm surprised her. The few men in her life had been laborers with rough hands, hard and weathered by years of manual labor, though her father's may have grown soft in later years when he'd not done much except wrap them around a mug of ale.

"Your dress is lovely. I would say that yellow is a particularly good color for you." He leaned back a bit and gave her a closer appraisal. "Yes. Yellow is definitely your color."

She wasn't certain how to respond. A man who decided what color complemented her complexion was something new to her. The only time she could recall a man commenting on her clothing was when her father ranted at the mention of her need of a new dress. Olivia was about to tell Mr. Howard that the dress belonged to Charlotte and that she herself owned nothing even vaguely similar to such finery when he interrupted her thoughts with a question.

"Would you prefer to visit the library, the shops in the Arcade, or perhaps stroll to the athletic fields and see if any of the teams are practicing this evening?"

Unlike Mr. Howard, she'd been on her feet all day, and the thought of walking held little appeal. "The library would be nice." There were chairs in the library where she could sit and rest her aching feet while perusing a book. And since the librarians enforced the Quiet signs in their domain to a fault, there'd be little opportunity for Mr. Howard's questions.

Though he'd requested she call him Samuel when they were alone, she hadn't yet been able to do so. Not that she didn't like him. It was just that his questions and demeanor continually reminded her of the power he possessed in this community. One mistake and she could find herself unemployed. Unfortunately, as time passed, it became more and more difficult to remember what she'd told to whom.

His shoulders sagged somewhat. "You're certain you wouldn't prefer the athletic island? I believe there's some rowing practice this evening."

Her choice had disappointed him, but Charlotte's shoes were already pinching her sore feet. Besides, Fred might be at the island practicing baseball or cricket, and she didn't want to make an appearance with Mr. Howard. Fred might think her arrival an attempt to provoke jealousy, which was the furthest thing from her mind.

"Why don't we stop at the drugstore for a glass of lemonade before going upstairs?" Mr. Howard suggested as they neared the Arcade.

She didn't want to stop for lemonade, but she'd already disappointed him with her choice of the library, so she reluctantly agreed. Still, she worried he would expect her to engage in lighthearted conversation, and she'd already exhausted her limited repertoire of small talk.

It was shortly after their lemonade had been served when she saw Fred walk into the shop. She averted her eyes, hoping he'd not seen her. Mr. Howard rested his arms on the table and leaned toward her. "Isn't that Fred DeVault, the man your cousin Albert rooms with?"

She turned a furtive glance to the other side of the room. Fred was looking at her, and her fingers went limp as she lifted her hand to wave. She turned her attention back to Mr. Howard, hoping Fred would soon depart. Instead, he paid the cashier and strode in their direction. She could barely breathe by the time he came to a halt beside their table.

His crisp shirt stretched tight across his muscular frame, and his dark wavy hair glistened beneath the gaslights. "Martha delivered your message," he said abruptly.

"Hello, Fred. It's good to see you." Heat rose in her cheeks and her voice warbled like a distressed songbird. So much for her attempt to remain calm. "You know Mr. Howard." *What an inane remark. Of course he knows Mr. Howard. Everyone knows Mr. Howard.*

Fred extended his hand. "Evening, Mr. Howard. I trust you and Olivia are enjoying your lemonade."

"Indeed we are. Thank you for stopping by to say hello." Samuel lifted his glass and took a sip of his drink.

Fred took his cue and, with an easy long-legged stride, crossed the width of the room and exited the store. Olivia watched him through the glass window as he headed down the interior hallway of the Arcade. Had Martha also told Fred of her engagement with Mr. Howard this evening?

"You have Martha deliver messages for you?"

She snapped to attention, surprised by his question. Next he'd want to know what messages she was sending to Fred and why. "You'll recall my cousin rooms with Mrs. DeVault—Fred's mother. Martha and Albert see each other every evening." She hoped her answer had been convoluted enough to allay further inquiry. In case it didn't, she decided to end with a question of her own. "How did you secure your position in Pullman, Mr. Howard?"

"I've worked for Mr. Pullman for years—it was a natural transition. He needed a company agent that he could trust and thought I was the proper fit for the job. So did I." He reached across the table and covered her hand with his.

Olivia hoped Fred wasn't watching through one of the windows that lined the interior passageway.

"Why is it you address Mr. DeVault as Fred, yet you won't address me as Samuel, even though I've asked you to do so on several occasions?"

She slid her hand from beneath his palm and took a sip of lemonade. "I'm afraid if I become accustomed to referring to you as Samuel, I might err during working hours." That was a true enough reply.

"I trust you wouldn't have much difficulty. Won't you at least try?"

He'd cornered her, and there was no escape. "Yes. I'll do my best."

He patted her hand, obviously pleased by her response. When they'd finished their lemonade, the two of them walked out of the shop and into the expansive Arcade hallway. Olivia never tired of this particular building. It had become one of her favorite places in Pullman. Sunlight spilled into the structure through a wide stretch of glass roofing that covered the central passageway and offered natural illumination during the day and a view of the stars at night. Though Olivia had never shopped in such a fancy place as this, Charlotte had been less impressed. She said the architecture imitated similar examples of the arcades in Paris, Berlin, and Vienna. Olivia didn't care if the idea had been copied or not—she found the building enchanting. She had expected Charlotte to tell her the American version was a poor example of those in Europe. Instead, she had been surprisingly complimentary. Of course, that had been immediately after their arrival and before Charlotte's world had come to an end, as she dramatically referred to her present life.

They strolled upstairs to the southeast corner of the second floor, and Mr. Howard escorted her into the library. The walk had been enough to set her feet to throbbing once again. She rounded one of the massive ornamental pillars supporting the roof and stained-glass dome and made a quick selection from a long magazine table in the center of the room. While Mr. Howard perused the contents of one of the mahogany bookcases, she selected a comfortable easy chair, thankful to be off her feet. She would never again borrow these shoes from Charlotte. She flipped through the pages of *Harper's New Monthly Magazine* and stopped at an illustration by George du Maurier titled "What Induced Him to Marry Her?"

"Obviously it wasn't her beauty that induced him, was it?" She hadn't heard Mr. Howard step behind her chair. He was leaning over the leather-upholstered chair, and his breath tickled her neck.

Olivia slapped the magazine to her lap. "I've been told that beauty is the only thing of import to men when choosing a spouse." Personally, she found the notion somewhat irritating.

"Well, you have no need to worry, Olivia. Your beauty surpasses that of most any woman I've ever seen. Any man would be delighted to have you as a wife." Moving to one side, he took possession of the chair alongside hers. He leaned much closer than necessary and lightly swept his fingers across her hand. "I know I certainly enjoy your company." He whispered his comments, careful not to provoke the librarian.

His words were disquieting in the extreme. Had Fred's unexpected appearance caused these surprisingly ardent remarks? Could he possibly consider himself in a competition for her affections? She didn't like that idea in the least. With Charlotte and her constant complaints, her own attempts to prove herself to Chef René, and her concern that every word she spoke could conflict with one of her previous falsehoods, Olivia had more than enough to keep her mind in a whirl.

She noted the book in his hand. "If you've made a selection,

I should soon go home. Since I'm attending the concert with you tomorrow, I promised Lady Charlotte I wouldn't be late this evening."

"*Lady* Charlotte? Are you referring to Mrs. Hornsby?" Mr. Howard's eyebrows were arched high on his forehead as he awaited her response.

Olivia wished she could snatch back that one word. What could she say to conceal her blunder? She swallowed and forced a smile. "Having worked for nobility, I seem to slip back to my former patterns of speech from time to time." She inhaled a deep breath. "And you must admit that Mrs. Hornsby commands a stately bearing."

He seemed to weigh her response and then nodded. "Yes. She does appear quite regal in her mannerisms."

Olivia wasn't certain she had convinced Mr. Howard with her feeble explanation. She could only hope it had been enough to set aside any suspicion. She waited while he checked out the book. Together they descended the wide stairway, walked the long hallway, and exited the building. Her too-tight shoes were now the cause of a slight limp, and she hoped her feet would recover by morning.

"I believe you mentioned you had met Mrs. Hornsby when she called at Lanshire Hall. What was her association with the Earl and Countess of Lanshire?"

Was he testing her? She'd never said any such thing. "I don't believe Mrs. Hornsby ever called at Lanshire Hall. If so, I'm not aware of such an occasion. I believe I told you we had met at a dressmaker's shop when she was having several gowns altered."

He placed his index finger to his lips and tapped lightly. "Yes. I do believe that's what you told me. It seems my memory fails me on minor details from time to time."

When they arrived in front of the house, Mr. Howard took both of her hands in his own. "I'm looking forward to the band concert." He moved a step closer. "And please tell Mrs. Hornsby you'll not be home so early tomorrow evening. I thought we might have dessert at the Arcade restaurant afterward."

His breath whispered across her cheek while he spoke. She wanted to move back, but her heels were lodged against the step. "I should go inside now, Mr. Howard."

He lifted her hand to his lips and kissed it. "And you've forgotten my name once again. What must I do to make you address me as Samuel, my dear?"

My dear? She wasn't his dear. When and how had this sudden change in Mr. Howard's demeanor occurred? What had she done to make him think of her in this possessive manner? She had accepted his invitations, but mostly because she feared losing her job, not because she found him irresistible company. The moment he released her hands, she turned around and raced up the steps. With a quick wave, she thanked him for the lemonade.

"I'll call for you at seven o'clock tomorrow evening. Do sleep well."

She thought she'd heard him add "my dear" to his final sentence, though she hoped she was wrong. Once inside, she leaned against the front door, wishing tomorrow would never come. The sound of Charlotte's tinkling laughter drifted into the hallway and was soon followed by a man's voice. Perhaps Albert and Martha had stopped by.

"Is that you, Olivia? Come see who has been visiting with

me this evening." Charlotte's melodious tone caused the hairs on Olivia's neck to prickle.

She walked to the parlor, where Charlotte sat beside Fred. They had turned the divan toward the front window to allow a perfect view of the front sidewalk. They'd been watching her. Heat fired in her cheeks. "Could we have a moment alone, Charlotte?"

Fred stood. "No need. I was about to leave when you and Mr. Howard arrived out front. I didn't want to interrupt, so I waited a few extra minutes."

Charlotte's blue eyes sparkled, a sure sign she was pleased to observe Fred's displeasure. Olivia's taffeta dress swished as Charlotte brushed by her.

"Please let me explain, Fred."

"No need. I believe I saw enough to tell me what I need to know."

How could she make him understand she'd done nothing to encourage Mr. Howard's advances? His cold eyes spelled out the truth. He'd already made up his mind, and nothing she could say was going to change things.

Olivia stood in the doorway and watched until his figure slowly faded into the nighttime darkness.

"Come along and tell me about Samuel and those kisses I saw him placing on your hands tonight."

Charlotte's words sliced through her like a slashing sword. Olivia whirled around and glared. "You made certain he would see me out there, didn't you?"

"But of course. I was extending an act of charity that you'll one day thank me for. What I did will eventually prove to benefit you greatly. Now, I believe I'll retire for the night." She grinned at Olivia as she continued up the steps. "However, I must admit Fred *is* rather good looking."

How did one deal with the likes of Charlotte? She was no match for the woman. Olivia dropped onto the chair and removed the unyielding leather shoes. Charlotte had placed the bouquet of flowers on a table near the divan. Had Fred noticed them and wondered if they'd been a gift from Mr. Howard? She shook her head. No need to speculate. As sure as the sun rose in the east each morning, Charlotte had told him.

Chapter Thirteen

When Olivia entered the hotel kitchen the next morning, Chef René crooked his finger in her direction. They didn't exchange words, for she'd learned not to question him early in the day. Following his lead, she trailed along until they entered the hotel lobby. As was his custom each morning, Mr. Billings sat perched behind the massive front desk calculating the guests' accounts. His self-aggrandizing mannerisms wilted, and he tugged at his starched white collar as they approached.

Chef René grasped Olivia's arm and pulled her up to the desk. "Mr. Beelings has something to say to you, Miss Mott."

Mr. Billings clutched his pen in a white-knuckled grip. "I apologize."

Olivia expected the writing instrument to crack in half and send ink spattering across her white jacket at any moment. Before she could respond, Chef René tightened his grip on her arm. "Not good enough, Mr. Beelings."

Mr. Billings slapped the pen atop his ledger and glared at

the ink droplets that spilled across the page. Teeth gritted, he directed an ominous stare in Olivia's direction. "I apologize for wrongfully accusing you of stealing liquor from the hotel bar. The culprit has come forward and admitted his guilt."

The chef clucked his tongue. "And?"

"And I will not accuse you of anything in the future. You are not my employee, and I will first speak to Chef René if I have concerns about any of his kitchen staff."

With a look of satisfaction, René pivoted on his heel and pointed Olivia toward the kitchen. "We must prepare breakfast, Miss Mott."

A thousand questions popped into her head, but this wasn't the time to ask. She would wait until they'd completed breakfast preparations; then she'd quiz Georgie. While she chopped and whisked, Chef René prepared a variety of the omelets and scrambled eggs that the hotel diners insisted upon each morning. Olivia was most confident with the morning meal. Perhaps because she'd made fewer mistakes, the preparation was simpler, and Chef René didn't insist upon a daily change in the menu.

"Eddie! These dishes need to be delivered to the hot closet."

Her mouth dropped open, and she twisted around to survey the kitchen. Surely the chef had erred. Why would Eddie still be working in the kitchen? Hadn't he been discharged for his thievery? The long-legged young man loped into the kitchen as if it were any normal workday. He came to an abrupt halt in front of the preparation table, his red locks bouncing up and down.

When he saw her staring, he winked and grinned. "Are these the dishes that need to go to the hot closet?"

She nodded her head, unable to speak. Now that she thought about it, she'd not seen Georgie since arriving at work. She sidled up to the stove when Eddie was out of earshot. "Where's Georgie this morning?"

The chef looked at her and shook his head. "Not now."

When they'd finally completed breakfast and the dirty dishes were being washed, Chef René signaled for her to follow him to his office. He closed the door and forced his corpulent body into his chair.

"Georgie has taken a position in the Paper Wheel Works. He will be paid a few cents more an hour than he received working in the kitchen."

She frowned and he held up his palm.

"Let me explain. He told me the truth about Eddie stealing the liquor, but he admitted he had been the one who had consumed most of the alcohol. He also confided that he feared retribution once Eddie discovered he'd come forth with the truth and therefore asked to change jobs."

She was surprised to hear that Georgie had been reassigned at his own request.

Chef René grinned and continued. "With the slight pay raise and opportunity for advancement, anyone would understand his leaving the kitchen. Georgie has moved out of the hotel and taken a room with a family here in town. In a few days, I plan to confront Eddie." He pointed to a cabinet in his office. "I have kept the empty bottles, and Georgie told me where Eddie keeps the tools of his trade. He'll lose his position in good time."

There was little time to dwell on Georgie's departure. They'd soon need to prepare for the noonday meal. And though having

Eddie remain on the employee roster for even a few short days was cause for concern, Olivia was pleased Georgie hadn't been discharged—even more, that he had escaped Eddie's poor influence.

Throughout the day, she caught Eddie watching her and wondered what Georgie had told him. She tried to convince herself that he was looking at her no more frequently than usual. Eddie had always leered at the girls. She was simply more aware of his behavior today. However, she was relieved when quitting time finally arrived.

After packing a few leftovers into a basket, she retrieved her hat and cape from the closet off the hallway. While tying the satin ribbons of her cape, Eddie approached and blocked the doorway with a menacing look in his eye.

"Some folks around this place know more than they oughta, Miss Mott." He stood too close and his unwashed clothing fouled the air.

"I wouldn't know about that, Eddie. Personally, I don't consider myself in that category. There is much I still need to learn. My soufflés are proof enough of that."

He glowered at her. "I ain't talkin' 'bout no soufflés, and you know it, don't ya?" He moved a step closer.

She could barely breathe. "Please move aside, Eddie. I'm not—"

"Eddie! What are you doing in there?" Chef René's question boomed through the narrow hallway and into the tiny coat closet. They both started and turned.

Eddie backed away, his menacing look replaced by one of fear or annoyance. He mumbled something as Chef René pushed him toward the kitchen.

Moments later, she departed by way of the side door rather than passing through the kitchen. Once outside she removed her cape and tucked it atop the basket. Even though she'd needed the added warmth early this morning, it wouldn't do for her walk home. She crossed through the park near the hotel, occasionally glancing over her shoulder as she continued onward. She hoped Chef René would keep Eddie in the hotel until she was well out of sight. The thought of having him follow her home was frightening. Moreover, she wouldn't want him to come to the house and alarm Charlotte.

When she reached the row house, she was winded, and the handles of the basket were cutting into her arm. One final look assured her that Eddie hadn't followed. She hurried inside and dropped the basket onto the kitchen table. Surprisingly, Charlotte was setting the table. Her ladyship must be famished.

After placing silverware at each place setting, Charlotte waved one of the napkins toward her. "Your face is as red as a beet. Has it warmed up that much outdoors or were you running?" Without waiting for an answer, she dropped the napkins onto the table. "You didn't need to rush. You've plenty of time to prepare for the concert."

Olivia simply agreed and unpacked the food. No need to worry Charlotte with talk of Eddie and his menacing ways. Besides, she was likely making a mountain out of a molehill. A young man such as Eddie would no doubt be occupying his free time with girls and liquor.

With the hot July sun finally heading westward, the afternoon's warmth had begun to subside by the time Fred mounted the steps of the Malloy residence. His invitation to the band concert had been extended to Mildred for all the wrong reasons. He wanted to prove to Olivia that there were plenty of other young ladies who would be pleased to accept his invitation. Now he regretted his hasty decision. Nonetheless, he would do his best to assure the evening proved pleasurable, for Mildred had done nothing but happily accept his invitation.

Before Fred had an opportunity to knock, Mildred whisked open the front door and greeted him. She was dressed in a pale green gown, and her auburn hair was piled high on her head and fastened with ornate combs. She'd obviously taken special care preparing for the evening. He hoped she hadn't read too much into his invitation, but he should have considered that possibility before he'd invited her.

They arrived early and stood chatting while beautifully attired attendees gathered near the massive, highly polished stairway leading to the west-central portion of the second floor. Fred watched the entrance, his emotions wavering. He hoped to capture a glimpse of Olivia, yet he knew that seeing her with Mr. Howard would only fuel his resentment that she'd chosen Mr. Howard as her escort.

Then he saw her. In reality, he first saw Mr. Howard, but his focus immediately shifted to Olivia. She was wearing a gown of pale blue silk with puffed sleeves, and narrow blue ribbons were woven into her hair. He inhaled a shaky breath—she looked beautiful. He wanted to look away. He tried to look away. But his gaze remained fixed upon her.

"Amazing that a chef's assistant could afford such a gown, isn't it?"

Mildred's comment shook Fred from his trancelike state. "I believe she probably borrowed it from Mrs. Hornsby."

"Mrs. Hornsby?"

"The widow who resides with Olivia," he explained.

"Oh yes. I've seen her with Olivia from time to time. She's expecting a child, isn't she? I believe I heard she's a widow."

Fred nodded and watched Olivia walk up the stairs holding on to Mr. Howard's arm. The town gossips likely knew everything about Charlotte Hornsby except her name.

Mildred tugged on his arm and motioned toward the stairs. "Shall we go up and take our seats?"

They followed a group of attendees, most with tickets admitting them to the main floor. Several of the supervisors and their wives walked toward the inner stairway of the theater that led to the boxed seating. While the usher directed Fred and Mildred down the aisle, Fred tried to covertly scan each of the elegantly decorated boxes that projected along the east and west walls of the theater. His breath caught when he spotted Olivia and Mr. Howard. The city agent held Olivia's waist in a possessive grasp while he pointed at the beautifully adorned stage. Fred inwardly cringed when he saw her laugh in response. She obviously was enjoying Mr. Howard's attention.

Fred imagined the man's ploys to hold Olivia's attention. He was probably reinforcing her perceptions of Mr. Pullman as a grand philanthropist while he expounded on the theater's exceptional features.

Disheartened, Fred slouched in his red leather–upholstered seat and stared at the huge chandelier that hung from the center of the fresco-painted ceiling.

Mildred leaned closer and pointed upward. "Look, Fred. There's Olivia with Mr. Howard."

Before he could stop her, Mildred stood and waved. "Oh,

look. She and Mr. Howard have spotted us. Olivia is signaling with her handkerchief." She grabbed for his arm and tugged until he stood up. "Wave at them, Fred."

He halfheartedly signaled and quickly settled back in his chair. "Do sit down, Mildred."

While preparing for bed after last night's band concert, Olivia had discovered a note propped on her pillow with brief instructions from Charlotte that she was not to be awakened for church the next morning. She did not plan to attend. Although Olivia shouldn't be pleased by such an announcement, she sighed with relief. She didn't want to begin the day explaining her lack of interest in Mr. Howard's advances, and there was little doubt Charlotte would insist upon a detailed report of the previous evening's activities.

Olivia quietly departed, thankful Charlotte hadn't stirred. Later in the day, she'd be better equipped to deal with the woman. And, if all went well today, Fred would ask her to remain after church services and join them for the noonday meal. She set off for the DeVaults' with a spring in her step—until thoughts of Mildred Malloy returned. What if Fred planned to escort Mildred to church today? She slowed her gait. Had she seen Mildred at church in the past? While she knew several other hotel employees regularly attended, Olivia didn't recall seeing the hotel maid there. She could only hope the young woman attended one of the churches in Kensington or Roseland rather than Greenstone in Pullman.

She was half a block from the DeVaults' when she saw Martha, Albert, Fred, and his mother walking down the front steps.

She waved and called to them. Certainly very unladylike behavior, but they were departing without her. She hastened her speed. Martha and Albert waited, but Fred continued onward with his mother by his side.

"Why were you leaving without me?" She gasped for air between each word.

"Catch your breath, Olivia." Martha rubbed her back like a worried mother. "After seeing you in that fine box at the concert last night, Fred said you'd surely be attending church with Mr. Howard this morning."

Olivia's stomach lurched at the remark. Why would Fred draw such a silly conclusion? Did he think her attentions could be so easily swayed? They hurried along and were soon closely following behind Fred and his mother.

"Good morning, dear." Mrs. DeVault glanced over her shoulder and offered a bright smile to accompany her chirpy greeting. Fred did neither.

Tilting her head close to Martha, Olivia whispered, "Is Mildred meeting Fred at church?"

Martha shook her head. "No. She attends over in Kensington. Besides, I don't think he asked her. Are you troubled because he escorted her to the concert last night?"

"Well, of course. Wouldn't you be worried, too?"

"I don't think he's fond of Mildred, but he didn't want his extra ticket going to waste. I suggested he give it to Luther Hughes, but I think he planned to fire some jealousy in your soul." She grinned. "Looks as though he succeeded."

Olivia tried her best to finagle a seat next to Fred, but it seemed as though he did everything possible to make her attempts futile. When all was said and done, Olivia was squished between Mrs. DeVault and Mrs. Verdon, a large woman who continually expanded her seating space throughout the service. By the time they stood for the benediction, the width of Olivia's pew space had decreased to no more than twelve inches. She'd listened to the sermon while seated on her left hip with her arms wrapped around her waist and Mrs. Verdon's feathered hat tickling her neck. She hoped to never repeat *that* experience again!

"Would you like to join us for dinner, Olivia?" Mrs. DeVault's offer was a welcome respite after more than an hour of pain and suffering beside Mrs. Verdon.

"I'd be de—"

"I'm certain she has other plans, Mother. It appears that Mr. Howard is heading in her direction."

Why had Fred been so quick to interrupt her acceptance? Perhaps Martha didn't know the depth of his feelings for Mildred. Had he planned to spend the afternoon in Mildred's company?

"I have no plans with Mr. Howard or anyone else, Mrs. DeVault. I'd be most pleased to join you." She turned to Fred. "However, if you and Mildred have arrangements to see each other this afternoon, don't let my acceptance interfere."

Fred glanced over his shoulder as he escorted his mother out of the pew. "We'll see if you come to dinner once Mr. Howard makes you an offer for an afternoon outing."

Before she could respond, Mr. Howard drew near and clasped her waist in an unforeseen and proprietary manner. Olivia twisted from his hold as Mrs. Verdon lumbered out of the pew and into the aisle.

"I thought you might join me for the afternoon. I've

arranged for a picnic lunch and rented a rowboat. I thought you would enjoy a surprise outing, so I didn't mention my idea last evening."

His assumption she would agree astonished her, especially after she'd turned down his invitation to attend church with him. "I'm sorry, Mr. Howard. I have previous arrangements. If you'll forgive me, I must hurry and join my friends."

"Next Sunday, then. I'll take care of everything." He made his way around Mrs. Verdon without waiting for Olivia's reply.

The man was certainly persistent. She would send him a note of refusal in the morning.

Chapter Fourteen

A piercing scream shattered the still warmth of the August night, and Olivia sat up in her bed with a start. Had she suffered another nightmare? Her heart wasn't racing, but she remained convinced a scream had wakened her. She sat on the edge of the bed and strained to listen. Had the shriek come from the park down the street or from a nearby house? Perhaps she was once again overreacting.

Since Eddie's discharge from the hotel, she had grown fearful and with good cause. Unlike Georgie, Eddie hadn't been offered another position with the company. Instead, he'd been banned from the town of Pullman. But before making his final departure, he'd caught Olivia outside the hotel and issued an ominous warning that she'd be sorry she ever got involved.

Olivia had been unable to forget his menacing words: *"Just about the time you think I'm out of your life, you'll find out different,* Miss *Olivia Mott."* With a dark look, he had angrily spewed forth the words at her. There was no doubt in her mind that Eddie Calhoun was a young man to be reckoned with.

A shiver coursed through her as another shrill scream sliced through the silence. It was coming from the next room. *Charlotte!* Shoving her feet into the worn slippers at her bedside, Olivia hastened to the room next door. Without knocking, she hurriedly entered.

Charlotte reached out and clutched Olivia's hand in a painful grip. "It's time. The baby is coming."

Using her free hand, Olivia brushed several strands of matted hair from Charlotte's forehead. Although the baby wasn't expected until next month, Olivia didn't argue. There was little doubt her ladyship was in labor. "Turn loose of my hand, Charlotte. I'll dress quickly and go fetch Mrs. DeVault."

The whites of Charlotte's eyes glistened in the starlit room. "Don't leave me, Olivia. I don't want to die in this house by myself!"

"You're not going to die; you're having a baby." Olivia attempted to wrest her hand free. "Let go of me so I can fetch proper help."

"No!" Charlotte tightened her grip, her fingernails now digging into Olivia's flesh. "*You* can deliver the baby."

If Charlotte didn't soon loosen her hold, Olivia would be in need of medical attention herself. "I've never delivered a baby. Let me go next door and see if Mr. Rice will go and fetch Mrs. DeVault."

"Promise you'll come right back. Don't go after her yourself." Panic clung to each word. "Promise!"

"I promise. No doubt you've already wakened them with all of your shouting." After wrenching her hand loose, Olivia didn't take time to dress. She grabbed Charlotte's wrapper from the foot of the bed and tied the robe around her waist as she went onto the porch and pounded on the neighbors' door. She didn't have to wait long for Mr. Rice to appear, his thin dark hair in complete disarray.

Dark circles surrounded his eyes, and he swiped the back of his hand across his mouth as he opened the door. "What's all the racket going on over there? Them screams could wake the dead."

"Mrs. Hornsby needs the midwife, and she's afraid for me to leave her. Could you go fetch Mrs. DeVault, please?"

"I s'pose I might just as well. Ain't gonna be able to get no sleep if she's gonna be hollering the rest of the night." He waved her away from the door. "Lemme get my shoes on, and I'll go fetch her. And tell Mrs. Hornsby to try keepin' it down a bit. Some of us got to work come morning."

Instead of offering a snappish rejoinder, Olivia clamped her lips together. She needed Mr. Rice's help more than she needed to vent her anger at the man. "Thank you for your willingness to help. I'll be certain to mention your need for sleep to Mrs. Hornsby."

Charlotte delivered another screaming cry that sent Mr. Rice scurrying inside to locate his shoes and Olivia back to their house. She would offer a few soothing words and then set some water to boil. Although she didn't know why, the few times she'd been at hand when a baby was born, someone always boiled water. If Mrs. DeVault didn't need hot water for birthing the babe, then there'd be plenty for a good cup of tea when her work was done.

Charlotte moaned and held out her hand when Olivia entered the room. "Help me! I'm in such terrible pain."

"Mr. Rice has gone to fetch Mrs. DeVault. She'll know what to do." Olivia brushed away the damp curls that had once again matted along Charlotte's forehead. The air outside hung warm and heavy, but perhaps a breeze would drift though if she lifted the window a bit more. "I'm going to put water on to boil; then I'll be back."

Charlotte had her eyes closed and didn't argue. Olivia couldn't tell if she'd fallen asleep or was too exhausted to argue. She offered a quick prayer that Mrs. DeVault would hurry and then decided it might be best to pray for Charlotte and her baby, too. With the water on the stove and no further cries coming from the bedroom, she removed several sheets and blankets from one of Charlotte's steamer trunks they'd begun to use for storage shortly after moving into the flat. She truly didn't know what would be needed, but she wanted to do her best to be prepared.

It seemed a lifetime had passed before she heard Mrs. DeVault and Mr. Rice approaching the house. "You might want to close that bedroom window so's to keep the noise down a bit. I'm hopin' to get me a few hours of sleep afore headin' off for work," Mr. Rice said.

Mrs. DeVault clucked her tongue and informed Mr. Rice that the room would be much too warm with the window shut tight. "You might try stuffing your ears with a bit of cotton if things get too noisy for you."

Mr. Rice mumbled something in response, but Olivia couldn't hear, and Mrs. DeVault didn't take time to respond. Instead, she hastened inside carrying an armload of supplies. Soon they were placing a piece of oilcloth, newspaper, and old blankets beneath a complaining Charlotte. Each time they forced her to move, she cried out in pain.

"Best I check her progress and see how much longer she's going to be. I'm glad I arrived before her water broke." She glanced over her shoulder at Olivia, who was retreating from the room.

"I'll go and fetch you a cup of tea, or would you prefer lemonade?"

Mrs. DeVault pulled back the sheet covering Charlotte's legs. "A cup of tea would be nice, dear."

Once she was certain Mrs. DeVault had completed Charlotte's examination, Olivia returned with a small tray bearing a pot of tea and two cups. "How much longer do you think?"

"Always difficult to tell with the first one, but she's progressing nicely. I'm guessing she'll be holding the babe in her arms by sunrise." Mrs. DeVault took a sip of her tea. "No need for both of us to sit here, Olivia. Just like Mr. Rice next door, you've got to be up and off to work come morning. Best you try and get a few winks of sleep if you're able."

She felt somewhat guilty leaving the room while Charlotte was in the throes of pain, but sitting by her bedside wouldn't decrease the intensity of her labor. The thought helped salve her conscience as she plopped onto the side of her bed. And soon she dropped off into a restless sleep.

"Olivia!" She jumped at the sound of her name. Mrs. DeVault was standing by her bedside. "You had best get up now or you'll be late for work."

"Charlotte?"

"You can stop in and say good morning to Charlotte and her son. A fine little fellow."

"I slept through it?"

Mrs. DeVault nodded. "Charlotte did quite well. She screamed only once after you went to bed. I imagine Mr. Rice got his few hours of sleep, too."

The baby was the sweetest little cherub Olivia had ever seen. Charlotte quickly offered him to her, and Olivia wished she didn't have to go to work. She'd much rather sit and hold the little fellow. His curly blond lashes flickered, and he opened his eyelids to reveal beautiful smoky blue eyes. He latched on to Olivia's finger with a firm clasp as his tiny lips formed a beautiful pink bow.

"He's beautiful, Charlotte," Olivia said, pulling the blanket more snugly around him. "And born on August fifteenth. My own dear mother's birthday. What will you name him?"

Charlotte shrugged her shoulders. "I care little. He'll assume no title, so it makes no difference. Perhaps I shall reverse his father's name and call him Morgan Randolph Spencer. Of course we'll be required to refer to him as Hornsby rather than Spencer. What think you of that, Olivia?"

"I don't know if that's—"

"Yes. I rather like that idea. Morgan, it is." She crooked her finger, and Olivia stepped closer. "I've told Mrs. DeVault that I plan to bind my breasts and want her to find a wet nurse for the baby. My figure has been ravaged by the pregnancy and birth while Randolph continues to deny his child. I find the idea of nursing a baby repugnant."

"Oh, Charlotte, I think you should reconsider."

"Well, I thought Randolph should reassess his denial of paternity, but that didn't occur. The child will at least carry his name, albeit in a different form."

The baby squirmed in Olivia's arms, and her heart ached for

him. Would Charlotte's angry feelings for Randolph Morgan spill over to this sweet infant? She had hoped Charlotte would develop into a loving mother, but her decision against nursing the baby didn't suggest such an occurrence.

"He's a beautiful little boy, and I'm confident he'll bring you nothing but joy." Olivia leaned down to hand the small bundle back to his mother, but Charlotte didn't reach out. "You best take little Morgan. I'm going to be late for work if I tarry much longer."

Instead of reaching for the child, Charlotte tucked her arms around her waist. "I think I'll ask Mrs. DeVault to take the baby home with her for a few days so I can rest."

Olivia's jaw went slack. "*What?* Why, that's the most preposterous thing I've ever heard. You don't want to be away from your baby. He needs *you*, not Mrs. DeVault." Olivia pried Charlotte's arms from her waist and cradled the child near his mother. "He may need his diaper changed. The blanket felt a bit damp."

Charlotte wrinkled her nose. "I'm not going to do *that*! If Mrs. DeVault won't take him home, we need to find someone to come to the house and help me." After a brief and rather sour look at the baby, she glared at Olivia. "Why didn't you *tell* me?"

"Tell you what? That babies dirty their diapers?"

Mrs. DeVault hurried into the room and pointed a warning finger at Olivia. "You better hurry if you're going to get to the hotel on time."

Olivia sighed with relief. She would let Mrs. DeVault set Charlotte straight. Perhaps when she arrived home this evening, the matter of the baby's care and Charlotte's surly attitude would both be resolved.

Carrying her chef's jacket and toque, she raced to the hotel at breakneck speed, skidding to a stop as she entered the kitchen. She nearly mowed down Chef René when he unwittingly stepped in front of her.

"If you went to bed at a decent hour, you might be able to get to work without the necessity of charging into the unfortunate souls who find themselves in your path, Miss Mott." Chef René frowned and tugged on the hem of his jacket as he spoke.

She donned her white coat and hat while offering an excuse for her tardy arrival. She completed the tale by adding, "He's a very pretty little boy."

Chef René grunted. "That's what all you women say about babies. I have never seen one *I* thought pretty, but I shall not argue the point." Shoulders squared, he marched across the kitchen with military precision. "Let us begin our breakfast preparations." Brandishing a wooden spoon overhead, he barked his commands like a general preparing to send his troops into battle. Olivia stifled a giggle.

Weary from a lack of sleep and the night's excitement, Olivia was thankful when the workday finally drew to an end. With luck, she would be able to rest for a short time this evening. She packed food for supper and was preparing to depart when Chef René called her to his office.

She stood in the doorway and leaned against the cool wood of the doorjamb, hoping Chef René would be brief. Charlotte would grow impatient if she was late getting home. Mrs. DeVault had agreed to remain at their flat until six o'clock. Olivia had been thankful for the offer, but Charlotte had complained she didn't want to be alone for even an hour. After Mrs. DeVault explained she'd be certain all was in order before departing, Charlotte had begrudgingly agreed to the arrangement.

It was when Olivia had been getting ready to leave that morning that Mrs. DeVault had suggested they discuss additional help for Charlotte and the baby this evening. *"I can come over about eight o'clock, and we'll talk."* But now Chef René wanted to discuss some matter. Who knew how long he'd keep her.

The chef pointed his thick finger at one of the chairs. "Sit! We will talk."

He'd given her no choice, and she did as he commanded.

Lacing his fingers together, he rested his arms across his substantial girth. "I was going to talk to you first thing this morning, but you were late arriving. So now we will talk." He sat on the edge of his chair and leaned across the desk. "We have been given a special privilege, Miss Mott. One in which I hope you will excel."

She bobbed her head. "I will do my best, Chef René."

Thoughts of Charlotte slipped from her mind as Olivia scooted back in the chair, curious to hear about this fine opportunity of distinction. Chef René knew her capabilities better than anyone. No one could deny the chef's expertise as an instructor, and she'd accomplished much under his tutelage, yet she remained unsure if she possessed the ability to *excel*. However, his words of confidence had bolstered her enthusiasm for whatever project he might suggest. She waited patiently while he shuffled through several piles on his desk. There was no doubt the chef was more organized in his kitchen than with the paper work on his desk.

"Ah, here it is!" His eyes gleamed with triumph as he clasped a piece of stationery between his thumb and forefinger and held it in the air. From this distance, she couldn't read the document, but the stationery appeared similar to the expensive linen paper Charlotte had stolen from her mother months earlier. She deciphered a large *P* monogrammed at the top of the page. Her hands quivered, and she wondered if this might be a special request from Mr. Pullman.

Placing the missive atop the center pile on his desk, he patted it gently. "Mrs. Pullman has requested that a special tea be prepared for guests who will be attending the sailing regatta and athletic competitions in late September, when all of her friends have returned from their summer sanctuaries."

Olivia waited. She wasn't certain what he expected her to say. Apparently he thought she didn't understand his reference to the elite returning home from their summer vacations.

"The wealthy all flee the cities during the hottest months. Most depart in June or early July to go abroad or travel to their vacation homes in other parts of the country. If the Pullmans aren't in Europe, they go to their resort along the shore in New Jersey or to Castle Rest in the Thousand Islands—both places I hope I'll never see again." He daubed the beads of perspiration that had gathered along his forehead with a giant white handkerchief.

Though Olivia couldn't imagine why he wouldn't want to revisit such lovely sounding places, the chef's attention was once again on the letter on his desk. He lifted the page by one corner and handed it across the desk. "Read this."

Olivia quickly perused the letter. Mrs. Pullman would be entertaining the wives of influential Chicago businessmen at a tea to be hosted at Hotel Florence. In addition to enjoying their tea, the women would be discussing plans to raise funds for the new Chicago Symphony Orchestra. Beyond that, the letter didn't state what else the women would be planning, which apparently was not something Mrs. Pullman thought of import to Chef René or the kitchen staff. The letter explicitly charged Chef René with impressing her guests with delightful delicacies and fine service throughout the afternoon event.

"Since the English are renowned for their teas, I thought this would be an excellent opportunity for you to exhibit some of the delights developed in the kitchen of Chef Partridge."

Olivia giggled. "Chef *Mallard*."

He shrugged. "At least I remembered his name resembled some type of edible bird. What do you think about this? The hotel will be filled with guests during the weekend, and I will need to direct all of my attention toward meal preparations. I would be most appreciative if you could handle this *tea*." He said the word as though it pained him. "If you do not believe you are up to the task, you must be honest with me." Wagging his index finger back and forth, he leaned forward and rested his chest atop the desk. "I don't ever want to see ants parading down my tables again. The ladies would run screaming from the hotel, and I would surely be discharged."

"No more peonies. Besides, they don't bloom in late summer." She wondered if Chef René would be pleased after he heard the honest reply he'd requested. "There was a pastry chef at Lanshire Hall, but it wasn't me. I wasn't even the regular assistant to the pastry chef."

He clasped a hand to his chest as though she'd mortally wounded him. "Ah *non*."

"I only performed as a helper when the regular assistant was not available, and I don't know if my pastries will meet Mrs. Pullman's expectations. If I could use my mother's recipes—"

"Good! I care little whose recipes you will put to use so long as they are worthy of being served in Hotel Florence." Suddenly he slapped his hands on the pile of papers. "Aha! I have the answer!"

His shout nearly caused Olivia to fall from her chair. "And that is?"

"You will prepare your recipes for me, and we will give them a taste test." He once again folded his hands across his great expanse of belly and grinned. "A good idea, non?"

"Yes. An excellent idea. I will bring my recipes tomorrow, and we shall begin."

He pushed on the arms of the chair and dislodged himself. "We shall begin tomorrow—after regular working hours."

"But—"

"After the others go home, you will bake and I will taste."

Olivia wanted to argue, but it appeared as if the matter was settled, and the timing couldn't be worse. When she disclosed she'd be working late every night for the remainder of the week, Charlotte would likely fly into a rage—or begin one of her crying episodes that could go on for hours. Olivia didn't know which would be worse. In the meantime, she wanted to select several of her mother's recipes before morning.

Approaching the house, she could hear the baby's cries coming through the open bedroom window. Picking up her pace, she ran up the front steps and hurried inside. A quick peek into the bedroom revealed the infant lying on the bed, his tiny arms and legs flailing in time with his lusty cries. Olivia looked into the parlor and noted Charlotte reclining on the divan.

"Could you do something to make him quit crying?" Charlotte asked as she waved her arm toward the bedroom. "He's been screaming ever since Mrs. DeVault departed, and I can't get a minute of peace."

"Did you consider holding him? He's kicked off his blanket." She had no idea when the infant had eaten. She hoped Mrs. DeVault had convinced Charlotte to nurse the baby. "And his diaper is probably wet. No wonder he's crying. When did he last eat?"

"Shortly before Mrs. DeVault departed at six o'clock." Charlotte tugged at the cloth strips around her chest. "These bindings hurt," she whined. "Why are you so late tonight?"

She chose to ignore Charlotte's question. "Did *you* feed him?"

Charlotte wagged her head back and forth as she continued to rearrange the bindings. "Mrs. DeVault found some woman. She said she'd return this evening and talk to you." She tightened her lips into a moue. "Are you going to do something about him?"

"Indeed I am." Olivia walked to the bedroom, picked up the baby, and carried him into the parlor. With as much decorum as she could muster, Olivia dropped a diaper onto Charlotte's lap and placed the child in her arms. "It's time you began taking care of your son."

[illegible]

[illegible]

[illegible]

[illegible]

[illegible]

[illegible]

[illegible]

[illegible]

Chapter Fifteen

The previous night's events had proved enough of a disaster that Olivia was actually pleased she had an excuse to remain at work this evening. Charlotte's childish behavior had bordered on intolerable. Instead of taking responsibility, she had acted like an uninterested party during the meeting with Mrs. DeVault and Mrs. Logan. Mrs. Logan agreed to supply milk, and Mrs. DeVault would continue to assist with the infant's care, but only if Charlotte agreed that she, too, would do her part. It was only when Mrs. DeVault threatened to withdraw her assistance that Charlotte had finally joined the conversation. Mrs. DeVault later explained that it was Charlotte's willingness to pay Mrs. Logan, rather than the woman's Christian love, that had been the deciding factor.

Mrs. DeVault remained hopeful that Charlotte would soon embrace motherhood, but Olivia had her doubts. At Olivia's insistence, Charlotte had changed a few wet diapers. Though she had retched, gagged, and whined, she'd finally managed to change one dirty diaper last night. This morning, with only a wet diaper to manage, she had done much better. However, she'd not been amused when she removed the wet diaper and young Morgan drenched her with an unexpected shower.

Chef René slapped his beefy hand atop the counter and all thoughts of Charlotte and the baby immediately dissipated. "The pastry kitchen is yours, Miss Mott. I hope to be impressed." He raised his eyebrows and looked at the clock. "I will return in one hour to check your progress."

The moment he departed, Olivia set to work, thankful the chef had not chosen to follow her downstairs to the pastry kitchen and watch. She lit the bakery oven, selected the temperature, and gathered the ingredients. She'd never been one to pray over the small things in life, nor over many of the big things, either, for that matter. But Mrs. DeVault said God was in the little things as well as the big, so she silently asked for guidance through these next few days of testing.

For the most part, she had already decided what she would prepare. Today, it would be pastry puffs with a variety of fillings, everything from lemon curd to chicken salad. By making the puffs in several sizes and adding an array of decorations, each would appear unique—a time-saving device learned in Chef Mallard's kitchen. Chef René hadn't set any particular rules regarding preparation. Therefore, Olivia had confiscated several pieces of leftover baked chicken for her chicken salad, as well as some chocolate custard, apricot cream, and rhubarb custard for her dessert delicacies.

She would have preferred more time for the puffs to cool before filling them and didn't hesitate to tell Chef René when he entered the kitchen. "You had best check the texture quickly, or the creams and custards will be in a complete meltdown."

Observing her plight, he didn't argue and immediately tasted the offerings. She'd drizzled the sweet puffs with chocolate or a dusting of icing sugar. In the chicken salad puffs, she had tucked a sprig of parsley or rosemary to add a dash of color. Unfortunately, there had been little time to arrange them in an attractive presentation that would be pleasing to the eye as well as the palate, something Chef René constantly emphasized.

Olivia anxiously awaited his response while he finished the final bite. "These will do nicely." He kissed the tips of his fingers. "Magnifique!"

She wanted to dance around the kitchen and celebrate; instead, she remained calm and offered her thanks. Hearing Chef René's praise had made her efforts worthwhile. When she began to gather the cooking utensils to carry them to the sink, he shook his head.

"You go home now. I've arranged for one of the kitchen boys to come down and clean up each evening when you finish your baking."

"Then I'll see you in the morning. Thank you, again, for your kind words."

"Time is limited in the evening, Miss Mott, but do not forget—*presentation*." The chef's final word floated across the room in a reverent tone.

She removed her toque and jacket. "The tables will be properly decorated, and I will use crystallized flowers and fruit to accent."

He popped another pastry into his mouth and gave an affirmative nod. "I look forward to tomorrow's offering."

Though René's praise had bolstered her spirits, her body

needed rest. Forcing one foot in front of the other, she wondered if she'd get any sleep tonight. And tomorrow would be another long day. Lost in her thoughts, she didn't hear the approaching footsteps and was startled when she felt a tug on her basket.

"May I carry that for you?"

"Fred! What a pleasant surprise." She loosened her hold on the basket and suddenly didn't feel nearly so tired. "What brings you here?"

"Mother returned to help Mrs. Hornsby with the baby, and I walked along with her." He shook his head. "That one's not much good with babies or the domestic life, is she?"

Olivia giggled. "No. She's certainly not."

"My mother says it may have something to do with losing her husband—that she's not gotten over grieving his loss. I'm not so sure. I think the woman tends to be self-centered and lazy. To my way of thinking, she should be pleased to care for the young lad. After all, he's all that she has left of her husband."

Fred's comments were a reminder that Charlotte must not forget her role of the grieving widow. Yet Olivia couldn't fault Charlotte too much. After all, she herself failed to remember their lies from time to time. Unlike the truth, she'd discovered it was much more difficult to recollect lies. The two of them had become rather lax of late. They'd better review the list of lies before bed tonight.

"People react differently in times of grief, I'm told." She hoped her cursory remark would be enough to forestall further discussion of Charlotte's behavior. "I'm pleased you happened along."

He laughed heartily and pushed his hair from his forehead. Her stomach flip-flopped at the sparkle in his eyes. "I didn't just happen along, Olivia. My mother said you had to work late, so I thought I'd wait in the park until I saw you heading toward home. Turns out I didn't have to wait at all."

Although they'd seemingly mended their disagreement over the night at the band concert, Fred had proceeded cautiously since then. They'd attended several outdoor concerts with Albert and Martha, she had accompanied Martha to watch the men compete in their soccer and baseball games, and they were together after church each Sunday. However, Fred hadn't invited her to spend time alone with him. Now she relished the moment and welcomed the pleasure of being with him, if only for a few minutes.

"I asked Mrs. Hornsby why you were working so late, but she merely said she thought you wanted to avoid being around the baby. I doubted that was true." He grinned.

She matched his stride as they continued along the perimeter of the park and then crossed the street, all the while savoring his presence and wishing he would slow his gait and they could spend the remainder of the evening alone. "I'm required to stay after regular hours each evening to make pastries for Chef René's evaluation. And while I'm preparing for the gala at the hotel, I understand that you and Albert have been practicing for the athletic competitions that will coincide with the regatta."

"Yes, though I imagine we're enjoying ourselves more than you are. Don't you resent spending so much time in the kitchen?"

She shook her head. “It’s hard work but an amazing opportunity.” Pleased at his seeming interest, she detailed several of the delicacies she would prepare. “I do want to please both Chef René and Mrs. Pullman.”

“Oh yes. We wouldn’t want to disappoint a member of the Pullman family.” His words dripped with sarcasm.

“Do you dislike Mr. Pullman and this town so much, Fred?”

“I’m not denying there’s a great deal of opportunity in Pullman. But these capitalists are building their empires off the little man’s sweat and toil. Wealthy visitors come to town and think this place is a utopia for the workingman. Instead, it’s just another means for Mr. Pullman to stuff more money into his own coffers.”

Fred’s slant on Mr. Pullman’s rise to wealth and fame differed dramatically from that of Mr. Howard. Of course, the two men possessed far different positions within the company and the town itself, so she supposed that wasn’t so odd. Mr. Howard thought Mr. Pullman’s rise to fame and fortune had been hard-earned and well-deserved. On the other hand, Fred painted a picture of a man willing to achieve success at any cost, even if it meant stepping upon the backs of hardworking, uneducated men to get there—a cold and indifferent man who cared little for anyone or anything other than the almighty dollar.

Yet she wondered aloud whether such a cold and heartless man would name a hotel for his daughter or take such care in beautifying the town.

Fred laughed at her remark. “I’m told Mr. Pullman has four children, but he favors only one—Florence. What kind of man gives such preference to one child over the others?”

Olivia didn’t think Mr. Pullman’s behavior such a terrible

offense. "He couldn't name the hotel after all of them, and she *is* the oldest child."

"No, he couldn't, but don't you see that it's not just the hotel? While the other Pullman children were absent the day his company began production, it was Florence who turned the valves to set the Corliss engine into motion and begin production at the Pullman Car Works. Her picture was in all the papers, yet there was no mention of the other children." He frowned and pointed toward Lake Calumet. "Have you seen the housing where the brickyard workers live?"

Although she'd not been to the area he referred to, he didn't hesitate long for a response.

"You haven't seen those places because they're well hidden, carefully tucked away so that Mr. Pullman's illustrious visitors won't know such ramshackle housing exists in this town. Those wealthy folks ride into Pullman on their private railroad cars and believe everyone living here has a perfect life—all thanks to our wonderful benefactor." Fred kicked a pebble and watched it bounce down the sidewalk before coming to rest in a well-landscaped patch of grass.

Although she didn't say so, Olivia had been satisfied with the town and its accoutrements—except for the library fees, which she deemed unnecessary. Of course, Charlotte said Olivia harbored low expectations, but she didn't consider Pullman a limited opportunity.

Fred shifted the basket to his other hand and paused to speak to a man walking the other direction with his wife and children. "That's John Wilsey," he said after the man moved out of earshot. "He works in the greenhouse. It's located near Lake Calumet and supplies the shrubs and trees for the town. He and the other gardeners also raise the cut flowers and bedding plants that are available at the Market."

Olivia wished she had known about the greenhouse and cut flowers sold at the town Market before she had picked the infamous peonies a couple months earlier. Since then, she'd purchased many of the beautiful varieties for use in the hotel. And she planned to utilize the greenhouse flowers to decorate the cakes, pastries, and tables for Mrs. Pullman's gala.

"Poor John got himself in trouble shortly after moving to Pullman," Fred commented. "He was sitting on his front porch in the middle of summer without his jacket. Mr. Howard happened by and told him that Pullman had parks where the residents could sit and relax and that people of refinement wore their suit jackets outside the confines of their homes. He added that Mr. Pullman expects the same behavior from those who live in his town."

Why did Fred have to bring Mr. Howard into the conversation? After all, making certain the rules in Pullman were observed was part of Samuel's job. She didn't think Fred should fault another man for performing the work for which he'd been hired. Olivia did agree the prohibition against sitting on porches was ridiculous, but Fred must agree that the parks provided a much more pleasant place to spend free time. As for the suit jackets, she simply assumed Mr. Pullman had good reason for requiring the formality. Perhaps she easily accepted rules because she'd lived with them all her life. She was exceedingly thankful for Chef René's kindness, especially after having worked for the lecherous Chef Mallard.

Sometimes Fred sounded like an angry zealot when he argued for the working class, like one of the union organizers she'd heard the hotel laundry workers whisper about. She wondered if he'd been swept into the tide of men who were promoting union shops. Surely he wouldn't do anything so foolish. Mr. Howard had told her just last week that any such men would be immediately discharged from employment. The company had made it clear that the rule against unions would be enforced and the men promoting such ideas would be dealt with harshly.

As they approached the house, Olivia spied Mrs. DeVault pacing in front of the parlor window. She carried young Morgan in her arms, rocking him back and forth. Charlotte was nowhere to be seen.

"Looks as though my mother hasn't been able to keep the young lad completely settled."

"I'm afraid Charlotte has been taking advantage of her kindness."

Fred chuckled. "She enjoys helping young mothers. That's why she continues with midwifery." He tilted his head closer. "However, I do think Mrs. Hornsby has been more of a challenge than most."

Olivia couldn't argue that point. Charlotte had proved to be a challenge even before the baby's birth. With her selfish attitude, most folks didn't find her particularly endearing.

As soon as they entered the house, Charlotte grabbed the basket, digging through it and helping herself to the food. Fred and Mrs. DeVault prepared to depart.

The older woman patted Olivia's shoulder. "Good luck with Charlotte this evening. You'll likely be the one caring for little Morgan during the night." Mrs. DeVault tucked the baby into the cradle she'd placed in the parlor. "I do wish she'd show the child a bit of affection. I know she's grieving and all, but even for a widow, her behavior's abnormal."

Fred grinned and motioned toward the kitchen table as his mother joined him at the front door. "Mrs. Hornsby may be indifferent to her young son, but she's surely interested in the contents of that basket."

While Olivia offered her thanks and bid their visitors good-night, Charlotte remained in the kitchen, already eating from a heaping plateful of food. Olivia hurried to the kitchen, hoping she had put aside enough food for tomorrow's noonday meal. She'd barely opened her mouth to ask when Morgan burst forth with a lusty wail. Olivia waited, certain Charlotte would hearken to the soulful cries, but she continued eating, acting as though nothing were amiss.

"Can't you hear the baby crying?"

Charlotte glanced up from her plate. "Yes." She looked toward the parlor and frowned. "And it's a most annoying sound. You had best pick him up before Mr. Rice from next door starts complaining about the noise."

Olivia hastened to the parlor. No sense attempting to win a battle while the child suffered. Lifting him into her arms, she held the baby close and wiped away the beads of perspiration that matted his soft downy hair. How could Charlotte remain so detached? Her heart ached for the boy. Just like her, he'd likely grow up without a mother's love. She wondered which would be worse: to lose your mother to death or to have her physically present and withhold her love. She decided the latter. For although she'd grown up without a mother, she'd always harbored the belief that her mother had loved her dearly before she died.

She carried the baby to the kitchen, cooing and fussing over him. "He's so beautiful, Charlotte. Don't you want to hold him?"

"No." Charlotte lifted the napkin and wiped her mouth. "I've told you I don't intend to care for him. As if it's not enough that Randolph has denied paternity, now he's refused my request for financial support, too."

"*What* request for financial support? Have you seen Mr. Morgan?"

"Of course not. You know I can't yet leave the house. How could I possibly go and see Randolph?" She pushed away from the table. "I had a letter hand-delivered to his office in Chicago today."

Olivia frowned. "Who do you know that would deliver a personal message to Mr. Morgan?"

Charlotte laughed. "As long as you're willing to pay, you can always find someone to do your bidding." While Olivia continued to hold young Morgan, Charlotte stretched out on the divan. "There's a young man who's been spending time near our building lately. He was outside this morning before Mrs. DeVault arrived, and he was most pleased to ride the train into Chicago and deliver the message. When Randolph discovered the missive was from me, he sent an immediate response." Her lips began to quiver. "Unfortunately, not the reply that I hoped for."

"You ought not invite strangers into the house, Charlotte. Martha says there are hobos that jump the trains, and some of them wander into Pullman when they're looking for a free handout. They can't be trusted."

"He wasn't a hobo, but he definitely was in need of a haircut. I've never seen such an unruly head of red hair."

Panic struck Olivia with a force that pressed her stomach into a tight knot. "Was he tall and gangly, with a space between his front teeth?"

Charlotte rested her chin in her palm for a moment and then bobbed her head. "Yes. He did have a gap between his teeth. Do you know him?"

Eddie!

Chapter Sixteen

Throughout the next week, Olivia maintained a close lookout as she walked about town, constantly expecting Eddie to pop out from behind a tree or lurch at her as she passed by a building. There wasn't time to dwell on him at work, but when she departed the house each morning or made a trip to the Market for supplies, thoughts of him were at the forefront of her mind.

She had considered asking Chef René for advice, but what possible counsel could he offer? *Be careful*? Or *Advise the bobbies if you see him*? She already knew she must maintain a watchful eye, and she certainly planned to alert the authorities if and when she made a sighting. She couldn't be absolutely positive it was Eddie who had appeared outside their house; at least that's what she told herself as she braced to leave the house each morning.

Olivia had been excited when Chef René announced her long workdays had ended, but she would miss having Fred arrive to walk her home each evening. Originally Chef René had said she would work late for one week, but then he'd extended the time period after rejecting a few of her offerings and substituting new recipes. On each of those nights, she'd been pleased to see Fred waiting for her when she exited the kitchen doorway. Now that his mother wouldn't be spending the evenings with Charlotte, Fred would be going directly to his own home after work, so Olivia decided to walk home with Martha whenever possible. Today, however, she'd be on her own, for Martha had agreed to work a later shift for one of the maids who'd taken ill.

Late in the afternoon Olivia had written out the final menu card, which Chef René would submit for Mrs. Pullman's approval. Olivia had no idea what would occur if the matron rejected her choices. But the chef was convinced Mrs. Pullman would find the selections delightful, and inspired by his air of confidence, Olivia departed the hotel with a spring in her step.

Still heavy with their summer foliage, the trees rustled in the late afternoon breeze, and the scent of a few lingering roses could be detected in the air. Before long, fall would arrive. She'd been told that the winters could be harsh in northern Illinois, but Olivia was enjoying each new season as it arrived.

"Olivia!"

Mr. Howard was waving his hat and running toward her. She couldn't imagine why he hadn't stopped by the hotel kitchen before she departed. He was panting when he finally reached her side, and she waited until his breathing slowed to a normal rate.

"I have a gift for the baby." He held out a beautifully wrapped package. She assumed he'd had it wrapped at one of the expensive shops in the Arcade.

"That's very kind of you. I'll give it to Charlotte." She held out her hand to accept the gift, but he shook his head.

"I'd like to see the baby, if you don't think Mrs. Hornsby will object."

"No. I don't believe she'll object. She hasn't appeared to take much interest in the child, which worries me."

"You poor girl. Working late hours preparing for the tea and all this, too." Without warning, he lifted her hand to his lips and kissed the back of her hand. "I do wish you'd let me help."

At the sound of footsteps behind them, Olivia glanced over her shoulder. "Fred!" She attempted to pull away from Mr. Howard, but he held fast. "I didn't expect to see you this evening."

He looked at Mr. Howard and then back at her, one eyebrow shooting almost to his hairline. "Obviously not." He stalked off without another word.

She wanted to run after him and explain Mr. Howard's presence was no more than an innocent encounter, but she would have to wait to vindicate herself. Right now, Mr. Howard was intent upon keeping her by his side. As they neared the house, she could hear Morgan's cries, and her anger mounted when they walked inside. Charlotte sat on the divan reading a book, a plate of cookies at her side. She didn't bother to look up when Olivia entered. The cradle was nowhere in sight.

"Where's Morgan?"

"I moved the cradle into the kitchen. I can't concentrate on my reading when he's crying in the same room." At the sight of Mr. Howard, her voice dripped with charm. "Would you care for a cookie, Samuel?"

Olivia wanted to throttle her. And had the baby not been

crying, she might have done so. She didn't wait to hear Mr. Howard's reply before heading off to retrieve the baby. His diaper, bedding, and undershirt were soaked—likely he'd not been changed since Mrs. DeVault's departure earlier in the afternoon. She scooped up Morgan and soon made short order of setting things aright.

"You look like you've been caring for babies all of your life." Admiration shone in Mr. Howard's eyes, and Olivia remembered his having spoken of a deep desire for children on at least two different occasions. She thanked him for the compliment and hoped he would soon bid them good-night.

Instead, he sat down opposite Charlotte. "You haven't opened Morgan's gift. I hope you won't think me presumptuous."

Charlotte looked bored as she offhandedly ripped the paper from the box and lifted the lid. "Very nice. Thank you."

"It's a christening gown. I thought . . . well, I didn't know if you had purchased one, but I saw this at a shop in the Arcade, and . . ."

Why didn't Charlotte tell him she appreciated his gift rather than allowing him to continue stammering? Olivia moved to the sofa and lifted the tiny dress from the box. "It is truly exquisite, Mr. Howard. How kind of you to provide such a thoughtful gift—one I know Mrs. Hornsby will cherish once she's feeling more herself."

Charlotte pinned her with an icy stare, clearly annoyed by the reproach. "Please accept my apology for my lackluster behavior, Mr. Howard." She reached into her pocket and withdrew a handkerchief and dabbed her eyes. "Since my dear husband's death, I haven't been myself. And now, with the added responsibility of the baby, well, life is sometimes overwhelming for me."

"Dear lady. Please don't feel you need apologize. Having trod the path of bereavement when my beloved wife died, I completely understand. But eventually you must start anew—for yourself and for young Morgan. If you can think of this as a new phase of your life and become excited over the possibilities, it will help." He leaned forward and rested his arms across his thighs. "I know Olivia has helped me toward making plans and moving on with my life."

Olivia gulped. How had she helped him? More than anything, she'd been trying to avoid him. Perhaps he'd misinterpreted something she'd done or said.

"She's done that for both of us, hasn't she? I don't know how I would have survived my grief had I remained in England." Though untrue, Charlotte's words sounded sweet and sincere. "And what are you and Olivia planning for your future?"

The color heightened across Mr. Howard's cheekbones. "We've not discussed the long term, but I hope she'll be pleased to learn she will accompany me to Chicago the day after tomorrow."

Chicago? The fact that the two of them were discussing her as if she weren't present was disconcerting enough, but accompany him to Chicago? When had he come up with that idea? He'd certainly not mentioned it to her. She would be at work the day after tomorrow. Obviously he'd overlooked the fact that she couldn't come and go whenever he took a fancy.

"How delightful! I do wish I could accompany you. Once

I'm feeling better, we can all go into the city for some shopping and perhaps the theater."

"There's no better theater than what is on stage here in Pullman, Mrs. Hornsby. However, Chicago does offer a greater variety."

"And a change of scenery. I do grow weary of seeing all this red brick, don't you?"

Mr. Howard's brows bowed like two arching cats. There was no doubt Charlotte's question had offended his sensibilities. "I find this town a picture of beauty and aesthetic pleasure, Mrs. Hornsby. I can't say that I find anything about the town tiresome or dull."

Never one to concern herself with the opinion of others, Charlotte offered him a placating look. "Before arriving in this country, I made my home in London and also traveled throughout Europe—Paris, Brussels, Vienna. As a result, I prefer large cities." As she spoke, she took on the air of her noble birth.

Mr. Howard's brow puckered. "Upon your arrival in Pullman, Olivia mentioned the two of you met in a dressmaker's shop, and she told me about the loss of your husband. But she didn't mention anything further. I'd enjoy learning more about your past. I could almost believe that you were born into nobility."

Olivia glared at Charlotte. Her loose tongue was going to submerge them in a pool of sinking sand from which they'd never escape. Vanity and pride had taken control of Charlotte's conversation. If they were going to survive, Olivia would need to divert his attention.

"What's this you said about Chicago? Did you forget I must work on Friday?" She felt like a silly imposter fluttering her lashes. However, her remorse quickly faded when the ploy succeeded.

"The trip to Chicago will be both business and pleasure. We're going to the Pullman residence, where you will meet with Mrs. Pullman and go over the menu for her tea."

"You mean in person?"

"Of course he means in person, Olivia. Did you think you'd talk to her through the back door?"

Olivia couldn't tell if she detected sarcasm or disgust in Charlotte's tone, but she was unwilling to permit the insult to go unanswered. "Sounds as though you're reverting to that brusque behavior you spoke of earlier."

Without waiting for a rejoinder, she turned her attention back to Mr. Howard. "Wouldn't Chef René be the proper person to speak with Mrs. Pullman?"

Mr. Howard shook his head. "Of course not. You're the chef in charge of the tea preparations, and you should be the one to discuss the event with Mrs. Pullman."

Whether she was in charge of preparations or not, she would find it surprising if Chef René were to delegate such a meeting to someone of her inexperience. "You're certain?"

"Not to worry. Chef René concurs with the decision. We'll depart on the one-o'clock train Friday afternoon, meet with Mrs. Pullman at two thirty, and have supper before our return."

The baby whimpered and Mr. Howard scooted forward in his chair. "I'll leave you ladies to the remainder of your evening. And I do hope to attend young Morgan's christening once you've made the arrangements."

For a moment, Charlotte appeared to not understand. "Oh yes, the christening. I'll be certain to notify you. By all means."

Olivia escorted him to the front door. He waved when he reached the sidewalk and then ambled off toward home. She leaned against the doorjamb, wondering when he and the chef had discussed this meeting in Chicago. It had been late in the afternoon when she had completed the menu card for Mrs. Pullman's perusal. Strange that Chef René hadn't mentioned it to her at that time.

A flash of movement across the street captured her attention, and she stood transfixed for a moment. Likely her imagination. As she pushed away from the door, she saw it again—a shuffling motion. It appeared someone might be hiding behind the row of hedges. She gathered her skirts to the side to avoid being seen and continued to peek out the door.

There! The hedge moved, and she could see something crawling behind in the shadows. A dog, perhaps. Suddenly realizing she'd been holding her breath, she inhaled a gulp of air. She strained to make out the figure rising from behind the bushes and clasped a hand to her chest when she recognized the lanky body and shock of red hair. *Eddie!* What was he doing watching their apartment? Was he hoping to earn more money from Charlotte, or was he lying in wait for her? In spite of the heat, she closed the heavy wooden door while the sound of her racing heart pounded in her ears.

Chapter Seventeen

Olivia had been up most of the night, fearful as she listened for unusual sounds at the doors or windows. On the few occasions when she'd dozed off, the baby's cries had awakened her. She'd written a note to Charlotte that they must develop a story about her "marriage" and her "deceased husband." Last night's near debacle was proof enough the issue must be resolved. Her head and body ached as she completed the note and then prepared for work.

No doubt she'd not be at her best today. Watching through the front curtain, she waited until she saw Martha coming down the street before she left the house. No need taking chances. For all she knew, Eddie could still be lurking nearby, and the sun remained hidden below the horizon until after she arrived at work each morning. After last night's sighting, her fear remained palpable.

"Good morning, Olivia!"

Martha's greeting was cheery—*she'd* obviously had a good

night's sleep. Olivia fell in step, and the two of them headed off.

"I hear you had a visitor last evening." She looped arms with Olivia. "Fred was in a terrible mood at baseball practice last evening. Albert thought it a good thing, for Fred scored two runs. He says that if you're trying to make Fred jealous, you're doing a fine job of it."

"But that's just it: I'm not trying to make him jealous. Mr. Howard appeared out of nowhere."

Martha giggled. "And you obviously didn't know Fred was going to show up."

Olivia frowned. "No. And I don't know how to discourage Mr. Howard. I've tried—truly I have. And each time things are going well with Fred and me, something like the incident last night happens."

Martha tilted her head. "It's because you're pretty, Olivia, and a little inexperienced with men."

"But it's a difficult situation. Even though Chef René manages the kitchen, Mr. Howard is the one who hires and discharges employees. He's an important man in this town, and I don't want to risk losing my job." A squirrel raced in front of them and skittered to a nearby tree. "I'm happy working at the hotel, and Chef René is a wonderful teacher—I've learned so much from him. But I don't know what to do about Mr. Howard's advances. What would you do?"

"I don't know, Olivia. I'd be happy to quit my job and marry Albert tomorrow." They circled around the hotel to the side door. "Have you considered asking God to direct you? He's the one who knows what's best for us and usually the last one we go to for help." She giggled nervously. "Well, I shouldn't speak for others, only myself."

Olivia offered her feeble thanks. She couldn't tell Martha the truth, that God didn't want to hear from the likes of her, for she was a liar of the worst kind. If she asked God to forgive her or help her, He'd expect her to confess to others, as well. She couldn't possibly tell Mr. Howard her letter of recommendation was a forgery and her employment was based on lies; moreover, Fred would never speak to her again if he knew the truth about her. He wouldn't want to court a woman he couldn't trust. No, she couldn't ask for God's help. He might forgive her, but the cost would be too great.

I died for you, Olivia. The words quietly blew into her mind like a gentle breeze, and she hurried into the hotel kitchen, where she could force them from her thoughts.

Chef René already had the ovens heated and was measuring out flour when she donned her toque. "We need to talk after the breakfast hour is complete, Miss Mott." He whisked the eggs and poured them into the dry ingredients. "In my office."

There was little doubt Chef René was unhappy. *Now* what had she done?

They worked through the early morning hours. When the breakfast preparations had been completed and the meal served to the many hotel guests, Chef René signaled for her to follow him. She didn't know which would prove worse—anticipating or discovering the cause of Chef René's discontent. One thing was certain: she didn't like these visits to his office.

As was their growing custom, he directed her into the office and then wedged himself into his chair. Hands folded, he leaned across the desk. "So! I am told by Mr. Howard that you will accompany him to Chicago and present your menu to Mrs. Pullman on Friday."

"I told him you would be the better choice, but he said you were in agreement. I'm afraid I'll make a fool of myself. Surely Mrs. Pullman will expect you to attend the meeting." She nibbled at her lip, frightened by the mere idea of the meeting.

"Interesting." The chef frowned. "When did Mr. Howard tell you of our *agreement*?"

"He stopped me as I was walking home from work last evening. He'd purchased a gift for Mrs. Hornsby's baby. During the course of our conversation, he told me of the arrangements."

Chef René tapped his folded hands on the desktop. "And what time did he leave your home last night?"

This meeting was more like an interrogation. She was giving out much more information than she was receiving. "I'm not certain. I believe it was shortly before nine o'clock."

"Just as I thought."

She waited, but he didn't elaborate. "You and Mr. Howard did agree I should make the presentation to Mrs. Pullman, didn't you?"

"Oui. He came to see me last night shortly after nine o'clock and told me he planned to take you with him. I offered no objection."

The usual gleam was absent from his eyes. Mr. Howard had neither asked the chef's permission nor sought his opinion. He'd merely announced she would be making the presentation, and Chef René had been forced to accept the decision. "I'll go straightaway and tell him that I cannot go with him tomorrow."

"Non." He shook his finger. "You will go, and you will make a fine presentation. I will practice with you so that you know exactly what you must do. You are my protégée, and you will make me proud."

Relief washed over her in a flood of emotion. The chef's generosity was more than she could have imagined. She jumped up and hugged him as he came around the desk. "Thank you." Tears formed in the corners of her eyes.

He waved his hand, obviously embarrassed by her show of emotion. "You will be a fine chef one day. When that time arrives, you tell people Chef René taught you everything you know about cooking. That will be thanks enough."

She wouldn't ask God to help or forgive her, but she did offer a prayer of thanks as she went back to the kitchen.

Chef René dismissed Olivia from her duties at noon on Friday. With his charming French accent, he bid her good luck and instructed her to remain poised and calm. "Be certain you enunciate your words so there is no misunderstanding."

Olivia grinned at his final remark and wondered if his French accent had been the source of some confusion in the past. "I'll do my best to make you proud."

She raced toward home with little time to change into another dress, arrange her hair, and meet Mr. Howard at the train station. Though Mrs. Pullman might expect Chef René to appear in his chef's jacket and toque, Mr. Howard suggested a dress would be more appropriate attire for her presentation. Still unable to fit into her dresses, Charlotte had recommended her pink-and-gray-plaid day dress. One of these days, Charlotte would doubtless cease her continual eating and regain her figure. When that happened, Olivia would be without a proper wardrobe. The thought was somewhat disheartening. She'd become accustomed to wearing Charlotte's pretty dresses and would miss the luxury.

The sound of Morgan's cries greeted her as she entered the house. Charlotte was sitting in the kitchen eating a piece of the leftover blueberry pie. Olivia scurried down the hallway. "Charlotte! Don't you hear your son crying?"

Charlotte licked her lips and pointed her fork at the pie. "This is excellent. Did you make it?"

"Yes. Now will you see to Morgan?"

"You could at least thank me for the compliment." Her lips tightened into her usual childish pout. "And for your information, there is nothing wrong with that baby. He's eaten and his diaper is dry. Mrs. DeVault has spoiled him, and he wants to be held all the time. Eventually he'll cry himself back to sleep."

From all appearances, it seemed Charlotte would never develop any motherly instincts. Normally Olivia would have seen to Morgan's needs, but today there wasn't time. If she didn't hurry, she'd miss the train. She carefully pulled on the dark silk stockings Charlotte insisted she wear and slipped her feet into a pair of Charlotte's gray kid shoes. After donning the plaid dress, she arranged her hair.

Charlotte strolled into the room and assessed her attire. She returned moments later with a wide gray-and-pink silk sash. "This goes around the waist and ties in the back." She circled the ribbon around Olivia's waist and tied a faultless double bow. "There! You look wonderful. Don't forget the hat."

Olivia turned her back to the mirror and peered over her shoulder. The sash set off the dress to perfection. She adjusted the pink flowers that curved around the wide-brimmed gray hat before placing it on her head. "I believe I'm ready." Lifting her purse from the bedside table, she thanked Charlotte for her assistance. "Please don't be angry with me, but I do wish you'd show Morgan as much attention as you've given me these past few minutes."

Charlotte shrugged. "He can't walk or talk. All he does is cry. And look at my figure. Having a baby has made me fat."

Olivia hurried down the hallway with Charlotte at her heels. When they reached the front door, Olivia stopped. "Did you ever consider that your constant eating, rather than your pregnancy, is what has caused you to gain weight? The baby isn't to blame for any of this, Charlotte. And he doesn't deserve to be punished because you're angry with his father. It's time you thought of someone other than yourself."

Charlotte didn't respond, and Olivia didn't have time for further discussion. She could only hope Charlotte would take heed and little Morgan would receive the affection he deserved. A train whistle hooted in the distance, and Olivia left the house, quickening her pace as she crossed Pullman Avenue. She scanned the area, hoping to catch a glimpse of Mr. Howard. Like her, he may have first stopped at home. She glanced back at 111th Street. Her breath caught in her throat as she spotted a lanky young man with red hair race toward the railroad tracks. This had to be more than coincidence. Her hands trembled. Was Eddie keeping her in his sights at all times? Would he wait to see which train she boarded and where she would go? She should have reminded Charlotte to lock the doors.

Silly! Eddie wasn't interested in Charlotte or the baby. At the very least, he wanted to frighten *her*. Hadn't he said as much? She should have mentioned the earlier sightings to Chef

René. At least someone would know about Eddie's behavior if something should happen to her.

The train slowed, squealing and hissing as it neared the station.

"There you are!"

Olivia startled and then breathed a quick sigh of relief when she saw Mr. Howard standing in the doorway of the station. "I was beginning to worry. Come along. I've already purchased our tickets."

Once they'd boarded the train, she peeked out the window and looked for any sign of Eddie. Should she mention her fears to Mr. Howard? She glanced in his direction and decided against the idea. Chef René would be the better choice. After giving him a report of her meeting with Mrs. Pullman, she'd tell him about Eddie.

"No need to be frightened. You'll find Mrs. Pullman very kind. And I have no doubt you are well prepared for the meeting."

Mr. Howard was staring at her trembling hands. She folded them together in a futile attempt to stop the shaking. "Chef René was most helpful."

He relaxed his shoulders against the leather upholstery. "Not many employees have the opportunity to visit the Pullman residence. You're a fortunate young lady." He tilted his head a bit closer. "I've a lovely supper planned. There is a fine restaurant in the Tremont Hotel, where I thought we would dine."

"Or if we finish early, we could simply return to Pullman." She hoped he would concur. Fred knew of this meeting with Mrs. Pullman and had asked what time she would be back. Though he'd acted as though he was merely inquiring how late his mother might be needed to help Charlotte with young Morgan, she suspected that he wondered much more.

Mr. Howard's eager smile faded at her suggestion. "I thought you'd be pleased by my invitation."

"Oh, it is most generous of you. But I worry about taking advantage of Mrs. DeVault and thought we could come back . . ." Her words trailed off like a vapor.

He patted her hand. "You are such a kind young lady . . . always thinking of others. I shall pay Mrs. DeVault for her services this evening. You'll have no reason to feel guilty, and she'll be thankful for the unexpected funds. A few extra coins will mean a great deal to her."

Olivia agreed Mrs. DeVault could use the additional income, but his solution would do nothing to solve her problem with Fred. While Mr. Howard chattered about the wonders of Chicago, her mind flitted back and forth between Eddie's reappearance at the train station and the possibility of a confrontation with Fred. She couldn't decide which was more harrowing. By the time the train arrived in Chicago, she'd decided she would more easily resolve her problem with Eddie than with Fred. A most distressing thought.

Chapter Eighteen

The carriage ride through the streets of Chicago proved as nerve-racking as her earlier trips to and from the train station with Charlotte. She was thankful for Mr. Howard's presence, for she couldn't have remained calm in the hubbub of activity otherwise. If anything, the city seemed even more formidable than she remembered. Everything, including carriages, street-cars, trains, buildings, and people, vied for space, and she never knew at any given moment who or what would win the battle. "This is a frightening city, don't you think?"

"There are those who say Chicago is much like Pittsburgh: hell with the lid let off. Of course, I tend to disagree."

Olivia wasn't certain where the city of Pittsburgh was located, but if it was similar to Chicago, it wouldn't be a place she'd soon want to visit. Once their carriage entered the posh residential area, the clamor of noise and incessant activity settled. Olivia peered out the window at the magnificent mansions of stone and brick, with their ornate roofs and fancy ironwork fences, and compared them to Lanshire Hall. Surprisingly, these houses appeared as stately and glorious as some of those belonging to members of the English nobility. Certainly as lovely as the home where she'd previously worked.

"This is the Pullman house." The carriage turned into a semicircular driveway that led to a three-story home of stone and brick. Connected to the east side of the house was what looked like a Grecian amphitheater she'd seen in one of Lady Charlotte's books. She could only imagine what the interior of the house must look like.

A Negro servant hurried to the coach. As she stepped down, Olivia stared at the huge portico that led to the front door. "Shouldn't we go around to the rear of the house?"

Mr. Howard adjusted his tie. "No. I am not a servant, and we are here by invitation. Mrs. Pullman is expecting us, Olivia."

She lowered her voice. "In England, I would be expected to use the rear door whether I was expected or not."

He grasped her elbow and moved her along. "This isn't England."

Of course, he was correct. The maid who took Mr. Howard's hat certainly welcomed them as though they belonged. Olivia tried to avoid gawking, but from what she'd seen thus far, the Pullman mansion was much grander than anything she'd expected.

From the entry, she viewed the twin-arched stairway of rich cherrywood winding upward to the second floor. Her heels clicked on the marble floor and echoed through the foyer as the maid led them into a room with thick Brussels carpet and velvet embossed wallpaper. Beautifully tufted gold brocade chairs flanked a marble-topped table, and a plush-cushioned divan was covered in a rich burgundy velvet that matched the wallpaper. Silk pillows rested in the corners of the divan, and a large oil painting of Mr. Pullman and a stately woman hung above the carved mantel. She leaned close to Mr. Howard. "Is that Mrs. Pullman?"

"Yes. She's quite a handsome woman, don't you think?"

Olivia agreed and continued to survey the room. Everywhere she looked, there were gold statuettes and ornate pieces of delicate glassware, tapestry-covered tables, and windows of stained glass. If what she saw in this room bespoke the rest of the house, the opulence surpassed the furnishings of Lanshire Hall. Before she had further time to take inventory of the room, Mrs. Pullman entered. An elegant woman, she crossed the room and bid them good afternoon. Her gown of pale green silk whispered like rustling leaves in a gentle wind.

Stepping forward, Mr. Howard signaled for Olivia. "Mrs. Pullman, may I introduce Miss Olivia Mott, our latest addition to the culinary staff at the hotel. Chef René has charged her with the preparations for your gala."

Mrs. Pullman glanced toward the hallway. "And Chef René is not in attendance today?"

Extracting a handkerchief from his pocket, Mr. Howard dabbed the beads of perspiration from his forehead. "His duties keep him in Pullman, but he has every confidence in Miss Mott."

Mrs. Pullman arched her brows. "*Does* he? I'm surprised he didn't personally advise me of this change in plans. He didn't mention Miss Mott when we last corresponded."

Although they were discussing her, Olivia felt like an intruder in a private conversation. Apparently Mr. Howard hadn't considered the possibility that Mrs. Pullman might disapprove of his change in plans.

"I believe you're going to find Miss Mott's menu much to your liking. She has excellent credentials."

Mrs. Pullman waved them toward one of the divans. "Do sit down." She patted her perfectly coiffed hair as she sat down opposite Mr. Howard. "I don't doubt Miss Mott's qualifications. I know Chef René would never hire an assistant without superb qualifications. I'm merely surprised he didn't advise me in advance that he wouldn't be at this meeting." She turned to look at Olivia. "Do you have a menu card prepared for my review, Miss Mott?"

Olivia withdrew the card from her purse. "I'll be pleased to discuss any changes you wish, Mrs. Pullman. Chef René has personally tested all of the recipes and given them his approval."

Mrs. Pullman scanned the card. "I think you've made some excellent choices, and if Chef René has approved the items, I'm confident they won't disappoint." She leaned back in her chair. "Now, what did you have in mind as a theme for the decorations?"

Olivia gulped. "Theme?"

"I much prefer decorations that convey a focused idea rather than a few floral arrangements scattered about. Don't you agree?"

"Yes, of course." How could she not agree? However, no one had mentioned the need of a theme for the decorations, and she'd planned exactly what Mrs. Pullman didn't want—flowers, candles, crisp white linens, and no focus. Mrs. Pullman was staring, obviously waiting for her to make a suitable suggestion.

"No flowers or candles," she muttered.

"Absolutely not."

"What about a sailing theme since your guests will be attending the regatta during their visit? Does that hold any appeal?"

Mrs. Pullman was still looking heavenward as though contemplating the idea when Olivia suddenly suggested a musical theme. "The tea is to raise funds for the symphony, isn't it? We could have musical notes on the menu cards, and if you would approve the use of a few flowers, we could arrange them around musical instruments. Perhaps we could borrow instruments from the Pullman band and orchestra members."

Mrs. Pullman's features softened while she contemplated the suggestion. "Yes. I do like that idea. Much more sophisticated than the sailing theme. If you would like some assistance with the decorations, I can have Regina come and help."

Mr. Howard leaned forward. "I don't think that's necess—"

Before he could say anything further, Olivia interrupted. "I would be most appreciative, Mrs. Pullman. The more elegant the event, the more funds you're likely to receive." Olivia didn't know who Regina was, but if the woman knew how to decorate and carry out a theme, Olivia wanted her at the hotel.

"Good for you, my dear. I'm pleased with your idea and the fact that you're willing to accept Regina's assistance. She's quite talented. I'll tell her I'm charging her with the responsibility of making the hotel's dining rooms and ladies' reading room into a veritable musical wonderland." She clapped her hands. "This is going to be delightful. I do want you to have one of the hotel staff see to the guest list and registry. I have the list of invited guests right here." She picked up several sheets of paper from the side table. "You may take it with you." She folded the sheets, handed them to Olivia, and then leaned back in her chair. "Based upon your accent, I would surmise you're from London?"

"Indeed she is. Olivia was an assistant chef at Lanshire Hall." Mr. Howard's chest swelled.

"Do tell? Now isn't that a coincidence. The Earl and Countess of Lanshire will be attending the regatta and athletic games. Of course, the countess will be in attendance at the tea, also. Won't she be surprised to see that we were fortunate enough to hire her assistant chef?" She chuckled. "Her loss is our gain, isn't it?"

Olivia watched Mrs. Pullman's lips continue to move, but she didn't hear anything further. Her mind was working overtime, attempting to digest what she'd just heard while wondering how this could possibly be happening to her. Had the earl and countess discovered Charlotte was in Pullman? No, surely not. If so, they wouldn't be planning to attend the regatta and a tea. Instead, they'd swoop into the city unannounced and take their daughter home to London.

The remainder of the meeting was a blur to Olivia. Before they'd even departed, her hands were shaking and her stomach roiling. The startling news settled around her in an oppressive haze, and she thought she might throw up in the carriage. Not until she extended her quaking hand to steady herself in the rocking carriage did Mr. Howard become aware of her overwhelming anxiety.

"You're trembling, my dear. Is it the excitement of meeting with Mrs. Pullman?"

She shook her head. "I'm unwell and wonder if we could immediately return home."

Mr. Howard's disappointment was palpable. "Perhaps once you've had something to eat, you'll feel revived."

At the mention of food, she swallowed hard, hoping she wouldn't retch. She would never live down such humiliation. "I don't think so. I'm sorry to spoil your plans, but I truly must go home."

"Then you must promise we'll come back to the city sometime so that I can show you some of the many sights I know you'll enjoy."

She murmured her agreement, thankful he'd not mentioned food again or forced her to set a date to visit the city with him. Their journey to Pullman seemed endless. Mr. Howard likely thought he was entertaining her with his ongoing monologue regarding the festive dedication ceremonies for the Columbian Exposition that were scheduled to take place in late October. Apparently Mr. Pullman and other wealthy men of Chicago had played a large role in ensuring the World's Fair would be hosted in their city. She did her best to appear impressed, but her roiling stomach prohibited much enthusiasm.

When the train finally pulled into the Pullman station, Olivia sighed with relief. She attempted to discourage him from accompanying her home, but Mr. Howard insisted upon escorting her. Certainly Charlotte and Mrs. DeVault would be surprised by her early return. What would Charlotte think when she heard the news about her mother and father? There was bound to be a hysterical scene, not that Olivia could fault Charlotte for any emotional outburst. After all, she'd nearly collapsed herself.

Olivia held fast to Mr. Howard's arm, but as he moved toward the front steps, she jerked back. "No need to come inside. I can make it on my own. I'm going to go and lie down the minute I'm inside the house." She loosened her hold on his arm. "I'm sorry for the change in plans."

He looked longingly at the front door, and for a moment, Olivia thought he might actually dart inside. Instead, he patted her hand like a doctor comforting an ill patient.

"I'll check on you tomorrow. And don't forget your promise."

Before he could say anything further about their next trip to Chicago, Olivia waved and retreated indoors. She was leaning against the front door when Mrs. DeVault hurried into the hallway with Morgan in her arms and a look of surprise on her face.

"Charlotte said you wouldn't be home until at least eight or nine o'clock. Did she misunderstand?" She drew closer and frowned. "You're pale, child. Are you ill?"

"Yes. We came home directly after the meeting with Mrs. Pullman."

"Let me make you a nice cup of hot tea. I say a cup of tea is always the first remedy for illness." She hoisted Morgan over her shoulder and patted his back as she made her way to the kitchen. A gusty burp soon followed. "There's the good boy. No tummy ache for you."

Olivia wished it would take no more than a hefty belch to relieve *her* upset stomach. "Where's Charlotte?"

Mrs. DeVault placed Morgan in his cradle. "She's resting. Said the boy kept her awake all night. I brought his cradle in here so he could keep me company while I prepare supper." She grinned at the cooing baby and placed the kettle on the stove. "I'm looking forward to the day when Fred will marry and give me some grandchildren to love. In the meantime, this little fellow is a nice substitute."

"He is a sweet little boy, and I do appreciate all your help. I don't know how we would have managed without you, Mrs. DeVault."

"When faced with a challenge, God's there to provide an answer. This time it was me." She pulled two cups and saucers from the shelf.

"Do you truly believe that, Mrs. DeVault?"

"Well, of course I do. You're a believer, Olivia. You know the first place to go when there's a problem is down on your knees. I'm not saying God has always given me the answer I wanted, but He always provides a way."

She supposed that was true enough for Mrs. DeVault. She was a woman of faith, a woman who lived what she professed. God was on call for people like Mrs. DeVault. But she doubted He was sitting up in heaven anxious to hear her problems. With all her lies and deceit, He knew she'd helped create the mess she was in. No, she wasn't like Mrs. DeVault. Sometimes she wondered if God would even claim her, much less help her solve her countless problems. Mrs. DeVault had called her a believer, but sometimes Olivia wondered exactly what that term meant. No one had ever explained what made a person a believer. Didn't everyone believe in God? So wouldn't that make everyone a believer?

She'd heard Mrs. DeVault talk about Jesus as if He was a personal friend one Sunday when a group of them had been sitting around the dinner table. Olivia had wanted to ask more, but she had been embarrassed. Everyone else seemed to know what the older woman was talking about, so Olivia had remained silent. After all, she didn't want to appear foolish.

Mrs. DeVault poured tea for both of them and settled in a chair beside her. "There now. Try that and see if you don't feel better."

Olivia took a sip. *Ask her*. She ignored the nagging voice and stirred a dollop of cream into the tea. *Ask her*. Her eyelashes fanned across her cheek as she stared into the cup and continued to stir. Without looking up, she gathered her courage. "What does it mean to be a believer, Mrs. DeVault? I mean, I know God is up in heaven and all, but is *that* what makes me a believer?"

Mrs. DeVault reached across the table and placed her work-worn hand beneath Olivia's chin. "Look at me, child."

"I've asked a foolish question, haven't I?"

"Of course not. You've asked the most important question of your life, and I'm pleased you chose me to ask."

Olivia didn't know who else she would have asked. Nobody else had ever mentioned the subject before, at least not that she recalled. Her father had had more interest in visiting the pub and tipping a mug than talking to her. And although Aunt Eleanor went to church and talked about praying, she'd never said anything about being a believer. Maybe it was a term that was used only in America.

"Being a believer means that you've accepted Jesus as your personal Savior, Olivia. It means you believe He's the Son of God, that He died and rose from the dead just for you. When you invite Jesus into your heart, He's more than your Savior: He's the best friend you can ever have. Someone you can go to with all your troubles and cares, and He'll never betray your confidence like some folks are prone to do." She grinned at the last comment. "Do you have a Bible, child?"

"Yes." Olivia did have the Bible that had belonged to her mother, though she seldom looked inside.

"When you have some time alone, I want you to read some special verses. I'll write them down for you." She ripped off the end of Olivia's grocery list. "You read these and then we'll talk." She pushed the page across the table.

Olivia glanced at the list. She folded the paper and tucked it into her pocket. "I'll read them after I go to my room for the night."

Mrs. DeVault sipped her tea. "I believe your color is improving. Are you feeling better?"

Olivia grinned. "I am. You're right about the tea. It seems to have—"

Before Olivia could complete her reply, Charlotte bounded into the room. "Olivia! I thought I heard voices in here. What are you doing home so early?"

After explaining her unexpected bout of illness, Olivia lifted her teacup and tilted her head toward Mrs. DeVault. "However, Mrs. DeVault's tea has done the trick. I'm feeling much better. I think we can finish supper preparations on our own and let Mrs. DeVault have a quiet evening at home." Without giving either of the ladies the opportunity to object, Olivia gathered the older woman's belongings and escorted her to the door.

"I'll be certain to read the verses tonight. I'll talk to you tomorrow."

Mrs. DeVault chuckled. "If you don't appear, I'll send Fred to fetch you."

Obviously Mrs. DeVault didn't realize Olivia regarded that

as pleasure rather than punishment, but she didn't correct the woman as she bid her good-bye.

When Olivia returned to the kitchen, Charlotte pointed an accusing finger. "Tell me the truth. Why are you home? You feigned illness hoping to discourage Mr. Howard's amorous interests, didn't you?" When Olivia didn't immediately reply, Charlotte sat at the table, crossed her arms across her waist, and insisted upon hearing a complete account.

Olivia inhaled a deep breath before she began her explanation. She had hoped for more time to formulate a prudent response. Though she attempted to choose her words carefully, the woman interrupted at every turn. Discombobulated by Charlotte's rude behavior, Olivia blurted out the unwelcome news in one impulsive burst.

Charlotte jumped from her chair and sent it crashing to the floor. The baby immediately squalled in protest from the cradle. "I find nothing humorous in your silly story, and I think it was downright cruel of you to say such things."

"I am not jesting with you. I have the guest list provided by Mrs. Pullman." She pulled the list from her purse and handed it to Charlotte. "See for yourself."

After scanning the paper, Charlotte grasped the edge of the table and fell into another chair. Olivia grabbed a damp towel and applied it to Charlotte's forehead before she could swoon and drop to the floor. She had expected a dramatic reaction. Charlotte hadn't disappointed.

She looked like a frightened animal snared in a trap. "What am I going to do?"

"It may not be as serious as you think. On the train ride, I considered the matter, and so long as you remain indoors, there's no reason your mother will know you're in Pullman. You've used a different name, so no one would assume you have a connection to the Earl and Countess of Lanshire." Olivia forced an air of bravado as she completed her explanation.

Charlotte bobbed her head, obviously wanting to believe all would be well. "But Mr. Howard knows of your connection to Lanshire Hall."

"Mr. Howard mentioned my previous employment to Mrs. Pullman, but I doubt that topic will be revived. By the time your parents arrive, I think Mrs. Pullman will have completely forgotten me and any connection to your parents."

Charlotte stood and paced back and forth as she considered Olivia's response. "Perhaps you're correct, but even the slightest comment could cause a remembrance."

"Why don't we eat supper and sleep on the matter. There's no sense fretting about it tonight."

Charlotte agreed more easily than Olivia imagined possible and made no further mention of her parents throughout the remainder of the evening. Apparently Olivia had misjudged Charlotte and her ability to deal with this latest predicament.

Later that night when Olivia retreated to the quiet of her room, she reviewed the Scriptures Mrs. DeVault had listed. Digging into her satchel stored beneath the bed, she retrieved her mother's Bible and fanned the whisper-thin pages until she located the book of Romans. She noticed that there were numerous underlined verses, and the corners of some of the pages had been turned down. Turning to the third chapter, she traced her finger to the twenty-third verse.

"'For all have sinned, and come short of the glory of God.'" She murmured the words and then exhaled a deep sigh. She probably shouldn't take pleasure in discovering the world was filled with sinners, but it eased her mind to know she wasn't the only one failing God.

After checking Mrs. DeVault's list, Olivia moved ahead to Romans 6:23. "'For the wages of sin is death; but the gift of God is eternal life through Jesus Christ our Lord.'" The first sentence caused her to quiver—she didn't like to think of death. But the second portion that mentioned eternal life was most encouraging. She flipped to Romans 10:9 and 10:13 and then backward to Romans 5:1.

Fortunately, Mrs. DeVault's listed Scriptures weren't scattered throughout the entire Bible, for although many young women her age were familiar with the Bible and its contents, such education had never been a priority in her father's house. When she finished reading the verses, Olivia slowly closed the cover and rubbed her palm across the leather cover. Had her mother studied the Bible? If she had lived, would she have taught her about eternal life? If her mother had truly believed these verses, they would meet in eternity. The thought was comforting—something she'd never before considered.

Olivia placed the Bible on her bedside table and wondered if *she* could possibly discover peace through Jesus Christ. Peace would be a wonderful thing, for she had never experienced absolute tranquillity in her life. Surely receiving a gift of such magnitude must be difficult. There had to be more to this issue of forgiveness and eternal life than what was contained in those verses. It sounded wonderful, but it seemed too simple to be true. She'd ask Mrs. DeVault.

Chapter Nineteen

With his white hat fluttering in the morning breeze, Chef René waved Olivia onward as she neared the kitchen door, then stepped forward to meet her. "So? I am anxious to hear a report of your meeting with Mrs. Pullman. Come along and tell me."

Olivia followed him into his office. Once they were seated, she spoke of Mrs. Pullman's pleasure with the menu. Chef René beamed and encouraged her to tell him more. She had nearly concluded her report, but then remembered Mrs. Pullman's request regarding a theme for the decorations.

Chef René's pleasant countenance faded to a frown. "You discouraged such an idea, did you not? Elegance is the key to beauty—not some ghastly *theme*." Disgust oozed from his final word.

Olivia squirmed in her chair. "I suggested flowers and candles, but she became insistent. I didn't believe I had the right to argue with her choice. So I made several suggestions." She muttered her final remark and bowed her head.

"Never, never suggest ideas for a theme!" He dislodged himself from the chair and edged around his desk. Lifting her chin with one finger, he stared into her eyes. "I am not angry with you, Miss Mott. You did not know. We may still be able to save Mrs. Pullman from herself. I will contact her and *suggest* she discard such a notion." He shook his head. "Men compete in sports. Unfortunately, women do the same with their teas and dinner parties. Take charge of the kitchen, Miss Mott. I must think."

She scampered down the hallway and set to work, but when the chef hadn't reappeared by midafternoon, her fears mounted. Several discreet inquiries revealed that none of the staff had seen Chef René, and he wasn't in his office. Though he'd instructed her to take charge, she hadn't expected him to disappear for the entire day. Had Mrs. Pullman's request for a theme distressed him so much he had taken to his bed? Surely not!

The supper menu consisted of simple fare, a fact for which she was now grateful. She scurried down the kitchen stairs into the pastry kitchen. Smells of freshly baked loaves wafted through the air to greet her. The crusty loaves of bread and blackberry pies were cooling on the large racks that had been specially designed and installed in the pastry kitchen. A sense of pride welled in her chest when she spotted the pies. The recipe was one she'd found in her mother's recipe box. After one taste, Chef René had declared Mrs. Mott's blackberry pie and her strawberry-rhubarb pie would be offered on the hotel's dessert menu when the fruits were in season.

She reached the top of the stairs with her mind racing, attempting to recall all that needed completion before the evening meal. Bustling around the corner into the kitchen, she ran headlong into Chef René. "*Where* have you been?" Unfortunately, her words sounded more like an accusation than a question.

The chef's eyebrows raised in perfect arches. "You question *my* whereabouts? When did you become executive chef of this hotel, Miss Mott?"

Olivia folded her arms across her waist and bowed her head, wishing she could form her body into a tight knot and make it disappear. "I apologize. My fear for your well-being caused me to speak out in an abrupt fashion."

He rubbed his jaw and contemplated her for a moment. "Oui. Most often you are soft-spoken and sweet-natured." He wagged his finger back and forth. "Today you forget. Come outside where we may speak privately."

She followed him until they reached the garden by the side entrance of the main kitchen.

He scanned the vicinity as though preparing to tell her a secret. "I went to visit Mrs. Pullman today, and we have agreed to dispense with a theme for her tea."

Olivia's mouth dropped open. "You went to—"

"Oui. With Mr. Pullman's permission. I took his private train back to Prairie Avenue, and after due consideration, we agreed upon ice sculptures, flowers, candles, and *elegance*. You, Miss Mott, will once again take charge of the décor."

Her spirits sagged. She had been pleased when Mrs. Pullman offered her assistant's help. Chef René's journey to Chicago had done nothing but cause her additional worries. He stared at her expectantly. "Thank you for your display of confidence in my abilities," she finally said.

He gripped her shoulder warmly. "You are an excellent protégée, Miss Mott. You will do a fine job. I will prepare the ice carvings for you."

She nearly giggled aloud. He'd best prepare them. Otherwise, the tables would be decked with nothing more than a chunk of ice direct from the Pullman icehouse, for she knew nothing of ice carving.

"Supper is well underway?" He held her elbow as they walked back to the kitchen.

"Yes. Everything is progressing smoothly."

"Then you may depart for the day. You've done a fine job, Miss Mott."

Olivia basked in the praise while she packed two pieces of pie, a chunk of bread, soup, and two servings of the leftover veal scaloppini into her basket and then headed off toward home. Since she'd have two extra hours of daylight to enjoy, she decided she'd leave the supper basket at home and go visit with Mrs. DeVault before Fred and Albert returned home from work. There would be more than sufficient time to ask her questions in private before the men arrived.

The sound of Morgan's cries broke Olivia's peaceful reverie as she neared home. His lusty wails drowned out the chirping birds and any other sound, save the whistling of a train nearing town. She'd grown accustomed to the trains that arrived and departed every half hour beginning at six in the morning and continuing until midnight. Though some considered the schedule a nuisance, others were thankful for the frequent trains back and forth to Chicago.

Morgan's cries continued. *Why doesn't Charlotte attend to him?* The woman's selfish behavior had been the cause of several arguments, though their disagreements had accomplished little. It was the boy who suffered, yet that fact seemed not to bother Charlotte in the least. Olivia shifted the basket on her arm and arched her shoulders to ease the ache in her back.

"There you are! It's about time *one* of you got home." Mrs. Rice rushed out her front door and thrust Morgan toward Olivia. "Take him. And tell Mrs. Hornsby she owes me more money. I've had the lad since one o'clock. He's wet and he's hungry."

Olivia set the basket on the porch and extended her arms for the baby. "Where is Charlotte?"

"Wouldn't we all like to know the answer to that one. She come over here this mornin' asking if I'd watch the baby for a couple hours while she dropped off her dresses for alterations at the Arcade. Ain't seen or heard a word since." She shook her finger under Olivia's nose. "And you tell her I ain't plannin' to be showing her any kindness in the future. She can take advantage of others, but not me."

Adjusting the baby in her left arm, Olivia unlocked the front door and then retrieved the basket with her right hand while Mrs. Rice continued to glower. She didn't know what the woman expected her to do. "I'll be sure to relay your message, Mrs. Rice." That said, she entered the house and closed the door. Morgan continued to cry, his tiny face as red as a ripe apple and covered with perspiration.

"There, there," she whispered. "A clean diaper and something to eat is what you need."

Exhausted by his ongoing crying episode, the baby fell asleep while finishing the remains of his bottle. "Let's get you into your cradle, young man," she murmured. Passing through the hallway, Olivia noticed an envelope propped against a small vase on the table and bearing her name. Her heart beat faster at the sight. A letter from Charlotte? Still holding the baby, she picked up the missive, went into the parlor, and placed young Morgan on the divan beside her. Her fingers trembling, she removed the folded pages and began to read.

Dear Olivia,

I know you will find my conduct unbefitting a mother, and I can only hope that you will forgive me for my abrupt departure. After learning my parents will soon arrive in this country and plan to visit this very city, I felt no other recourse was available to me. I will not chance encountering them during their visit here. As you can well imagine, they would be humiliated to find their daughter in such circumstances.

Olivia glanced at the baby sleeping soundly at her side. How could Charlotte leave Pullman without her son? She returned her attention to the letter.

I leave young Morgan to your care. I chose to leave on Saturday in the hopes you could make proper arrangements for him on Sunday after church services. Perhaps with proper payment, Mrs. Rice would be willing to assume his care while you are at the hotel. I've left money for his expenses in the top drawer of my chest, and I've paid Mrs. Logan for milk until the end of the month. I realize the funds won't last long, but it's the best I could do for now.

Fondly,

Charlotte

Fondly? Olivia turned the page over, anxious to locate the

portion of the letter stating when Charlotte would return, but there was nothing more. She reread a sentence from the last paragraph aloud. "'I've paid Mrs. Logan until the end of the month.'" It was only the first week of the month. And the tea wasn't scheduled for another two weeks. Why had she departed so soon? Surely she'd be back to check on the baby's welfare before then. Wouldn't she?

Olivia tucked the letter into the envelope and lifted the baby into her arms, her thoughts jumbling to and fro like a frantic hummingbird batting its wings. Perhaps Mrs. DeVault could offer her counsel. She had planned to go and talk to her before this difficulty had been unexpectedly dropped in her lap. She'd take young Morgan with her and seek the older woman's advice.

First, she'd need a few diapers for the lad. She rounded the corner into the hallway and glanced out the door. Fear clutched her throat, and she fought to take in a breath. She stared across the street, unwilling to look away lest she lose sight of the young hooligan. Finally, when she was about to give up, the thatch of red hair reappeared. For a brief moment she and Eddie stared at each other before he raced down the street. Suddenly remembering the mention of money in Charlotte's letter, she closed and locked the door before hurrying to check in the bedroom.

Olivia peeked into the envelope just long enough to assure herself of the contents. Obviously Eddie hadn't been in the house, but she certainly didn't want money lying about. Should she go to the bank? Like the shops in the Arcade, the bank would be open all evening. Yet she longed to talk with Mrs. DeVault. She could carry the money along with her and, if time permitted, stop at the bank on her way home. But what if Eddie lurked down the street and accosted her along the way? Would he do such a thing? Tucking a loose strand of hair behind one ear, she considered the idea. She'd be carrying an infant in her arms. Surely Eddie wouldn't be so malicious as to risk harming a baby.

Her thoughts were soon interrupted by a loud knock. Eddie? Instinctively she hugged the infant closer to her chest. *Silly!* Eddie wasn't going to knock on the front door like a guest arriving for a cup of tea. Still, she peeked through the glass before opening the door.

"Fred!" She pulled open the door, grasped his hand, and pulled him inside. "I'm so happy to see you."

A hint of pink colored his neck and crept up into his cheeks as he lurched forward. He grinned and removed his hat to reveal his tousled brown hair. His blue eyes twinkled. "This is a pleasant surprise. I didn't know you'd be so pleased to see me."

She cringed, embarrassed by her behavior. Fear had caused her to make a fool of herself. She stumbled over her words in her haste to explain Charlotte's unexpected departure. He led her to the parlor, listening intently while she talked. Overwhelmed by his sympathy and understanding, a stream of tears rolled down her cheeks.

He extended his arms toward the baby. "Here now, none of that. Let me hold Morgan while you wipe away those tears." With a natural ease, he took the child from her. The baby snuggled close, nearly lost in the crook of Fred's muscular arm. "Come, let's sit down for a minute, and you can gather your thoughts."

Olivia swallowed, forcing back her tears. "To make matters worse, I'm afraid I've angered Eddie Calhoun."

A frown creased Fred's handsome features. "Who is Eddie Calhoun? I've never heard of him."

Fred occasionally commented or asked a question as the story of Eddie Calhoun and his wayward activities unfolded. When she completed the telling, he shifted the baby onto his shoulder. "And what kind of message was this Eddie delivering for Mrs. Hornsby? I didn't realize she had acquaintances in Chicago."

Olivia faltered. In her fear and concern, she'd forgotten her list of lies. She'd unwittingly said too much. "Charlotte didn't confide the exact mission for which she'd obtained Eddie's services." *Another lie.*

He lightly patted Morgan's back. "I will discreetly inquire regarding this Eddie. In the meantime, you must be careful to lock the doors." He pointed a warning finger. "And you should have an escort with you at all times. Martha continues to walk with you each morning?"

"Yes, but I can't wait until I have someone to go with me every time I want to leave the house or walk home from work. Martha leaves in the evening before I do, and most of the others reside in other parts of town."

He shrugged, and the baby shifted his head on Fred's shoulder. "I'll call at the hotel for you each evening." He tilted his head to the side. "Unless you prefer Mr. Howard's company."

She laughed. "I think not. You made the offer, and now I'm going to hold you to your word."

He chuckled, and his deep voice caused the baby to stir. Returning young Morgan to the crook of his arm, he glanced at the parlor clock. "My mother sent me to fetch you. If we don't soon arrive, she'll be sending Albert to find me. I will escort you to the bank on the way back home—best we not keep Mother waiting any longer."

Apparently Mrs. DeVault had meant what she'd said yesterday. When Olivia hadn't appeared, she'd sent Fred. She hoped Mrs. DeVault had plenty of time, for Bible questions weren't the only ones for which Olivia needed answers after today's events.

Still holding the baby, Fred waited while she locked the door. She scanned the park across the street as they headed off, thankful when she saw only young families and children in the park. No one who remotely resembled Eddie Calhoun. She smiled at Fred's attentiveness to the baby but quickly looked away when he glanced in her direction. She didn't want him to catch her staring at him. He would make a fine father one day.

"I'm interested in hearing about your journey to Chicago with Mr. Howard." His jaw tightened as he awaited her response.

"There's not so much to tell. We met with Mrs. Pullman, and she approved the menu I brought. Then we came home."

He raised his eyebrows until they nearly disappeared beneath the brim of his hat. "He was anxious to immediately return to Pullman? Hard to believe."

She shook her head. "I wasn't feeling well and asked to come home directly after our meeting."

"If the weather cooperates, I shall have to take you to Chicago next Sunday after church. We can visit Humboldt or Garfield Park. Perhaps not so fancy an afternoon as you might experience with Mr. Howard, but I believe much more enjoyable." He grinned broadly and winked.

Her stomach fluttered at the gesture and she readily

agreed—until she remembered the bundle Fred carried in his arms. "Oh, but I can't. I have Morgan to care for now. I had best not make plans for my time away from work."

Fred shrugged. "We'll manage to arrange something. Who knows? Morgan may enjoy an outing in the park if the weather permits." He grinned down at the baby. "What do you think, Morgan? Would you like to see the big city?"

Olivia recalled the noise and hubbub of the city and shivered. "I'm not certain Chicago is a place for young Morgan."

As they approached Market Hall, Olivia admired the selection of blooms one of the flower vendors offered through the open air windows. Her heart tripped in a choppy beat when she spotted Mr. Howard approaching. *Please. Turn away. Don't come any closer.* Although she managed to avoid eye contact and pretended not to see him, the silent plea went unheeded.

The man was sprinting across the street, waving his hat overhead and calling her name. Fred stopped as Mr. Howard approached. "What does *he* want?"

Placing a hand atop her hat as a gust of wind coursed down the street, Olivia shrugged. "I'm certain I don't know."

Fred frowned, obviously unconvinced.

"Mr. Howard?" Olivia waited for his response.

"I saw the three of you and wondered . . ." His brows furrowed. "That is, it would be easy to mistake you for a young family out for a stroll." He glanced at Fred and then looked intently at Olivia. She couldn't decide how to respond. He hadn't asked a question, yet he obviously expected some reply.

Fred took a step closer to Olivia's side and grasped her elbow with his free hand. "If you'll excuse us, Mr. Howard, my mother is expecting us for supper. We don't want to keep her waiting."

Mr. Howard looked down at Morgan for a brief moment. "I trust Mrs. Hornsby isn't ill."

"Not to our knowledge," Fred said as he tightened his hold on Olivia's elbow. "Come along, Olivia. We're already late."

She tipped her head, thankful Fred had taken control of the situation. "Good evening, Mr. Howard."

He nodded formally before donning his hat. "Miss Mott. Mr. DeVault. I trust you'll enjoy the remainder of your evening."

Olivia sighed, relieved to be away from the sticky situation. But she'd taken only a few steps when Mr. Howard called after her. "Don't forget that you owe me an afternoon in Chicago, Miss Mott."

She noted the twitch in Fred's jaw and steeled herself for his questions.

Chapter Twenty

A week later, Olivia arrived at the hotel kitchen, harried and exhausted. Mrs. DeVault was filling the void during the daylight hours, but Olivia was required to care for young Morgan each evening and throughout the night. The lack of sleep was taking its toll. Unlike Charlotte, Olivia hastened to still the infant when he cried, pacing the floor or rocking him—whatever was needed. For that, she'd received Mr. Rice's thanks but little slumber for herself. The infant was colicky, due in part to a change in his milk—at least, that's what Mrs. DeVault advised.

The older woman had forecast a bleak result with such a change, and she had been correct. However, there had been no choice. Though Charlotte's letter clearly stated Mrs. Logan had been paid for the remainder of the month, the woman contradicted the declaration and refused to supply further sustenance for Morgan. With an immediate resolution needed, Mrs. DeVault had decided upon fresh goat's milk as a substitute. But young Morgan had objected to the new arrangement.

Although Mrs. DeVault had said he would adjust within two weeks, Olivia didn't know if she would survive. She trudged up the steps and into the kitchen. Her feet felt as though heavy weights had been attached to them, and dark circles rimmed her eyes. Chef René had declared she resembled a raccoon, in spite of her attempts to obscure the offending discoloration with powder.

Turning from the giant stove, Chef René glanced in her direction and shook his head. "When will you get some sleep, Miss Mott? You cannot continue to work in this condition. The guests arrive for your tea at the end of the month. You must be prepared, Miss Mott." He pointed his spoon in her direction. "If you are to be a chef, your first concern must be the kitchen."

Olivia dropped onto a nearby chair. They would be alone for another fifteen minutes before the kitchen boys arrived. "But there is a baby at my house who needs care. I can't disregard his needs because of my own desire."

He pushed the pot of simmering oatmeal, one of the daily breakfast offerings, off to the rear of the stove and joined her. "His *mother* did. Why do you feel this child is now your responsibility? I am told there is a home for orphaned children in Chicago. Perhaps you should go there and see if they will take the infant."

Olivia cradled her arms across her chest, thinking of her own motherless childhood. How could she do such a thing to little Morgan? He deserved more than a home filled with unwanted children. Though her father had never shown her love or attention, she'd always known that Aunt Eleanor loved her. Furthermore, she'd seen the dark, dank places in London where these children lived. She had passed one each time she walked to visit Aunt Eleanor. No, her heart would not permit such a thing. She couldn't provide Morgan with a luxurious home, but a child needed love more than finery—of that she was certain.

Chef René sat down beside her. "What do you think? You can take the child to the orphanage in Chicago tomorrow morning. I will permit the time away from work."

"No." Her word was a mere whisper. "The child is more important than my dream."

"Non! I would agree if he were your own baby. But this is someone else's child, Miss Mott." He tapped his finger on the band of his white toque. "You must think of your future!"

"I'm too tired to think, Chef René. Today I'll do well to make it through my tasks that require little thought."

"What's this I hear? Too tired to think?"

Both of them shifted around at the sound of Mr. Howard's voice. He'd obviously been listening to their conversation. Olivia hoped he didn't plan to intrude. He seemed to think he had the right to direct both her work and personal life. She was aware that his insistent behavior revealed affectionate feelings that were more than a passing fancy. But to date, her attempts to dissuade him had proved unsuccessful.

Fred was likely correct: if she truly didn't care for Mr. Howard, she shouldn't accept his invitations. Thus far, the power he held over her employment with the company had controlled her decisions.

"Miss Mott?" Mr. Howard interrupted her thoughts, always careful to address her formally during working hours.

"Yes, Mr. Howard?"

"May I speak with you privately, please?" He then turned his attention to René. "May we use your office?"

Mr. Howard knew they would both comply, for the questions weren't actually requests. They were commands posed in a gentlemanly fashion. Before either of them responded, he motioned for her to follow him. Olivia glanced over her shoulder, but Chef René shrugged and raised his brows. He obviously had no idea what Mr. Howard wanted.

Once Mr. Howard closed the door, he pulled Chef René's chair around the desk and sat down beside her. "I'm a bit embarrassed to admit it, and I hope you won't consider me rude, but I overheard your entire conversation with Chef René."

What should she say? That she thought his behavior highly improper? She merely gave a slight nod.

"I believe I have a solution for your problem with the infant. However, I want you to think on what I'm about to suggest—for several days. Then you may give me your answer." He reached across the arm of his chair and lightly grasped her hand. "You know that I am very fond of you, Olivia. We've not known each other long, but from the first moment I saw you, I knew I was ready to move forward with my personal life."

How could he have known such a thing the moment he saw her? Clammy beads of perspiration rolled down her back. She wanted to withdraw her hand yet feared his reaction should she pull away. Her mind raced. Exactly what was Mr. Howard suggesting? Apparently he construed her silence as agreement, for he continued.

"If you married me, we could provide a loving home for young Morgan. He's a fine infant, and I have the means to give him an excellent upbringing. You'd be able to quit your job and give him the nurturing he deserves. I believe this is a perfect solution—for all three of us."

The warm air wrapped around her like a suffocating wool blanket. She feared she might swoon. And with the door closed, the small room provided little ventilation. Gathering her courage, she withdrew her hand, plucked a piece of paper from the desk, and frantically fanned herself.

Mr. Howard immediately joined in and waved his white linen handkerchief back and forth in front of her. "This is why I want you to take time to consider my solution. I knew you would be—"

Olivia held up her hand to stave off further explanation. She inhaled deeply, carefully choosing her words. "You and Chef René forget that Charlotte—Mrs. Hornsby—may come back at any moment. As I explained to Chef René, Mrs. Hornsby's letter didn't say she wouldn't return."

"And it didn't say she would. We must assume that if she intended to do so, she would have clarified her plan."

"I could argue the opposite, but there's no way of knowing for certain. A decision of any type cannot be made at the moment." She checked the clock. "I must get back to the kitchen, Mr. Howard."

He slid forward and once again captured her hand. "But you'll consider my proposal?"

The urgency in his voice matched the eagerness in his eyes, and she wanted to run from the room. She couldn't believe he would suggest they should wed. They barely knew each other. Surely he couldn't love her. The man could have his choice of many women. Why had he selected her? She had little to offer him . . . couldn't even offer love. He was a nice enough man but not the man for her, not the man she hoped to marry one day. At least she didn't think so. And she had no interest in a marriage of convenience. Did Mr. Howard believe she would grow to love him? Was he willing to take such a chance in order to provide a home for Morgan?

Her legs wobbled as she stood, and he placed a supporting arm around her waist. "I'm fine, Mr. Howard. It's the heat; it's stifling in here."

He leaned forward and turned the doorknob. Thankfully, a faint breeze drifted into the room. She glanced at his arm that continued to circle her waist, and he immediately released her. He wouldn't want the staff to see him clutching the waist of the assistant chef.

"We'll discuss this further next week. Perhaps when we have our belated supper in Chicago?"

She stepped into the hallway and twisted around. "I have the baby to look after now. I'm not formulating any plans for my days or evenings away from work."

The sparkle she'd noted in his eyes only moments ago disappeared. "In a city the size of Pullman, I imagine I could arrange for someone with excellent references to care for the child."

Unwilling to offer an affirmative response, she pointed toward the kitchen. "I must return to work. I'm certain Chef René is in need of help with the breakfast preparations." She hurried off before he could detain her.

Chapter Twenty-One

On several occasions throughout the day, Chef René broached the topic of her conversation with Mr. Howard, but she immediately silenced his inquiries with comments about the seating arrangement in the dining room or with a question regarding one of the recipes. By day's end, he'd ceased his questions, though she knew he was more than a little interested in what had transpired.

He followed her outside as she prepared to depart for the evening. "I trust Mr. Howard didn't speak ill of me during your meeting this morning?"

The man didn't give up easily. "Of course not. This was a . . . a private matter." She sighed with relief when Fred rounded the corner of the hotel. She waved him forward. "I thought you'd forgotten me."

A gust of wind whipped his hair, and he ran his fingers through his mass of dark curls. Chef René glanced back and forth between the two and then rested his arms across his rotund belly. "Ah, so *that* is how it is."

Olivia arranged her white jacket across one arm and held her toque between her fingers. "We are friends. His mother is caring for Morgan."

Chef René tipped his head back and laughed, his sagging jowls jiggling. He wagged his head back and forth. "We, too, are friends, but you do not look at me with this same affection that I now see in your eyes." He lowered his voice and winked. "I think Mr. Howard will be worried if he sees the way you look at this young man."

"Who knows what will or won't worry Mr. Howard?" Olivia attempted a nonchalant shrug and bid the chef good-night. She quickly fell in step alongside Fred. With the familiarity of a couple who'd known each other much longer, he took the food basket and swung it in one hand as they walked. His easy ways calmed her, and she laughed as he jested with her. Once their laughter ceased, he grew more serious.

"I made a few inquiries about Eddie Calhoun. One of the janitors at the train station has seen him hanging around over there on a couple of occasions, but that was several days ago—probably when you last saw him hiding across the street. I may try to locate young Georgie and see if he has any information. I know a couple fellows who work at the paper wheel factory, and they can probably tell me if he's living here in Pullman or over in Kensington."

Olivia didn't think Georgie would have maintained his friendship with Eddie—not if he wanted to remain employed at the factory. But she remained silent. Better to keep her thoughts to herself or she might discourage Fred from assisting her. Another Eddie Calhoun sighting was the last thing she wanted. The sooner the redheaded miscreant was out of her life, the better. She had enough worries with the approaching gala, Mr. Howard's proposal, and young Morgan's care.

Fred lifted the basket a notch. "You probably don't need this food today. Mother is planning on your joining us for supper tonight. She said the two of you had never completed an earlier conversation, and she intended to do so tonight."

Although she detected the curiosity in his voice, she merely agreed that his mother's company would provide an enjoyable evening. "Besides, I thought you and Albert were practicing your baseball or rowing this evening."

He laughed heartily, causing tiny lines to crinkle at the corner of his eyes. "You sound like my mother. She says I'll never find a wife who'll be willing to put up with my still wanting to play games like a young boy."

"I think most any young woman would gladly accept a marriage proposal from you." A blush stole across her cheeks, and she quickly looked away, embarrassed by her response. What must he think of a woman who would make such a bold remark?

"I'm flattered by your assessment." Fred tipped his head closer, his lips twitching to force away his natural grin. "And do you count *yourself* among that number?"

Without thinking, she joined in his banter. "I don't think my heart could withstand two marriage proposals in one day." Her eyes widened, and she bit her lower lip the moment the words escaped her lips. In the pleasure of their repartee, she'd let down her guard and forgotten to mind her tongue.

His brow furrowed.

She forced herself to giggle, relieved when he quickly followed suit.

"So you're attempting to make me jealous, are you, Miss Olivia Mott?"

The heaviness slowly lifted from her chest, and she inhaled a shallow breath. Placing her hand on her heart, she feigned mock indignation. "I would *never* do such a thing."

Fred guffawed loudly. "On first meeting, a person would miss the depth of your humorous nature, Olivia." His blue eyes softened.

A twinge of guilt nagged her conscience. *I didn't lie! But you still deceived him.* The argument raged in her mind until they arrived at the DeVault home. Albert greeted them at the front door with Morgan cradled in one arm.

Olivia greeted Albert with a kiss on the cheek. "Getting in practice for one of your own, I see."

He vehemently shook his head. "No! Marriage maybe, but I haven't had enough preparation for fatherhood just yet."

Olivia removed her bonnet and cape and hung them on one of the hooks in the hallway. "That's what all men say, but you appear quite at ease with Morgan."

Albert grinned. "I'm simply helping out where needed. I'm waiting for supper, and Mrs. DeVault can't tend to the boy and cook, too." Morgan whimpered and Albert bounced his arm. "You've got him spoiled, Livie."

She slapped her cousin's arm. For the first time since Olivia's arrival, Albert had reverted back to the childhood name she detested. "Don't call me that. You know I dislike it. And he's not spoiled—he's got a case of the colic. Just ask Mrs. DeVault and she'll agree. Now out of my way so I can go and assist in the kitchen. I trust the two of you strapping men can handle this teeny baby."

Without waiting for a response, she removed the basket from Fred's hand and marched off toward the kitchen.

Mrs. DeVault's clear blue eyes sparkled as she greeted Olivia. Her ample figure was wrapped in a cotton apron that covered her plain brown dress. The heat from the stove had turned her cheeks rosy. "Olivia! I'm pleased to see you, child."

She offered the words as though she hadn't seen her for a month instead of just earlier this morning. The woman certainly had known that she'd be arriving—both to partake of supper and to retrieve Morgan. Her tone exuded a warmth usually reserved for family and close friends. She crooked her finger and Olivia stepped closer.

"I was hoping we would have some time alone to visit. What with Mrs. Hornsby's unexpected departure and all of the upheaval with the baby, we haven't had an opportunity to resume our discussion about those Bible verses."

"I do have several questions for you, Mrs. DeVault."

The older woman beamed and rubbed her palms together. "Good. I'm pleased to know you followed my advice and read the Scriptures."

"Oh yes. I read them that very night." Olivia reached into her reticule and retrieved a scrap of paper. "I wrote down a few notes."

Mrs. DeVault beamed her approval. "Well, you ask away. If I don't know the answer, I'll find someone who does."

While Mrs. DeVault removed a beef and potato pie from the oven, Olivia posed her questions, hoping she didn't sound foolish. But Mrs. DeVault didn't frown or laugh at her. On the contrary, she appeared pleased by each inquiry.

The older woman wiped her hands across the corner of her apron and sat down next to Olivia. "Let's start with your first question. Receiving eternal life is every bit as easy as the Bible says. It's a gift—pure and simple. But here's the thing, Olivia. We have the right to accept or reject it. This isn't something that's forced upon us. If you believe what the Bible says, you ask for forgiveness and invite Jesus into your heart."

"But how do you know if He really forgives you?"

Mrs. DeVault's expression became somber. "That's called faith, Olivia. And even though He forgives us, we must be prepared to suffer the consequences of our sins."

Olivia tilted her head and stared out the kitchen window while considering what the cost of her sins might be. "What if I sin again?" Her voice trembled.

The sparkle returned to Mrs. DeVault's eyes as she patted Olivia's hand. "We're imperfect creatures, Olivia. But once we accept Jesus, we try to do better by following His Word and listening to the Holy Spirit." The older woman touched her palm to her heart.

"Is that the little voice I keep hearing that tells me I should or shouldn't do something?"

"That's exactly right. We need to do what *God* wants us to do, Olivia, not what other folks tell us. You look to the Bible for your answers, and you'll not go wrong." Pressing her hands atop the table, Mrs. DeVault stood up. "I believe that pie's rested long enough to thicken. Don't want to leave it too long; the men will complain if it's cold."

Even though Mrs. DeVault seemed to know a lot about the Bible and faith, she obviously thought it important that Olivia search out answers on her own. Likely so she'd become more acquainted with the contents while she looked. Olivia considered the size of the book and its feathery pages. Finding the answers to her questions could take many an hour!

When Olivia had placed the final pieces of silverware on the table and poured steaming coffee into the heavy earthenware cups, Fred walked into the kitchen with Morgan on his shoulder. Mrs. DeVault wagged her head back and forth and pointed him toward the door.

"Put that boy down and let him sleep. You keep carrying him around like that, and he's going to think that's the way of things, and I'll never complete my chores when you're at work." Her voice was brusque, but her eyes twinkled.

Fred nuzzled the baby's downy hair and whispered his apologies to the infant as he carried him from the room. "I won't tell young Morgan a soft heart lies beneath those gruff words."

Mrs. DeVault shooed him from the room without comment, and when he returned a few minutes later, his arms were empty. His mother wasted no time putting him to work. Using thick towels, he lifted the pie from atop the stove, careful to protect his fingers from the edge of the dish.

"In the center of the table?" he asked his mother.

She pursed her lips into a tight knot. "How can you serve if it's in the middle of the table, Frederick? Put it in front of your plate. You will serve tonight."

Olivia moved a step closer. "Frederick?" she whispered.

With a look of disgust, he plopped the hot dish onto the table. "*Fred*, to you. Only my mother can get away with calling me by my formal name."

Mrs. DeVault turned on her heel. "What? Frederick is an

excellent name! You are ashamed of the name your father and I gave you?"

"No, of course not, Mother. It's just that I prefer the shortened version. It's not so . . . stiff and proper sounding."

She muttered something under her breath, then asked, "Where is Albert hiding? Does he think he's permitted to be late to the table?"

Albert strode into the room with Martha following close on his heels. He reached around and pulled her forward. "I hope you won't mind that I've invited Martha to join us, Mrs. DeVault. She stopped by Olivia's apartment and, not finding her there, decided to see if she was here. I told her we were just sitting down to supper and that—"

"Oh, stop with your rambling explanation, Albert. You know there's always plenty for one more." She flapped a linen towel in his direction. "I'm always pleased for Martha's company. Olivia, would you set another place, please?"

Soon they'd all taken their places, and Mrs. DeVault signaled for Fred to offer the blessing. Olivia liked the way Mrs. DeVault had everyone hold hands. It made her feel as though the prayer was from all of them instead of just from Fred.

After the prayer, Albert tucked his napkin into his shirt collar, just as he'd done when a little boy. It hung in front of him like a triangular bib, but Martha seemed not to care a whit. "Any word from Mrs. Hornsby, Olivia?" he asked.

Fred spooned a large serving of the pie onto Albert's plate. The inviting fragrance of the meat and vegetables drifted toward Olivia as she passed the plate of food to her cousin. "No, I've not yet had any word from Charlotte."

Once Fred had finished serving all of them, Martha dipped

her fork into the pie. "I think you should consider finding a more permanent place for the baby. After all, you can't continue to care for him. He'd be better off with a mother and a father."

Olivia's breath caught. She placed a hand to her bodice. "He's not a sack of flour that I can drop on someone's doorstep."

Martha apologized, but her words of regret sounded hollow. Moreover, her eyes betrayed what she truly thought: Olivia should take Morgan to the orphanage in Chicago where they *might* find him a home. Martha sounded just like Chef René.

Olivia knew that placing Morgan in an orphanage wouldn't guarantee him a nice home with a mother and father. She'd seen some of the orphanages in London where many children remained until they were old enough to be sent into the factories to earn a few quid. For now, at least, it was better if the baby remained with her.

She thrust out her chin. "I'll keep him with me for a while longer. Charlotte may yet return. I've even considered giving up my position at the hotel if necessary."

Martha flashed a pitying look. "Really, Olivia. Don't be foolish. How would you support yourself and the child? Wasn't Mrs. Hornsby paying a portion of your rent? Anyway, if you don't work for the company, you can't live in Pullman. I thought it was your dream to be a chef." With a woeful grimace, she wiped the corners of her mouth. "Do you plan to give up your dream and leave Pullman? How will you survive?" She dropped her fork and stared at Olivia, bug-eyed. "Unless you plan to wed in the near future."

Heat traveled up Olivia's neck and spread across her cheeks as she remembered the conversation with Mr. Howard earlier in the day. Had Martha been listening in the hallway outside Chef René's office? Could she have heard Mr. Howard's proposal?

Fred stared at her, and she longed to escape his questioning eyes. Was he thinking of her comment earlier in the day when she had mentioned a proposal? She could only pray he wouldn't ask. She didn't want to lie.

Chapter Twenty-Two

For the fourth time within a two-hour period, Olivia trudged up the long flights of stairs leading to the top floor of the Arcade. Everything appeared to be in readiness. The crystallized flowers added a perfect touch to the simple decorations Chef René had insisted upon. They shimmered in the glow of the copious candelabra strategically situated throughout the lodge rooms on the third floor of the Arcade. On September 24, Mrs. Pullman had sent word of her decision to change the location for her tea. She had suddenly decided she disliked the idea of having her guests divided between the ladies' reading room and the dining room. With the hotel lobby located directly between the two rooms, she had determined the arrangement would be *unacceptable*. At least that's the word Chef René had used when he advised Olivia. They'd been left with only a week to make the necessary adjustments, and the logistics were exhausting.

Specific members of the kitchen staff and the wait staff had been assigned to assist Olivia, and loaded wagons had transported many of the amenities that would be needed for the party. In addition, Chef René had recruited a host of young men to carry the items up the sweeping staircases to the third floor—for a fee, of course.

Like all of the formal buildings in Pullman, the lodge rooms were luxurious. Once decorated, they provided an excellent ambiance. Olivia checked the clock. The guests would arrive in less than an hour. Chef René had promised that the ice sculptures, surrounded by linen towels and wrapped in hay, would depart the hotel kitchen a half hour before the first guests were due to arrive. *"This will allow sufficient time for delivery and proper placement on the tables,"* he'd said. She would have preferred an earlier arrival, but from the set of his jaw, she knew he would brook no argument.

The waiters in their starched white shirts, freshly pressed jackets, and creased pants were lined up in readiness while the kitchen staff flurried in the Moose Lodge room at the far end of the hall—Olivia's choice for a makeshift storage and preparation room. The ornate chairs and furnishings had been moved into the other rooms to provide additional seating.

Now she could only hope the staff had remembered all of the utensils and supplies needed. Should an emergency arise, she would keep two boys, Walter and John, at the ready to fetch anything needed.

"Here come the ice sculptures. Hey, Thomas! Up here." Walter was leaning out of a third-floor window while hollering to one of his friends on the wagon. Olivia hoped none of the elegant guests who were arriving for the festivities had observed Walter's unceremonious behavior.

She yanked the stripling's shirt and motioned him back

inside. "The town is awash with distinguished guests, Walter. Do *not* hang out the windows and yell at your friends like a young ruffian."

With a hearty laugh, Walter moved away from the window. "If I can't holler at my friends, can I at least toss some water on my enemies?" He slapped his leg and guffawed.

Chef René appeared just then and pinched the boy's ear between his finger and thumb. "Whom do you think you are speaking to, Walter? Miss Mott is my assistant, and you will treat her with proper respect. Do you understand?"

Walter squirmed and wriggled as he lifted onto his toes, likely hoping to relieve the pressure on his right ear. "Yes, Chef René."

The chef released the boy and pointed toward the door. "Now go and help carry the ice sculptures. And don't stumble. If you drop them, there will be no pay for you!"

The bug-eyed boy raced from the room with Chef René's ominous warning following him out the door.

"You've become quite the tyrant," Olivia observed with a twinkle in her eyes. "I didn't even know you were in the room until I heard you bellowing at young Walter. He must be frightened out of his wits."

"Ha! It would take more than a pinched ear and a stern warning to alarm him. The boy needs a father's direction to guide him. Unfortunately, his father is no longer living, and his mother is busy trying to earn a living for the family." He waved his hand. "We don't have time to discuss Walter Young's troubles. I can't stay long, but I wanted to ensure everything is in order."

Olivia knew why he'd truly arrived: he wanted to make

certain she'd properly placed the mirrors that would reflect light on his ice sculptures. And, of course, he wanted to be the one to position the creations on the tables. Not that she faulted him. He accompanied her throughout the rooms, and when he'd finished the tour, he took hold of her shoulders and placed a fleeting kiss on each cheek.

"*Formidable!* You have surpassed my expectations, Miss Mott. You have created elegance." As the boys carried the first of the carvings up the steps, he glowed with satisfaction. "After the ice sculptures are in place, Mrs. Pullman will never again mention the idea of themes for her social events."

The young men had received their instructions before departing the hotel, and all remnants of hay had been removed from Chef René's creations before they ascended the stairs. Olivia remained in the background while he orchestrated the final maneuvers and strategically positioned each of the swans on the smaller tables. When the final sculpture was ready to be unveiled, he motioned her forward.

Slowly he removed the toweling. Olivia gasped. In the center of the large serving table sat a perfect ice replica of Hotel Florence. She grasped the older man's arm. "It's beautiful, Chef René! Mrs. Pullman will be delighted."

"Oui!" He stepped back to take in the entire setting. He pointed to the far end of the hallway. "Even with that awful sign that says *Moose Lodge*, we have managed to create elegance, Miss Mott."

With an admonition to keep the trays filled and the tea hot, he bid her good-bye and lumbered off to prepare an elegant supper for the many guests and dignitaries visiting Pullman for the several days of festivities. Mrs. Randolph Morgan had been among the guests slated to attend today's tea, and Olivia wondered if both she and her husband would be in Pullman for the entire weekend. Would Mr. Morgan chat and exchange pleasantries with the earl and countess? Would he mention Charlotte's presence in Pullman? The thought all but knocked her to her knees. Before this moment, she'd not considered the idea. Had Charlotte feared Randolph might reveal her presence in Pullman and avow she had wrongfully accused him?

"Miss Mott. *Miss Mott!*" One of the waiters tapped her shoulder and pulled her from her introspection. "Mrs. Pullman is arriving." All thoughts of Randolph Morgan vanished from her mind, and Olivia assumed her position beside the polished cherry balustrade at the top of the wide staircase to await Mrs. Pullman's appearance.

The staff stood at attention, their eyes fixed upon the stairway. Moments later, attired in a plum gown accented with crystal beads and a stand-up collar, Mrs. Pullman appeared with her husband at her side. With wrist flounces and a jabot of ecru lace, Mrs. Pullman was the epitome of beauty and grace. Then, before Olivia had completed her assessment of the ensemble, she caught sight of an aristocratic couple following Mr. and Mrs. Pullman. It was the Earl and Countess of Lanshire. Olivia clutched the cool wood of the banister and inhaled deeply. She didn't want to faint. How she wished Chef René hadn't departed. She wanted nothing more than to escape into the recesses of the back room and hide. Without thinking, she uttered a silent prayer. *I know I don't deserve it, but could you help me through this? Please?*

Not one of the foursome acknowledged Olivia's presence as they passed by. Perhaps God had heard her prayer. The thought comforted her. She followed at a distance while the group made their way around the rooms, surveying the tables and occasionally murmuring a comment. When they had finished their rounds, Mrs. Pullman turned to speak with the countess. Olivia held her breath, fearful the woman would disapprove of the décor, for the countess was renowned for her impeccable taste. One word of censure could signify disaster for the chosen design.

The countess scanned the room one final time. "Exquisite!"

Mrs. Pullman beamed at the praise.

"The ice carving of the hotel is a superb focal point for this event," the countess continued, gesturing with her gloved hand. "I couldn't have suggested anything more perfect. I'm pleased you didn't choose to use some tedious theme like so many of your American counterparts. The practice never was completely embraced in European social circles and is utterly *taboo* this season." Mrs. Pullman flushed at the praise. "But, of course, you already knew that, didn't you, for your tables are exquisite. The crystallized flowers add a perfect touch."

Mrs. Pullman waved Olivia forward. Both the earl and Mr. Pullman had stepped to the other side of the hall and were engrossed in conversation, obviously uninterested in conversing further about the décor. Olivia momentarily gave thought to retreating from the building. Both Mrs. Pullman and the countess were staring at her, but she couldn't force her feet to move any more rapidly.

With charming grace, Mrs. Pullman grasped Olivia's hand. "I believe you may remember this talented young woman?"

The countess frowned as her gaze traveled from the tip of Olivia's white toque to the shine on her black leather shoes and then returned. She peered into Olivia's eyes. How Olivia wanted to turn away, yet she dared not.

The older woman slowly shook her head. "I'm sorry, girl. I don't believe I recognize you. Your name?"

"Olivia Mott. I was employed in your kitchens at Lanshire Hall." Olivia curtsied and forced a smile. "Of course, Chef Mallard conducted all meetings with you, so we never actually met."

From all appearances, Olivia determined the countess was pleased she didn't have to think further on the matter. And Olivia was thankful to have the situation so easily resolved. At least it *had* been resolved until Mr. Pullman strode across the room, the earl at his side.

"I'd wager you were sorry to lose this fine young lady as a chef in your kitchen," Mr. Pullman commented. "However, she's a testament to the fine training given at Lanshire Hall. I hired her based upon your excellent letter of recommendation, Countess."

At a loss for words, the countess glanced at her husband.

The earl shrugged his shoulders. "Mr. Pullman has asked me to join him for a meeting with some other investors," he said. "I'll join you back in our rooms before supper?"

Olivia took the opportunity to slip away while the foursome discussed their plans. The guests were ascending the staircase as she scurried down the hallway and into the preparation room, where she finally exhaled a sigh. After a final review of the serving trays, she dispatched the waiters. One thing was certain: for the rest of the day, she would remain with the kitchen staff in the Moose Lodge meeting room.

Olivia dropped into bed exhausted. She shifted positions, but sleep wouldn't come. Too many thoughts cluttered her mind. The remainder of the day had passed in a whirlwind, but there had been no further dealings with the countess.

She stared at the ceiling, remembering Mrs. Pullman's grand entrance into the preparation room at the conclusion of the tea. The older woman's effusive compliments had embarrassed Olivia. In order to divert attention away from herself, she had eloquently praised the staff. After hearing her acclaim for the workers, Mrs. Pullman promised each of them that a small bonus would be added to their pay the following week. The staff had offered her a hearty cheer once the guests had departed. Olivia grinned, remembering how Walter, using flowers from the table decorations, had fashioned a daisy chain, placed it atop her toque, and declared her their champion.

She drifted into a restless sleep after reminding herself she must keep to the kitchen tomorrow. Although most of the guests would be attending the regatta and athletic games, a few might linger behind. She would take no chance of further contact with the countess.

Fred had hoped Olivia could be in the grandstands or along the waterfront cheering him on during the sculling or the baseball game, but he knew she would be hard at work in the kitchen. There would be no time off for those employees required to take care of preparations and accommodations for the guests. However, the men participating in the games were excused from work all day on Saturday.

The oarsmen had been at the island since early morning and

now were anxious to begin the first sprint of the day. The contestants held their boats steady at the starting line. Mr. Pullman, Mr. Howard, and a number of other dignitaries stood together near the water's edge. Though the race could be observed from the grandstands, most spectators enjoyed cheering their favorite teams from the waterfront.

Mr. Pullman made it a point to station his group near the finish line so that he could congratulate and hand out medals to the winning team. His guests and a few of the company supervisors, all clad in look-alike dark suits, white shirts, and ties, circled around their host. Mr. Pullman's expectations were high. He predicted the Pullman teams would win or place in the top three of every race or game this day.

Fred cared little if he pleased Mr. Pullman, but he did harbor concern for his teammates, for jobs could be affected when losses occurred. Right or wrong, some of the participating employees had been hired solely based upon their athletic prowess, and George Pullman expected to be rewarded. As with everything else, the town's namesake left little to chance.

The gun sounded. Fred hoped for a cohesive start that would allow their team to quickly build momentum. They completed six partial strokes in a three-quarter slide followed by a quick cadence of half, half, three-quarters, three-quarters, and then a full-length stroke. The moment the full-length stroke had been completed, they moved into their high ten before settling into a slower stroke tempo. As they neared the finish, the Pullman team remained slightly ahead of a team that had traveled from St. Louis to participate.

In a desperate voice, the coxswain of the St. Louis team called for a flutter. Instead of boosting the men to a win, the demanding strokes further exhausted his team, and the Pullman team stroked to a relatively easy win. Once on shore, they were greeted with cheers and jubilation, along with the presentation of their medals by Mr. Pullman.

Although many of the supervisors participated in the games, Fred had never seen Mr. Howard take to the playing field or join the oarsmen or sailors on the water. He encouraged the workers and often spoke of his own desire to participate, but thus far he'd not done so, often stating his work kept him from practice. Fred wondered how he managed to eke out time to escort Olivia when he didn't have sufficient time to take to the practice field.

Fred moved down the line, and Mr. Howard extended his hand in congratulations. "Good job, Fred. Let's hope you do as well in the baseball game this afternoon."

Fred accompanied Albert to the athletic field and wondered if Mr. Howard's comment had carried an ominous message. Perhaps he was overreacting, yet why had the comment been directed solely at him? Fred slapped Albert on the shoulder as they ambled along. "Our team worked well today, don't you think?"

Albert grinned and held his medal aloft. "Absolutely. We pulled out a victory!"

"For Mr. Pullman, too. Did you think there was a warning of some kind in Mr. Howard's comment?"

"You mean about winning the baseball game?"

Fred frowned and nodded.

Albert laughed. "You worry too much, Fred. You need to quit looking for trouble around every corner." He clasped his hand on Fred's shoulder. "Besides, we're going to win, so there's no need for concern."

They stopped at a grove of trees along one end of the field and found a spot to relax and enjoy the refreshing breeze wafting across the lake. Families strolled by carrying picnic baskets laden with food for their noonday meals while children raced back and forth, urging their parents on at each event.

Soon Mrs. DeVault arrived with a basket of food and cool drinks for them. When they'd finished eating, the two men sauntered to the far side of the grandstands to watch a rival game before taking to the field to play the winner. Mrs. DeVault headed off for the grandstands.

"They're good," Fred declared when the game ended. The winning team was from a small town in Indiana, and they'd never before participated in the games. "Seems they've come with the intent of taking home a medal."

Albert stood up and brushed the grass from his uniform. "Well, we'll have to show them we're made of stronger stuff than the team they just trounced. And we'll have the advantage of being rested."

A short time later the Pullman team ran out onto the field. Albert's words rang in Fred's ears throughout the game, energizing him, and when they entered the final inning, the score was tied. The crowd rose and roared in anticipation as John Burke came up to bat for the Pullman team. The first ball whooshed past him, and the umpire called a strike. John stepped away from the plate, hit the dirt from his shoes with the tip of the bat, and then returned. This time the bat connected with a loud crack and sent the ball flying into the grandstands. John's home run was the final score of the game. The Pullman team won by a single run.

Chapter Twenty-Three

There was much Fred didn't know or understand about Olivia, and he'd hoped Albert would shed a ray of light on some of her behavior. He'd waited until they were alone to broach the topic. Unfortunately, the fact that Albert and Olivia were cousins hadn't been of great assistance. Albert had been able to relate that Olivia had grown up without a mother and that she hadn't shared a close relationship with her father, but Olivia had already told Fred that much. It was her secretive nature that baffled him.

She'd been reticent to share much about her personal life or her work at Lanshire Hall. Yet her work at Hotel Florence seemed of great import to her. Why would she hesitate to discuss her position at Lanshire Hall? He thought her achievements should be a topic of great pride, one she'd wish to elaborate upon. At first he'd decided she didn't want to appear boastful, for by his measure, she was a humble young lady. However, he could see no reason for her to withhold so many details. It all seemed peculiar to him.

He'd even spoken to his mother about his lack of success in learning much about her. In her wisdom, she had advised that he should move slowly. She thought Olivia so wounded by her past that it might take years before she would feel comfortable sharing all of her history.

His mother's words had evoked a deeper thankfulness in Fred for his family. They had never had much money, but there had always been a great deal of love. Love for each other and a deep love for God. Guided by his parents' instruction, he had come to faith early in life. And so it had caught him by surprise when he'd become angry with God after his father's death. For two years he'd wrestled with his grief, and though he continued to miss his father dearly, he had finally accepted God's will and returned to the foundations of his faith.

Hoping Olivia would come to trust him, he had shared the tumultuous events of his past with her one sunny afternoon as they'd walked along the Calumet River. But his attempts to put her at ease had fallen short. Perhaps tonight would prove more successful. With the conclusion of the athletic activities and Mrs. Pullman's fancy tea, he hoped Olivia would be pleased with his invitation today. He'd been scrimping and saving for weeks in order to afford the events he'd planned for their outing. Even Chef René had offered his cooperation and agreed Olivia could depart work earlier than usual on Saturday. His mother had agreed to care for young Morgan, but she had warned him he ought not be disappointed if Olivia didn't want to go into the city. Still, he hoped she would accept his offer.

He mustered his courage as he walked off to meet her at the hotel. Though there had been no further sightings of Eddie

Calhoun, Fred continued to maintain a watchful eye. He hoped his presence established a sense of protection that had forced the young hooligan to abandon his menacing ways. In some ways, however, he was thankful for Eddie's miscreant behavior, for Fred enjoyed walking Olivia home from work each evening.

Olivia was pacing in front of the rocking chairs that lined the hotel's wraparound front porch where guests whiled away their leisure afternoons reading a book or visiting with one another. She waved and descended the steps. Fred hurried to meet her. Concern shone in her soft brown eyes as she came alongside and quickened her pace.

He tugged on her hand and laughed. "We're not in training for a race, are we?"

She slowed only slightly and shook her head.

"Difficulty at work today?"

"I thought we'd seen the last of this barrage of guests, but Chef René tells me some of them plan to return in a couple of weeks."

"After successfully preparing an elegant tea for all those finicky socialites, you will have no problem. You and Chef René should count it a compliment."

He had hoped his lighthearted banter would cheer her, but when she didn't respond, he wondered if there was more to her mood than an onslaught of guests. Now he wasn't certain if his invitation would be met with a cheerful response or an immediate refusal. He considered waiting until tomorrow, yet proper etiquette required more than a day's notice.

He decided to go ahead. Reaching into his pocket, he produced two tickets to *Hearts of Oak,* a play scheduled to open in Chicago's Auditorium Theater. He handed them to Olivia.

"Look what I've purchased for us."

She tipped her head and gave him a sidelong glance, then studied the tickets. Before she could offer an objection, he turned around and walked backwards like a schoolboy while he told her he'd made arrangements for Morgan's care and for her early departure from work on Saturday.

"I hope you won't think I overstepped my bounds. My plan was to relieve you of any worry so that you could simply enjoy the outing." He raked his fingers through his hair while he awaited her answer.

"You had best turn around and watch where you're going before you fall and hurt yourself."

He took her banter as a good sign and pointed to the tickets she continued to hold between her fingers. "I'd be willing to fall flat on my back if it meant you'd agree to join me for supper and accompany me to the theater."

"I can't let you do that, Fred. The cost is far too much. These tickets alone—"

"I've invited you to be my guest, and I wouldn't have done so if I couldn't afford the expense. The tickets have already been paid for." He grasped her hand, unconcerned what any passerby might think. "Please say you'll accept my invitation, Olivia."

"How could I refuse?"

Without thinking, Fred put his arm around her shoulder and hugged her close. "I'd shout for joy, but it would likely bring all of the women and children out to gawk at us."

She laughed at his remark, delighted he'd planned a special outing for the two of them. And his embrace evoked emotions that surprised her. He held her close to his side in a way that made her feel they belonged together. For the first time in years, the ache of loneliness lessened its hold, and she secretly hoped he wouldn't release her. She liked this sensation of belonging—and she liked Fred even more.

Chapter Twenty-Four

A twinge of guilt assailed Olivia as she fingered the silk and taffeta gowns of differing styles and colors. These dresses, the very finest of Charlotte's attire, had been tightly stuffed into one of her three wardrobes. Truth be told, the woman could have filled another one had there been space for an additional piece of furniture in the bedroom.

Though Charlotte's wardrobes had overflowed, none of the clothing had fit her for more than a few weeks after their arrival. And the dresses still hadn't fit her after Morgan's birth. Olivia didn't know if the contents of the wardrobes had been left behind because they were useless to Charlotte or because Charlotte planned to return. She hoped it would prove to be the latter, though as the days progressed, Olivia had become apprehensive. If Charlotte had departed only to avoid meeting her parents, she should have been back by now. Olivia found herself torn by the decision that must be made.

She placed a gown the shade of ripened wheat across the

bed. After spreading the skirt and stepping across the room, she assessed her choice. Yes, it would be perfect! With her brunette hair fashioned in soft curls and Charlotte's pale brown cashmere wrap around her shoulders, she should look as fashionable as any lady attending the theater this evening. Perhaps more so, thanks to Charlotte's excellent taste.

An hour later, she glanced at the clock and forced her fingers to move more quickly at fashioning her curls. She thought she'd given herself ample time to prepare, but she'd not included the time she had needed to press the skirt of her dress. She was shoving the final pins into her hair when she heard Mrs. DeVault's distinctive knock on the front door, a precaution devised by Fred to protect her from possible problems with Eddie. She hurried to the door with the cashmere wrap over her arm and a beaded reticule in her hand.

Fred stood beside his mother in the doorway, wearing his dark blue Sunday suit and carrying a black topcoat and derby. He looked most handsome with his wavy hair slicked and combed to the side.

She felt the warmth of a blush rise in her cheeks as he approvingly assessed her. "Do come in. Morgan is asleep and shouldn't awaken for another half hour or so."

Mrs. DeVault unpinned her hat and dropped it on one of the hooks in the hallway. "You two go on and catch your train so you're not late. I think I can handle young Morgan without instructions. I *do* look after him most every day."

Olivia giggled as she nodded her agreement. "Thank you so much—"

"No need to thank me now. I can hear the train whistle in the distance." She patted Olivia on the shoulder. "Off with you and have a fine time. I'll want to hear all the lovely details of the theater over supper tomorrow."

Neither of them responded as they departed. Outside, they greeted several couples passing by, and Olivia couldn't help but notice the admiring looks she and Fred received. One young girl commented to her mother how much she liked Olivia's gown.

Fred tilted his head closer. "I agree the dress is pretty, but the lady wearing it is beautiful, both inside and out."

Feelings of guilt attacked her, filling her thoughts with self-condemnation. Fred wouldn't think her so beautiful if he knew the truth about her. God may have forgiven her, but she doubted that Fred would absolve her of her ugly secrets so readily. They boarded the train and took their seats, her mind still fraught with guilt.

He leaned close and rested his arm alongside hers. "Is that one of Mrs. Hornsby's dresses?" His voice was no more than a whisper, and she suspected he didn't want to embarrass her with his question.

"Yes. Since she encouraged me to wear her dresses before her abrupt departure, I've taken the liberty of wearing this one without her permission."

"I'm sure she wouldn't mind. Furthermore, I'm certain she wouldn't look half so wonderful as you in the dress."

His words of praise were more than she could imagine. Someone who believed she looked finer than Lady Charlotte? The idea anyone would compare her favorably to Charlotte would have seemed preposterous less than a year ago. "Thank you, Fred."

As the train pulled out of the station and slowly gained speed, Fred brought up her work at Lanshire Hall. She wasn't sure what had suddenly sparked his inquiry into her past, but she soon found herself tiptoeing around each of his questions. She truly didn't want to tell any further lies. If this discussion continued, she'd have another list of lies to be forgiven before they ever arrived in Chicago.

In utter frustration, she looked out the window and commented on the weather and scenery. Shades of evening were falling across the flat prairie, and the setting sun reflected off Lake Michigan in a blaze of rusty gold. Her efforts were soon rewarded when Fred pointed out several barges on the lake. As they continued the short journey into Chicago, he didn't miss the opportunity to direct her attention to the same luxurious homes she had seen when she had traveled to Pullman with Lady Charlotte.

"They are lovely, aren't they?" she said.

He grimaced at the sight. "The rich should be ashamed of their opulence. They compete for the biggest and best home while their workers struggle to get by."

Olivia didn't want their evening ruined by a discussion of the wealthy capitalists who lived in Chicago's finest section of town. Instead of commenting, she merely nodded, relieved when the train's shrill whistle announced their arrival a few minutes later. Although the idea of once again navigating the streets of Chicago unsettled her a bit, Olivia was confident in Fred's ability. He exuded a sense of self-assurance that enabled her to trust him.

The journey from the train depot to the theater didn't seem nearly so harrowing as her previous trip to Chicago. Either she was becoming more accustomed to the hubbub of the city and what to expect, or Fred had a calming effect upon her.

Fred removed the tickets from his jacket pocket when they neared the auditorium. "I do wish you would have agreed to supper."

Olivia removed Charlotte's gloves from her reticule and slid her hands inside. She fastened the small buttons at the wrist and straightened her shoulders. "I couldn't permit you to spend so much. Furthermore, your mother is spending too many hours already caring for Morgan. It would be unfair to ask more of her. After Charlotte returns—"

"Yes. We'll come to the city and have supper during the holidays. Chicago is quite festive then. The stores are richly decorated to entice the shoppers, and more of the buildings for the Columbian Exposition will have been completed by then, too. When the Exposition opens, you must promise to attend with me."

"Oh, I would very much enjoy that. I've been hearing bits and pieces of information from hotel visitors about the plans and expectations. It all sounds so grand and exciting." She placed her hand in the crook of Fred's arm, and they entered the lobby.

Though the outside of the enormous auditorium was of a simplistic design, Olivia gasped as a formally attired attendant led them into the extravagantly decorated theater and directed them to their seats. Her attention was immediately drawn to the ceiling, where majestic arches, highlighted with gold leaf, and plaster reliefs, inlaid with carbon-filament lamps, gleamed like mellow gold and gave the entire theater a luminescent glow.

"What do you think? This is quite a place, isn't it?"

"Oh, Fred. I thought Mr. Pullman's theater was magnificent. But it pales in comparison." She quickly placed her gloved fingers to her lips. "I hope nobody heard me say that."

Fred laughed. "I doubt we'll see anyone we know, and if they dislike our remarks about George Pullman, let them tell him. He won't suspect they came from us. He wouldn't believe any of his factory workers could afford such a fine place as this."

She patted his arm. "Do give him credit for providing the town with a wonderful theater, Fred."

"I'll agree the theater is very nice, but we're not going to discuss work or Mr. Pullman any further this evening. Agreed?" He grinned and then pointed out the elliptical arches situated throughout the theater. "Those arches are beautiful, but would you believe there are ducts concealed inside that carry steam heat in the winter and cool air in the summer so the theater always remains comfortable?"

Olivia thought he must be teasing her. "Surely not. How could they possibly cool such a place as this?"

"It's true. The ducts carry cooled air that has been passed across blocks of ice that are sprayed with water. Rather ingenious and much more comfortable than sitting in a stifling, overheated building in midsummer."

Fred was impressed with the construction and mechanics of the vast building while Olivia marveled at the intricate architectural design. On the back of their programs, Olivia discovered a reprinting of the newspaper article that had been published regarding the opening night at the theater on October 2, 1889.

While fastidiously attired couples made their way into the theater, Olivia pointed to a sentence midway down the page. "Look at this, Fred. It says that on opening night the sidewalks around the building were carpeted, gaslit, and covered with a canopy for the over five thousand guests in attendance. Even

President Harrison was in the audience." She looked about the theater in wonder. "Just imagine. I'm attending the same theater as did the president of the United States."

He chuckled and tapped the program. "And don't forget the mayor, the governor, and the vice-president. From the sound of it, this place is nearly fine enough for the two of us."

The lights dimmed and voices hushed as the curtain opened and the play began. Even from their seats in the upper gallery, Fred and Olivia could hear the performers' voices with perfect clarity. The acting was magnificent and the costumes delightful. Olivia was enthralled and sat with rapt attention. Never before had she seen such a brilliant performance.

During the intermission, Fred purchased coffee, and they sat at a small table in the lobby, discussing the first acts of the presentation and watching the many theater attendees milling about and purchasing refreshments.

When the play had ended and the final applause quieted, the crowd slowly migrated toward the exits with murmurs of approval on their lips. As they descended the wide staircase to the lobby, Olivia took Fred's arm. She considered the evening a complete success in every aspect.

However, her mood altered when they reached the last stair and she saw Mr. Howard waving from across the lobby. He approached with a determined step. "Why, Olivia, how wonderful to see you. I thought I captured a glimpse of you from my box shortly after the intermission." Formally attired in black tie and tails, Mr. Howard seemed to assess Fred's dark blue suit before turning his full attention back to Olivia.

"I'd like the two of you to join me for a late evening dessert and coffee at the Grand Pacific Hotel dining room." He tipped his head closer as though he planned to tell them a secret. "Sometimes the actors come to the hotel dining room after their performances and visit. I believe you'd find it most enjoyable."

Before consulting with her, Fred offered regrets and mentioned their need to get home due to Morgan. But Mr. Howard didn't give up easily. He offered to arrange for their transportation home at his expense, but Fred adamantly refused to hear of it.

Once they were settled on the train, Fred grew quiet.

"Is something amiss, Fred?" Olivia asked.

He rubbed his thick, callused fingers across the back of her hand. "Mr. Howard is a better choice for you, Olivia. He can give you the things you deserve: a life filled with beautiful gowns, the opportunity to meet famous people and attend fine parties, and a better future than I ever could." He studied their entwined fingers.

His words pierced her. "Is *that* what you think of me? That I'm no more than a shallow woman interested only in pretty dresses and parties?"

Intensity darkened his blue eyes, and he released her hand. "I never said you were shallow. But it makes sense that most any woman would be interested in making a better marriage than what a Pullman factory worker can offer."

"Well, I'm not 'most any woman,' Fred. If and when I marry, it will be a marriage based upon love and respect, not upon how much finery my husband can heap upon me throughout my life."

He bowed his head for a moment. "I like that—love and

respect. And truthfulness. That's important, too, don't you agree?"

Truth. Couldn't love and respect have been enough? Why did he have to add truth? It was almost as though he knew she was hiding something. Or was it her guilt that caused her to question his motives?

She agreed. "Yes. Truth is very important." She understood that fact more than most. After all, her lies were constantly popping up to wreak havoc in her life. What would Fred do if he knew her truth? If she told him all her secrets, would he consider her a fraud and never want to see her again? *Tell him. Better sooner than later*. But the tiny voice of encouragement wasn't quite loud enough. She didn't want to lose Fred. Should he declare his love for her, she'd tell him then. But doing so now would only complicate matters. It might terminate their relationship completely. A *most* disturbing thought.

Chapter Twenty-Five

Nearly a week had passed since Fred escorted her to the theater, but the images were still vivid in Olivia's memory as she locked the front door on Friday morning and stood near the railing watching for Martha's familiar face in the predawn light. The rustling of leaves drew her attention and a trickle of fear inched through her belly. She scanned the nearby foliage but couldn't see anyone there. Most likely just the wind, she told herself.

She peered down the street, hoping to catch a glimpse of Martha. There was no one in sight, yet Martha hadn't mentioned any change in her work schedule. If she waited any longer, she would be late for work.

The snap of a branch captured her attention, and then a squirrel scampered nearby, as if to ease her fears. After gulping a quick breath, she descended the porch steps and crossed the street. She'd taken only a few strides when fallen leaves and twigs crackled behind her. Before she could turn, an arm wrapped around her body and a hand grabbed for her purse. She clung to the handle, unwilling to turn loose of the handbag or its contents. Only yesterday she'd withdrawn five dollars from the bank to make several purchases at the market after work. She would not easily hand over her hard-earned money.

In a swift, jarring move, she tilted sideways and screamed while fighting to wrest herself from the bruising hold. After several more yelps, she heard the clopping of heavy footsteps and a loud shout. Before she could catch her breath, both she and her assailant toppled to the ground. When she looked over her shoulder, her neighbor Mr. Rice held the fellow in a chokehold.

Olivia scooted away from the two men and squinted. Even in early morning shadows, she could make out the thatch of red hair. "Eddie!"

Mr. Rice pulled the young man to his feet. "What do you think you're doing, young man? I think I best take you over to the stationhouse in Kensington."

Eddie twisted around. "No, please don't do that. I'm sorry, Miss Mott. Truly I am. I was just trying to get back at you for losing my job."

Olivia detected the fear and anguish in his plea. "Let me have a few minutes alone with him, Mr. Rice."

"Are ya sure?"

Olivia bobbed her head.

"I'll watch from across the street, but you holler out if he makes one move toward you."

Olivia waited until Mr. Rice was out of earshot. "You nearly scared me to death, Eddie. And if Mr. Rice hadn't come out when he did, you would have run off with my purse. Isn't that the truth?"

His hair waved in wild abandon as he readily agreed. "Yes. But I don't have a job because of you."

"*I* wasn't the reason you were fired, Eddie. You're the one who stole the liquor."

"I know." He bowed his head. "And I'm paying for what I did. I know I shouldn't be mad at you. Trouble is, when I apply for a job, they always ask where I worked before. Then they want a recommendation. Of course I don't have one, since I was fired."

Eddie's need for a recommendation struck a chord that reminded Olivia of the forged letter she'd used to gain employment. God had forgiven her, yet a renewed guilt washed over her. "I can't help you in that regard, Eddie, but I'll agree to let you go if you promise you'll quit stalking me. Give me your word that you'll stay away from me and out of Pullman."

"You've got my word, Miss Mott. You won't see me around town again." He scratched his head. "I know I got to suffer the consequences of my wrongdoing. I'm lucky I ain't in jail."

Olivia didn't know if it was his comment about consequences, the sadness in his eyes, or her own guilty conscience, but she opened her reticule and handed him a dollar. "It's not much, but it's the most I can spare."

"Thank you, Miss Mott." He appeared embarrassed, but he tucked the money into his frayed pocket and then glanced across the street. "I'll be on my way, if it's all right."

"You go on. I'll explain to Mr. Rice."

Several hours later Olivia was bent over one of the chopping tables slicing onions, with thoughts of her talk with Eddie still fresh in her mind. While Eddie suffered the consequences of his wrongdoings, she continued her life of lies without the slightest penalty. Even Chef René had been willing to overlook her deceitful behavior. The pungent smell of the onions drifted upward, and she blinked several times to ease the stinging in her eyes. Tears rolled down her cheeks, and she wiped them on the sleeve of her white jacket.

Without warning, a hand grasped her shoulder. Startled, she lost her grip on the knife and jumped backward as it spiraled to the floor. Mr. Howard stood by her side with the knife lying beside his foot. She gasped. The blade had barely missed plunging into his shiny black shoe.

Heart racing, she leaned down and picked up the knife. "I'm *so* sorry. I could have wounded you."

"You've already wounded me, Olivia." He whispered the words into her ear. Then, speaking loud enough for all to hear, he instructed her to join him in Chef René's office for a meeting. Why today? Hadn't the incident with Eddie been enough to set her nerves on edge? Now a meeting with Mr. Howard.

She followed along, wondering how she had possibly wounded Mr. Howard. Granted, the knife had come close, but it hadn't done any more than touch the sole of his shoe. Once he closed the door, she again offered an apology, but he held up his hand.

He beckoned her toward one of the chairs. "Please, no more. You've already apologized, and I'm not injured in the least."

She removed her toque and sat down. "But you said I'd wounded you."

"Perhaps I should have spoken more plainly. You've

wounded my heart, Olivia, not my foot."

She swallowed hard. Was he going to speak of his earlier marriage proposal? From beneath an errant curl that had come to rest above her left eye, she peeked at the door. How she wished she could bolt down the hallway and back to the kitchen. But she couldn't—not without Mr. Howard's permission. So she clutched the chair arms and waited to hear what he had to say.

"I was disappointed when I saw you in Chicago with Mr. DeVault." He leaned back into the thick padding of Chef René's chair. "Especially since you've declined my invitations to dinner and the theater. Every day I've hoped you would suggest we meet and continue our earlier conversation. Am I such poor company, Olivia?"

His eyes clouded with sadness, and she considered how lonely he must be without his wife to keep him company each evening. Much like her own, his life had changed without warning. She preferred to spend her free time with Fred, but she hadn't intended to hurt the man.

She picked at the frayed edge of her cuff. "You are a fine escort, Mr. Howard. A gentleman in all respects. My refusals were always truthful."

He rested his elbows on René's desk. "Then how is it you were able to overcome all obstacles and accompany Mr. DeVault to Chicago?"

"Fred took care of all the details. He arranged for his mother to care for Morgan and made certain my work schedule didn't conflict with our departure—all things that made it possible for me to easily accept his offer." She didn't add that Chef René had given her permission to leave work earlier than usual.

"I see. So will you attend the theater with *me* if I do the same?"

She now found herself boxed into a tight corner of her own making. How was she to escape? "I doubt whether Mrs. De-Vault would be agreeable to such an arrangement, and except for Charlotte and me, she's the only person who has cared for the baby."

His brows puckered, and he appeared deep in thought for a moment. "Correct me if I'm wrong, but shortly after Mrs. Hornsby's unexpected departure, I believe you mentioned the baby was left in Mrs. Rice's care. If Mrs. DeVault isn't willing or is unavailable, perhaps Mrs. Rice would be an acceptable alternate. The woman has children of her own, does she not?"

Olivia thought of Mr. Rice's angry voice as he hollered at his own children and his impatience when Morgan would cry. "Possibly. Though I don't think Mr. Rice likes the idea of extra children in the house. Mrs. Rice only agreed to help when her husband was at work."

"Well, I suppose I had best put on my thinking cap and locate a suitable person to care for the lad. I didn't plan to press you for an answer regarding my marriage proposal, but I do hope you are keeping it under consideration."

He said he wasn't pushing for a response, but she heard the insistent question in his voice. She couldn't bear to look at him, for his words were filled with a pleading despair that she'd likely see reflected in his eyes. She didn't want to hurt him any further, yet she couldn't agree. The silence in the room was deafening. When he finally spoke, it startled her.

"My dear Olivia, you'll be hard pressed to continue renting the row house with your income. And I doubt if Mrs. DeVault plans to continue caring for Morgan indefinitely." He leaned forward and stretched his arms across the desk. "Surely you've accepted the fact that Mrs. Hornsby is not going to return. She's abandoned the child and she's abandoned you. I'm offering you and the child a wonderful future." He sighed. "Would it be so difficult to love me?"

She stared at her folded hands and shrugged. "I'm not an expert in matters of the heart, Mr. Howard, but I would never marry a man unless I truly loved him."

"The only way you can discover your feelings is if you and I become better acquainted. And the only way for that to occur is for you to agree to spend time with me. I'm certain I can locate a suitable person to care for Morgan." Mr. Howard pressed his open hands atop the desk and stood.

Olivia considered his statement. "Please understand that I won't leave Morgan with anyone I don't consider capable of offering excellent care. I'd have to be acquainted with the person."

She stepped toward the door, surprised when he casually grasped her hand. He turned the knob and escorted her into the hallway.

"Of course. And I admire your commitment to the child." Before releasing her, he brushed a kiss on the back of her hand. "You might advise Chef René that the Earl and Countess of Lanshire are expected to return on Monday. He may want to make some special dishes during their stay."

His news erased the vexation that she'd experienced when he had kissed her hand. "That's only a few days away." Her voice sounded like a croaking bullfrog.

"Indeed. But Chef René is accustomed to preparing for

royalty. He needs little notice." With a brief wave, he departed using the side door.

She watched out the window until he passed through the iron gates and onward toward the administrative offices. She would talk to Fred and explain what had occurred. Surely he would understand her dilemma and offer sound advice. Of greater concern was the news that Charlotte's parents were returning. She had secretly hoped they would change their plans and decide against another visit to Pullman. She'd have to keep to the kitchen once they arrived.

As soon as Mr. Howard disappeared from sight, she turned away from the window. She must deliver the news to Chef René.

The chef wasn't nearly as composed as Mr. Howard had predicted. Moreover, he acted as though the entire idea of the returning nobility was her fault. He banged his pots and pans, barked orders at the staff, and overcooked the fish course, which he then insisted upon re-creating.

When Olivia could take no more, she yanked on his sleeve. "I didn't invite them, you know. I'm only relaying the message from Mr. Howard. The kitchen staff is not to blame, either."

He plopped his ample body onto a nearby chair. "Oui, I know it is not your fault, but this makes me angry. I have already planned next week's meals for the hotel guests. With nobility here, the menu will need to be changed. I cannot serve them the normal fare." His heavy jowls wobbled as he shook his head in disgust. "We will be prepared when they arrive, but it will take extra work. I'll need your assistance completing the menus, and you'll go to the Market Building tomorrow to alert the merchants."

While the rest of the kitchen staff prepared to depart, Olivia jotted down notes of the chef's preliminary ideas of what he would prepare and what tasks must be completed prior to preparation of the first meal. Of course, neither of them knew exactly when the earl and countess would arrive. They didn't expect the guests before breakfast on Monday, but they needed to be prepared in any event.

Though she knew Chef René wanted to continue planning, Fred was likely pacing back and forth outside, wondering when she would appear. "Please, Chef René, could we continue this in the morning? I must get home to the baby."

He sighed and waved. "Go on then. I'll work on this by myself, but be prepared for a full day of work tomorrow."

"I'll plan to stop by the Market on my way to work and tell the vendors you must have their full cooperation with fruits, vegetables, and cuts of meat."

"Non. Wait until later in the morning, after we have decided upon the menus. And you may need to come in on Sunday after your church meeting."

She wanted to shout she couldn't possibly work on Sunday afternoon, for she would be spending her afternoon with Fred and Morgan, enjoying a stroll in the park if the weather permitted. Instead, she suggested they work in earnest so they could complete their tasks on Saturday. "That way we can both attend church."

"The food—that is what is important, Miss Mott."

"Indeed, I read in the Bible that Jesus is the bread of life. Maybe going to church would be the best thing to help us with this food situation."

He waved her toward the door. "I don't need you sending

me to church, Miss Mott. As a little boy in France, my mother made sure I lit my share of altar candles. Now off with you, or I'll put you back to work."

Olivia scurried out the door before he could change his mind. Descending the steps and rounding the corner, she wondered what Chef René had looked like as a little boy lighting church candles. The thought made her grin.

Fred's collar was turned up against the cool evening air. "I was about to come inside and see if you'd left without me."

She laughed and tucked her hand into the crook of his arm, enjoying the warmth and safety she always felt when she was near him. "Problems concerning the arrival of guests next week."

While they walked, she explained about the Earl and Countess of Lanshire and Chef René's worries. But she didn't mention her meeting with Mr. Howard, his marriage proposal, or his invitation to the theater. In spite of her lateness, Fred's mood was lighthearted, and she didn't want to spoil their time together. There would be time to talk about Mr. Howard later.

Suddenly she came to an abrupt halt. "I nearly forgot to tell you what happened this morning."

Fred listened attentively while she explained the incident with Eddie. She didn't mention she'd given him money, only that she'd taken pity upon him.

"I know what you did was kind, Olivia. But I wonder if Eddie would have been so kind had Mr. Rice not come to your rescue."

She shrugged. "We'll never know. But I no longer fear him, and I'll no longer have to be looking over my shoulder when you're not around to protect me."

"Wanting to get rid of me as your evening escort, are you?"

"No. Of course not. I'd find it most pleasing if you continued to meet me after work." Surely he must realize how much she cared for him.

"Just the answer I was hoping for." When they reached the front of the house, he stopped and faced her, then cupped her face between his hands and lightly kissed her lips.

The staff had nearly completed serving breakfast Monday morning when Chef René blustered into the kitchen. "They've arrived! Mr. Beelings informs me they prefer to have their noonday meal in the private dining room. This is good news!"

Olivia understood his meaning: they needed to prepare the special dishes only for the earl and countess. Something of a more simple nature would be offered to the remaining hotel guests. As for the staff, the report signaled less drudgery in the kitchen and the probability that their workdays would end on schedule. For Olivia, it decreased the likelihood she would encounter her former employers. She could only hope the earl and countess would continue the practice during their entire stay.

"Did Mr. Billings report how long the earl and countess intend to remain in Pullman?"

"Non! They said at least three days, but who can tell with nobility? Unlike us, they can come and go at their pleasure."

She knew that was true enough, but she also recalled that the countess disliked being away from home for long periods.

During Olivia's employment at Lanshire Hall, the couple had always returned from their sojourns within six weeks. She could only hope the countess hadn't changed her perspective. The sooner they departed, the better for all concerned.

Chapter Twenty-Six

Morgan's eyelids fluttered and then drooped as he finished his bottle. He was a beautiful child, and Olivia had become much too fond of him. She'd tried hard to remain detached, but it was proving an impossible task. She kissed his soft cheek and settled him in his cradle. She was looking forward to relaxing with a good book after a second day of catering to the demands of the earl and countess.

Footsteps clattered across the wooden porch just as she was tucking Morgan's blanket around him. She tensed at the knock but quickly remembered Eddie's promise.

Still, the need for caution had been imbedded in her memory, so she peeked through the window of the front door. *The countess.* Her heart thumped so loudly she wondered if Mr. Rice might hear and bang on the wall. *Mr. Rice.* If he or his wife saw the countess, he'd be outdoors questioning her at any moment. She had best let the woman inside.

Her fingers trembled as she opened the door. "Why,

Countess. To what do I owe this honor?"

"May I come in?"

Olivia stepped aside and waved her forward. "Yes, of course." She forced a feeble smile. "I hope you'll understand that I was taken aback to see you on my porch."

The countess removed her kid gloves. She glanced at the cradle while she unfastened her cloak and handed it to Olivia. "I see you have an infant. I wasn't aware you were married."

"Oh, I'm not married," Olivia quickly responded. "Won't you please sit down?"

The countess's eyebrows arched as she took the seat offered. "I wouldn't announce that fact to the world, Miss Mott. It's certainly not something of which you should be proud."

"Oh! He's not my baby. He belongs to a friend." Olivia sat down, as well.

"I see. Well, then, let us get to the crux of why I'm here, shall we?"

Olivia scooted back in her chair while the countess fumbled in her reticule and then removed a black velvet box. She opened the lid and dangled a necklace from two fingers.

"I'm certain you will recognize this, as well as two other pieces I have in my bag."

Olivia wondered if she might lose her supper. She swallowed hard, her stomach churning. *Don't lie!* The tiny voice repeated the command several times. "Yes, I do recognize them. They belong to Lady Charlotte."

The countess narrowed her eyes. "They belong to *me*. And I have just purchased them from Mr. Capper, a jeweler in the Arcade. I'm sure you know him quite well."

Olivia shook her head. "No. I've never met the man."

The countess returned the necklace to its case and snapped it shut. "Your name is on these papers as the person who sold my jewelry, Miss Mott." She tapped the page but snapped it back when Olivia attempted to see exactly what had been written.

"I assure you, I never sold the jewelry, Countess. There is a mistake." *Tell her the truth!* "If you are willing to listen, I'll explain exactly what has occurred."

The older woman silently listened while Olivia detailed Charlotte's forced intrusion into Olivia's plan to come to America and the many problems the two of them had encountered since departing London. Though the countess appeared anxious to believe her daughter was alive, she frowned and shook her head in disbelief when Olivia revealed Charlotte had stolen and sold the jewelry and that Morgan was her grandchild.

"Impossible! You've gone too far with this story, young lady. You should be ashamed of yourself. The truth is, you worked at Lanshire Hall, you stole my jewels, and then you sold them to Mr. Capper. You're attempting to cover your own crimes by accusing my daughter." Anger shining in her eyes, the countess whacked her gloves across the arm of the settee.

Olivia flinched. "At Charlotte's instruction, I did sell two pieces in London to cover our passage. Other than that, I've had nothing to do with the sale of the jewelry. I assure you that my claims can be proved."

The countess pursed her lips and nodded. "I'll listen, but you had best have some convincing evidence."

"In order to avoid revealing her true identity, Charlotte took the name of Hornsby. Any of the neighbors can tell you she was pregnant and gave birth to Morgan. If you doubt it was

Charlotte, you'll find many of her gowns hanging in the wardrobes in her bedroom. Should you still doubt my word, you could speak privately with Randolph Morgan—he's the baby's father. Charlotte met with him right here in Pullman. Though he'd likely deny paternity, he'd possibly falter under the earl's questioning."

Suddenly Olivia remembered Charlotte's letter. She jumped up from her chair. "I do have something tangible that will prove I'm telling the truth." Without waiting for the countess to object, she hurried to the bedroom and retrieved Charlotte's letter from the bureau drawer.

All evidence of composure vanished when the countess read the letter. Her shoulders slumped, her complexion paled, and her hand trembled as she refolded the letter. "I can't deny this is Charlotte's handwriting." She bowed her head. "With the evidence you've produced, I fear I've misjudged you."

The countess glanced at the child. "Morgan? Charlotte named the infant after his father." She pinched the bridge of her nose. "I do recall that a few weeks after Mr. Morgan visited, Charlotte was ill nearly every morning, unable to partake of the morning meal."

Olivia leaned forward. "I believe she truly loved him, but—"

"But he is married."

"Yes. And already has several children."

"Where is my daughter?"

"That letter is the last I've heard from her. As you can see, she didn't advise me as to where she was going, and I have no idea of her present whereabouts. If you still doubt my word about the jewelry, I'll accompany you to the shop. The owner can't possibly identify me as the person who sold the jewels to him. However, I do admit that I benefited from the sale of your jewelry. As I earlier mentioned, Lady Charlotte paid my passage to America, and since our arrival in Pullman she has also paid a portion of the rent and expenses."

The countess remained silent, staring across the room as though she couldn't believe all she'd heard this day. The baby stirred and she looked his way again. "May I hold him?"

"Yes, of course." When she hesitated, Olivia lifted Morgan from the tiny bed and placed him in her arms. "He's quite a fine little lad, isn't he?" The infant wrinkled his nose and stretched. His eyelids fluttered opened, and he looked up at the countess.

"He has Charlotte's fair complexion and her blue eyes." She settled back on the divan and gently patted the infant. "What are we to do about you, Morgan? And how are we to find your mother?"

With those few words, it seemed the countess had accepted Morgan as a member of her family. Suddenly Olivia realized she would be parted from the child. She tamped down the feeling of panic rising in her chest. "You don't have to make a decision tonight, Countess."

"What? Oh, but we're leaving in the morning. Decisions must be made immediately. I want you and Morgan to accompany me back to the hotel. We'll talk to my husband. He'll know what should be done."

Olivia thought to argue against the plan, but she dared not disagree. She wondered if the woman planned to take custody of Morgan and then accuse her of thievery. Not once had she mentioned absolving Olivia of blame. Guilty or not, she might end up in jail.

"Come along. It's getting late and we haven't much time. Where are the baby's wraps?"

"Wraps? He doesn't have a coat, but his cap is in my room. I bundle him with a blanket if the weather turns cool." She thought it inappropriate to point out that the weather had been quite warm since the infant's birth. And though it was October, she'd made do with his cap and a blanket when she took him outdoors during the evening. A coat hadn't fit into her tight budget—especially since she'd been so generous with Eddie Calhoun.

"No jacket? What *can* you be thinking? He might contract a case of pneumonia or the croup."

"I haven't had time to purchase his winter necessities, but I had planned to acquire a warm coat by the end of the month." Olivia hurried off to retrieve the baby's cap while the countess wrapped him in the blankets.

Olivia wasn't certain what the woman expected. It wasn't as though she'd ever been responsible for an infant before. And Morgan had certainly flourished under her attention. Mrs. DeVault had even applauded her care of the baby.

She pulled back the blankets and tied the cap on Morgan's head. He was enclosed like sausage in a tight casing. Tiny beads of perspiration dotted his tiny upturned nose. Already he was too warm, but Olivia feared retribution should she attempt to remove even one of the layers.

Outside, pale grays and charcoal etched long lines across the horizon as nightfall blotted out the final hues of gold and orange from the sky. Olivia fought to keep pace with the countess's long stride. Her shorter legs and the burden of carrying the baby made the process difficult. Throughout their short journey, she lagged behind.

"We can go in through the kitchen. I have a key." Olivia panted to catch her breath.

The countess stopped and waited until Olivia was beside her. "Why on *earth* would we go through the kitchen? I am a *guest* in the hotel."

"Perhaps to avoid any prattle by the staff?" She didn't want to be seen accompanying the countess. The questions would prove innumerable and the conjecture even worse.

"I care not a whit what the staff in this hotel have to say. Do come along."

They entered through the ornate front doors, the ones through which Olivia had entered on her first day in Pullman. Mr. Billings was at the desk. Why was he working so late? She had hoped one of the members of the night staff would be on duty. She refused to look in his direction as she followed the countess to the stairway.

"Good evening, Countess. Good evening, Miss Mott." Both of them ignored his greeting. The countess was on a mission, and Olivia wouldn't give him the satisfaction of a reply.

Fortunately, Olivia was required to climb only one flight of steps. The earl and countess were assigned to the second floor, where the rooms were of the finest quality and reserved for important guests. Going up the flight of stairs, the countess didn't slow her pace. By the time they entered the sitting room in the suite, Olivia was gasping for breath. She didn't even curtsy to the earl. Instead, she hastened across the room and, still clutching the baby, dropped to the settee.

"Do sit down." The earl's sarcasm hung in the air like a

damp fog. "What is this about, my dear?" he asked his wife.

Olivia didn't attempt to rise and show proper English decorum. She was too exhausted. Though a twinge of guilt attacked, she pushed it aside and reminded herself that she was no longer employed by the Earl of Lanshire and was no longer a resident of England.

The countess sat down in the chair beside her husband. Her quiet murmuring served as a backdrop while Olivia peeled away the layered blankets and freed Morgan from his sweltering cocoon. Perspiration dotted the folds of his chubby arms, and his damp blond hair clung to his head in tiny ringlets. In spite of the heat and bouncing journey in her arms, he offered a tiny smile and cooed when she wiped his clammy face and arms with a cloth. Moments later, she recognized the anger in the earl's voice as he argued with his wife.

"Bring me the child," he commanded Olivia.

She placed the baby in the earl's arms. His features slowly softened as he looked at the child and examined him closely. "You want me to believe this is my daughter's child, but you have no knowledge of her whereabouts. Is that correct?"

"Yes, Lord Spencer." Years of training prompted her to offer a small curtsy.

Before she could offer further explanation, the countess removed Charlotte's letter from her pocket and handed it to her husband. "Don't say anything you'll regret, my dear," she whispered and reached for the baby. While the countess held Morgan in one arm, the earl read the document. Olivia remained transfixed. When he finished reading, he massaged his forehead, as though the simple act might eradicate the problem.

He finally looked up and waved Olivia toward the divan. She

backed away and pretended she couldn't hear as they discussed Morgan's future and debated the veracity of all she'd told them. Olivia fidgeted with the ties of her cloak and longed to be anywhere but in this room with her former employers.

The clock on the carved mantel ticked off the minutes at a steady rate. "Perhaps I should take Morgan home and the two of you can make your decision in private. He'll be more comfortable in his cradle."

The earl's dark eyes flashed, and Olivia scooted into the corner of the divan. She'd overstepped her bounds, speaking when she'd not been asked a direct question. Nevertheless, she had chores at home needing her attention before bedtime. A matter that would be difficult for the earl and countess to understand. They had servants to perform any daily tasks.

"We will take the child home with us—to London. Neither my wife nor I can refute the proof you've offered. I do hope you aren't withholding information regarding Charlotte's whereabouts." One of his bushy eyebrows arched.

"I would tell you if I knew anything further."

He nodded. "I would prefer to remain and personally take charge of a search for her, but my obligations at court forbid my delay. We must depart as scheduled."

"Tomorrow?" Olivia's voice trembled.

The couple nodded in unison. "He will remain with us tonight. My wife tells me there are shops in the Arcade where any items needed for the journey can be acquired. She'll send one of her servants to make the necessary purchases."

The decision was final. Now Olivia wasn't certain that telling the truth had been such a good thing. She hadn't had sufficient time to adjust to parting with Morgan. And she still held out hope that Charlotte would return to claim her child.

She summoned her courage. "I wonder if it might be best for all concerned if you waited a few days. You could adjust to Morgan. See to his needs during the daytime while I'm working here in the hotel. I could answer any questions—"

"Enough! Were you not listening to what I said, girl? There will be no delay."

The earl's command silenced her.

"We will depart in the morning as planned. My wife and our staff can adequately care for the child."

Olivia knew she had no choice but to acquiesce. "I am pleased Morgan will be in good hands with a family that loves him. And if Lady Charlotte should return?"

"I will be making arrangements before we depart Chicago tomorrow. You will be advised if anything is expected of you regarding our daughter." Worry tightened the earl's features, and he turned his attention back to the infant.

"I would be pleased to fetch Morgan's cradle. Lady Charlotte purchased it for him only weeks before his birth."

The countess gently touched her husband's arm. "Please, my dear? I would like to take the cradle with us."

He hesitated but then agreed. "Miss Mott, have you written any of your relatives at home about my daughter or the child?"

Olivia shook her head.

"The countess tells me Mr. Morgan denies he fathered the child. Did Charlotte speak to anyone else regarding Mr. Morgan's involvement? Mr. Pullman or Mr. Howard, perhaps?"

"Not to my knowledge. She did write a letter to Mr. Morgan after the baby's birth. She had the missive delivered to his office, but I'm unaware of the contents."

He hadn't yet advised what she was to tell anyone who questioned her about the child. Mr. Billings would want details, especially when he saw the earl and countess depart with the infant tomorrow morning.

"What would you prefer I tell anyone who might inquire about the infant?"

The earl stiffened and squared his shoulders. "Tell them it's none of their business, and if they have further questions, they may direct them to me." He rang a bell, and one of the servants immediately appeared from the adjoining room. "Go along with Miss Mott and retrieve the cradle she gives you. Bring it back to our rooms posthaste. The child needs a proper place to sleep."

Morgan was nestled in the arms of the countess, and Olivia looked longingly in their direction. "Might I hold him one final time, Lord Spencer?"

The earl muttered and waved her toward his wife. "Of course. Say your good-byes to the child."

Olivia gathered Morgan into her arms and kissed his chubby cheeks. She whispered words of love into his tiny ear and then quietly sang him a soft lullaby. Suddenly, she no longer cared that mending and laundry needed to be completed before morning. Morgan cooed and gurgled, and she beamed at him. Such a lovely child.

The countess removed the baby from her arms. "I know this is difficult for you, but we have much to accomplish if we are to depart on schedule tomorrow morning."

"Yes, of course." Olivia placed one final kiss on Morgan's forehead and then motioned for the servant girl to follow her. "I wish you all a safe journey back to England."

A surprising tenderness shone in the earl's eyes as he acknowledged her. "And we thank you for the fine care you've provided the boy, Miss Mott."

Olivia offered a deep curtsy. "It was my great pleasure, Lord Spencer."

As Olivia and the servant descended the stairway, Mr. Billings rushed toward the front desk. With his glasses perched across his thick nose, he leaned across the front counter, lying in wait to attack. She'd barely touched one foot to the bottom step when he waved his lanky arm in a wide circle, motioning her to him.

She shook her head and continued walking. "I'm on an errand, Mr. Billings. I don't have time for idle chatter."

He removed his glasses and frowned but made no further attempt to detain her. However, she knew he'd seek her out tomorrow. She could hardly wait to deliver the earl's message to him.

Chapter Twenty-Seven

Except for the sounds of her own grief, the house had been much too quiet since Morgan's departure. Though Olivia had been awake most of the night, she remained uncertain what she would tell Mrs. DeVault. She'd considered going to visit last evening but had feared she would be overcome by her tears and a lack of words.

Tell the truth—no more and no less. The same message had been playing over and over in her head since the servant left with Morgan's cradle last evening. She wanted to keep her promise to God and tell the truth. She uttered a silent prayer that Mrs. DeVault wouldn't ask too many questions.

The older woman arrived with her usual smile and the daily weather report. As she entered the parlor, she scanned the room and then turned to Olivia. "Your eyes are puffy and red, child. Tell me what's wrong." She unfastened her cloak and frowned. "Did you leave Morgan in your bedroom this morning?"

"No. Morgan is gone." Tears threatened and a lump formed

in her throat as she whispered the words. She gathered her courage and forced herself to continue. "Surprisingly, the Earl and Countess of Lanshire spoke to me about their desire to rear Morgan as their own child. They plan to depart this morning for their return journey to London." Her lips quivered as she inhaled deeply.

Mrs. DeVault gasped and then placed her open hand across her lips. "So *that's* why your eyes are swollen. You've been awake and crying most of the night."

Olivia didn't want to talk about the difficult night she'd endured. If she did, she'd begin crying and never regain control. "He needed the stability of a permanent home. Even you had mentioned the fact that I couldn't continue to care for him indefinitely."

"But with a family of nobility? At their age, I can't imagine why they would want the child."

Olivia glanced at the clock, hoping Mrs. DeVault would take her cue. "Who knows what causes people to make such decisions? I know they will provide the boy with an infinitely better life than I could have hoped to give him." Lifting her cape from the divan, she tossed it about her shoulders, thankful when Mrs. DeVault followed suit.

Offering a feeble smile, the older woman walked alongside Olivia to the front door. "I'll need to get back home and take the remainder of the day to remember how I filled the hours before young Morgan came into my life."

Olivia held her emotions in check. "I do appreciate all the assistance you've provided. I couldn't have done it without you. I believe this is the proper decision for the lad."

Mrs. DeVault swooped Olivia into a warm embrace. "How

selfish of me! Here I should be offering you sympathy, and I'm tied in a knot worrying about myself." She loosened her embrace but continued to pat Olivia's hand. "It's going to take a while for you to adjust to life without the boy. You must come over to the house and spend your evenings with us. Too much time alone isn't good, and I don't want to have you moping about."

Olivia followed Mrs. DeVault to the porch and locked the door. Once they descended the front steps, they headed off in opposite directions. "I'm setting a place for you at the supper table. Don't disappoint me."

Olivia turned and waved. "I wouldn't think of disappointing you."

She had told the truth, and Mrs. DeVault had easily accepted her explanation. Her prayer had been answered. She smiled at the thought and then uttered another prayer. There would be many explanations to make over the next several days. She would need God's help with each one.

From the set of Chef René's jaw, she knew he would likely be the first to question her. She surmised Mr. Billings had already cornered the chef. His thick arms rested across the soft ledge provided by his paunchy stomach.

"You know I dislike seeing Mr. Beelings armed with information about my employees."

The accusation wasn't exactly what she'd anticipated. Nonetheless, Mr. Billings had obviously been gloating about the tidbits of gossip he'd managed to gather last night.

Members of the kitchen staff were at their workstations preparing for the first meal of the day. Olivia didn't want to discuss this matter in front of them. She tipped her head toward the hallway.

His bushy eyebrows arched. "So now *you* give *me* orders?"

She shrugged. "I thought you might prefer a bit of privacy."

"Oui. We will go to my office."

She stifled a chuckle. So long as it was *his* suggestion, they would go to his office.

He closed the door and reached into his pocket. "Mr. Beelings said Lord Spencer left this for you." The chef handed Olivia an envelope. "He says the earl and the countess had Morgan with them when they left this morning. Is this true?"

"Yes. They plan to rear him as their own child. He will have an excellent home."

"This is good. The child has a good home, and I will once again have my protégée's full attention." He pointed toward her eyes. "Too much crying is not good. You must keep busy so you don't have too much time to think. You can read the letter this evening. We have breakfast to prepare for our guests."

With that said, he marched back to the kitchen, with Olivia following in his wake. He obviously planned to ensure she didn't have time to think. She shoved the letter into the pocket of her navy blue skirt and hurried to keep pace.

Though she'd successfully avoided Mr. Billings throughout the morning, Mr. Howard entered the kitchen after the noonday meal and immediately summoned her to Chef René's office. "I've been advised the Earl and Countess of Lanshire departed this morning with Morgan in their custody. Is this information reliable?"

It seemed that today she was going to spend more time in the chef's office than in the kitchen. She knew Mr. Billings was responsible for passing along the information, for Chef René discouraged gossip among the hotel staff. This was one of the many reasons he and Mr. Billings failed to get along. How many times would she be forced to answer the same questions? Perhaps she should just write a brief announcement, post it on the front desk, and be done with all the probing questions! Of course, she would never do such a thing, but the idea was appealing.

"Yes, the earl and countess departed. Yes, they took Morgan with them. And, yes, your information is reliable." The startled look on Mr. Howard's face reflected she had been much too abrupt with her response. "Forgive me. I've already grown weary of answering the same questions."

His features softened. "In that case, I won't interrogate you any further. If, at some time in the future, you'd like to offer additional details, I'd be pleased to listen."

"Thank you for your understanding. Now, if there is nothing else . . ." Pressing her open palms against the chair arms, she pushed herself up.

Before she could escape, Mr. Howard interrupted and waved her back to her chair. "Not yet." Fingers tented beneath his chin, he waited until she sat down. "With the baby no longer in your care, you are apt to be lonely. I would count it a pleasure if you would allow me to help you fill the void. Indeed, I believe this would provide the perfect opportunity for our postponed visit to Chicago. You choose the day and time, and I shall make the arrangements."

Olivia's brain ceased functioning. She couldn't think of any response to sidestep his offer. His open-ended invitation had placed her at a distinct disadvantage. She wanted to ask for time to think, yet she feared offending him. Instead, she decided to pick a distant date and hope something would arise in the interim. Not an excellent idea, but under the circumstances, it was the best she could do.

"What about a Saturday in mid to late November?"

He laughed, and then quickly sobered. "You are jesting, aren't you? Surely you have several free hours before then."

No more lies. Why did those words come to mind at this moment? She prayed for clarity of thought, for a response that would hold Mr. Howard at bay yet permit her to speak the truth. "I have much to accomplish over the coming weeks. I can no longer afford to remain in the flat I shared with Mrs. Hornsby."

He straightened in his chair. "I can assist you in that regard. I'll have a list of available housing to you by late afternoon. We can go and check what's available after work this evening."

For a brief moment, panic constricted her chest. Then she remembered Mrs. DeVault's invitation. "I've already accepted an invitation to supper this evening."

"Then tomorrow or the next day or the next. You surely haven't engagements for every night this week." Holding out his hands in entreaty, he awaited her response.

That idea certainly hadn't worked to her advantage. But she needed to move, and if he insisted upon helping, his involvement in the process could be easily explained to Fred. "I believe tomorrow after work will do." Before departing, she decided upon a final tack. "Quite frankly, there's no reason to clutter your busy schedule with my search for housing. A list of available flats would suffice."

"Miss Mott! If I didn't know better, I'd think you were

attempting to avoid my company. I deem it a pleasure to escort you. In addition, I believe I can provide the services of several men who will assist with the move."

She shook her head. "Oh, that's not necessary. I'm confident Fred and Albert can manage. If not, they'll solicit help from members of the soccer team."

Her refusal appeared to annoy Mr. Howard, but he didn't comment further. He pressed his hands against the top of the desk and rose. "I'll meet you at the kitchen entrance to the hotel tomorrow evening at six o'clock."

Olivia jumped to her feet, pleased finally to escape the confines of the room. She'd have this evening to explain to Fred.

The meeting hadn't produced the outcome Samuel had hoped for. He still didn't understand why Olivia had willingly allowed the earl and countess to take custody of young Morgan. It made no sense. At their last meeting, she'd professed her belief that Mrs. Hornsby would return. And handing over the child to surrogates who would take him to England seemed an odd choice. After all, Mrs. Hornsby had come to America in an effort to begin life anew. It was doubtful whether she would want the boy living in England.

On the other hand, perhaps Olivia had decided the baby's English heritage was important and decided this arrangement a good choice. Given the age of the earl and countess, the entire affair was odd at best, though Olivia likely felt a sense of comfort in sending the infant with people who she knew would love and care for him. Samuel hoped one day she would trust him enough to share the entire story.

He made his way to the lobby and stopped for a moment at

the front desk. Mr. Billings sat at the desk working on the accounts but hurried to the front counter. "Anything further to report, Mr. Billings?"

The hotel supervisor shook his head. "My guess is that Chef René will know the entire story by week's end. The girl trusts him. However, he reveals nothing to me . . . or to anyone else, for that matter."

Mr. Howard raised his brows. "A trustworthy man. I applaud him."

The desk clerk's smile faded. "I, too, consider myself trustworthy."

Mr. Howard tipped his head and laughed. "*Do* you? A wagging tongue is of value to me, Mr. Billings, but it does not make you trustworthy. Try talking to Chef René. Perhaps he'll blunder and repeat something of importance."

"He doesn't slip up, and he doesn't like me in his kitchen. If I'm to gather additional information, I'll be required to find another way."

Samuel departed, uncertain whether Mr. Billings had been completely forthright. If the man had additional information, he'd likely been put off by Samuel's comments just now. But Mr. Billings couldn't keep his lips sealed for long. Eventually he'd come around. If nothing else, he'd succumb to the lure of a promotion or a promised pay raise. Unlike Chef René, the man was devious, but he had demonstrated his worth on several occasions and always proved himself loyal to the company.

Samuel stopped outside his office and asked one of the clerks to prepare a list of all available flats and boarding rooms currently available for rent. He dropped into his chair and swung around to face the window. There was no question Olivia had feelings for Fred DeVault. Her eyes sparkled at the mere mention of his name. And Mr. Billings had pointed out that Fred met her every evening after work. Of course, there was the attachment to Mrs. DeVault to consider, also. Obviously Fred had him at a disadvantage. Perhaps he could do something to shift matters to his benefit.

He lifted a large ledger to the top of his desk and traced his finger down the entries. *Fred DeVault.* He worked in electroplating. This should prove easy enough.

Within fifteen minutes, his clerk returned and escorted Mr. Godfrey into his office. "Sit down, Mr. Godfrey." The man was obviously nervous. He was crushing his hat between his large hands. "No need to be concerned. Nothing's amiss."

The man sighed as he slid into the chair. "Always a fearsome thing to be called to the business offices."

"Well, we've had nothing but excellent reports about your performance, Mr. Godfrey, so you need not worry any further. There is, however, the need to switch some of your men to different shifts. I'm certain you'll understand that I'm not at liberty to divulge the reasons."

"Oh, of course not, sir." He bobbed his head at a dizzying tempo. "Just tell me who you need changed around, and I'll see to it."

Samuel handed the list to Mr. Godfrey. "I believe these changes will work quite well. If any of the men complain, you let me know."

"Yes, sir. But I don't think you'll hear any complaints. All my men are pleased with their work. Is that all you need, then?"

"Yes. And if you could have those changes go into effect beginning tomorrow, that would help immensely."

"Tomorrow? You don't want to change over at the first of the week? It would give the men a few days to make the adjustment."

"No, this needs immediate attention. If any of the men inquire, you can advise that this is Mr. Pullman's order. The two of us are merely the messengers."

Mr. Godfrey jumped to his feet, once again massaging his hat with both hands. "Yes, sir. Good day to you, Mr. Howard."

When the door had closed, Samuel studied the changes he had noted in his ledger. Perhaps with Fred working the late shift, Olivia would be more inclined to spend her evenings with him. Though he harbored a modicum of guilt, he forced it from his thoughts. Fred had enjoyed the advantage for far too long. If Samuel was going to have a chance at winning Olivia's hand, he must create his own opportunities.

Chapter Twenty-Eight

The leaves crunched beneath her feet as Olivia ran around the corner of the hotel. After her recent encounter with Eddie, she had wondered if Fred would continue to meet her after work. When he had appeared that first day after revealing the news, she had been pleased. Apparently he considered their walks home more than an obligation. She waved as he approached. He frowned and offered a halfhearted greeting.

"What's wrong? Have I done something?" She tucked her hand into the crook of his offered arm and matched his stride, thankful the fall breeze wasn't cold enough to force them home in a rush.

He shook his head and jabbed at the air with his free hand. "If it weren't for my mother, I'd quit this rotten company." His eyes blazed with anger as he spewed the words.

She tugged on his sleeve and came to a halt. "Fred! I've never seen you like this. What's happened?"

He turned to face her, his eyes still shining with a fury that frightened her. "Mr. Godfrey announced shift changes this afternoon. Beginning tomorrow, I'm assigned to the late shift."

"Permanently?" She wanted to remain calm, yet she knew what this change would mean. Fred wouldn't get off work until midnight. They'd seldom be able to see each other.

"Yes. One of the men offered to trade with me, but Mr. Godfrey said no one would be permitted to exchange hours. He said the orders had come from Mr. Pullman without any explanation, and he was not authorized to change them."

He calmed a bit, and they continued onward. When he started to turn toward her house, she pulled him in the other direction. "Your mother invited me to supper tonight at your house. I have something to tell you, too."

Fred's sullen look changed to surprise. "I hope it's good news."

She hadn't yet decided if it was good news or bad. For certain, it would change her routine. "Morgan is gone." He opened his mouth to speak, but she went on. "Let me explain." As they continued down the street, she offered him the same minimal report she'd given the others. If she added or detracted information, there would be too many questions to answer, too many lies to unravel.

He waited a moment, obviously expecting more. "That's it? You have nothing more to add?"

"The earl asked that I keep my explanations to a minimum, and I believe I should honor my word." What she had told him was the truth. She'd been careful. She didn't want to lie.

"But I have so many questions. This doesn't seem reasonable. Why would they want Morgan? And why would you let them have him? I thought you believed Charlotte would return."

These were the same questions Mr. Howard had asked. "He will have a better life with them than I could provide. I truly can say no more, Fred."

He shook his head. "Just when your obligations decrease and we could share more time together, I'm assigned to the late shift." He opened the front door. "Life plays strange tricks on us, doesn't it?"

"What's this I hear about strange tricks?" Albert bounded into the hall, a grin splitting his face. His cheerful demeanor faded when he caught sight of them. "You two look like you've been at a wake. What's happened?"

Before either of them could respond, Mrs. DeVault bustled toward them, wiping her hands down the front of her faded apron. "Supper's ready." She glanced among the threesome. "What did I miss?"

"Give us a chance to wash up," Fred told her, "and we'll talk further at supper."

"I hope it isn't something that's going to ruin our appetites." Mrs. DeVault placed her hands on her hips. "I prepared a fine meal, and I don't want it going to waste."

Fred patted his mother's shoulder. "I doubt there's much of anything that would ruin our appetites. At least mine or Albert's. I'm not so sure about Olivia's."

Once they were seated around the table, the four of them joined hands and bowed their heads, and Fred began to pray. Olivia peeked at him from beneath her thick lashes. He was uttering the usual words, but they were emotionless. She must remember to ask Mrs. DeVault about prayers. She hoped they all counted, even the ones like Fred was praying, or the ones when she said no more than, "Please help me." Perhaps they'd have a few moments alone after supper.

The food was everything Mrs. DeVault had promised: chicken, oven-roasted to perfection, mashed potatoes with creamy gravy, fresh peas, and fluffy biscuits with apple butter. Had Fred's change of shifts not occurred, it would have been the perfect end to the day. He quickly complimented his mother on the meal, but the remainder of the supper conversation consisted of the men's grievances and talk of unions. Olivia squirmed in her chair and attempted to change the conversation on several occasions, but Fred continually returned to the topic. If only Fred had received the job he'd been promised, she was certain he would be happy in Pullman. Unfortunately, this latest problem had only added fuel to the fire.

Olivia struggled to think of some way in which she might help. What if Fred *could* change jobs? What if there was an opening for a designer or an etcher? Mr. Howard would surely know of any possible vacancies. After this latest incident, she knew Fred wouldn't go to his supervisor and inquire. But she could ask Mr. Howard. Perhaps he might be willing to help. Of course, she wouldn't want Fred to know. She could ask Mr. Howard when he accompanied her tomorrow evening.

Mrs. DeVault patted Olivia on the arm. "I don't want you sitting at home alone every evening. Even though Fred won't be here, I'm going to expect you for supper the remainder of the week. We'll keep each other company."

"That's very kind, but I have plans after work tomorrow. With Fred's change in hours, you may want to reschedule your evening meal."

Mrs. DeVault shook her head and chuckled. "I'm an old lady. I can't eat my supper at midnight. Besides, I've still got Albert to think of." She gave Olivia's cousin a wink. "Tell me, what plans do you have for tomorrow evening?"

With as few details as possible, Olivia explained her need to move. "I plan to begin looking at flats after work tomorrow."

Fred helped himself to another spoonful of mashed potatoes. "You'll need to request a list of available housing. Since I won't be working in the morning, I'll go over and ask one of the clerks in the Administration Building to prepare one. I can drop it off at the hotel."

She chased several peas around her dinner plate, worried he'd become angry with her if she divulged the truth. On the other hand, if he went to the Administration Building and said the list was for her, he'd likely discover the list had already been prepared at Mr. Howard's request. Better to be truthful. Isn't that what she'd promised God? "That's kind of you, Fred, but Mr. Howard has already requested a list."

Fred's fork dropped from his hand and clattered against the china plate. "Mr. Howard? How did *he* discover you'd be moving before any of us knew?"

Olivia's stomach muscles tightened into a knot. Fred didn't miss a beat with his questions. "Word travels quickly around the hotel. He came to the kitchen today and inquired about my circumstances."

Fred tilted his head back and laughed. "Now isn't that something, Albert! I don't think Mr. Howard would come to the electroplating shop and offer to help either one of us, do you?"

Mrs. DeVault pointed her finger at Fred and gave him a

stern look. "Stop with your bantering, Fred. Let's just enjoy our supper."

"I wasn't jesting, Mother. I was making a point. Mr. Howard has more than a passing interest in Olivia." He narrowed his eyes. "And I'm not at all convinced Olivia hasn't given him a bit of encouragement along the way."

How *dare* he make such an insinuation! Heat rushed to her cheeks, and she stared at him in disbelief. "That's unfair of you. We've already discussed the fact that he has enough power to have me terminated at any moment. I don't want to anger him."

"There comes a time when you have to draw the line, Olivia. Just how important is your job?" His eyes were dark and brooding as he awaited her response.

"What are you implying?" Olivia jumped up from the table and sent her chair clattering to the floor. She leaned down and retrieved the chair before slapping her napkin on the table. "I believe I should take my leave."

Fred shook his head. "Please! Sit down, Olivia. I apologize. My comment was uncalled for, and I beg your forgiveness. I know you would never compromise yourself."

Ever the peacemaker, Mrs. DeVault frantically tugged on Olivia's hand. "Yes, please forgive him. He's not himself with these happenings at work today. Please do sit down."

Olivia couldn't deny the older woman's request. But Fred's outburst and judgment of her behavior had wounded her.

Fred had no choice but to listen. His mother had reared him to respect his elders, and he'd not abandon her teaching, no matter what his age. It didn't mean he must agree with what she said, only that he'd listen and consider what she said. On this occasion, he knew his mother was correct. He deserved her censure, for his words to Olivia had been rude and hurtful. Little wonder that Olivia had pointedly requested that Albert escort her home. And Fred's mother hadn't wasted a moment telling him so. The minute Olivia and Albert had departed the house, she'd ushered him into the kitchen and handed him a dish towel. While she washed dishes and scrubbed the pots and pans, she lectured him. He dried and listened. Yet he was glad that she was finally winding down.

"You had best do more than say you're sorry or you'll lose that young lady. She's a nice girl, Fred." She waved a soapy finger in the air. "And I like her!"

He couldn't help but laugh at his mother's antics. Now she was playing matchmaker. However, his mother was correct. He needed to do something to make amends—something beyond a simple apology. He could purchase flowers or take her out to supper, but Olivia would appreciate something out of the ordinary . . . something original—like her. But what? As he placed the dishes on the shelves that lined the far kitchen wall, he noticed his mother's recipe box. Olivia had spoken to him of her mother's recipes and how important they were to her. A new recipe box! Yes, he would make her a box that would hold her mother's old recipes and would be large enough to include the new recipes from the hotel kitchen.

His mother heartily approved the plan but was of little assistance when he asked about dimensions for the new box.

Mrs. DeVault wiped her hands on her apron and shrugged. "I don't know how many recipes she has. Maybe you need a very big box, but if she has only a few of her mother's recipes, then not so big." She removed her apron and hung it on a hook near the sink. "I know! I have a key to the house. You can go and measure Olivia's recipe box after she departs for work in the morning. That way you can purchase the wood and begin right away. Perhaps you could make a matching rack for her spices, too."

He grasped his mother by the shoulders and kissed her cheek. "You always could figure out a way to solve my problems."

"Go on with you. If you're thinking you'll wheedle another piece of pie with your compliments, you should know me better than that."

He laughed, pleased with his plan. First thing in the morning he'd go and take the measurements. Then he'd head off for the lumberyard, where he'd purchase some scraps of wood. With luck he would find some nice pieces of cherry. He would frame a glass lid for the box and etch her name in the glass. Then again, maybe glass wasn't such a good idea. It would break too easily in the kitchen. He'd think of something to make it extra special, though.

The next morning, Fred paced back and forth in the hallway, checking the mantel clock each time he passed the parlor. He didn't want to hurry to Olivia's flat while it was dark outside, for Mrs. Rice might mistake him for an intruder. He decided that if Olivia's next-door neighbor saw him enter the house, he'd explain that he was preparing a surprise for Olivia. If Mrs. Rice was anything like his mother, she'd relish the role of a willing participant in his secret. When the clock chimed at eight-thirty, he hurried out the door. The streets were quiet, with only an occasional shopper hurrying toward the Market and a few dawdling children, who would likely be tardy for school. Anyone scheduled for the morning shift would already be at work.

Mrs. Rice didn't make an appearance when he approached the house. He'd make a point to knock on her door before departing. Better to take time and explain his presence rather than to fuel any gossip should she be watching him through the gauzy curtains. He put the key in the lock, heard the familiar clunk of the receding bolt, and turned the knob. The door opened easily, with only a faint creak to announce his entry. He walked inside—a trespasser. The thought stirred an eerily disturbing sensation deep in the hollow of his belly. Did thieves have these same feelings when they broke into someone's home?

The moment he located the recipe box and checked the measurements, he would be on his way. He made his way to the kitchen, pleased when he immediately saw the oblong box sitting beneath one of the shelves near the stove. It was of rough pine, bigger than he'd expected. Perhaps he'd made a mistake in thinking she might need a new box, though if it was full, she'd soon need something larger. He lifted the lid. The box certainly appeared full, but mostly because of several bulky folded sheets in the front. Perhaps these were recipes Olivia planned to transfer onto smaller paper that fit in the box. He withdrew the pages and unfolded them.

He struggled to make sense of what he was reading. At the top of the page were the words *Details for us to memorize*. A list of sorts had been written directly beneath the heading. *Charlotte will now be known as Mrs. Hornsby. Her hypothetical husband died. We supposedly met at a seamstress shop while she was having her mourning clothes altered. Don't address Charlotte as Lady Charlotte.* More details continued down the page. At first he thought it might be Olivia's journal. But this wasn't a diary. Instead, it was a list of strange information about Charlotte and Olivia.

He continued to read until he finally realized what he held in his hands. This was a list of lies the women had committed to memory and spoon-fed to everyone they met. Charlotte and Olivia had woven together a web of lies that were memorialized on these pages. He didn't want to continue reading, yet he couldn't look away. When he'd read the final page, he folded the pages and put them back in the box. Fingers trembling, he slowly closed the recipe box with a sense of revulsion.

Who was Olivia? What about her was true, and what was false? There was no doubt that she was Albert's cousin. She obviously was an expert liar, for even Albert had believed all she'd told him. When had the lies begun, and who, exactly, was Mrs. Hornsby? She obviously was a woman of wealth and class if she had been *Lady* Charlotte. He couldn't sort it out. Not here. Not now. He needed to get out of this house.

He shoved the box back into place and hurried out the front door. Too late, he remembered his plan to speak with Mrs. Rice but pushed the thought aside. If Olivia questioned him, he'd merely say her neighbor had been mistaken. He'd see if his lies were as believable as hers had been.

His mother turned from her dusting when he entered the house. He shrugged out of his jacket and waved when she peeked around the doorjamb. "That was a hasty trip. Where is the wood?" She stepped into the hallway and scanned the area.

He shook his head. "I decided the recipe box wasn't such a good idea. I'm not feeling well. I think I'll go upstairs and get some sleep. I wouldn't want to be sick my first day on the new shift. Mr. Howard would probably consider my absence a protest to the change in hours and fire me."

"Is it your stomach or head that's bothering you? I can go to the druggist and request something to help, or I can make you some soup from the leftover chicken."

He continued up the stairs, the truth of what he'd seen weighing down upon his chest. "Don't go to the pharmacy. If you want to make soup, I'll eat some before I go to work." He looked over his shoulder and noted his mother's frown as she peered up the staircase. "Don't worry. I'll be fine. I merely need to rest."

He sat on the edge of his bed and covered his face with his palms. Only last night he had thought of Olivia as someone extraordinary and special. This morning's revelations had proved his belief to be true, but not in the way he'd thought. The fact remained that he had no idea who she was or what was truth and what was deceit. Right now, he didn't even want to attempt to sort out fact from fiction.

So far as he was concerned, she was no more than a chimera, a fleeting illusion of the woman he had hoped to one day marry. In the time it had taken to read those few pages, the young woman he'd grown so fond of had disappeared. He fell back across the bed and stared out the window. Instead of moping, he should be thankful he'd discovered the truth before he'd fallen in love with her. Unfortunately, that thought didn't heal his intense sorrow, for deep within he knew he'd already committed his heart to Olivia.

Chapter Twenty-Nine

Mr. Howard waited outside the kitchen door, holding his felt derby in one hand and a single yellow rose in the other.

Chef René glanced up and arched his bushy brows. "A rose?" His question was no more than a whisper.

Olivia removed her toque and white jacket, then stepped closer. "That's a *yellow* rose, not red. Yellow means friendship."

Chef René bent over a cookbook and traced his finger down the page. "It may be yellow to you, but to him it is red."

Olivia shook her head in denial, but she feared the chef's assessment was correct. Mr. Howard's eyes sparkled with anticipation, a look she longed to receive from Fred, but not from the company agent.

She thanked him for the rose and suggested a small vase in the kitchen would keep it fresh until tomorrow. She didn't want to walk about town carrying a rose in her hand. What if someone saw her and mentioned it to Fred?

Furthermore, she didn't want Mr. Howard to consider this

search for new living quarters as anything more than one friend helping another. Of course, he wasn't really her friend, but he wasn't a beau, either. He waited patiently while she poured water into the vase and placed the rose inside.

The moment they walked outdoors, he offered his arm. She wanted to refuse, but her courage waned. He patted her hand as she tucked it into the crook of his arm, a much too possessive action. First the flower and now patting her hand as though they were a couple. She didn't want to encourage his affectionate behavior.

"Did you bring the list?" Perhaps she could break this arm-in-arm arrangement by perusing his inventory of available apartments.

"No need for a paper. I have them all up here." He tapped his head.

Nearing the far corner of the hotel, he made a sharp turn. She tugged on his arm. "I can't afford to rent rooms on this street." Though she didn't mention it, she doubted any of the well-paid supervisors who lived on 111th Street would even consider renting out rooms.

"My next-door neighbor, Mrs. Barnes, mentioned she would be delighted to have you as a boarder, and I thought you'd like to look there first." He continued walking. "Her daughter recently married. Only last night she mentioned being lonely for another woman in the house. Needless to say, I thought of you, and she was delighted with the idea."

"That's kind, but I'm on a strict budget, Mr. Howard."

Once again he patted her hand. "Samuel. I *insist* you quit addressing me so formally when we're alone. As for the room and board, she's not in need of funds. Unlike the other women who rent out rooms, she is willing to take a lesser amount." He tipped his head close. "One I know you can afford."

Certainly he was well aware of her wages. He'd hired her. Still, she thought him presumptuous to assume he knew what she could or couldn't afford. He had no idea what other obligations she might have. She feared he was already persuaded she'd take the room. And though she didn't want to live next door to him, she worried his preplanned arrangements would make it difficult to refuse without a credible excuse.

"Here we are." He escorted her up the front steps and knocked. Mrs. Barnes had obviously been awaiting their arrival, for she immediately opened the door. A pleasantly plump woman, she greeted them with a welcoming smile. The woman's soft brown eyes reminded Olivia of Aunt Eleanor. Tucking a strand of her graying auburn hair behind one ear, the woman invited them inside. Despite the fact that Mrs. Barnes was evaluating her suitability as a tenant, Olivia was drawn by the woman's comforting air of kindness and gentility. She appeared genuinely pleased to have them come calling.

"I do hope you'll forgive my husband's absence. He had some additional work to complete in his office." She smiled and shook her head. "Horace can't sleep unless his books are reconciled each night. I'm sure you understand, Mr. Howard."

"Of course. Horace is a dedicated and valued employee."

Mrs. Barnes beamed at the compliment. "Why, thank you."

She directed them into the parlor. Unlike Olivia's flat, the stairway and woodwork were a lustrous cherry that had been finished in its natural color, and the double parlor they entered was extravagantly appointed and spacious.

"Would you prefer to see the rest of the house before we visit?"

Olivia didn't have an opportunity to voice her opinion, for Mr. Howard immediately agreed to the offer. Mrs. Barnes waved them forward, and they entered the dining room, situated directly off the parlor. Four sizeable china closets and pantries were located in the kitchen and dining room, and Olivia nearly gasped aloud when she saw the laundry room. Three stationary washtubs lined the wall and were supplied with hot and cold water. In the basement, she viewed additional shelves lined with canned goods, cupboards for additional storage, and the room that contained the steam coils for warming the house. Steam heat—yet another benefit of rooming with a supervisor who lived across the street from the factories.

"Let me take you to the third floor, where you can inspect the three rooms my daughter occupied before . . ." Her voice trailed off, and she dabbed her eyes. There was no doubt Mrs. Barnes missed her daughter terribly. When they arrived at the second-floor landing, she hesitated in the large front alcove room. "This is one of my favorite places. I sit here and read most afternoons." She motioned to the rear of the house. "There are two bedrooms on this floor—and the bath, of course."

The walls throughout the house were papered in small floral patterns, and the ceilings had been tinted in harmonious shades to match the paper in each room. Venetian blinds were topped with sumptuous draperies and lacy curtains. On the third floor, the three large rooms had been converted into a dressing room, bedroom, and sitting room. To say the rooms were lovely wouldn't do them justice. Olivia couldn't believe she'd been presented with an opportunity to reside in these exquisite surroundings.

"My daughter chose the wallpaper and furnishings for these rooms." Mrs. Barnes surveyed the area one final time before leading them downstairs. Once they'd returned to the parlor, Mrs. Barnes sat down beside Olivia. "Mr. Howard tells me you're the assistant chef at the hotel. Mr. Barnes and I enjoy partaking of a meal in the hotel dining room from time to time." She tipped her head toward Olivia. "The food is excellent. I'm afraid you won't find our meals nearly so fancy. Mr. Barnes says I should hire a housekeeper like the other supervisors' wives. I do have occasional help, but mostly I prefer to keep my own house in order—just like Mrs. Howard always—" She stopped short and covered her mouth with her hand. "Oh, I'm so sorry, Mr. Howard."

"No need to apologize, Mrs. Barnes. You're absolutely correct. My wife enjoyed cooking meals and managing on her own. And she performed admirably until her illness."

"Indeed, she did. And a finer neighbor couldn't be found in all of Pullman." Mrs. Barnes straightened the edge of a crocheted doily on the side table. "When did you arrive in Pullman, Olivia?"

"A little over five months ago. This will be my first winter in Pullman. I'm told to expect a lot of snow and cold weather."

Mrs. Barnes nodded. "True enough. But working in the hotel, you don't have to concern yourself with the cold. And if you decide to reside with us, you'll be plenty warm without the worry of coal or wood."

"The rooms are lovely, Mrs. Barnes. I'm certain you're aware of the rental rates in Pullman. Your rooms far surpass anything

I could afford. I do appreciate seeing them, however."

The older woman waved her hand. "The rent we charge for these rooms is between you and us." Mrs. Barnes went on to explain how much she missed her daughter. "Having you in the house would ease my pain. I do hope you'll agree. We'd not accept anything over seven dollars a month."

Seven dollars? Too late, Olivia realized she couldn't say no to this kind woman. She shouldn't have agreed to visit the house and meet Mrs. Barnes. Why hadn't she simply said she wanted to look elsewhere? But surely Fred would understand. She could meet him elsewhere if he didn't want to call on her at a supervisor's house.

Mrs. Barnes cast a pleading look in her direction. "Do say you'll agree, Olivia."

"I'd be pleased to accept, but only if you'll agree to let me cook for you and your husband several times a week."

The older woman grasped her hand. "Oh, we're going to have a *fine* time. I can tell."

Mr. Howard leaned forward and rested his arms across his thighs. "You must remember that, unlike your daughter, Olivia works long hours each day. And she'll be busy with her own social life part of the time." He grinned broadly. "At least I hope she will."

"Oh, absolutely. You would have freedom to come and go as needed. In fact, I'll have a key made for you tomorrow morning. When would you like to move in?"

"I believe the second week in November would be best for me. Is that agreeable?"

Mrs. Barnes clapped her hands together like a delighted schoolgirl. "I can hardly wait. It will be much more lively having another woman in the house." She glanced at Mr. Howard. "As Olivia's time permits, of course."

Despite the fact that she argued against it, Mr. Howard insisted upon escorting Olivia home. "I thought we'd stop at the Arcade restaurant. Surely you must be hungry." He placed his palm on his stomach. "I know my supper is long overdue."

She would have preferred to hurry home unescorted, eat something light, and gather her thoughts. She'd need to carefully explain this move to Fred, or he'd once again accuse her of putting her job first. But this hadn't been about her job. It was an opportunity to live cheaply in the best possible accommodations. And the house was only half a block from the hotel, a true blessing for her when the snow began to fall. However, she doubted whether any of those assets would erase the fact that the apartment was located next door to Mr. Howard. Fred's mistrust of the Pullman supervisors ran so deep that he'd likely accuse Mr. Howard of marrying off the Barnes's daughter in order to provide Olivia with the apartment.

Olivia was thankful the restaurant wasn't crowded and even more pleased when the waiter led them to a table away from the windows where passersby would see them. Not that many people knew her, but all the residents in Pullman were acquainted with Mr. Howard, and talk traveled quickly through the town.

While they waited for their supper, Olivia searched for the proper way to broach the subject of Fred's job. Perhaps a general question about the workers would let her ease into the topic. "If a person applies for a specific position with the company, do you hire the person for only that position?"

He furrowed his brows. "I'm not certain I understand your

question. You were hired to work as an assistant chef, and that's the position you were given."

She agreed. Obviously he'd thought she was preparing to offer a complaint about her job in the hotel. "I was thinking of factory positions. If I had applied to work as a seamstress, would I be sure to receive a position as a seamstress? Or if a laundry worker was needed, would you simply send me to work in the laundry?"

"I suppose it would depend on the circumstances, such as the rate of pay and whether you would be willing to accept the position. Why all these questions about job placement? Has this something to do with your cousin Albert?"

Without realizing it, Mr. Howard had given her the perfect opening. "Yes, it's about both Albert and Fred. They mentioned having been hired for specific positions with the company, but when they actually began work, they were assigned to lesser jobs that didn't make use of their skills."

They stopped talking while the waiter placed a plate in front of each of them. "That sometimes occurs," Mr. Howard said, "but I'll look into it and see if I can't find something that would allow Albert to utilize his skills. I'll review his application. I'm sure I can locate something."

She clenched her napkin between her hands. "And Fred?"

His features tightened into a frown at the mention of Fred's name. "I believe Mr. DeVault is in electroplating." He shook his head. "For some reason, Mr. Pullman recently requested shift changes in that department. I wouldn't be able to do anything for him."

"I see. Well, thank you for offering to help Albert. I know he'll be grateful." He was watching her closely, so she forced a tepid smile. She didn't want him to see her disappointment. "Albert is quite fond of Martha Mosher, who's with housekeeping at the hotel. I think they may decide to marry soon."

"Truly? Martha is a fine young woman. Mr. Billings tells me she's a good worker. If Albert's planning to marry, I'll need to find him a position that offers higher pay." He took the final bite of his supper and wiped his mouth with the linen napkin. "I'm going to have a slice of pie. Would you like some dessert?"

Olivia shook her head. She didn't want dessert; she wanted to go home. But she would be required to remain until Mr. Howard finished his pie and coffee. This evening certainly hadn't accomplished what she'd intended. Granted, she'd arranged for a lovely place to live, and it looked as though Albert would be considered for a new position at a higher rate of pay, but she'd done nothing to help Fred. In fact, she wondered if mentioning his name had been ill-advised. Mr. Howard had been blatantly annoyed. Olivia could only hope her inquiry wouldn't cause any further problems for Fred. Too late she realized she should have considered the possible ramifications of speaking out before plunging headfirst into company business.

"Oh, *Mademoiselle* Mott, would you be my *friend*?" Chef René's heavy French accent rolled off his tongue the next morning in a lilting tune. He stood framed in the kitchen doorway, holding the stem of the yellow rose between his folded hands.

"You are most humorous, Chef René." Olivia was forced to bite her lip to keep from laughing.

"Does that mean you will be my friend?" He grinned and thrust the rose at her. "Please."

"Stop! What do you want to hear? That you're right and he is interested in more than friendship?"

The chef shrugged his broad shoulders. "There is no doubt of that. I merely wanted to make you laugh."

"Then you accomplished your intent." She shoved her arms into her white jacket. "I did find a perfect place to live. At the very first place I looked."

"And the only one, I would guess. You are to become Mrs. Barnes's tenant?" He lifted a large crock from one of the shelves.

"How did you know?"

"In this hotel, word travels quickly. But you have our wonderful Mr. Beelings to thank for your lovely new home. He suggested the possibility to Mr. Howard, who then spoke with his next-door neighbor. You see? Even Mr. Beelings has detected Mr. Howard's interest in you." Chef René whisked the eggs he had cracked into the bowl and poured them into a sizzling skillet of melted butter. He set the empty crock on the worktable. "Don't be discouraged. You are young and naïve when it comes to men."

Naïve? She'd admit to her inexperienced behavior in England and even in the first few months after she'd arrived in America. But after that, she'd outgrown her innocence. At least she thought she had. Obviously not.

The remainder of the day passed without incident. Mr. Howard didn't appear, and she managed to avoid Mr. Billings. She'd not be thanking the hotel manager for prying into her private business. He no doubt hoped to gain a stronger foothold with Mr. Howard and the company with his snooping. She wondered if Mr. Howard frequently amassed information on company employees from their higher-ranking counterparts. She shivered at the thought.

Chapter Thirty

After work, Olivia stopped at home only long enough to pen a note to Fred before hurrying to the DeVault residence. She was certain tonight's supper would be more enjoyable than last night's dinner with Mr. Howard. Passing the park, she captured a glimpse of a young mother pushing her baby in a carriage. The scene stirred feelings of loss for little Morgan. Perhaps moving out of the flat would help ease the pain of the baby's departure.

Olivia watched as the woman leaned over the baby carriage, and she wondered if Charlotte missed Morgan. Each day she hoped to receive a letter from the young woman, but each day she was disappointed. At times it felt as though Charlotte's existence in Pullman had been no more than a fleeting dream. Yet Olivia's longing for Morgan remained very real.

Mrs. DeVault pulled open the front door and greeted her with a smile. "I thought you might have forgotten."

"No. I stopped at home for a few minutes. I hope my tardiness didn't ruin your supper, but I wanted to write a note for

Fred." She withdrew the envelope from her skirt pocket. "Would you give this to him?"

Mrs. DeVault winked as she accepted the letter. "I'll put it on the table so that he'll see it the minute he gets home." She took Olivia's cape and hat and hung them in the hallway.

"I've invited him to spend Sunday afternoon and evening with me. I didn't know if he'd be attending church after working so late."

"He'll be at church, and if I catch him dropping off to sleep during the sermon, I'll flick him like I used to when he was a little boy." She laughed and snapped at the air with her thumb and index finger. "Albert won't be joining us for the evening meal. He's taken Martha to the Arcade for supper. Said he had a surprise for her."

Olivia perked to attention. Surely Mr. Howard hadn't already located a new position for her cousin. "Did he confide in you?"

"Do you think I'd let him out the door before discovering such information?" She laughed and waved Olivia toward the kitchen. "He received a promotion today. A new job with a nice raise in pay, too." She tipped her head close. "He's going to ask Martha to marry him." She squeezed her shoulders forward and rubbed her hands with delight. "Isn't that wonderful news? Now you mustn't let on I've told."

"I'm very pleased for both of them. I'm sure Martha will be surprised." But her words were stilted, and she was unable to force any genuine joy into her voice. Fortunately, Mrs. DeVault was so excited she seemed not to notice.

"Now I'm praying Fred will come home and tell me that he has been promoted to another position, too. Wouldn't that make for a memorable day?"

Olivia wanted to tell Mrs. DeVault not to get her hopes up, because Fred would receive neither a new position nor a raise. Instead, she simply agreed. She didn't want to admit she'd played a role in Albert's success while she'd likely doomed Fred's career.

While Mrs. DeVault filled their bowls with thick beef stew, Olivia sliced the loaf of fresh bread and voiced a topic she'd been wanting to discuss. "Could I ask you a question about praying, Mrs. DeVault?"

"Why, of course. I don't profess to have all the answers, but I'll do my best."

Olivia summarized her thoughts about the many differing prayers she'd heard people offer. She didn't want Mrs. DeVault to think her question foolish. "Do you think God hears all of our prayers, or only the ones that sound genuine?"

"Come and sit down at the table. We can talk while we eat our supper—after we pray." Once she'd offered thanks for their meal, the older woman raised her head and motioned for Olivia to eat. "You know, the Pharisees' prayers consisted of beautiful words that sounded genuine, and they could quote the Scriptures word for word, yet the Bible says they were condemned to hell. Prayer isn't about sounding good to other people, Olivia. It's about what's in your heart. Even when the words won't come, God knows your heart. What sounds pitiful to mankind may be amazingly beautiful to God's ears." She picked up a piece of bread and spread it with butter. "Have I answered your question?"

"Yes, but I have another." Olivia enjoyed another bite of stew before continuing her query. She pointed her fork toward the bowl. "This is delicious." She almost didn't want to stop long enough to ask her question. "You told me that if we repent of a wrongdoing and ask for God's forgiveness, then we're forgiven."

"That's correct." Mrs. DeVault sipped her coffee.

"When someone is a Christian and has been wronged, must that person forgive the one who wronged him?" Olivia held her breath while she awaited the answer. Fred professed to be a Christian. She hoped he would forgive her if he discovered she'd discussed upgrading his job with Mr. Howard.

Mrs. DeVault lifted her napkin and wiped the corner of her mouth while seeming to contemplate her answer. "As Christians, we are supposed to forgive. Yet even for Christians, forgiveness can be difficult and sometimes doesn't come quickly or easily. If a wound is deep, it can take a long time to heal. Likewise, if we cause profound pain to another, we can't expect immediate forgiveness. You could say that's one of the consequences of sin in our lives."

"What if we go to the person and admit what we've done? Do you think they would more readily forgive the offense?"

"Possibly. There's no way to be certain. But I think it best we admit our shortcomings, both to God and to the person we've offended." The older woman's eyes twinkled. "Have you been studying your Bible, Olivia? Is that what has caused these questions?"

Olivia wished she could say she'd been reading her Bible every day, but some nights she fell into bed too weary to read. Sometimes she even fell asleep while praying, though she didn't want to make that admission. Mrs. DeVault would likely never fall asleep while conversing with God Almighty. "Not as much as I should," she admitted. "Sometimes I don't find enough hours in the day."

"Perhaps you could rise a few minutes earlier in the morning? I'm often too weary at night. I fall asleep if I read at bedtime.

Years ago I discovered I enjoyed the quiet of the morning for my Bible reading. Try it and see." She offered an encouraging smile. "Is there someone you need to forgive, Olivia?"

Offhand, she could think of any number of people she needed to forgive: her father, Chef Mallard, Charlotte. The list could go on and on, for she harbored resentment against more people than she cared to admit. And there were any number of people she'd deceived with her lies. However, she was more concerned about being forgiven than forgiving others. The thought fluttered through her mind and then returned with a gentle nudge. "There are many people I need to forgive, Mrs. DeVault."

The older woman scooped up their bowls and silverware. "Well, there's no time like the present. That's what Mr. DeVault used to tell me all the time." She grinned. "I always found it an annoying comment."

Olivia giggled.

"Believe me, Olivia, you'll know when the time is right for you to forgive each of those people. God will give you a little nudge." She laughed. "Sometimes He has to give me a big push."

Olivia thought Mrs. DeVault must be joking, for she couldn't imagine the woman would ever withhold *her* mercy. At least she hoped not. If someone like Mrs. DeVault had difficulty with forgiveness, she wondered about others—particularly Fred. The multitude of fabrications that Olivia had extolled as truth marched through her mind like an endless parade. Could he possibly forgive her all those untruths? The thought was daunting. She doubted his forgiveness would come easily. For the present, she'd continue to live as though those lies were her truth. She didn't want to chance losing Fred.

Mrs. DeVault tapped her finger on the table. "I want a full

report on your search for a new place to live. You've not mentioned one word. Do tell me if you found something suitable."

Olivia would have preferred to keep the news to herself, but she couldn't deny the older woman's eager request. First she elicited a promise of secrecy. "I want to be the one to tell Fred. Please don't say anything to him or to Albert. Please?"

"It's your news, my dear. I won't breathe a word." After pouring herself another cup of coffee, Mrs. DeVault leaned back in her chair and rubbed her hands together. "Now, let me hear all the details."

A couple of days later one of the kitchen boys clattered into the kitchen and pointed a thumb toward the hallway. "Miss Mott! Mr. Howard wants to see you in Chef René's office."

Chef René approached and tipped his head. With his lips close to Olivia's ear, he whispered, "He probably has another yellow rose for his *friend*."

A smile broke across her face, and they laughed until tears trickled down Olivia's cheeks. The kitchen boy frowned and tugged on the sleeve of her jacket, his concern evident. "I think he wants you to go *now*." The boy obviously feared he'd be accused of dallying if she didn't soon make an appearance in the office. Gratefully she accepted the handkerchief Chef René offered and wiped her damp cheeks. Waving the white handkerchief like a flag, she marched out of the kitchen.

She might need to warn Mr. Howard that all of his "invitations" were beginning to cause gossip among the hotel staff. Somehow she hoped to put an end to these private meetings during work hours.

The office door was open, and he motioned her forward. Always the gentleman, he stood as she entered. "Do sit down." He closed the door before returning to his chair. "Since you no longer are responsible for the care of young Morgan, I believe I have a bit of good news. A proposal of sorts." He rubbed his hands together as though warming them over a fire.

Proposal? Surely he wasn't going to ask her to marry him again. As far as Olivia was concerned, the reasoning for such a marriage had departed with the earl and countess. She nibbled her lower lip. "What type of offer?"

"I'm proposing that you accept a position that will permit you the opportunity to travel, yet you'll remain the assistant chef at the hotel and continue your duties when you're in Pullman."

Her eyebrows puckered. She thought Chef René had been pleased with her performance. Only this morning he had complimented her. "I don't understand. I'm happy with my position in the kitchen. Has Chef René voiced displeasure with me?"

He rested his arms on the top of Chef René's desk. "Not at all. It's your fine ability that leads me to offer you the new position. It would entail traveling in the Pullman cars. You would be evaluating the performance of our chefs, waiters, porters, and other employees working in Mr. Pullman's railcars."

She inhaled deeply, confused by the proposal. "Why would you offer me such a position? I'm not qualified to assess the work of those employees. I don't even know what their jobs entail." Outside of his marriage proposal, this was the most ludicrous thing he'd said to her since they'd first met. "I don't understand why I can't remain in the hotel kitchen."

He leaned forward and grasped her hand. "You can. However, this is an opportunity for advancement within the company, and Mr. Pullman believes you would be the perfect candidate."

Mr. Pullman? Could she possibly refuse if *he* had suggested her for the position? "I believe I need time to consider the idea. Is that possible?"

"Of course. I wouldn't expect you to make an immediate decision. It's always best to carefully consider decisions that will affect one's future employment with the company." Placing his palms on the desk, he pushed himself upright. "You take all the time you need."

Bewildered by the offer, she thanked him and walked out of the office in a daze. She walked headlong into Chef René as she entered the kitchen. He took hold of her shoulders and looked into her eyes. "You appear bewildered, Miss Mott. Did Mr. Howard request your hand in marriage?"

Stunned, she shook her head. "No. He offered me a job."

"What?" His question thundered throughout the kitchen, and all work came to a halt. He waved to the kitchen staff. "Get back about your work! Miss Mott, follow me!" He led her into the carving room instead of heading off toward his office.

She sighed, grateful she'd not be a witness to any discussions between Mr. Howard and Chef René. He closed the pocket door and placed his hands on his hips. "What is this about a job? You are unhappy in my kitchen?"

"No, of course not." There was barely enough room for the two of them in the small room—especially given the chef's rotund form. The heat from the warming ovens engulfed the room, and Olivia longed for a breath of cool air.

"Then what is this foolishness about a job?"

While she explained as succinctly as possible, the damp heat inside the room seemed to wilt her in both body and spirit, and her explanation wasn't nearly as clear as she'd intended. The chef questioned her at length. She pulled a handkerchief from her pocket and wiped away the beads of perspiration forming along her forehead and upper lip. Taking her cue, Chef René opened the door, but only a crack. A breath of air entered the room, and she longed to throw the door wide open. "I wonder if this is what hell must be like." She muttered the words under her breath. The chef arched his brows.

"I believe hell will be *much* hotter than this carving room, Miss Mott. Now, then, I can see that there may be an excellent opportunity for you in this job you've been offered. However, I must first talk to Mr. Howard. If you agree to take the position, I do not want him sending you off during the busy season. And not for long periods of time."

His agreement surprised Olivia. "Then you think I should accept the position?"

"I think you should consider it carefully. When an offer comes directly from Mr. Pullman, it should be declined only if there is significant reason." He shrugged his broad shoulders. "That is my opinion."

She doubted any of them would consider her interest in Fred a significant reason. Though she didn't want to be away from him or give up her work with Chef René, the idea of refusing Mr. Pullman's offer was a fearsome one. This matter would take a great deal of thought—and prayer.

Chapter Thirty-One

Olivia could barely wait to arrive at Mrs. DeVault's the following evening. All day she'd been anxious for quitting time. Even Chef René had noticed her eyeing the clock and had accused her of lackadaisical performance when she'd forgotten to instruct the kitchen boys to heat the metal covers for the soufflés. Consequently, two of the soufflés had collapsed in the short distance between the hot closet in the carving room and the customers' table. Chef René had insisted she go into the dining room and offer her apologies. Fortunately, the guests, both women who understood the difficulty of soufflé preparation, agreed to accept alternate selections, along with a downward adjustment to their check. Mr. Billings would likely suggest they deduct the amount from her pay, but at least the women hadn't been unkind.

As she rounded the final corner, the brisk November wind slapped at her skirt. She gathered her cloak against the biting chill and bowed her head, grateful she had only a half block more to walk. Mrs. DeVault wouldn't worry about her arrival this evening. She'd departed work on time and hadn't stopped at home, her anticipation being too high. If there wasn't some response from Fred awaiting her, she'd try to hide her disappointment.

She knocked and immediately opened the door. Mrs. DeVault had given her instructions to simply walk in, but she couldn't bring herself to act in such a bold manner. "It's Olivia, Mrs. DeVault."

The older woman peeked around the door at the end of the hallway. "Hang up your wraps and come join me in the kitchen."

The older woman's cheeks were flushed from the heat of the kitchen. Olivia imagined her own were pink from the brisk weather. "Um, it smells wonderful."

Mrs. DeVault lifted the lid from a kettle and spooned dollops of dough into the boiling broth. "Chicken and dumplings for supper. Good hearty food—not fancy like you can make, but it sticks to your ribs."

"And tastes as good as what we make at the hotel."

The older woman beamed at the praise. "There's a note from Fred on the dining room table. He said to be sure I gave it to you this evening."

Olivia's attempt to act nonchalant failed. In her hurry to retrieve the missive, she tripped over her feet and nearly landed face first on the floor. Fortunately she managed to get hold of the doorjamb and remain upright, preserving a modicum of aplomb, although her feet continued to skitter as though she'd stepped upon a sheet of ice. Thankfully, Mrs. DeVault didn't laugh at the spectacle she'd made of herself.

Her fingers trembled as she ripped open the envelope and removed the note. The paper was folded in half, but even before opening the page, she could see there were only a few lines of writing. The brevity surprised her, though he'd likely been in a hurry. At any rate, it would take only a few lines to say he'd be delighted to spend his Sunday with her. She unfolded the page and gasped upon reading Fred's message.

I have plans to see Mildred Malloy on Sunday. In the future, arrange to spend your free time with Mr. Howard or any other man of your choosing. Fred DeVault

She dropped to the chair and reread the message. No salutation, no closing. No explanation. Only the barest minimum required to drive home the point that he was no longer interested in keeping company with her. She traced a finger over his signature. Why had he signed his surname? Was it to make his terse response even more cold and formal? Had someone reported having seen her in the restaurant with Mr. Howard? Fred had known she would be with Mr. Howard while conducting her search for a new apartment. Surely he couldn't fault her for accompanying him into the restaurant. She could think of no reason other than the location of her new apartment. Had his mother told him?

Her throat constricted as she attempted to swallow down the panic that had risen in her chest. After inhaling several deep breaths, she regained a bit of composure. Remaining calm would help her maintain a clear mind.

She folded the note and tucked it into her pocket while she walked back to the kitchen. "Did you mention the apartment to Fred, Mrs. DeVault?" Her voice trembled slightly, but Mrs. DeVault didn't seem to notice.

The older woman glanced up from the bubbling chicken broth and shook her head. "These dumplings are done. If Albert doesn't arrive soon, he'll be eating a cold supper." She continued to ladle their supper into a china tureen. "Would you put the green beans in the vegetable dish, Olivia?"

"Yes, of course." She absently scooped the beans from the pan. "You're certain you didn't say anything to Fred about my moving in with Mr. and Mrs. Barnes?" she asked as she placed the pan on the worktable.

Mrs. DeVault placed the lid on the kettle and frowned. "No. In fact, other than asking me to give you the note, your name wasn't mentioned." She turned to face Olivia. "Why do you ask? Did he mention something in his letter?"

"No. I just thought . . ." She shrugged. "It isn't important. Did Fred mention anything about his job?"

"He didn't receive a transfer, but he was pleased for Albert." She carried the tureen to the table and returned for the bowl of green beans. "I'm praying his supervisor will recommend him the next time the company has an opening for a glass etcher. It's a waste of his God-given talent." Mrs. DeVault tipped her head toward the dining table. "Sit down and let's enjoy our supper."

"But what about Albert?"

"He knows what time I serve supper. If he's late, he knows I forgive him, but he'll eat a cold supper." She grinned. "Similar to what we talked about the other night. Even though we're forgiven, we can still suffer the consequences of our actions." She grasped Olivia's hand in her own. "Let's pray."

Olivia lay in bed and stared at the ceiling. The covers were too tight and bowed her feet in an uncomfortable arc. She lifted her knees and tugged on the covers until they loosened enough for her to wiggle her toes, but even that didn't help. Sleep wouldn't come. She'd been unable to escape the recurring snippet of conversation with Mrs. DeVault—the part about paying the cost for sin. Though she'd attempted everything from planning next week's menus for the hotel dining rooms to reciting the alphabet backward, nothing had helped her get to sleep.

Suffering the consequences of her lies wasn't something she wanted to dwell upon, yet she'd been unable to force the comment from her thoughts. Truth be told, she'd rather not confess she'd been a willing participant in the web of lies. What purpose would it serve to confess her past misdeeds? After all, Charlotte had departed for parts unknown; Chef René had accepted her as his protégée; Morgan was safely in the care of his grandparents; the earl and countess had absolved her of any wrongdoing regarding the jewelry and blamed their daughter for the forged letter of recommendation. There was no need to divulge the truth now. Best to keep it tucked away like a horrible nightmare. She tossed to her side and plumped the pillow beneath her head. If only that still, small voice would quit nagging at her.

The following morning, she arose a half hour earlier than usual. Half awake and uncertain what time she'd finally drifted off to sleep the night before, she lifted her mother's Bible from the table. If her drooping eyelids were an indicator, she'd not been asleep for long. She opened the book. *Proverbs*. She didn't want to read from Proverbs. She'd located too many passages in Proverbs that troubled her concerning her own behavior.

She closed her eyes and edged her finger into the pages. Flipping to the New Testament, she began to read in the book of Ephesians. This choice should prove to be new and different. She scooted back in her chair and began to read after deciding upon the first five chapters. She was moving along rapidly until she reached verse twenty-five of the fourth chapter: *Wherefore putting away lying, speak every man truth with his neighbour: for we are members one of another*. She snapped the Bible together and slapped it onto the bedside table. The words seared her conscience like a hot iron. Why had she decided to read from Ephesians?

I led you there.

Olivia whirled around. The words had played so loudly in her mind she wondered if someone had entered the room. She shivered and wrapped a shawl around her trembling shoulders. Her nightgown was threadbare; she'd merely experienced a slight chill, she told herself as she hurried into the kitchen to prepare her morning coffee.

Olivia contemplated attending a different church on Sunday morning or not going at all. After Mrs. DeVault's comment about Fred's presence, there was no doubt he would be in church. She wondered if Mildred Malloy would be seated by his side. The mere thought caused a queasy tug in the pit of her stomach, and she thought she might be sick. Looking into the hall mirror, she adjusted the faux raven's wings that adorned the Persian-lamb hat. It was Charlotte's hat, but she now considered it her own. Her features were wan and her complexion lacked color. She pinched her cheeks before slipping into Charlotte's blue velvet coat. The lamb's wool collar matched the hat and muff, though the lovely ensemble did little to raise her spirits.

The brisk north wind was too cold for a mere cape, and she had nothing else except the threadbare jacket she'd brought from England. There was little doubt she'd be overdressed compared to other ladies of the working class, but at least she'd be warm.

Edging through one of the far doors of the church, Olivia stood at the rear of the sanctuary and scanned the seated congregants. She sighed, pleased she hadn't spotted Mildred. The usher led her down the aisle to the pew where Fred was positioned in the aisle seat with his mother alongside him. Albert and Martha leaned forward and waved from their usual places on the far side of Mrs. DeVault.

As the usher came to a halt beside the pew, Fred stood and stepped aside to permit Olivia entry. "Please move to the other side of my mother. I'm expecting Mildred."

The icy wind she'd endured walking to church seemed balmy compared to the chill in his voice.

She glared at him. "Of course, *Mr. DeVault*. I wouldn't want to interfere with your romantic pursuits."

"Nor *I* with *yours*." Anger burned in his eyes. "Mr. Howard is several more rows toward the front of the church."

The usher remained in the aisle, awaiting further direction. He leaned close to Olivia's ear. "Will you be taking a seat in this pew, miss?"

"Indeed I will!" The skirt of her velvet coat clung to Fred's suit. Circling her arm around the bulk of fabric, she freed the coat from his pant leg and entered the pew as decorously as possible. Given the embarrassing circumstances, she silently applauded herself for ignoring the urge to stomp on one of Fred's highly polished shoes.

Mrs. DeVault clucked her tongue and patted Olivia's arm. "Don't let him upset you, dear. He's not in the best of moods this morning. Likely a lack of sleep."

Before Olivia could respond, the reverberating chords of the organ filled the sanctuary. Olivia and Mrs. DeVault shuddered. The instrument, a gift to the church from Mr. Pullman, was touted as the very finest available. Unfortunately, the organist was not. The man was in dire need of additional lessons before he would do the instrument justice.

The minister waved his arms for the congregation to stand, and Olivia glanced over her shoulder. Mildred had not yet entered the church, and Olivia selfishly hoped the young woman wouldn't make an appearance. She desperately wanted to speak with Fred and discover what had precipitated his terse response to her note.

While still listening for the clank of the church door, Olivia scooted back on the hard oak pew. She folded her hands in satisfaction. It seemed improbable Mildred would make an appearance so late, especially since the minister frowned upon latecomers disrupting his sermons—a fact he didn't fail to mention each Sunday.

As the preacher launched into his sermon, Olivia's attention strayed to the front of the church. She stared at the stained-glass window and allowed her thoughts to wander. By the time the congregation stood to sing the final hymn, she'd not heard much of the sermon. Truth be told, she hadn't heard any of it.

But she didn't lament her inattentive behavior for long.

Instead, she calculated when she might find a few private moments with Fred. One thing was certain: if and when she was alone with Fred, she *must* control her tongue. She didn't want to say anything she'd later regret.

As they exited the pew, Mrs. DeVault took Olivia's hand. "Come along. We're going to have a nice meal today."

Fred stood behind his mother and shook his head, obviously hoping to discourage her. Ignoring his signal, Olivia stepped alongside the older woman and accepted the invitation. Though she realized her decision displeased Fred, it would likely prove the only opportunity she would have to see him for another week. Occasionally she looked over her shoulder to chat with Martha and Albert, but she carefully avoided looking at Fred.

When they neared the house, Fred came alongside his mother, hastened up the front steps, and unlocked the door. Once his mother had entered the house, he waved Martha and Albert forward.

However, the moment Olivia started toward the doorway, Fred grasped her arm. "Why don't we remain out here for a few minutes? I doubt there will be any privacy inside." Olivia patiently waited while Fred hurriedly explained to Albert that he'd be in shortly. "Tell Mother I'll not be long." He closed the door and turned to face her. "I want you to go home, Olivia. I think my note was very clear."

"Your note wasn't clear at all, Fred. I don't know what has happened. Are you acting this way because I'm going to room at the Barnes's house or because someone saw me at supper with Mr. Howard? You knew he was escorting me the other evening."

She took a step closer, hoping he'd understand she was

determined to clear the air. Though he stood facing the stinging wind, his complexion was pale.

"You're going to rent rooms in the house adjacent to Mr. Howard's?" His loud guffaw rang with sarcasm. "While the choice doesn't surprise me, be assured I didn't know anything about your new living arrangements until now." He leaned against the porch railing and glanced down the street. "Let's hope Mr. Howard doesn't come looking for you. I'll be given a lecture that the good citizens of Pullman shouldn't loiter on their front porches."

She sighed. "This has nothing to do with the town rules. I want you to explain that note you wrote to me."

He raised his brows. "You do? Strange, because I think *you* owe *me* quite a few explanations. Too bad today's sermon didn't touch upon lies."

She took a step backward and leaned against the house for support. "Lies?" Her voice faltered.

"Yes, Olivia. You know—falsehoods, deceit, untruths, dishonesty—*lies*." His eyes turned dark and he clenched his jaw. "Lie after lie, neatly recorded. Am I helping you remember? Surely your memory isn't so weak that you don't recall your handwritten notes."

He'd seen the pages she had folded and placed in her recipe box! But how? He couldn't have seen them—they were in her house. He hadn't ever been alone in the kitchen. Was he baiting her? Had Charlotte returned and told him something? Her mind whirred as she attempted to sift through his comments. If she denied his accusations, he might reveal more information. She opened her mouth, but before she could speak, she hearkened to the sound of the inner voice whispering, *Don't lie*.

"Exactly what is your question, Fred?"

"I've seen your list. The one inside your recipe box." He curled his lip as though she sickened him. *"Who are you?"* He held up his hand to stave off her response. "Don't say anything, Olivia. You'll only make matters worse. I don't want an explanation. I don't want to know who you are. In fact, I don't want anything to do with you. Now please go."

Tears stung her eyes as she bounded down the porch stairs. She hurried toward home, her footsteps echoing in the cold wind. For a moment she slowed her pace, but his angry words pursued her like a hungry dog nipping at her heels, and she immediately increased her speed. There was no denying she should have revealed the truth long ago. In fact, she should never have lied or agreed to any of the misdeeds. But she couldn't change the past.

God had granted His absolution, but Fred's scathing words had been clear. He wouldn't be quick to forgive, that was certain. She wondered if he'd ever forgive her.

The consequences of sin. She didn't like them. And right now, she found little solace knowing of God's forgiveness when Fred hadn't even been willing to listen to her.

Her cowardly act to hide the lies had failed miserably. She should have confessed everything to Fred when Charlotte departed. Instead, she'd continued to deceive him. A disastrous choice.

[illegible]

[illegible]

[illegible]

[illegible]

[illegible]

Chapter Thirty-Two

Removing one hand from the lamb's-wool muff, she turned up her collar and bowed her head against the bitter wind. What would Fred tell his mother? Would Olivia ever again be welcome at the older woman's table? The thought of not having Mrs. DeVault's companionship added yet another wound. She wouldn't let that happen. Surely they could remain friends.

"Miss Mott!"

Someone was calling out to her. Keeping her head bowed, she peeked up only far enough to glance down the street. *Mr. Howard.* She had nearly made it home. If she'd walked a bit more rapidly, she would already be inside. Of all the people she didn't want to see right now, he was first on her list. Her shoulders drooped in defeat. She didn't want to smile and make idle chatter when only moments ago Fred had ended their relationship. The only thing she wanted to do was bury herself beneath the bedcovers until time for work tomorrow. She didn't acknowledge him. There was no need. He was trotting down the sidewalk and had reached her side before she could think of any response other than *Go away*. But even in her troubled state of mind, she couldn't be so rude.

Panting slightly, he came to a halt as she approached her house. "I'm pleased I caught up with you. I was detained after the worship service—a meeting regarding church finances."

Apparently Mr. Howard was involved in *every* aspect of the town. If he harbored any curiosity about why she was only now arriving home, he didn't ask.

Samuel rubbed his gloved hands together. "Might we step inside for a moment?"

"Mrs. Rice is watching us from behind her parlor window. She thinks I can't see her hiding behind the curtain. She is quite the nosey parker." Olivia arched her brows. "Do you think it would be wise for the two of us to be alone in my apartment?"

"No, you're correct. Word would be about town before sunset." He motioned her closer to the door, where they'd be out of the wind. "Mr. and Mrs. Barnes asked that we join them for dinner."

"We? Now?" He made it sound as though Mr. and Mrs. Barnes considered them a couple and that she would be available at any given moment. She frowned. "I spoke to Mrs. Barnes at church, and she didn't mention—"

"That unfortunate mistake was my blunder. I asked the dear woman if I could extend the invitation on her behalf. Unfortunately, one of the ushers stopped me with a question immediately after services. You were out of the church before we could speak." A gust of wind swooped down the street, and he moved a step closer. "If you'll agree to accompany me, we could begin walking."

"Why don't you go on without me? I don't believe I'd be good company this afternoon." Anxious to escape into the warmth of the house and try to forget the day's events, she moved closer to the door.

He grasped her arm and shifted to the left, effectively blocking the door.

"Trust me, Mr. Howard. I would not be good company."

His eyes shone with determination. "Mrs. Barnes will be most disappointed if you decline her invitation. She very much wants you to meet her husband. As for being good company, you need not worry. Even if you remained silent the rest of the day, your beauty would be enough to delight me." He offered his arm. "I won't take no for an answer, Olivia."

Beleaguered by his persistence, Olivia avoided his piercing stare. The Rices' lace curtains flickered. Obviously Mrs. Rice remained positioned at her parlor window. Olivia didn't have the energy to argue. The cold weather, Mrs. Rice's annoying behavior, Fred's scathing words, and Mr. Howard's determination finally wore her down.

They walked in silence, with Olivia secretly wishing she'd been forceful enough to stand her ground and Mr. Howard clutching her arm as though he feared she might bolt and run. The prospect had actually crossed her mind several times before they reached the Barnes's residence, and she wondered if she had enough energy remaining to put on a cheerful face in front of the couple. Or if she even wanted to.

When they approached the house, Mr. Howard faced Olivia. "Please promise you'll address me as Samuel. I'd greatly appreciate this one concession."

"I'll do my best."

He stared at her, waiting.

"Samuel."

"There, you see. That wasn't so difficult, was it?" He beamed as though she'd achieved a major accomplishment.

She shivered, uncertain whether Mr. Howard's annoying insistence or the weather had been the cause. "I'm quite cold. May we go in now?"

"Yes, of course." He patted her hand and rang the doorbell. "Remember now—you're to address me as Samuel."

"I'll do my best, *Samuel*."

Mrs. Barnes opened the door and greeted them warmly, then quickly ushered them inside. Her amiable chatter continued while she led Olivia into the parlor.

"Horace, this is our boarder, Miss Olivia Mott."

The tall, thin man jumped to his feet and patted down the fringe of hair that circled his balding pate. "Pleased to meet you, Miss Mott. I want to add my hearty welcome to our house." He affectionately patted his wife's hand. "Luella's been far too lonely since our daughter, Lucinda, married and moved back East. You're going to add a ray of sunshine to our lives, Miss Mott."

Mr. Barnes's words were kind, yet Olivia thought them somewhat disconcerting. If the man was seeking a companion for his wife, Olivia feared she would prove to be a disappointment. "Thank you, Mr. Barnes. I, too, am looking forward to the arrangement. However, I do spend long hours at the hotel . . ."

He bobbed his head. "Of course, of course. But many's the evening I return to my office and Luella is left to her own devices. Occasionally the two of you might want to visit the

Arcade for some shopping or enjoy a cup of tea together. With the holidays approaching, I'm afraid my wife will be experiencing the loneliness even more."

At the mention of the holidays, a glistening tear shone in the woman's eye. Olivia hastened to respond. "Yes, of course, shopping and preparing for the holidays would be lovely." Mrs. Barnes sniffled, and Olivia decided a change of topic was in order. She motioned toward the rear of the house. "Is there some way I could assist you with today's meal preparations?"

Mrs. Barnes pulled a lace hankie from her pocket and dabbed her eyes. "Oh, but you're our guest. I couldn't impose."

Olivia looped arms with the woman. "Nonsense. Nothing pleases me more than working in a kitchen. How may I help?"

Mrs. Barnes sauntered toward the kitchen with Olivia in tow. "Horace says I should hire a maid when I'm having guests for dinner, but I don't agree. I think it's much more hospitable to prepare the meal and serve the guests myself."

"There are certainly excellent points for both sides. I enjoy cooking and believe it has a more personal touch if I prepare and serve the food. However, it does take you away from the pleasure of visiting with your guests." Olivia hoped her answer had been diplomatic. She didn't want to be accused of taking sides with either member of the family on her first visit.

The older woman offered Olivia an apron. "I suppose you're correct. There are generally two sides to everything—even this serving platter." She giggled as she turned over the plate in an exaggerated motion and emphasized her point.

Olivia made an effort to join in her laughter and slipped the apron over her head. "How may I help?" She tied the strings around her waist and stepped farther into the kitchen.

"Would you consider making the gravy while I mash the potatoes?"

"I'd be delighted." Secretly glad to have a task on which to focus her attention, Olivia immediately set to work while Mrs. Barnes drained the potatoes.

"I can't tell you how pleased I am that Samuel suggested inviting you to dinner today. Most Sundays it's just the three of us. This is much more enjoyable."

Olivia ceased stirring and turned from the stove. "Mr. Howard *suggested* you invite me to dinner today?"

Mrs. Barnes glanced at Olivia while she continued to mash the potatoes. "Yes. I do believe he's taken a genuine liking to you, my dear, but don't tell him I said so. It's flattering he would go to such lengths in order to spend time with you, don't you think?"

A light flush colored the older woman's cheeks, either from the heat in the kitchen or her careless remark. Olivia couldn't be certain which. But she *was* certain she didn't like Mr. Howard's tactics. Yet she dared not tell Mrs. Barnes, for the woman thought his behavior totally charming.

Well-intentioned or not, the man hadn't been forthright with her regarding the dinner invitation *or* renting rooms from his neighbors. Though Mrs. Barnes might find Samuel's behavior flattering, Olivia did not necessarily agree. His honesty would be preferred. Odd she would feel so strongly about the issue after her own behavior with Fred. With a pang, she realized Fred had likely felt *much* more deceived when he'd read her lengthy list than she did now.

After they were all settled at the table, Mr. Barnes offered thanks for their meal and then carved the roasted beef while his wife encouraged all of them to eat their fill. "Otherwise, my husband will have little variety for his noonday meals next week."

Samuel lifted his plate to receive a thick slice of the beef from Mr. Barnes. "You'll be pleased to hear that I've arranged for several young fellows to move your belongings, Olivia."

Mrs. Barnes gave Samuel an approving look as she passed the squash to Olivia. "How thoughtful of you, Samuel! Isn't he the most thoughtful man you've ever met, Olivia? We've found him to be the best neighbor we could ever hope for, and I'm sure you'll feel the same once you've moved into your rooms."

Olivia glanced at Mr. Howard as she handed him the vegetable dish. "He obviously takes great pleasure in planning for others."

Mr. Howard's brow furrowed. She'd likely annoyed him. Nevertheless, he remained cordial throughout the meal.

After dinner, Olivia insisted upon helping with the dishes while the men excused themselves to investigate a problem with Mr. Barnes's accounts. Slipping into their overcoats, they promised to be at the company offices for only a few minutes.

"You see what I put up with? Even on a Sunday afternoon, he can't set aside his concerns." Once the dishes had been washed and put away, Olivia removed her apron and followed Mrs. Barnes to the front room. She'd been surprised the men would work on Sunday, but it obviously wasn't an unusual occurrence for either of them. The two men had been gone for nearly an hour when Olivia decided Mr. Howard's absence provided a perfect opportunity to depart.

"I do hope you won't be offended if I hurry off. I must be at work early tomorrow, and I've a number of matters needing my attention—not the least of which is packing my belongings so that I may move into your house." She detected the disappointment in her hostess's eyes.

"I know you're a busy young lady, and though I'd very much enjoy your company, I won't attempt to dissuade you." She retrieved Olivia's coat and hat. "I do hope Samuel won't be displeased with me for permitting your departure. I know he'd insist upon escorting you home."

Mrs. Barnes held her black wool muff while Olivia peered into the hall mirror and arranged her hat. "I don't need an escort, Mrs. Barnes. It would be a poor use of his time to walk me home when he lives next door and has other important matters that require his attention."

Mrs. Barnes wavered, seeming to weigh the possibilities. "Still . . ."

Olivia patted the woman's hand. "Please tell him I insisted." She retrieved the muff and impulsively kissed the woman's cheek. "Thank you for a lovely dinner, Mrs. Barnes."

Though the temperature remained cold, the sun was bright and the breeze had diminished. The walk home would be pleasant. Olivia rounded the corner and lengthened her stride, pleased she'd been able to escape before Mr. Howard returned. Mr. and Mrs. Barnes were kind, generous people. Living under their roof would surely prove a blessing. If only Samuel didn't live next door.

Fred tapped on the front door and waited. No answer. He looked down the street and wondered if Olivia had retreated to the library rather than spend the remainder of her Sunday afternoon alone. A twinge of guilt assaulted him, yet he pushed the feeling aside. He wasn't the one who had been living a life of lies. Why should he feel remorse if she endured an afternoon of loneliness? Yet deep inside, he knew why. He cared for her. More than he wanted to admit, even to himself.

With a heavy thud, he plopped down on the porch, his feet resting on the front steps. He'd wait. His mother would expect him to do no less. After all, she was the one who had insisted he come. If Olivia didn't arrive within the hour, he could comfortably report he'd done his best. He rubbed his gloved hands together and watched for any sign of Olivia.

He'd nearly convinced himself he could leave when he spotted Olivia in the distance. She shaded her eyes, and he knew she'd seen him—or at least she'd become aware someone was sitting on the front steps. She waved and quickened her pace. Did she know it was he, or did she think Mr. Howard was awaiting her?

Olivia's lips curved into a broad smile, and she broke into a near run as she approached him. "Fred! I'm so pleased to see you. How long have you been sitting out here in the cold?"

Her pleasure at seeing him appeared genuine. Did she think he'd come to tell her he'd had second thoughts and they could continue on as though nothing had happened? He stood as she reached the porch. "Not long. I thought perhaps you'd gone to the library, so I decided I'd wait a short while."

He followed her glance toward the front windows. Mrs. Rice, the next-door neighbor, stood behind the lace curtains watching them—a reminder that nothing escaped the watchful eyes that inhabited this town.

Olivia fidgeted with her purse. "Has Mrs. Rice been talking

to you? About me? Or Charlotte?" she hastened to add.

"No. We haven't spoken. I didn't know she was watching me until just now." Olivia appeared relieved yet he wondered why it made any difference.

Olivia dug in her handbag and withdrew her key. "Why don't we go inside?"

He nodded his agreement. "I can't stay long. It wouldn't be proper."

She offered to take his coat, but he refused. The sparkle in her eyes faded, and he realized she truly did expect more from this conversation than he was willing to offer. Best get it over with.

"My mother insisted I come and apologize for my rude behavior earlier today." Before he could complete his apology, Olivia gasped.

"You told her?"

"About the lies?" He shook his head. "No, Olivia. I'll leave that for you. I told her we have differences that make it impossible for me to consider continuing to see you. She insisted I come here and tell you that you are welcome in our home and she still counts you a friend."

Olivia dropped to the settee and buried her face in her palms. He hoped she wouldn't cry. Discomfort had begun to take hold when she finally lifted her head.

"You never did explain how you found my list, Fred. Since it was located in my recipe box, I can't imagine how you happened to discover it."

Fred wrestled with how much he should tell her. He didn't want her to think he'd broken into the house and rummaged through all of her possessions. "I had planned to make a new recipe box for you—a gift. I wasn't certain what size box would be best, and my mother suggested I measure your old one. She gave me her key to your house and said I'd locate the box somewhere in the kitchen." He inhaled a deep breath. "I didn't go through any of your other belongings, if that's your concern."

She shook her head. "No. There's nothing else hidden away. Will you please let me explain what occurred and why I developed that list?"

He raked a hand through his wavy hair. He didn't want to hear her excuses. Nothing she told him would change his mind about the way she'd deceived him, but he couldn't bring himself to say so. "If it will make you feel better to tell me, I'll listen."

He leaned back in the chair and listened carefully. His resolve began to weaken as she told him about her life in Lanshire Hall and the unwelcome advances she'd endured from Chef Mallard. However, he steeled himself against being swayed. Piece by piece, she revealed the detailed web of lies she and Charlotte had orchestrated and their subsequent need for a method to keep their stories coordinated.

She exhaled a deep sigh. "I know it was wrong—all of it. But in order to protect everyone, it seemed necessary. I've already discussed the forged recommendation with Chef René, and he accepted my explanation and apologies."

He couldn't believe she'd confessed her behavior to Chef René yet hadn't mentioned any of this to him. Now he doubted she would have ever told him if he hadn't discovered her list. "Chef René knows everything you've told me?"

"Only about the letter being a forgery. Albert knows none of this." She bowed her head. "After Charlotte disappeared and the earl and countess claimed custody of Morgan, I convinced myself there was no reason to reveal the past."

He leaned forward and rested his forearms across his thighs. She had confirmed his doubts. She had planned to base their possible future on a history of lies. He shivered at the thought.

"I've asked God's forgiveness for my sins. I'm striving to be truthful. I can't change the past, Fred. I can only tell you that if you'll give me another chance, I'll do my best to always be truthful."

He remained in his slouched position and slowly shook his head. "Not now—maybe never. I don't know if we could build a relationship out of the few truths that remain between us." He inhaled a ragged breath and stood up. "At present, I don't even want to try. In fact, I think it's best if we move on with our lives—separately. I'll not repeat anything you've told me today. You have my word."

She stepped closer as he neared the door. "I had hoped you could find it in your heart to forgive me, Fred." Her voice was no more than a whisper.

"I do forgive you, Olivia, but I want a relationship that's been built on trust." He buttoned his coat. "I must go. I've remained here far too long."

She didn't attempt to forestall his departure any longer, and for that he was thankful. There was nothing more he could say.

Chapter Thirty-Three

Olivia stood in the doorway a few moments longer. With the back of her hand, she wiped away a single tear that trickled down her cheek. She'd created quite a mess of things with her list of lies. How she longed for a friend in whom she could confide. She could talk with Mrs. DeVault tomorrow evening, but she wondered if such a discussion would be prudent. Fred might think she was overstepping her bounds by confiding in his mother. She had few options. She trusted Mrs. DeVault to maintain her confidence, yet offer wise counsel. To trust anyone else might prove disastrous. Gossip traveled quickly through Pullman. The thought of her name being bandied about town held little appeal.

One thing she knew: being home alone would permit ample time for chores. There would be no need for fancy gowns the remainder of this day. She trudged into her bedroom and removed the green silk dress. With a gentle tug, she pulled her dark blue skirt and an old shirtwaist from the wardrobe.

Before returning to the parlor, she retrieved her sewing basket and several stockings that were in dire need of repair. Dragging the rocker near the window where the late afternoon sun provided excellent light and a bit of added warmth, Olivia threaded her needle and slid the wooden darning egg inside one of the stockings. She deftly moved the needle in and out until the unsightly hole finally disappeared. With a gentle squeeze she popped the wooden egg from deep inside the stocking, surprised when it briefly flew through the air like an overweight bird. She thrust her arm outward, hoping for a midair retrieval. Instead, the needle pricked her finger and the darning egg fell to the floor with a thud. Even her mending had become a disaster. A tear of self-pity slid down her cheek as she reached deep inside her skirt pocket.

Instead of the soft cotton handkerchief, her fingers scrunched around a thick piece of paper. She withdrew the object and stared at the crest in the corner. It was the envelope the earl had left at the hotel before his departure. She had shoved it into her pocket and completely forgotten about it.

Placing it on the table, she pressed her hand across the rumpled edge and smoothed the corner before finally running her finger beneath the seal. Her mending now forgotten, she removed the letter. Inside the folded page lay a business card. She held the finely printed card by one corner while she read the simple directive. *You are to make personal contact with this man*. The earl's signature had been affixed beneath the one-line instruction.

The piece of stationery fluttered to her lap. She leaned back in the rocking chair and studied the card. *Montrose J. Ashton, Esquire*. A Chicago solicitor with an office on LaSalle Street.

She shivered. The combination of solicitors and Chicago couldn't be a good thing, yet the earl's few words didn't sound ominous. He had merely directed her to visit with Mr. Ashton. She hoped he hadn't assumed she visited the city on a frequent basis.

She tucked the business card into her reticule. Perhaps she'd go and visit Mr. Ashton on her next day off work. Then again, navigating the streets of Chicago seemed a daunting mission. Could she muster the courage to make such a journey on her own? If only Fred could accompany her—she'd feel much safer having his strength to rely upon. She sighed. Her reliance would need to be placed in the Lord, for Fred surely wouldn't be available.

When she was slipping her arms into her heavy woolen coat the next evening after work, Chef René approached. "You have been gloomy all day, Miss Mott." Using his thumb and forefinger, he pulled his lips downward into an exaggerated frown. "Is there something I can do to cheer you?"

For a moment, she considered telling him of Fred's decision to end their relationship, then decided against it. Chef René would have no answers for her. "No. Everything is fine, but I truly appreciate your kind offer." His eyes continued to reflect concern, as though he didn't believe her. She forced a bright smile. "See? No need to worry."

"You are not so convincing, Miss Mott, but I'll not force the subject further. I am here if you need me."

His kindness touched her, and she impulsively kissed his

fleshy cheek. "You're a kind man, but I promise I won't tell the rest of the staff."

Unaccustomed to receiving any acclaim from his staff, his cheeks colored at her praise. He waved his hand with bravado. "Off with you now. And if nothing is amiss, I expect to see you happy and vivacious come tomorrow morning."

"I'll do my best." She hurried out the door and toward the DeVaults'. Fred would be at work, and she'd soon discover whether she could remain friends with his mother. She hoped they'd have a few minutes alone before Albert arrived. Not that she minded her cousin's presence. But Albert's friendship with Fred ran deep, and he might inadvertently repeat some snippet of conversation.

With her heart thumping an irregular beat, she approached the front door. What if Mrs. DeVault sent her away? She had to anticipate the woman's allegiance to be with her son. Still, the woman had specifically said that she still considered Olivia a friend. Olivia knocked and waited.

Mrs. DeVault opened the front door, a wide smile curving her lips. The erratic beat of Olivia's heart immediately settled.

"Olivia! Come in, my dear. What a pleasant surprise."

She hesitated on the threshold. "Has Fred told you of our . . . um . . . circumstances?"

"A little, but do come in. No need to warm the outdoors." She grinned and pointed at the hall tree. "Hang your coat and come join me in the kitchen. I need to make certain my rolls haven't burned."

Olivia did as the older woman requested. Soon the aroma of the warm yeasty rolls wafted down the hallway. She inhaled and followed the familiar smell into the kitchen. Mrs. DeVault was lifting two baking pans from the oven. The rolls were browned to perfection. "If Chef René sees those, he may offer you a position in the pastry kitchen."

Mrs. DeVault laughed. "I've no interest, but thank you very much for the compliment. I find it hard enough to keep up with Fred and Albert." She set the pans on a cooling rack and closed the oven door. "I'm pleased you stopped by, Olivia. I had planned to come see you later this evening, but this is even better. You can join me for supper."

"Oh, I didn't want to impose upon you for supper. I had just hoped for a few minutes to talk before Albert arrives home." She removed the rolls from one of the baking pans while Mrs. DeVault busied herself with the other.

"No need to concern yourself about Albert. The foreman asked for volunteers to work a few hours overtime, and he offered." She carried the empty pan across the room to a pan of dishwater. "He's saving as much money as possible. He's decided he and Martha are going to need extra funds to furnish their apartment."

The thought of preparing for marriage caused a sudden wave of wistfulness. "Did Fred explain that he doesn't plan to call on me in the future?"

Mrs. DeVault glanced in her direction. "He said he'd rather not discuss it any further than to say he doubted whether the two of you would have a future together and that I shouldn't interfere." She shrugged. "I told him that he'd not dictate my friendships, and he couldn't dictate the content of my prayers, either." She carried two bowls to the stove and ladled a hearty serving of chicken and noodles into each of the bowls. "Shall we sit out here in the kitchen?"

Olivia quickly agreed. The room was warm and intimate. Mrs. DeVault placed several rolls into a napkin-lined basket and set it between them. She grasped Olivia's hands in her own before she offered a prayer of thanks for their supper and one for God to straighten out Fred's thinking.

After raising her head and releasing Olivia's hands, she flipped open a napkin and spread it across her lap with a flourish. She offered the warm rolls to Olivia and then buttered one for herself. "Nothing better than warm bread, don't you think?"

At the moment, Olivia could think of several things—namely, an ongoing relationship with Fred. However, she agreed that warm rolls were one of her favorite foods. "I didn't come to tell you all that occurred between Fred and me, but I want you to know I did withhold information from him. Because of my dishonest behavior, our relationship was based upon a foundation of deceit." She stared into her cup of coffee. "How I wish I could change that, but I can't. Fred wants a trustworthy woman, and I can't fault him for that. Even though I believe I'm now trustworthy, he has no way of knowing I've truly changed. Do you think he can find it in his heart to ever trust me again?"

"I can't speak for Fred. But if you continue to show him through your actions and deeds that you have made a permanent change, who can say? Perhaps he will have a change of heart."

Olivia knew the older woman was correct. If she was going to restore Fred's trust in her, she would need to do more than offer a simple apology and say she had changed. "All is not lost, I guess, for he did say that he's forgiven me." She forced a feeble smile.

Mrs. DeVault patted her hand. "Don't despair, Olivia. Give him time. The two of you need to discover whether you're truly intended for each other. If it's meant to be, God will redirect your paths. In the meantime, you must not pull away from the Lord. Promise me that you'll continue to study your Bible and pray."

Olivia traced her fork around the edge of the bowl. "I promise." Should she ask Mrs. DeVault about the railroad position? Other than Chef René, the woman was the only one who would likely give her forthright advice. Deciding she valued Mrs. DeVault's opinion more than most anyone else's, she plunged forward. She explained the little she knew about the job offer and then asked what her friend thought.

"Well, it certainly would give you the chance to see some of the country—which is an opportunity offered to few of us. And as the song says, absence makes the heart grow fonder. Perhaps if you're occasionally away from Pullman, Fred will realize how much he misses you." She took another bite of roll and then leaned forward an inch or two. "But you must first pray about this decision, Olivia. If God directs your steps, then that's what you should do. If you don't feel Him nudging you along—don't take the position."

By the time she departed, Olivia had experienced a rising sense of relief. She'd been assured of Mrs. DeVault's ongoing friendship, advice, and prayers—sufficient encouragement to buoy her spirits.

That night she kept her promise and read her Bible. In addition, she uttered prayers throughout the entire evening. She hoped God would lend a listening ear and give her a quick reply.

Mr. Howard would expect an answer before many more days passed.

She fell asleep with a prayer on her lips, and when she awoke the next morning, she continued to pray. The result was not what she'd expected. In place of a simple answer to her prayer, she felt an urgent prompting to tell Mr. Howard she had been hired under false pretenses. Olivia considered the folly of such action, but the conviction continued to plague her. If she followed such urging, she would likely find herself without a job. Holding fast to the belief that she would soon receive a simple yes or no, she continued to pray.

One of the kitchen boys entered the carving room shortly after she arrived. "Mr. Howard wants you to come to his office at ten o'clock."

She gulped down the knot in her throat and thanked the boy. "Did he say why?"

"Huh-uh. Am I s'posed to go pick up eggs this morning? Don't look like we got enough for this afternoon's baking."

No matter the weather, all of the boys liked to escape from the kitchen for the daily trip to the Market. Not that she blamed them. They could visit with the vendors, who were quick to spread the latest gossip, as well as give their advice on the best bargains. Occasionally they even favored the boys with a few extra eggs or vegetables to take home to their families. Olivia glanced at the schedule posted on the wall. "Sorry, but you don't go until Friday. You have trash duty today."

His eyes twinkled a bit. The boys disliked trash duty, but in the late afternoon they enjoyed going outdoors and setting the refuse afire. He hurried off when Chef René bustled into the kitchen.

The chef assessed her for a moment. "You were supposed to return in high spirits this morning."

She forced her lips upward and hoped her effort would meet his expectations. "I have to meet with Mr. Howard at ten o'clock." The chef's left eyebrow raised, and she saw the question in his eyes. "I don't know what he wants."

Chef René shook his head. "I'm sure he wants an answer about the position he's offered you. Have you decided?"

"Not yet. I'm still waiting on an answer."

Now both of his eyebrows arched. "From?"

"God, of course."

He waved a spoon in the air. "But of course. Silly of me to ask such a foolish question." Leaning his body across one of the wooden worktables, he looked into her eyes. "And when are you expecting this answer from God?"

She shrugged. "Any minute now, I hope. But who can tell. He seems to keep a different time schedule than I do."

René shook his head and looked at her as though she were a lunatic. "God has His own time schedule, Miss Mott, and I suggest you be prepared with an answer for Mr. Howard." With his ample belly resting on the worktable, he swung the spoon like a pendulum. "Such as yes or no."

Shortly before ten o'clock, Olivia removed her toque and headed toward the door.

The chef's voice followed after her. "Your answer, Miss Mott?"

"It hasn't yet arrived."

She could hear his chuckling laughter as she hurried out the kitchen door. All the while, she continued to whisper to God. She stood outside the front doors of the building for a brief moment. "I really need an answer, God."

The clerk ushered her directly into Mr. Howard's office. She had hoped for a lengthy wait, one that would give God a little more opportunity to respond, since He seemed to be off duty except for that voice whispering she must reveal the truth.

"Good morning, Miss Mott." Mr. Howard greeted her with enthusiasm and motioned her toward a chair near his desk. The clerk closed the door as he exited the room.

Samuel walked around the desk and perched on the corner nearest to her. "I was wondering about your decision, Olivia. I know I told you to take your time, but Mr. Pullman is eager to fill the position with a quality employee. Quite frankly, he's anxious for you to accept the offer."

She listened, but still no answer came from above. Olivia opened her reticule and pulled out a lace-edged handkerchief. Mr. Ashton's business card fluttered to the floor. Olivia reached to the side of her chair, but Mr. Howard bent forward, swooped up the card, and effectively thwarted her effort. Setting aside all manners, he studied the card and visibly paled.

His fingers trembled as he handed her the card. "How did you happen to come by one of Mr. Ashton's business cards, Miss Mott?"

His brash disregard for proper etiquette surprised her, and she wondered at the change in his appearance and demeanor. "A friend gave it to me."

"For what purpose? I can't imagine why anyone would refer you to a lawyer."

She shrugged. "I don't know, either, Mr. Howard. However, there is something I must tell you." Without further hesitation, she blurted out the truth.

His eyes grew wide when she revealed that her letter of recommendation had been a forgery, that she hadn't possessed any of the necessary requirements for the position of assistant chef. Though she'd expected a barrage of questions, he was stunned into silence. She decided to move forward. "Under the circumstances, I imagine you will want to withdraw your offer of a new position with the company." She stopped short of mentioning her current position of assistant chef and sent a prayer heavenward.

Mr. Howard returned to the other side of the desk and assumed a formal posture. His eyes were somber. Gone was his earlier sense of informality. Silence permeated the room for several long minutes. He finally lifted his gaze. "I can't imagine why you've stepped forward with this information, Miss Mott. I can only assume you feared someone would betray your confidence and decided my personal feelings for you would permit an escape from discipline if you came forward on your own. However, now that the truth has come to the forefront, I am required to set aside my personal feelings and fulfill the duties for which I have been employed."

He rubbed his jaw and stared across the room. "I've had no complaints about your performance from Chef René. And since he is a man who prefers solving his own problems, I doubt he would have mentioned any difficulties. Given your recent performance at Mrs. Pullman's tea, it appears Chef René has provided you with excellent training. In other words, the company has had the dubious *privilege* of paying you a generous salary while teaching you the skills you were hired to perform." His eyes softened momentarily. "Dear Olivia, what am I to do?"

Olivia nibbled her lip. She wondered the same thing. What

would he do? And if he fired her, what would happen? She'd be just like Eddie—jobless and lacking a recommendation.

Once again his posture stiffened and the softness disappeared. "You signed a contract when you were hired, Miss Mott. You may recall that your employment contract contained an oath."

"Yes, I remember," she whispered.

"That contract stated that if you were hired under false pretenses, you would be subject to discharge and repayment of wages." He leaned back in his chair and tented his fingers beneath his chin. "I do care for you, Olivia, and what you have done does not change my personal feelings for you. Still, you must be disciplined for your behavior the same as any other employee. I am not going to discharge you, but you must repay the wages you received during the first four months of your employment."

His words sounded far away, and for a moment she thought she might faint. "I don't have any money, Mr. Howard. How can I repay the company?"

He tapped his finger on a ledger book. "We will withhold a percentage of your current pay until you have met your obligation." He leaned back in his chair and glanced at the ceiling. "I believe we have reached an amicable resolution to this problem."

"Thank you, Mr. Howard." She began to stand up, but he waved her back into her chair.

"You will begin your new position riding the rails in the near future, Olivia."

She snapped to attention. This hadn't been what she'd

expected to hear. Surely he had misspoken. "You still want me to take the new position?"

"Absolutely. In fact, I'm even more convinced that you are exactly the person we need to fulfill the duties." He stood and moved back around the desk. "None of this changes my personal feelings for you, Olivia. I realize there is much more to this story than you have told me. Perhaps one day . . ."

She shook her head. "I believe I've said enough."

The moment Mr. Howard dismissed her, Olivia hurried from his office. Deep inside, she had expected him to exonerate her of responsibility for her actions. Instead, he had substantiated Mrs. DeVault's observation: Transgressions reap consequences. The reduction in wages would prove difficult, yet the decision had been fair. It had been more than fair. Thankfully, Mr. Howard hadn't discharged her. And God had provided her with an answer. Not the simple yes or no she'd expected, but nonetheless an answer.

She took comfort in the realization that she had neither betrayed the Earl and Countess of Lanshire, nor had she been required to disclose Lady Charlotte's identity. In addition, her confession had halted Mr. Howard's interrogation regarding Mr. Ashton and his business card. Mr. Howard might question her more thoroughly in the future, but if and when that time arrived, she'd trust God for the answers. She'd done what she believed God had required of her. Now she must trust that He would see her through the months ahead. And if Mrs. DeVault was correct, perhaps Fred's feelings toward her would eventually soften.

Did absence make the heart grow fonder? She wasn't certain. But God answered prayers. And if she and Fred were meant for each other, she could do more than hope: she could pray. She would let God see to the rest.

Because of Olivia's love of cooking and aspiration to become a chef, I thought it would be fun to present some of the recipes that she prepares or that are mentioned in this book. If you enjoy cooking or baking, you may want to try one or two.

Judith Miller

Sunday Morning Scones

2 cups flour
2 Tbsp. sugar
2 Tbsp. baking powder
½ tsp. baking soda
½ tsp. salt
½ tsp. ground nutmeg
½ cup cold butter, cut up
1 cup raisins
¾ cup buttermilk
1 egg white, lightly beaten
Sugar and cinnamon mixture (if desired)

Preheat oven to 425°. Mix together flour, sugar, baking powder, soda, salt, and nutmeg in large bowl. Cut in butter until mixture resembles large crumbs. Stir in raisins and buttermilk. Roll dough into a ball and knead for a couple minutes on floured surface. Roll out to ¾-inch thickness. Cut out 3-inch triangles and place on greased baking sheet. Brush tops with egg white and sprinkle with mixture of sugar and cinnamon. Bake for 15 minutes or until golden brown. Makes 12 scones.

Olivia's Chicken Salad Puffs

Chicken Salad

2 cups cubed cooked chicken
1 cup seedless green grapes, halved
½ cup shredded Swiss cheese
½ cup chopped celery
3 Tbsp. sliced green onions
½ cup sour cream
¼ cup mayonnaise
¼ cup chopped cashews or toasted sliced almonds
Salt to taste
Parsley for garnish

Combine chicken, grapes, cheese, celery, onions, sour cream, salt, and mayonnaise. Chill until ready to serve. Add cashews and mix before filling puffs.

Cream Puffs

¼ cup margarine
1 cup boiling water
1 cup flour
¼ tsp. salt
4 eggs

Preheat oven to 400°. Add margarine to boiling water and stir until melted; add flour and salt all at once. Stir until well blended and ball forms. Set aside to cool for 10 minutes. Add eggs to flour mixture, one at a time. Stir briskly after each addition until thoroughly blended. For miniature puffs, drop batter from teaspoon onto greased baking sheet. Bake for 25–30 minutes or until lightly browned. Cool and cut top from each shell. Remove any dough and fill with chicken salad. Replace top and decorate with a sprig of parsley tucked between top and shell.

Chef René's Aubergines Bohémienne—Bohemian Eggplant

Translated from La Cuisinière Provençale by J. B. Reboul, 1897

1 large eggplant (or 3 normal-size European aubergines)
5 medium zucchinis
2 green peppers
2 red peppers
2 tomatoes
2–3 Tbsp. olive oil
Garlic (as many cloves as you like, minced)
Thyme (to taste)
Salt & pepper (to taste)
Grated Gruyère (Swiss) cheese

Cut the eggplant into large dice (do not peel). Cut zucchini into dice. Remove seeds from the peppers and the tomatoes; chop. Heat the olive oil in a skillet. When it begins to smoke, throw in the eggplant and peppers. Stir several times. Add the zucchini and tomatoes. Cook until the vegetables become soft. Season with garlic, thyme, salt, and pepper. Serve hot with grated cheese.

Mrs. Mott's Strawberry-Rhubarb Pie

¼ cup flour
1 ¼ cups sugar
2 cups diced rhubarb
3 cups (heaping) sliced strawberries
Piecrust for 9-inch double-crust pie
Butter

Preheat oven to 425°. Combine flour and sugar. Mix ¾ cup of flour-sugar mixture with fruit and set fruit aside. Line bottom of 9-inch pie pan with piecrust. Sprinkle remaining flour-sugar mixture over bottom piecrust and then pour in fruit. Dot with butter. Top with remaining piecrust. Slit openings in top crust and bake for 50–60 minutes or until crust is golden brown and fruit is bubbly.

ACKNOWLEDGMENTS

Special thanks to:

Linda Beierle Bullen and Mike Wagenbach of the Pullman State Historic Site, who answered my many questions, furnished copies of printed resources, and provided me with their excellent insights, as well as tours of the hotel, car works, and the town of Pullman.

Also, special thanks to:

Kristofer Thomsen for his gracious hospitality and the private tour of his home, the former residence of Pullman surgeon John McLean.

A MESSAGE TO MY READERS

I hope this series whets your appetite for further exploration into the life and times of the residents and community of Pullman, Illinois. As you continue to read the second and third books, or perhaps in between each release, you may want to visit the town or check some Web sites to learn more. If you have the opportunity to visit, I would encourage you to do so. The residents of the town are proud of their community, and restoration is an ongoing process.

I would particularly suggest you consider visiting during the month of October, when the Historic Pullman Foundation and the Pullman Civic Organization cosponsor the annual Historic Pullman House Tour the second weekend of October. The Pullman State Historic Site, which includes the Hotel Florence, the Pullman Factory, and the Greenstone Church, is open that weekend for tours. You may learn more about the opportunity for tours and events throughout each year by going to *www.pullman-museum.org* and clicking on "Current Events" or *www.pullmanil.org* and clicking on "Programs" and then "Calendar." Walking tours of the town are conducted on the first Sunday of the month from May through October.

More information on the Pullman era is available at the following Web sites: *www.pullman-museum.org* and *www.chipublib.org/008subject/012special/hpc.html*.

There are also numerous books of interest regarding both Mr. Pullman and his community.

While researching for this series, I visited Pullman and fell in love with the history of the town and its people. I hope you will experience that same pleasure.